P9-DML-080

PRAISE FOR THE BAST NOVELS

"I loved it. . . . It's beautifully crafted [and] really gives the reader a feel for life in the neo-Pagan community."
—Marion Zimmer Bradley on
Speak Daggers to Her

"With a brilliantly balanced combination of humor, sympathy, and sardonic wit, Rosemary Edghill has created the perfect voice to present the feminist, Wiccan, fringed edges of New York—and what's more, she's done it while simultaneously writing a definitely-not-traditional, locked-door murder mystery."
—Tanya Huff, author of *Blood Pact*, on
Speak Daggers to Her

"Clever and compelling, and good PR for the broomstick crowd."
—*New York Daily News*

"Bast is feminist, smart, down-to-earth, and funny. . . . The books are charmingly off-beat as they explore witchly reality on the cusp of the millennium."
—*New Orleans Times-Picayune*

"Bast's voice is genuinely engaging, and her perspective is fresh and bracing, while the aura of magic adds a decidedly fresh note to this murder mystery."
—*Minneapolis Star Tribune* on
The Bowl of Night

BELL, BOOK, AND MURDER

Speak Daggers to Her
Book of Moons
The Bowl of Night

ROSEMARY EDGHILL

A Tom Doherty Associates Book
New York

BELL, BOOK, AND MURDER

This is an omnibus edition, consisting of the novels *Speak Daggers to Her*, copyright © 1994 by Rosemary Edghill, *Book of Moons*, copyright © 1995 by Rosemary Edghill, and *The Bowl of Night*, copyright © 1996 by Rosemary Edghill.

This book is printed on acid-free paper.

A Forge Book
Published by Tom Doherty Associates, Inc.
175 Fifth Avenue
New York, NY 10010

Forge® is a registered trademark of Tom Doherty Associates, Inc.

Library of Congress Cataloging-in-Publication Data

Edghill, Rosemary.
    Bell, book, and murder / Rosemary Edghill.
       p. cm.
    "A Tom Doherty Associates book."
    Contents: Speak daggers to her — Book of moons — The bowl of night.
    ISBN 0-312-86768-9
    1. Bast (Fictitious character)—Fiction. 2. Women detectives—New York (State)—New York—Fiction. Witchcraft—New York (State)—New York—Fiction. 4. Occultism—New York (State)—New York—Fiction. 5. Detective and mystery stories, American. 6. New York (N.Y.)—Fiction. I. Title.
PS3555.D475A6 1998
813'.54—dc21   98-19088
                                      CIP

Printed in the United States of America

0 9 8 7 6 5 4 3 2

CONTENTS

SPEAK DAGGERS TO HER

I

I could say this was any large Eastern city, but you'd know it was New York. I could say my name was Isobel Gowdie, or Janet Kyteler, or even Tam Lin, but what's on my paychecks and phone bills isn't important. My name—my real name—is Bast.

I live in New York and I'm a Witch.

Put away your pitchforks—or more likely, here in the nineties, stifle your yawns and stop edging toward the door. It's just my religion, into which I put about as much time and money as you do into whatever you do that isn't for the biweekly paycheck. I'm not inclined to criticize any way a person might have found to waste excess money, and I'm not having as much fun as you probably imagine I'm having. No naked orgies under the moon, for example; the Parks Commission would object and it's no way to have safe sex. When modern Witches meet, the main concern is usually how to fit eight people and the couch into a room the size of a Manhattan living room *and* make sure you leave with your own Reeboks. No lubricious fantasy there.

Just one more thing about the *W* word and then I'll leave it, since it's a subject that either bores you silly or you've got all the wrong ideas and won't change them for anything I say. Personally, I'd rather we called ourselves anything else, from Pagans to Earth Religionists to Aquarians. It would fit most of us better: over-educated ex-hippies trying to unscrew the inscrutable, trying to make sense of life through ritual and gnosis. But we got stuck with the *W* word back in the forties, when a lovely half-mad Brit picked up Dr. Margaret Murray's anthropological dream-mongering about the witch trials in western Europe and tried to weave a modern religion out of it, patching and piecing from everything that caught his fancy.

By the time Gerald B. Gardner was done, his *"wicca-craften"* had damn little resemblance to the Witches out of history and fairy tales, and so do we. Now we're stuck with the name and a tag-end of faded glory that some of us spend a lot of time justifying to anyone who shows the least interest.

I don't. What I was trying to justify, this particular Friday, was a left-hand margin the typesetter had accidentally set ragged and the client didn't want to pay to get reset. Since the typesetter didn't want to eat the cost and reset it for free, that left me, a Number 10 single-sided razor blade, and a lot of freelance hours.

The Bookie Joint—Houston Graphics if I answer the phone before 5:00—is one of those places you've never heard of unless you're in the business—a freelance studio that does layout and pasteup, turning piles of typeset galleys into pages of type. They call the people who do it artists, which is the only glamorous thing about the job. Layout artist is a dead-end job in a dying field; most books these days are set page-for-page, and desktop publishing is taking over for the really small presses.

But if you don't mind earning less than ten dollars an hour with no bennies and no guarantees, it's a great job. Everybody who works here is something else—actors, writers, artists. Your schedule is flexible to fit around your other jobs. You can get as many or as few hours a week as you need—except when something like the job in front of me comes up. I'd promised Raymond I'd finish it before I left tonight. He's our art director and takes it almost as seriously as he does modern dance. Ray's a dancer—at least he was while he still had his knees. We have some framed stills on the walls. Jazz Ballet of Harlem. Pretty.

Ragged left instead of ragged right. You'd think StereoType never typeset a sheaf of poems before.

The phone rang and I was glad to answer it.

"Bookie-Joint-Can-I-Help-You?"

"Bast?"

This narrowed the caller down to a member of my immediate world.

"Bast?"

"Yo?"

"Miriam's dead."

It was Lace on the phone, which meant that Miriam was Miriam Seabrook, and Miriam was my age. People in their middle thirties don't just up and die.

"Bast?" Lace sounded half a step away from hysteria. "We were going out to dinner and I used my key and she was lying there on the bed and I thought she was asleep—" Lace took a deep breath and started to cry in high, weepy yelps.

"Did you call the police?"

I thought I was fine—after all, I wasn't the one who'd walked in and found my lover dead—but my jaw muscles ached when I pushed the words out. Not Miriam. Not dead. I didn't even know her very well, I plea-bargained.

"I can't. You know I can't. You know what they'll do to me—oh, please, *please*, can't you come over?" Lace started to cry in earnest, a real Irish peening for the healins.

Lace is a dyke radical, which means she has a lot of not-quite-paranoid fantasies about what the Real World will do to her just for breathing. Not quite paranoid, because her mother got a custody order to take her kids away from her and the U.S. government revoked her passport when she came out of the closet. She used to be some kind of engineer until she joined the lunatic fringe.

"Lace. Listen. Call 911 and tell them. You don't have to tell them who you are. Just do it. I'll be right over."

Muffled breathing. Too late I wondered if Miriam had been murdered and was the murderer still lurking around her apartment waiting to make it two for two.

"Lace? Are you there?" Fear is contagious; I was all alone in the studio and it had seemed a friendly place until the phone rang. I could see late afternoon sunbeams white with dust. Sunshine. Daytime. Normalcy. Right?

"Lace."

"I'm here." A tiny little whisper.

"I'll be there as soon as I can, okay? Okay?"

Lace hung up on me.

I barely remembered to lock all three of the inside locks at Houston Graphics, and I was halfway down the block before I realized I'd forgotten to lock the inside lobby door. By then I had no intention of going back.

New Yorkers are supposed to have this inborn instinct for

getting cabs. I don't. Hell, I can't even figure out the bus routes. Fortunately, Miriam's is right on the subway. I caught the D at Broadway/Lafayette, changed to the A at 59th Street, and headed uptown.

I got off at the 211th Street stop, staggered up the stairs (still under construction, as they have been for ever and aye) to the late afternoon howl of sirens and car horns, and into the building on Park Terrace East.

No answer on the buzzer. I punched buttons at random until somebody who should have known better buzzed me in. The elevator was broken so I took the stairs, and by now I was sure what I was going to find.

Fifth floor. Five flights up. Miriam's door was open.

My mouth tasted like burnt copper. I almost called for Miriam, but Miriam was dead, so I heard, unless it had all been somebody's idea of a sick joke.

"Lace?"

I stood in the open doorway. The apartment sounded empty. So I went in and hunted through the whole place real fast. No alien muggers with chain saws. No Lace, either, and no way of knowing whether she'd called the cops. Her set of keys to Miriam's place was on the living room table, right where she'd probably dropped them.

Miriam was in the bedroom on the bed. And she was dead.

I don't know why they always say in books that people weren't sure or couldn't quite believe it. You *know*—in the pit of your stomach, instantly, beyond doubt. This is no longer a person.

She didn't look quite real—like a waxworks, almost-not-quite life-size. She had on her underpants and a khaki T-shirt, and she was flopped there just like she'd gone to sleep. There was a wet spot on the sheet—gritty reality of the relaxed sphincter—but the sense of peace, and rest, and *absence* was almost numbing.

Or maybe I was just in shock.

For something to do I went back out and put Lace's keys in my purse. It'd been over an hour since she'd called me, and it was starting to look like a safe bet Lace hadn't phoned 911. I wondered why she'd phoned me.

So I could do it, of course. And I knew I was going to, which irritated me. But first I was going to take another look around the place, which wasn't as stupid at a time like this as it sounds. Miriam was a wannabe Witch, and a Neopagan, and I didn't want a bunch of people who couldn't tell the difference between that and Anton LaVey splashing "Satanist" all over the *New York Post*.

But all the posters on the walls looked more feminist than anything else, and no one who didn't know what they were looking at would recognize Miriam's altar.

I went back to Miriam. Priestess of the Goddess and death is all part of the Great Cycle of Rebirth and all that crap, but I still didn't want to touch her. She had an intense perfume, like a cross between pine needles and fresh bread. I couldn't concentrate on anything, and all the details except the body on the bed kept slipping away. Finally I made myself hook my fingernail under the silver box-chain around Miriam's neck. It would be just as well if she didn't go to the morgue wearing a pentacle.

Morgue. Miriam was dead. Damn it, she was *my* age, maybe even a few years younger, and people my age just don't curl up and die.

And now I was stripping the body so no one would know she was a Neopagan.

And I call *Lace* the paranoid one.

I was more keyed up than I thought, which was why I yelped and jumped and jerked the chain so her head rolled toward me as the pendant slipped out of her shirt.

Because Miriam wasn't wearing a pentacle—that nice chaste star-in-a-circle that's the badge of office of practically everyone here on the New Aquarian Frontier. What Miriam was wearing on that long silver chain was little and brown and nasty, and eventually my heart slowed down and I saw it was a mummified bird claw of some kind, with the stump wrapped in silver wire so she could string it on the chain. The nails were painted red.

"Oh, *fuck* . . ." I said very softly. Then I unhooked the chain and slid it free, because out of civic spirit I did not want Miriam found wearing a dead chicken foot either. And I didn't want it touching her.

I didn't want it touching me, for that matter. I put it in her bedside table drawer. Then I went and called 911, and it wasn't any work at all to sound convincingly rattled.

The books have another thing all wrong, too. I'd expected the apartment to be swarming with police just like on "Murder, She Wrote." I got two EMTs and a bored policeman, none of whom cared about my careful, plausible story. We'd had a dinner date. I got here and used my key. I found Miriam.

I lied because even with my limited experience I felt that police do not like to hear about people who find other people dead and just leave, and because if I told the truth they'd probably come down on Lace and Lace already has enough problems. She was going to have some more when I got ahold of her, too.

And if anyone had to pitch an idiot story to the heat, it might as well be me, since I had a number of advantages over Lace. I looked like something I was in most respects: a straight white blue-eyed thirtysomething wage-earner, dressed off the racks of Macy's Herald Square and five foot eight in my stocking feet. Hair the same color I was born with (black), no makeup, no earrings, and no bizarre jewelry out where it could push John Q. Lawdog's buttons. I was highly plausible, in my humble opinion.

But nobody was asking for my opinion this evening, and even the EMTs didn't seem that interested in my story. They zipped Miriam up into a gray plastic mummy bag and wheeled her away. I got out Miriam's phone book for next-of-kin and the policeman copied out her sister Rachel's name and address.

That was it. He made me leave the apartment first and then he took a sign that said NOTICE followed by some type it was too dark in the hallway to read, and put it on the door and told me not to go back in, and that was that.

The police probably wouldn't get around to notifying Rachel Seabrook until at least Monday, he said, if I wanted to call first.

He was nice. I guess he was nice. I'd just found someone I knew dead and lied to the police on top of it and my stomach was full of old scrap iron and I was going to ring Lace's chimes but good and something was *wrong.*

I wanted to cry.

The cop got into his cop car and I went back across the park and down the steps to Broadway. The motorists were still at it—the only thing more dangerous than the subways in New York is the streets—and when I went to put the token in the turnstile at the subway platform I found I was still carrying Miriam's address book in my hands.

Miriam was dead.

"You're so together," Bellflower tells me. Yeah, sure.

I came to New York from the Real World about fifteen years ago. Everybody comes to the Big Apple for something they can't get anywhere else. In my case it was Craft. The One True Polytheism. Wicca.

Unlike a lot of other people I got what I came for.

Miriam was one of the others.

I first met Miriam about five years ago hanging around The Snake — the largest and most out-of-the-broom-closet occult shop on the East Coast. It's been named, at various times, The Naked Truth and The Serpent's Tooth, and is known to its intimates as The Sneaky Snake, or, more briefly, The Snake.

Most of us in what I laughingly call the New York Occult Community, which includes Pagans and Witches and ceremonial magicians and Crowleyites and permutations of all of the above too numerous to catalogue, have been through its doors at one time or another, and about half of us have worked there. It's a nice place to spend Saturday, helping Julian the-manager with the jewelry inventory and watching the tourists gawk.

Miriam stood out like a sore thumb, striking up bright little conversations with the other browsers in the "Witchcraft and Women's Mysteries" section (Tris, the actual owner, is nothing if not conservative), copying the notices of "Covens Forming" off the bulletin board, and earnestly attending every event the shop offered, from "Enochian Invocation, Calls and Chants" to the Sunday afternoon semi-open Neopagan circles.

I avoided her. The new ones are always trouble, looking for god or guru or someone to tell them the True Facts, and ready to latch onto anyone who will hold still long enough and "Yes, my Lady" her to death.

There are some people in the Community who enjoy that, like Risha the Wonder Witch with her forty-member coven of eternal First Degrees.

I don't. If I had the nerve and the energy to start my own coven, those are the last sort of people I'd pick. They stick forever, they don't learn, and they don't grow. If they wanted to sit in the chorus watching a priest perform, why didn't they stay in the monotheism they came from?

But I digress.

I saw Miriam, and I heard about her (Newbies are an eternal source of gossip. They're so cute when they're dumb), and I met her at just about every "open" event in the city, and we had some conversations and I suggested some books that would probably settle her head on straighter than the moonshine she was reading. Her eyes bugged out when she realized a Real Live Initiate was willing to talk to her and practically oozed down her face when she found out I was entitled to wear the Third Degree silver bracelet and be called "Lady" in A Real Wiccan Circle. Then she got disappointed because I was still a clay-footed human being and wouldn't tell her that what I had was The Answer. Eventually she worked her way through that, too, and forgave me, and we became "sort of" friends.

I even showed her to Bellflower, who is *my* High Priestess, but Miriam wasn't the kind of person who was comfortable with the kind of coven Belle ran, and I sometimes get the feeling that actual religious passion makes Belle nervous.

It's the same old story. Some people just don't manage to click. Every coven is different, and covens with styles that would suit them are full, or gossip of one sort or another ensures they don't get asked when there is an opening, or they just drift away. Score one for the Goddess's winnowing process.

Miriam was one of the ones who drifted. After a year or so on the fringes she gave up on being what she called a "real Witch" when none of the Welsh or Alexandrian or Gardnerian covens would take her and started trying the evanescent trads that spring up and vanish overnight. She even tried Santeria and the O.T.O.—in fact, after a while, every time I saw her she was into something new.

I tried to steer her back toward the safe stuff; that was how she met Lace, shopping the Dianic trads down at Chanters Revel, which was where I was heading now. Lace worked there.

But Miriam hadn't really been "womyn" enough to suit the Dianics. She'd kept looking. Or drifting. And now she was dead. And she had The Answer, if there is a The Answer.

Hard and jagged and unwanted I remembered the chicken claw she'd been wearing around her neck, and I felt a niggling in the part of my brain I reserve for jumping to conclusions. I beat it down because I was not, damn it, a flake like Lace. I'm a charter member of the Conspiracy to Prevent Conspiracy, and I don't look for hidden meanings.

The subway jerked to a stop. The niggle would stay flat for a while. I got off the A at West Fourth Street and started walking toward the Bowery. It was about eight-thirty on a Friday night in June.

Once upon a time a bunch of devout, right-thinking lesbian separatist Goddess-worshipers got fed up with The Sneaky Snake and decided to start their own occult bookstore.

Chanters Revel first opened its doors about five years back, and contrary to conventional wisdom—which is that 50 percent of all new businesses fail every year—is still going strong. They don't cater as much to the dried-bats-and-floorwashes crowd as The Snake does—the Revel shopper is more likely to be shopping for homeopathic herbs and crystal jewelry, along with the hottest new titles on how to start your own feminist ecosystem. The Revel also brews a mean cup of Red Zinger tea, twenty-five cents and bring your own cup.

I pushed open the door and slid into the shop. For reasons involving rents and overhead, the Revel is located in an area that only the most depraved real estate agent could call SoHo. It's south of Houston, all right—and probably east of the sun and west of the moon as well. It's also one of the few establishments of any sort that has its own herb garden out back.

It was Friday night, and Tollah, who is one-half of Tollah-and-Carrie, the Revel ownership, holds a TGIF Ritual every Friday around nine P.M., East Coast Pagan Time. Which means, in practice, around ten-thirty, but the Friday ritual is mostly for regulars and they don't mind.

The Revel doesn't have indoor ritual space like The Snake does, so Fridays are held in the Revel's little back garden, or with everybody crammed inside if it rains. Tonight was going to be a back garden night, Goddess willing. People were already queuing up to drink quarter-a-cup tea and stand around and gossip.

Tollah waved from the cash register beside the door. I headed for the tea urn. I didn't see Lace anywhere.

I fished my cup out of its hiding place—rank hath its privileges—and dropped a quarter in the box. I poured myself some Zinger. I had a number of reasons for wanting to see Lace, number one or possibly two on the list being that if she'd phoned the police about Miriam before I had and got herself on tape with it, I was probably going to have some really awkward questions to answer eventually.

And for no good reason I wanted to ask Lace why Miriam was wearing a chicken foot around her neck when she died.

I'm not a religious bigot, and I can't have an opinion on something I haven't studied. This leaves me voting "No Award" on a lot of New Age so-called spiritual pathways. Most people are turned off by the Santerios sacrificing chickens to their gods, but exactly how is that different from a kosher butcher slaughtering baby goats for Passover?

Mostly the difference is that the *fleisher* is pulling down $80,000 a year and has a condo in Palm Beach, and the *oshun* is on welfare and lives in a fifth-floor walk-up in Queens. Never tell me money doesn't talk. Money's the left-hand path, the ruler of the things of Earth.

So my self-image requires an open mind. Fine. And some gods require blood sacrifices. Fine. It's between them and their worshipers and the legal code of the United States. And some spiritual paths have window dressing that's a real cage-rattler (ever check out Tibetan Buddhism?). This is also fine.

But since all these things were so fine, why was I getting grue and goose bumps because Miriam was wearing a piece of a chicken that the chicken certainly wasn't going to miss now?

Oh, it isn't that I don't believe in evil. It's just that it's rarer than the funny-mentalist televangelists like to think. I prefer to distinguish among evil and stupid and weird. Maybe if I could talk to Lace I could be sure which category Miriam's jewelry fell into.

And maybe I could get some kind of handle on why she was dead. It made no sense. There hadn't been a mark on her that I remembered—not AIDS, not drugs, not terminal cancer—and if she had any medical kinks from diabetes to a bad heart she would have been sure to mention it at some point as proof of her great psychic power. People do.

Miriam Seabrook was dead. For no reason, without even the excuse of traffic accident or urban violence. I wanted to talk the experience to death and bury it in words and the only person I could do that with wasn't anywhere.

If it wasn't unfair, you wouldn't know it was Life.

I poured myself a second cup of tea and tried to distract myself with the bookshelves. There wasn't much there I wanted: I do my book buying at Weiser's or The Snake—my kind of Wicca is too masculinist and hierarchical for the good ladies of Chanters Revel, which is where I do my fraternizing. A foolish consistency is the hobgoblin of little minds, as someone said just after he jumped political parties.

I took one more hopeful look around to see if Lace had come to Earth. It has often been said that a significant percentage of Grateful Dead groupies make their living by touring the country following the band and selling Grateful Dead memorabilia to other Grateful Dead groupies who also make their living by touring the country following the band and . . . You get the idea. For sheer incestuous symbiosis, Neopagans have them beat all hollow. Without moving from my place under a "Women Hold Up Half the Sky" poster, I could count two occult silversmiths, one mail-order herbalist, a candlemaker, a guy who sandblasts mirrors with the holy symbol of your choice, a pretty good (and very expensive) astrologer, and a couple people who regularly read Tarot at The Snake on Wednesdays. It's a wonder Tollah and Carrie don't go broke—half the customers at the Revel are their suppliers.

No Lace.

I suddenly realized that I could not face a TGIF Ritual tonight. Miriam's death didn't belong in it, and I wasn't sure I wanted to tell anybody about that just yet anyway.

I also realized I'd promised Ray I'd finish those damned galleys still sitting on my board at work. Before Monday.

Weekends are for sissies.

I decided to circulate a little more in the name of showing the flag and also to give Lace one last chance to show up and make me a great excuse for leaving. I saw everybody else but I didn't see Lace. Just as the party was starting to move outside—Tollah pulled the shade with the picture of Mama Kali and the "Closed" sign down over the glass part of the door—I managed to corner Carrie.

"Seen Lace?"

Carrie frowned—which made her look cute and ultramundane both and made me wonder yet again what life would be like if I weren't so painfully straight—and made a sincere effort to remember every personal interaction of the last twelve hours.

"She left here about five. She was going to meet that Miriam Seabrook—" Carrie wrinkled her nose in a way that indicated Miriam was Not One Of Us, and from Carrie that was the equivalent of anyone else's screaming phillipic—"and go to that new Greek place to eat. Lace was supposed to bring us back some falafel—but it's okay because Lugh brought in pizza and we split that," she finished in a rush, just in case I might think she was—Goddess avert—*mad* at Lace.

That settled it. If Carrie said Lace hadn't come back, she hadn't. And in a store that measured ten feet by thirty, someone Lace's size wouldn't exactly be invisible.

"Well, okay," I said, which Carrie could take any way she liked. I went out the back door of the Revel with everyone else, and then down to the bottom of the garden and through the gate and down the alley and out.

And I wondered what Miriam Seabrook, dead space cadet, could possibly have done in life to put that look on gentle Carrie's face.

It was pretty late when I finally got home. New York, you may have heard, is a summer festival: I'd wandered around until I fetched up in front of that bar (you know, the one with no windows and the walls painted black) that seems to be a favorite with all my friends.

Not me. It's not that I mind five bucks for a beer. It's that for that I want light to see and room to drink it afterward.

Despite that, I went in and blew twenty bucks on Tsingtaos until the Real World got to be more irritating than the show I was replaying in my head and I headed for home sweet ungentrified home.

Not that they aren't trying—the gentrifiers, I mean. It was worse back in the eighties when there were still yuppies, but you can feel the hot breath of the real-estate developers panting down your neck six blocks away even now. Let's go co-op! Condo! Loft!

And when there is nothing anywhere on Manhattan Island but studio apartments renting for $1500 a month, they'll say "Where is the charm of the old neighborhoods?"

Sure they will—I don't think. It's the social equivalent of strip mining: They'll be laughing all the way to the bank for the twenty seconds or so it takes their jury-rigged wonderland to turn into slums that'll make Calcutta look like Westchester County, and for the New York economy to crash because nobody but drug lords and lawyers can afford to pay the kind of money that lets people live in places that cost that much.

It's not wanting things like that to happen that leads to block associations (and you thought they were only to stop the spread of crack), and banners across the street saying "Help Save Our Neighborhood," and large informational signs discussing New York City's tax structure as it relates to Alphabet City. And other land-marks of my neighborhood.

Never mind what I pay in rent, or that even if I could afford to live uptown I might not. Think instead about the cultural fallacy

that holds that the idea of making money is so sacred that the
means by which it is made cannot be questioned—and that anyone saying that sometimes it isn't a good idea to get all the cash
profit you possibly can would probably be arrested for heresy if
there was a Holy Vehm for the First Church of Money.

When I drink I think too much.

I walked up five flights of stairs and I was home.

The light on my answering machine was blinking as I came in—
welcome to the wonderful world of consumer goods. Stupid, but
it's my one techno-toy: I can't stand not knowing who wants to
talk to me, and since I do a bit of freelance artisting, it's actually
a deductible business expense.

I closed the door and flipped the three locks back into place and
walked over and pushed the button next to the flashing red light
before doing anything else. I have one window and it has no shade;
there was enough light to do that by.

The thing obediently played through the part about "leave your
name and number after the beep" and got to the point.

"Bast? It's Miriam. Seabrook?"

I am not superstitious, but for a moment I wondered wildly if
they had pay phones in the county morgue. But Miriam must have
called earlier today, while she was still alive.

Right. Real bright, girl.

"—and I've got to see you," the ghost in the machine went on.
"I've really got to see you. It's—" Recorded Miriam drew a shaky
breath. I hit "Save" and the tape went back to the beginning and
started flashing again.

I went over and turned on the lights. White walls, cracked
linoleum, kitchen table old enough to be a Deco-era collectible that
isn't. One long room with a bed at the other end and a bathroom
with no bath. Home.

And Miriam on my answering machine, person-to-person from
the Twilight Zone. Once I played it back she'd be gone for good;
the next message coming in would record right over her.

I thought about it for a minute or so, feeling very lucid, and
rummaged around until I found my old rinky-dink Sony that I use
for taping lectures and stuff. I popped out the tape—music, Sangreal, live, at *Rites of Spring*—and stared at it while my mind helpfully provided the information that there probably wasn't another
blank tape in the place and if there were I wasn't in any shape to
look for it. So I flipped Sangreal over to Side B and hit "Record"

and let it tape a few seconds of my not-too-steady breathing before I went over and hit "Play" on my answering machine again.

Sometimes I just love my life.

"Bast? It's Miriam. Seabrook? I know it's . . . I haven't been in
touch, but I've really . . . I need to . . . There's this weird stuff, and
I've got to see you. I've really got to see you. It's —" the long pause
again, and this time, listening, I could hear tears. "It's too weird.
I'm scared. I think they're going to —" The voice stopped abruptly,
and when it started again it was bright and upbeat and jarringly
fake. "So anyway, call me, okay? Or I'll be down at the Revel, until
eleven?"

Clatter of phone hanging up, and then a beep and my message
again and Miriam calling back to leave her number. Long hiss of
open line, as if she'd waited, not hanging up, hoping I'd come in
and pick up the phone and save her. But the answering machine
cut her off with a little self-satisfied choodle, and there weren't any
other messages on the tape.

I stopped the recorder and rewound the tape and popped it out,
and popped the answering machine tape out too, and stuck both
of them in a Ziploc Baggie, and put that in a cookie jar that holds
subway tokens and incense charcoal and other things that
roaches won't eat.

Then I went to bed and tried to convince myself that Miriam's
death was from all-natural causes, that Lace's paranoid disappearing act had nothing to do with knowing too much about something, and that Miriam hadn't died as a direct result of being in
over her head somewhere.

And I couldn't.

2

My alarm blitzkrieged me out of bed before the sun had come down into my neighborhood, and I was already in the shower before it occurred to me that this was probably Saturday. Further investigation revealed that it was, but by this time I was curious enough to want to try to find out why I'd set my alarm.

Somewhere over the second cup of Morning Thunder I remembered that I had to get back to Houston Graphics and finish that job for Ray. And I might as well call Rachel Seabrook from there while I was at it.

What else I had in mind to do today I wasn't admitting even to me—at least not before breakfast. And maybe lunch.

I got to Houston Graphics about eight and unlocked all the locks I'd locked the night before. I'm not the only one who comes in on weekends—anybody who's worked for the place five years has a set of keys—but if I wasn't the only one today at least I was first. I turned on the lights and the wax machine and the stat camera and the coffeemaker, and when the coffee was ready I poured myself a cup and turned on my light table and settled down to the finicking business of salvaging that type job.

Three hours later—still alone—I straightened up and tried to work the crick out of my lower back. Ray's bitch-kitty of a job was within shouting distance of being done; only another spread to go. And it was late enough so that I could call the time zone next door and be pretty certain I wouldn't wake anyone up.

I didn't want to make that call. How do you tell somebody that their sister is dead? *"Hello, I'm a total stranger and I'm calling to fuck with your head. . . ."* Sure.

I pulled out Miriam's address book. The other numbers in Miriam's book were in every color of the rainbow, decorated with doodles and pentagrams and cryptic notes in massed initials. Rachel Seabrook's number was carefully written in blue-black ink, like a penance. I punched all eleven digits firmly, not giving AT&T a chance to get cute.

Three rings and answer. "Hello?" The authentic Midwest sound of chronic sinus trouble. Area Code 317. Indiana.

"Hello, this is—" I had to think about it for a minute before identifying myself "—Karen Hightower. May I speak to Rachel Seabrook?"

"This is she." Third person peculiar is alive and well in the Middle West.

"I'm afraid I have some bad news for you, Ms. Seabrook. I'm afraid—" no, I'd said that already "—I'm sorry to tell you. Your sister Miriam is dead."

"How do you know?" Hostile, but not unreasonably so. The telephone is a great leveler. You can't judge what you can't see. All she knew about me was that I knew Miriam.

"I found her body."

There was a pause while we both listened to the long-distance hiss.

"I see. I'm sorry, Miss . . . ?"

"Hightower."

"You must think I'm very cold. But Miriam and I were never close."

"Your number was in her address book. I gave it to the police. They have— She was lying on her bed. She died in her sleep. They should be calling you."

Normally I put sentences together better than that. Grace, wit, charm, adverbs . . . But not today. Death is the only really rude thing anybody can do anymore, it seems. People will forgive rape, murder, theft, and arson, but dying is the unforgivable act. We don't even want to mention anyone crude enough to do it.

"I see. I'm sorry. It must have been very difficult for you. Have you . . . Do you have any idea of what I should do now?" A hesitant laugh: *I'm sorry to be such a bother. . . .*

"I'm sorry," I sorried back, "I don't really know. Maybe the po-

SPEAK DAGGERS TO HER   25

lice will be able to tell you. I don't think she had a will. There's her apartment—if you like I could get together her personal papers and send them to you."

That's right, Bast, offer to burgle dead Miriam's apartment for the sister so you have a good excuse.

"I . . . I really can't just drop everything and fly out to New York. We weren't really close." *Tell me it's okay to do it this way. I know I'm supposed to make a big fuss over the dead sister, but this would be easier. Tell me it's all right.*

"If you like I can send you her things."

"Thank you. That would be very kind."

We were never really very close. You might steal everything, but I don't really care. I can say a friend of hers in New York took care of things. We weren't really very close.

"If there is anything you would like. A memento. Please let me know. . . ."

"Thank you, Ms. Seabrook. Let me give you my name and address and phone number. I'll need a UPS address from you."

Thank you. You're very kind. We weren't close. I wrote letters and numbers on my blotter with a technical pen. A rural route in Shelbyville.

By the time I hung up on Rachel Seabrook I had her permission to rummage the length and breadth of Miriam's apartment and strew her worldly goods to the four winds. It was understood that anything with a high resale value would go to Rachel. There wouldn't be much. Not by Shelbyville standards, anyway.

I knew somebody from Shelbyville, Indiana once. He spent so much time being *from* Shelbyville that he never paid much attention to where he actually was. I think he's dead now.

And it was lunchtime, and by now it was obvious even to me how I was going to spend my afternoon. Because Miriam had been afraid when she died, and I wanted to know why.

I finished up the work for Ray, tidied up the studio, and filled in my time sheet. Eloi came in while I was leaving—he was working on a long job, medical textbook with lots of dead babies. He spun his hat the length of the room and made a ringer on the tensor lamp over his board. He didn't say much. He never does. I think he thinks he's Humphrey Bogart but I've never dared ask. At least because he was there I didn't have to lock up again.

I caught the Uptown train. When I got to Miriam's apartment

I took the police notice off the door and used Lace's keys to get in. Crime number one.

Inside, the place looked and smelled like an abandoned hotel room. I had a flash of Stephen King–land cyanotic zombies shambling out of closets, which was stupid. Death is a part of life. If the dead interact with the living at all (insufficient data), it is not reasonable to think that they will be any more antisocial than they were while they were alive. Miriam had been my friend, sort of, and anything else on a day-trip from Between The Worlds I could deal with.

Meanwhile, here was a quick introduction to Death, Twentieth Century–style. You die, and two weeks later the landlord rents your apartment. Everything you scraped to buy or collect is suddenly worthless, and all people can think of is how to get rid of it gracefully.

There's something to be said for the old custom of funerary goods. One big bonfire and all the fuss would be over.

I opened the windows and put on the kettle. Miriam's purse was still on the microscopic fold-down Conran's kitchen table. I left it there and rummaged around a little until I found about what I expected: two joints wrapped in foil in the freezer compartment of the fridge and half a Baggie of magic mushrooms in a recycled Skippy jar in the cupboard next to the vervain. The Sixties are alive and well and living in the Craft in New York City.

I threw the 'shrooms and the pot into the trash and hoped there wasn't anything worse around—and if there was, that I'd recognize it. The vervain went, too—not that it's illegal; it's a harmless herb used in a lot of Wiccan and Pagan banishing rituals. On the other hand, I only had Miriam's word for it that the gray-green stuff in the jar marked "Vervain" was vervain and not, say, oregano.

The tea-water boiled while I finished denuding the kitchen of occult and counterculture additives. The stuff that was legal, semimundane, easily identifiable, and still useful I left lined up on the counter for later collection. Then I took my tea out to the living room.

I'd never been in Miriam's apartment before last night. Whatever her day job was she'd made decent money on it or had outside financial help; this place probably rented for between six and seven hundred a month. I wondered if there was any way on earth to collect her security deposit for Shelbyville.

It was a typical New York apartment: kitchen on the right,

bathroom behind it down a hall, bedroom opening off the hall, and living room straight ahead.

The living room looked like everybody else's I hung out with. Not much here to excite Shelbyville: the couch was a curbside rescue, the end tables were wooden crates, the coffee table was an old trunk. The room was a first-class job of urban scavenging, but the standards of Fly-Over Country are not our own. All Rachel Seabrook would see was junk.

Across from the couch was the standard brick and board bookcase, with the standard authors: Adler, Valiente, the Farrars, Buckland. Some Crowley, and even a copy of the Sumerian-style *Necronomicon* somebody published as a stunt a few years back. It's a complete grimoire of Sumerian magic, all right, but it doesn't contain any banishing rituals. The system was written without them, and so it's worthless. Who ever heard of drawing without an eraser?

Records and tapes, all harmless. A pile of magazines: *Gnostica* and *Green Egg* and *Fireheart*. A few copies of *Ms.* and *Mother Jones,* for variety.

Copies of *The White Goddess* and *The Golden Bough,* both paperback and full of Miriam's marginal notes. But nothing here you couldn't show your mother, if your mother happened to be Sybil Leek.

On the right-angle wall there was another, lower, bookcase that had her altar on it. Most Pagans have one—it's just a flat surface, sometimes covered with a cloth, where you keep chatchkis that are meaningful to you. Light a candle, burn some incense, reaffirm your personal belief system.

Like everything else in the room, Miriam's could have been issued stock from Pagan Central Supply: A blue pillar candle, an incense burner, some big quartz crystals, a Goddess figure. Hers was a museum shop replica of the Goddess of the Games, from Crete.

The little Goddess was dusty, and so was the top of the candle. Well, we aren't any of us demon housekeepers. To coin a phrase.

But the coffee table wasn't dusty. Neither were the tapes piled on the bookshelf. So Miriam did clean.

But not her altar. Not even so much as you'd expect from handling the things—lighting the candle, and so on.

Theory: Miriam hadn't been near her altar in weeks.

Miriam, if you can hear me, the next time I see you I'm going to thump your punkin' haid in. What the hell were you up to?

The answer, of course, was in the bedroom.

I felt the energy as soon as I crossed the threshold. It's not a particularly witchy trick—you do it all the time: Ever walk into a room full of people and *know* a fight's in progress? Or come home, and not even bother to give a yell because you *know* there's nobody there? Maybe you don't talk about things like that, but Witches do, and we have to call the reason-for-knowing something. So we call it energy, most of us. Whatever it is, it's the thing that changes.

The energy in Miriam's room was not good. I thought about Stephen King again. But I'd been here yesterday and the only energy I'd felt was Miriam being dead.

This was not that.

I went back out to the living room and stopped at Miriam's dusty altar. There were matches on a lower shelf. I lit the candles and got out the charcoal. I couldn't find any incense around the altar, but I'd seen some in the kitchen.

I went back in and came out with a self-seal Baggie of something that looked like coarse sand. The grains were red, yellow, and black. I'd saved it because I knew what it was. Russian Church incense—the heavy smoky stuff, all copal and frankincense and myrrh. It made a nice familiar smell as the smoke made Jacob's Ladders up to the ceiling. The little Goddess seemed to shine brighter, as if she liked being remembered. And I knew that nothing bad could get at me while She watched.

Most adults lose that sense of serenity, the idea that somebody else is going to shoulder the load and do the looking-out-for. Maybe wives had it before Women's Lib, when Hubby took all the heat, or maybe that's another myth of the Golden Age that there's no way to check. But it's one of the things that religion has always promised to provide.

Not, mind, that I'm going to leave my door unlocked and expect the Great Goddess to keep the muggers away. She encourages independence.

But I felt better now.

I went back into the bedroom and opened the window, and a bunch of Austrian crystal suncatchers that Shelbyville might like went spinning. They sent little light-flies spinning over the walls that Miriam had lovingly painted with a pastoral landscape in shades of violet, and wickedness popped like a bubble.

I'd known Miriam was a wannabe artist as well as a wannabe Witch. I hadn't known she had this much talent. It made her death worse, somehow, which is unfair.

I looked around. Mattress on a platform. One nightstand a salvage job with a drawer, the other one of those cheap metal footlockers from Lamston's. There were another two footlockers at the foot of the bed.

Bedside lamps—cheap copies of Art Nouveau. You used to be able to buy them down at the Canal Street Flea Market. Mirror (cracked) and discard-chest of drawers, a gift of the Garbage Goddess, painted lavender and decorated with painted vines. A straight chair and a square hassock, also secondhand.

The closet, as always, was tiny, narrow, and deep. It held sneakers, Tibetan tie-dye vests, and one or two suits of mundane clothes that had that indefinable look of being a couple of years out of style. For the second time today I wondered what Miriam did for a living. There wasn't enough in the way of "straight" clothes here for a work wardrobe. Of course, maybe she had a job like mine, in which case they wouldn't care if she showed up naked, so long as she got the work done.

But Miriam wasn't going to be working anymore. Miriam was dead.

Why?

And what had left that bogeymonster feeling in the room?

The actual cause of death in every case is the same: The heart stops. What coroners call the proximate cause is *why* the heart stops. Miriam was young (thirtysomething), not overweight by more than a few pounds, in fair-to-good physical condition, and if she was seeing Lace she was certainly watching what she ate— Lace is a combat vegetarian. From the way she'd looked when I found her I ruled out those nineties charmers, AIDS and cocaine.

Which left what?

Forget it, Bast. Lots of people die of lots of things.

Poison, for example.

But that would make it suicide, unless Lace had killed her.

"There's this weird stuff, and I've got to see you."

And I didn't think someone who'd left a message like that on my answering machine would kill herself a few hours later. She'd meant to be at the Revel's TGIF. She'd said so.

I went back to the closet and did a thorough job this time. Nothing but clothes, nothing in the pockets. A standard-issue black polyester ritual robe like The Snake sells. Miriam—or somebody—

had embroidered it all around the yoke, hem, and sleeves. Silk thread. I took it out and laid it on the bed.

The top of the dresser was covered with more of the usual stuff: New Age cosmetics from the Revel and elsewhere, half a dozen bottles of essential oils. Hairbrush, earrings, bracelet, watch, ring. Little ceramic Ho-Tei with his fat celadon belly.

The top drawer of the dresser held more jewelry, some unopened mail, and a passbook and checkbook from Chemical with the ATM card stuck in the passbook. A set of numbers that I was betting was Miriam's access code was written on the card in gold ink—and, damn it, they tell you and *tell* you not to do that.

She had about two hundred in checking and nearly a thousand in savings, no recent withdrawals. Her last paycheck was also in the drawer, already endorsed. I made a note to deposit it. I also took out Miriam's address book and made a note in the back: Chastain Designs, up on West 47th. The Diamond District, for you out-of-towners.

Nobody calls West 47th "Diamond and Jewelry Way," just as nobody calls Sixth Avenue the "Avenue of the Americas." We started with numbers and we'll stay with them. Or maybe numbers are just easier to spell.

At least the paycheck explained Miriam's lifestyle. Chastain Designs—I knew from my Saturdays at The Snake—was a wholesale jeweler; from the hourly rate on Miriam's paycheck she did some kind of scut work—probably assembly—that netted her about enough to pay her rent and utilities without too much left over. Assembly-line jewelers aren't paid a lot—they're just hired hands—but if Miriam was doing any freelancing at all she could be making good money. Could have been.

I wondered if she did design. If she did, it was a good bet she'd asked the Revel to handle some of her pieces on consignment. I wondered if Carrie'd turned her down.

I started a second pile on the bed: Jewelry, bank stuff. I put the paid bills and the letters on top of the ritual robe. Triage. After a minute I opened the nightstand and added the chicken foot to the robe pile.

One of the lockers at the foot of the bed held correspondence. Miriam kept everything. There were copies of Pagan newsletters and flyers for festivals and membership applications for groups and catalogs and, occasionally, personal correspondence with members of this group or that. There was no insurance except an on-again-off-again policy with Blue Cross that didn't seem to be on right now.

My tea got cold while I read through the antique mail, and after an hour or so I had an empty footlocker, a full wastebasket, two more neat piles, and an urge to raid Miriam's kitchen.

You get to know the groups that are taking the risk of going public. I recognized all the names from their notices in the back of all the Pagan newsletters that Miriam got and I get, too. All innocent. All mainstream (for Neopaganism). Nothing here that could explain the look on Carrie's face last night at the Revel when she mentioned Miriam. Gentle Carrie, who never wanted to say anything bad about anybody.

I went off to the kitchen and made more tea and a sandwich and congratulated myself that Miriam didn't have a cat. If she did I'd probably end up adopting it, and I didn't want to do that.

Don't get me wrong. I like cats; what Witch doesn't? (Although, if you want to get technical, the historic and traditional familiar for practitioners of northwest European–based non-Christian religion traditions is the toad, because the English garden toad secretes the same hallucinogen—bufotenin—when upset as that found in Carlos Castenada's favorite mushroom, *Amanita muscaria*—which is why so many ancient potions call for toad sweat as one of their ingredients.)

But I digress. The trouble with cats versus me is that cats, like all animals, are looking for something. Their range. The other members of their pack. A warm spot in the sun. Company. Locking a cat up alone for twelve hours a day in a coffin-shaped and coffin-sized apartment is not my idea of giving an animal these things.

Stewardship is a pretty outmoded word these days, but if you love something—or even if it just belongs to you—you take care of it, right?

Anyway, I was glad Miriam didn't have a cat.

While I ate I went through her purse. Wallet first. Miriam had a Macy's card, a secured Visa, a New York Public Library card, and was a member of the Park Terrace East Neighborhood Watch and her building's tenant association and Greenpeace.

Everything so normal it hurt. I kept digging. It was a big purse. More letters. I made a note to write all these people and tell them why Miriam wasn't going to be writing anymore. A pair of Chastain Designs earrings still on their showcard—very upmarket. A candy bar. More nameless keys. Wallet, paperback, comb, hand mirror, Tarot cards (Waite design), stubs of a couple candles, Ziploc bag of granular incense. I opened it and sniffed. More Russian Church incense.

And down at the bottom, the paydirt I didn't want to find. A little brown book.

In the olden days, around 1500 C.E. (Christian Era), most books were this size. In modern days, A.X. (after xerographic replication), lots of books are this size again. The *Book Of The Law*, say, or *The Sayings of Chairman Mao*. The size of an 8 1/2 × 11 sheet of paper, cut in fourths.

The book in Miriam's purse, however, had never seen the light of copier, Xerox or otherwise.

It was, as previously intimated, about four by five. It was a thin book, maybe a quarter of an inch thick, and the front cover was much thicker than the back—maybe half the total thickness. The book was bound in pale grainy leather—pigskin, maybe. The covers and spine were blank, but it had the look of a professional binding job.

I opened it. The inside front cover was thick because it had a thin sheet of painted wood bound into it: color on black, and the colors faint and hard to see. It reminded me of an icon, but their backgrounds are gold.

Got it. Russian lacquerwork. There used to be a display of it up at the Crabtree & Evelyn in Citicorp Center, and Brentano's (when there was a Brentano's) used to carry it. Gorgeous stuff, fabulously expensive and all done in the traditional manner, right down to the final polish with a wolf's tooth.

I wondered if this piece I was holding had been polished with a wolf's tooth.

Had Miriam gone bonkers and converted to the Eastern Orthodox Church?

I flipped through the book.

The first page said: "Khazar Wicca—Invokations" (sic), in fake-medieval illumination. The rest of the pages were plainer, but they were all hand-done, calligraphed in brown ink. I recognized Miriam's penmanship from the samples I'd seen in her bedroom. Every few pages there was a large four-color initial; the last two were just pencil ghosts and their pages were blank. The book seemed to be a series of poems or prayers (or even, as the title almost said, invocations), with the occasional word in a different alphabet lettered painstakingly in. I read what I could.

* * *

As I have said before and will continue to say, I know just about enough about the history of worship on this planet not to judge religions on the basis of their window dressing and not enough to judge them in spite of it. Religious art consisting of pictures of horrible tortures and a liturgy celebrating blood and slaughter does not mean that the priests or congregation of said religion intend anything similar. Case in point: the modern Catholic Church, whose dogma would be truly hair-raising if you thought they meant any of it. Or the Tibetan Buddhists, some of the gentlest people I know, despite their *raokshas.*

Having said that, I proceeded to judge Miriam's latest religion on precisely that basis. Because it was calling itself Wicca, and there are some things that are simply not Wiccan. Any spiritual path that celebrates them, and calls itself Wicca anyway, is doing so with intent to deceive. And a religion that starts out lying to you about what it is isn't likely to be healthy for seekers and other living things.

The poems were all about death. Not death as an inevitable and sometimes frightening stage in the Great Cycle of Rebirth, but death as an end in itself—something to be celebrated.

And the death the poems were celebrating was the planet's.

"When winter comes forever and the dream of green is gone—"

"Black sky bleak with no stars rising, where the sun is found no more—"

"Come, Wintermother, bring an end to all that lives—"

The literary level was about what you'd expect—rather silly rewarmed Kipling—but the subtext was spooky and nasty. This was one artifact that wasn't going to make its way back to Shelbyville.

Before I closed it I took one last look at the icon. Someone other than Miriam had done the work on it, trying hard to fake a traditional lacquerwork style. Now that I knew what to expect I could make out the design, but somehow the poems had more power. In a world where the *Nightmare on Elm Street* movies are light entertainment, visual images no longer have the power to shock. Two monsters—one red, one blue—tearing a naked woman in half in the middle of a blasted heath was strictly amateur hour.

Except for one thing.

The tiny painted woman was recognizably Miriam. And she was wearing something around her neck. It was a yellowish blob, at this size. Maybe a chicken foot.

Oh, Miriam, you stupid git, I told you and told you the things to look out for. These woods are dark and dangerous, and in them lurk lots of people whose only interest is in being worshiped.

Sad but true, and at least now Miriam was free to try again, which didn't make me feel a whole lot better, to tell the bedrock truth. I wondered if Lace knew anything about the group Miriam had been with; it would be good to put the word out on them as being people to avoid. I finished my sandwich, picked up the book and purse, and started back into the bedroom.

The phone rang.

I debated whether to answer it through six rings. It was unlikely it was the New York Police calling to see if any house-breakers were home, and nobody else knew that Miriam was dead—unless Lace had mentioned it, which, knowing Lace, was unlikely. It might even be for Miriam—or at worst it might be Rachel Seabrook, checking to see if I was here. At any rate, answering the phone could not get me in more trouble than I was in now. I thought.

I picked up the phone in the middle of a ring.

"Hello?"

There was a —choke? —cough? —gasp of surprise? from the other end of the line.

"Holy shit! It's Miriam! She's—" There was a loud hang-up and then a dial tone in my ear.

I stared at the phone meditatively. Adult male voice, slight bor-oughs accent. Not expecting the phone to be answered by Miriam in a big way.

Because he'd killed her?

You've been reading too many murder mysteries, Bast. Nobody killed Miriam—and if they had, why would her killer be phoning to tell her about it?

Because he'd poisoned her and wanted to see if it had worked?

Unfortunately that was too plausible for my peace of mind. The fact that I'd managed to give him one hell of a scare did little to compensate for the fact that now he—my mythical murderer—would be looking for Miriam to finish the job.

But Miriam Had Not Been Murdered.

If she had been, would the police notice?

And why, on the basis of, let's face it, no evidence at all, was I so convinced someone had killed her?

I didn't know.

So I did the first sensible thing I'd done since yesterday. I called Bellflower.

Lady Bellflower, to give her her proper liturgical title, is the High Priestess (HPS for short) of my coven, Changing, and has been in the Witch business longer than I have. She's short, round like the Venus of Willendorf is round, has exophthalmic baby blue eyes and frizzy ash-blond hair that is usually standing out in all directions. Like most of our native New York Crafters, Belle comes from a Jewish humanist background, got fed up with the man-centricity of Judaism, and went looking for the Goddess. If you'll read the Old Testament (Jeremiah 44:15–19), you'll see this is not the first time Jews have gone looking for the Lady.

Belle took her training a generation or so out from the original Long Island Coven. The Long Island Coven was founded in the early sixties by an American couple named Rosemary and Raymond Buckland, who were trained by Gerald Gardner in England. I'm Gardnerian lineage; since Belle is the one who trained me, so is she. But after running a traditional Gardnerian coven for over a decade (a wonder in itself when the median burnout time for leadership in the Community is about five years), Belle decided to take a more eclectic approach to life. This has made her something of a scandal in the strictly Gardnerian part of the Community. It also makes her one of the few Witches with her own weekly radio show on WBAI.

I call Belle's approach the New Hope of the Craft. She laughs, but it's ecumenicism that's going to carry us into the next century. If you think that's a good idea, you'd like Belle.

The phone rang several times and I sat through the "leave your name and number" message that Belle uses to screen her calls.

"This is Bast," I said after the beep. "Belle? You there? Okay; today is Saturday, June 16, it's around three—"

"Bast?" Belle's voice has two registers: basso profundo and squeak. To save time she uses both together.

"Hi. Look, you got a minute for me to dump my problems on you? A friend of mine is dead. You remember Miriam Seabrook—"

Belle is a good listener; it didn't take me long to unload the last twenty-four hours. I left in Lace and her phone call but left out the Khazar chicken-foot conspiracy, for reasons I wasn't quite sure of at the time.

"Do you want us to do a Crossing for her?" Belle asked when I finished.

Crossing is short for Crossing Over; I understand the Witches borrowed the term from the Spiritualists, though most of us won't admit it now. Most Neopagans (who borrowed it from us Witches) believe that after death people go to a paradise (which most of us call the Summerland, another Spiritualist borrowing) to rest, relax, and make plans for their next incarnation, in which most of us also believe.

Sure it sounds stupid, but try explaining Christian heaven with a straight face ("You die, see, and then you get to wear wings, and a halo, and a long white robe. And they give you this harp. And then you stand around a giant glowing throne, singing. Forever. That's right. No, you don't do anything else. When you're dead you *want* to sing.")

Anyway, Crossing Over is about sending good thoughts and good energy to the person currently on their way to the Summerland. At worst it's harmless and does what all good funerals do, which is comfort the living. At best, well, that depends on your belief system, doesn't it?

So: "Yeah, sure. That'd be good. When?"

"Well, Changing's meeting next Friday anyway. Why don't you just pass the word; I'll make it an open circle."

Open means that any friendly person can attend, regardless of affiliation. Most of Changing's circles aren't exactly closed, but guests generally have to be cleared with the Priest/ess of Importance for the Rite; usually Bellflower.

"Yeah. Thanks. Lace'll want to be there. Damn it, Belle, how could Miriam go and do a shit thing like that—she was thirty-two and she just dropped dead!"

I was crying, to my utter astonishment. Belle just hung on the other end of the electronic umbilical and let me snivel. I mopped my eyes on my sleeve and did counted-breathing exercises.

"Who's making arrangements for the mundane funeral?" Belle asked after a while.

"Damned if I know. I think there's an autopsy. It'd have to be after that. Her sister is from Indiana, and not exactly wild to do much of anything. So I guess there's not going to be any funeral."

"Yes there is," Belle said firmly. "Ours. Look, why don't you come on up after you're done there? You're only a few blocks away."

"Yeah. Okay. Maybe. Look— Thanks."

Belle sighed, the way she does when she suspects she is not getting through to someone. "Blessed be, Bast."

"B-B, my Lady. Ta."

I hung up and went into the bathroom and did a better job of drying and cleaning my face than my sleeve could provide. I splashed cold water on it and looked in the mirror. Same old white-bread wonder Witch. My eyes were living refutation of the fact that blue and red make purple. I looked like a cross between the American flag and an albino raccoon with leprosy.

Bellflower says that the reason I haven't left Changing is because I can't find any trainees who would be up to the standards she says I'd set for any coven I ran. She says I'd rather go along with the familiar even if I disagree with it (we've had discussions about how Changing is run) than put my own ideas out on the line and be forced to change them. She says that I'll be a happier, healthier, calmer person when I stop feeling that there is one right way to do anything, especially in Wicca.

Maybe. Maybe there isn't one right way. But there are a lot of ways that are demonstrably better than a lot of other ways, and there are some ways (Belle and I differ on this) that are just plain wrong.

Had I been the wrong kind of friend for Miriam? Had I spent so much time insisting that she find the right path in the right way that I steered her away from all the almost-as-goods right down the one she died in?

Or (admit it to yourself, Bast), died *of?*

Okay, it was a stupid idea. But dead didn't have to mean murdered. Hundreds of people die of Christian Science every year, and it isn't called murder. Or even suicide. If Miriam's current spiritual path had included eating things out of boxes marked "Not To Be Taken Internally," it would explain her death. And any competent, responsible, or at least cautious guru would have stopped her—if he could and if he knew.

I wanted to find out who Miriam's guru was. And if he *had* known. And if he was a responsible person.

And, bottom line, I wanted to find out just how much guilt I ought to cop to.

I went back to finish rousting Miriam's personal possessions. I figured I'd give Lace first pick of the stuff and then the rest could go

to her friends and mine on a first-come basis. Everything that
Shelbyville was likely to want was already piled on the bed—I
didn't think that the arrival of three crates of books on Witchcraft
and Paganism would make Rachel Seabrook's life any happier.

I found Miriam's altar tools, the ones she'd use to set up a circle. I found her personal workbooks, all crammed full of dreams,
rituals, poems.

What I didn't find was her *athame.*

Remember that old Dorothy L. Sayers mystery where Lord Peter,
arriving on the scene of the crime, is dead certain it's murder because he cannot find the one thing that absolutely, positively, *must*
be there in the kit of a working artist?

This was like that. There is one thing that almost every Witch
and Pagan has—and a wannabe conservative like Miriam certainly would have. In fact, I knew she had one, because I gave it
to her myself.

There was a knife-smith named Ironshadow who was in the
Community a while back doing all the local Pagan festivals and
Society for Creative Anachronism events. Ironshadow had a nice
line in inexpensive ritual daggers—*athames*—that had about a six-
inch double-edged blade, ebony-wood handle, and your choice of
decorator pommels.

I'd bought one for Miriam after hearing her whine for two hours
about that hoary old piece of Craft folklore that says you can't buy
your own ritual blade, it must be given to you by a friend. We'd
both been at Panthea Festival. Ironshadow's table had been right
there. The one I picked had an amber pommel. I'd always felt guilty
about how happy it made her. She didn't see the meanness in the
gesture at all.

Was that what my tie was to Miriam? Guilt?

Anyway, she took it back to Ironshadow and had him engrave
her magical name—Sunshrike—around the pommel-bezel, and
he signed the blade up near the tang, and I'd know it anywhere.

Except it wasn't anywhere. And it had to be.

I turned the place inside out in good earnest this time, looking
for every place a paranoid ex-hippie might hide the most precious
thing she had, the thing that symbolized her spirit—the thing that
was, in occult terms, Miriam/Sunshrike. The phone rang again
while I was looking and nearly stopped my heart, but it was only
Belle, wondering where I was.

"Uh, it's going to take me longer than I thought to finish up here. Why don't we just give it a miss?"

"You're still coming Thursday?"

Thursday was Midsummer, one of the Eight Great Sabbats In the Wheel Of The Year. It would be Just Family—all the members of Changing who would manage to juggle work and world to get there.

"I'm still coming Thursday," I said, as much to the Goddess on Miriam's altar as to Belle.

By seven o'clock I was starving, and I knew for a fact that Miriam's *athame* was not in the place. Where it was if it wasn't here was a nagging question that didn't manage to seem too urgent, at least on this empty a stomach. After all, Miriam was dead. Her *athame* didn't matter to her now.

Did it?

I gathered up my two piles. Rachel's went into an old suitcase I'd found. Mine went part in my purse, part bundled into Miriam's ritual robe and lashed together with her belt cord.

I made a fast circuit of the apartment to make sure everything was tidy for extended absence—closed the windows, stripped the soiled bed (afterthought), doused the candles and the incense on the altar.

The Goddess looked at me, and I picked her up and put her in my purse, taking off the scarf I was wearing to wrap her in.

Good-bye, Miriam. I guess you might have been a better friend than I thought.

And I was a worse one.

3

I'd meant to go down to Chanters Revel and see if Lace'd ever turned up, but going through Miriam's apartment wiped me out worse than I thought. I got home about eight-thirty Saturday night and there were, thank God-or-Goddess, no messages on the answering machine. So I lay down for half an hour and when I woke up it was about five in the morning. So I did what any sensible person would do: turned over and went back to sleep.

The next time I woke up it was to the sound of my own voice telling somebody to leave their name and number and I would get back to them. Lace was starting to do just that when I grabbed the phone.

"Lace? It's me." Which is a damned stupid thing to say when answering your own phone, but answering machines do that to people.

"I thought I better call you." Lace sounded like she had a major head cold—or like she'd been crying for a long time.

"I think you'd better talk to me, Lace. Did you call the police Friday?"

"No." Defiantly.

Well, that was one weight off my mind—assuming Lace was telling the truth.

"Look, you know where I live. Come on up and I'll fix you a cuppa. And I've got some of Miriam's things for you."

Lace foghorned something unintelligible and hung up. But

she'd come. Getting Miriam's things would get Lace here. She didn't have Miriam's keys anymore. I had two sets now—Lace's and Miriam's—and at the moment I could see no good reason to give Lace either one.

I piled the jewelry I'd earmarked for Lace on the table and set the tea-water to boil.

For a wonder in our neck of the woods, Lace is actually Lace's real name. Georgina Lacey Devereaux, from some place down South before she came here to the Big Empty. You can't tell where she's from by the way she talks—unless she gets really mad, when it comes out in her swearing.

Lace is actually an inch shorter than I am, but she gives the impression of being really big, in that broad-shouldered, husky, breastless way some dykes get. Her hair is cut I-dare-you short and bleached-out white: in her army surplus, spikes, and leather she looks like a cheap Rutger Hauer clone from *Bladerunner*.

When I looked through the door at her her eyes were so red and swollen she reminded me of one of those white mice the government spends millions giving cancer to in an attempt to prove that nicotine may be harmful. I popped my locks and let her in.

"Want a drink?" I said. Ten-fifteen in the morning. But she stopped looking so hostile. I put the tequila and the orange juice on the table.

"No harm done, Lace. It was real heavy, okay?"

She smiled at me and began to cry, so I turned away and started working on what would be scrambled eggs and tofu with red pepper. Lace assembled most of the working parts of a Tequila Sunrise and made it go away.

Like I said, Lace is a vegetarian. Distilled vegetables are her favorite kind.

When I'd reached the point of charring some bagels in my toaster oven, Lace had reached the point where she was poking through the jewelry.

"I called her sister Rachel," I said. "She asked me to pack up Miriam's things, so I went up there yesterday and went through all her stuff. I'm sending Rachel the official papers and bank things, and some of the jewelry. I thought you'd want these, and if there's anything else in Miriam's apartment you think maybe somebody could use, I don't think Rachel's going to mind."

Breakfast was ready. We ate eggs. Lace piled the pieces of jewelry on each other. I'd packed the gold for sending back to Shel-byville, along with the most mundane of the silver pieces. This was the snake ring and ax earring stuff—and a pentacle I'd found tossed in the back of a drawer, as if Miriam'd found something better.

"There was this thing she used to wear around her neck," Lace said. "Where's that?"

It was in a Ziploc Baggie with the Khazar book, but I wasn't going to tell Lace that. Lace is the violent type. "Where's what? She wasn't wearing anything." I was gambling, just a bit, that Lace wouldn't remember too clearly her last sight of Miriam.

Lace frowned. "She always wore it. It was . . . It was like this rabbit's foot, only a bird."

If I'd never seen Miriam's pendant, I'd never have recognized it from Lace's description.

"She wasn't wearing it? You're sure?"

Lace sounded more upset than seemed reasonable over the ab-sence of a piece of jewelry.

"I checked the place over before I called the cops. No ritual jew-elry on her, and nothing out in plain sight in the apartment. What was Miriam into lately, Lace?"

"Why?"

Lace had been mellowing out under the combined influence of tequila, sympathy, and my respect for the fine art of paranoia. Now she looked wary.

"Well, you know, I kind of got the feeling that Carrie didn't want Miriam around the Revel anymore, and Changing is having a Crossing Over for her next Friday, and I didn't know whether to tell them down there. . . ."

"Damn that Carrie bitch." The words came out flat and evenly spaced, with no inflection. "She never did like Miriam. She was al-ways going on about how Miri had to make a commitment—and then when she did, Carrie just couldn't hack it. Miriam was al-ways more C.M. than she was," Lace added plaintively.

I could believe that. C.M. is Community shorthand for Ceremonial Magic—or Magick, if you prefer. C.M. is mostly Christianity-based, hierarchical, sexist, and very expensive to practice. From what I'd seen in Miriam's apartment, Lace didn't mean it literally—except that the Khazar book I'd seen had a whole lot more in common with Ceremonial Magic than with Wicca.

"Well, you know, Infinite Diversity in Infinite Combinations," I said. The First Church of Star Trek has a lot to answer for. "What did you think of Miriam's group when you met them?"

"I didn't meet them. She wouldn't take me. She said they weren't very out—of the broomcloset, you know—and real hetero. She was pretending she was straight."

Lace's mouth made a shape you usually only see on tragedy masks—and no wonder, if her lover had decided to join a homophobic group. Miriam must have had to work like hell to find one, too; the trendy phobia on the New Aquarian Frontier is hetero.

I made encouraging noises, but Lace wanted to forget the whole thing and I didn't get much. Miriam'd found her new group about three months ago. Lace didn't remember its name, but thought it was called "something like Baklava." Once she was in, Miriam dropped most of her other Community contacts. In the first flush of conversation she said some things about the group—and against some others—that got Tollah and Carrie's back hair up. Some hard words about collaboration and party-Paganism were said.

"I'm sure they'll want to know about the Crossing Over anyway," I said soothingly. I wondered what Miriam could possibly have said to make Carrie hold a grudge for three months. I'd probably have to die ignorant; Carrie'd never tell.

Lace finished her second or maybe third spiked orange juice and had tea, and I wrote out all the information about the Crossing Over on a 3 × 5 card to post down at the Revel. I changed my mind and gave Lace one of the sets of Miriam's keys—how much trouble could she get into in an empty apartment?—and we made a date to get together about the stuff in Miriam's apartment—maybe next Saturday, the 23rd, before the rent that Miriam wasn't around to pay anymore was due. Then she left.

After Lace was gone I made myself another cup of tea and got out the stuff I'd taken from Miriam's apartment. That reminded me about the little Goddess, so I got her out, too, and unwrapped her and put her on my own altar. She wasn't displacing anybody; I figured she'd get along with my thunderstone just fine.

She looked a lot brighter here than she had at Miriam's, all gold and ivory (although considering where she came from, it was probably cast resin and gilt paint). Goddess of the Games, Lady of the Wild Things, Maid and Mother but never Bride.

There are some people who think I have an overromantic imagination.

I picked up the rest of the stuff and put it on the table.

Ritual robe. Four 8 × 10 blank books that were Miriam's occult diaries. The Khazar prayer book. The chicken-foot necklace.

No *athame.* That still bothered me. And I didn't know why.

Even assuming that Miriam had, as I was starting to think, gotten involved in a really coercive power-tripping occult group calling itself (with no justification) a Wiccan coven, what that was, was sad. Not a case for Denny Colt, aka The Spirit, superhero investigator.

So why was I trying to make Miriam's death into a crime with a victim and a victor?

Tidiness, probably. Man is the pattern-making animal; the idea that some things Just Happen offends us. If Miriam died, it had to be for cause. Even murder was better than a random cosmos.

It is thinking like that which has led to most of the witch hunts of history. Sometimes things *do* Just Happen—if you're of a philosophical bent, call it a part of the Lady's pattern that's just too big for you to see. But stop looking for a villain, Bast.

Right? Right. Good advice.

And in order to take it I wanted to find out more about "Baklava," alias the Khazar Tradition. Maybe they didn't use *athames.* Maybe Miriam had broken hers, or lost it, or given it away.

Sure.

I glanced through the diaries just enough to put them in chronological order, then started going through them in good earnest. Accounts of dreams, bad poetry, artwork never meant for anyone else to see.

Miriam wasn't a diligent archivist, but enough of the entries were dated for me to be able to figure out what was going on. Every few pages the same entry, some variation of: "This time I think I've found It, The Answer. . . ." and then a flurry of pages done in the style of her newest find. Over and over, for three books and four years. Miriam never changed. She never stopped looking for an answer that came from outside, that she could lace on like a corset to make her life the right shape. She didn't learn anything from all the "The Answer"s that turned out not to be.

We bring the answer with us. All the traditions, all the paths, teach us to see what is already here. That is the central Mystery of our Mystery that I had never convinced Miriam of. The secret is that there is no secret.

The fourth book started in spring of this year. Miriam was still using the dating style of her last fling, so the year appeared to be seven thousand something and the date was 28 Inanna, but after that she started talking about the vernal equinox, so I knew it was March 21. It started out as a series of dreams—ice and snow images—and then, rare for Miriam, an actual diary entry:

"Dark Moon Waxing." (That would make it around March 28. I consulted my pocket ephemeris to be sure.) "Tonight I met a Man of Great Power. He was at The Snake, and he says that he was looking for *me* because he heard me *calling* him—"

The trouble with lines like these, that were old when snake oil was new, is that they are also literally true. The urge that makes you pick up the phone and call a long-lost friend who, it turns out, was thinking about you—what is that, if not what Miriam was describing?

Coincidence? Thank you, no. If I believed in magic as hard as some people believe in random chance and coincidence, by now I would have walked off a building thinking I could fly. But you don't have to believe in something to use it. No one ever had to believe in a chair, you'll notice. Some things are, some things aren't. Use your five sound senses and any more you may have been given, can develop, or encourage. And make up your own mind, not somebody else's.

Here endeth the lecture. So far the only thing wrong with the Mysterious Stranger was that it's bad manners to say these things (even if true) to total strangers. I went on with my reading.

He knew, wrote Miriam, that she had Power, but that it flowed in different channels from that of her peers and so they didn't understand her. He, while not presuming to understand her, had been working with the energy she was attuned to for quite some time. He had a group. Would she care to come to one of their meetings?

Of course she would—who wouldn't, with a sell like that? And Miriam, bless her heart, had written the directions he gave her into her magical notebook.

I copied them—it involved taking the F train to Queens and a bunch of other things. She hadn't written the address, just something on the order of "third building on the left, seventh floor, ring bell." But I could find the place if I had to. If I wanted to. If I was stupid.

The next couple of pages were lists of godnames, herbs, the Cyrillic alphabet copied out with its English equivalents next to it. Do you know that the Cyrillic alphabet has thirty-three letters, of which three are double consonants? I thought you didn't. Apparently her first meeting with the group had gone well, and

Miriam was working on learning all the in-group trivia of yet another spiritual pathway.

Then there was a shopping list of sorts. It looked like Miriam was going to a ritual and had a list of things to bring. Probably a dedication. Innocent enough. Most groups have them—they give the seeker something to hold on to emotionally while s/he's being trained for initiation. Moon in Pisces; we were in April now.

One of the items on the list was a good recent photo. I thought of the likeness in the front of the "prayer book." Somebody had taken Miriam's measure in more ways than one.

Another was an *athame.* Or any double-edged knife. Miriam would have taken them the best she had. Her Ironshadow blade.

So where was it now?

The next several pages were rituals, probably copied out from typed Xeroxes they'd given her once they decided she was trustable. It was pretty standard stuff, based heavily on the Gardnerian model with a lot of Crowley thrown in, and garnished with heavy pseudo-Russian Old Gods.

There was certainly a pre-Christian religion in Russia—in fact several of them, since the now-defunct Union of Soviet Socialist Republics (which everybody calls Russia and which isn't) covered one-quarter of the Earth's land mass. This religion was probably nasty, brutish, and shamanic, as so many of the subsistence-level cold-climate Paganisms are.

But we don't *know.* And probably never will. And anything calling itself a reconstruction is going to be nine-tenths fantasy and one-tenth plagiarism. Miriam's group's stuff was just Russian-flavored pseudo-Gardnerianism with a ritual magic chaser. Miriam probably would have moved on from this, too.

The rest of the pages were blank, I thought, but I flipped through to be sure. In the last few pages toward the end I found that Miriam had taken up her diarizing again.

Unlike her usual flowing hand these were written tiny and crabbed, as if Miriam didn't want to see them herself. None of them was dated, but after a few minutes I realized the earliest one was the last—which meant you had to start at the end and work backwards—and after that it was fairly easy.

But oh, what they said. My heart hurt for Miriam, and at the same time I was so mad at her that if she'd been here right now I would have strangled her. How could anyone be that stupid? I asked myself. How could she stay when they did that to her?

The people at the battered women's shelters ask that every day. And the ones in Children's Services. And the cops. How could he-she-they-it let anyone do that?

Miriam (I guessed) was dedicated into the Queens coven. The next thing they asked for was her blood and bone. I don't know where she got the bone. Baby teeth probably, if she'd saved any of hers. The blood had been drawn at a covenmeet. The site had become infected. She'd started having nightmares.

Put it on paper and it sounds laughable—the "Saturday Night Live" version of *Rosemary's Baby*. But the fear came through even in the cryptic notes that were the only thing Miriam allowed herself to write.

That, and her justifications for what the coven did. How she was stupid to make a fuss. Stupid to be afraid.

They asked for more and more, but what they asked for didn't make it onto paper—only Miriam's anger with how afraid they made her, her triumph each time she managed to do something against all her better instincts. Her statements about how her fear was the last barrier between her and Power. How it would pass. Soon.

Oh please Goddess soon she wrote. And started to cross it out. And didn't.

How could she let them do that to her?

Easy.

She forgot she was a grown-up.

Our childhood is spent doing things against our will. Against our instincts, our desires, our judgment (such as it is) we're compelled to do things we don't want to do. Eat our vegetables. Wash. Go to school. And usually we look back on those things later and realize they were the right things to do at the time.

Childhood is about trust. And somewhere in most of us the trusting child lives on. And sometimes, years later, it can be lured into horror, step by step, by the voice that says: *Just do it. I know what's best. You need to do this. It's best for* you.

The icons of Manson and Jonestown are never far from us, and sometimes adulthood is the easiest thing to give away when people ask us to give them things. Some people thrust their adulthood into any hands even halfway willing to take it. I didn't know where to assign the blame. I only knew my chest hurt.

I tucked my extended museum collection of Miriam's life in a safe place and hit the streets, burying anger in motion. I spent the rest of the day making the rounds—Aphrodisia, Weiser's, The Snake—and telling people about Miriam's death and Changing's open circle.

I should have stopped in at the Revel, too, but then I would have had to admit to Carrie that I'd known about Miriam's being dead when I'd been there Friday and hadn't told her.

Actually, social cowardice can be a rewarding, self-affirming life path.

Chores done and social outrage put away, I picked up a six-pack of Tsingtao I couldn't really afford and headed home to share it with the little Goddess. Work in the morning. So much for a wild weekend in the earthly paradise.

But if the Khazar coven was so goddamn medieval in its arts and graces, where *was* Miriam's *athame*?

Raymond was pleased with the work I'd done on the poetry spreads—which was nice, but what really matters is what the client thinks. Most of them have an annoying ability to expect the impossible and see what isn't there.

As a reward for my yeoman service, Ray gave me a mammoth job that'd just come in from Flatiron Press—one of the last great independent New York publishers, down on 23rd Street. It really was a reward, even though it looked like a bitch of a job, because it meant I'd have no trouble working enough hours to pay my rent for the foreseeable future.

I carted it back to my table and looked it over. It was unusual for us to get a job from Flatiron. Flatiron still does most of their stuff in-house, unless they get something like this. My life's partner for about the next three months: weight about ten pounds, all found. It was a huge, messy manuscript—and stats, and boards—that seemed to be about "how to build your own Victorian house from granite rocks." It had twelve million pictures and drawings that all had to fall on the same spread as their call-outs, no exception.

A call-out is book-design jargon for the reference in the text. When the text says: "The Adam-style fireplace, with ornamental liripipe and ruched gonfanons, represents—" the picture or drawing it cites has to be on the same spread—which is design jargon for any two facing pages. Even-numbered pages are always on the left side of a spread, because page one always starts on the right and has a blank facing page.

It didn't take me long to learn that. Anyone could. But then, nobody wants my job.

So I spread it out and settled in to a nice, peaceful, noncreative fug, which should carry me safely into the fall, when there are more interesting things to think about than work. At lunch I deposited Miriam's last paycheck, emptied her account as far as the ATM would let me, bought a money order, and dropped my package for Shelbyville off at the UPS.

On Tuesday Rachel Seabrook called, to tell me the UPS package containing Miriam's personal effects had gotten there and to tell me what the police had said when they called. There would be an autopsy of Miriam's body, as in all cases of accidental death. It was a routine procedure. On the other hand, Rachel couldn't expect to see results, death certificate, or body until the end of August.

"What am I going to do? I can't just pretend she's still alive!"

I recommended a lawyer and a memorial service. I told Rachel there would be a memorial service here on Friday. I told her she could almost certainly get Miriam cremated and scattered without having to fly her home. I got off the phone before I promised to arrange any of these things.

Maybe it wasn't going to be such a quiet week after all.

Thursday, June 21, was the summer solstice—the longest day of the year. It was also the last day before the dark moon, which probably explained my mood. It's a little-known fact that human craziness shows a measurable upswing on the dark, or new, moon as well as on the full, but I didn't feel crazy. I just felt depressed. It was a real effort to leave Houston Graphics right at five and catch the Uptown train for Bellflower's.

Belle lives mostly by herself in a rambling apartment in Washington Heights and does not believe in spending money on furniture. The elevator was broken again, so I walked up the five flights of stairs and leaned on the bell. This week it was wired up to a recording of a kazoo playing *Ode to Joy.*

"We ordered Indian take-away," Dorje said, once I finished hugging Belle hello. "You want to go in on it?"

"Sure," I said.

I looked around the living room, counting heads. Since this was a weekday, and Changing has frequently been accused of being a yuppie coven (meaning most of us have nine-to-five jobs that prefer we show up for them), anybody who couldn't afford a late night was doing private ritual at home to mark Longest Day and would gather here tomorrow for Miriam's Crossing.

Counting Belle and me we were five so far (Changing is an actual thirteen-member coven, when we all show up). The Cat was here, of course—she's a student who lives, none too happily, with her parents and appreciates any chance to get away from them. Sundance has a car and a night job out on the Island Thursday through Monday, and Dorje lives two blocks away, so they were here, and Glitter and Beaner might make it later, dea volente.

These are their Craft names—the names they took when they decided to become Witches. Their "real" names are none of your business—or mine, although I know most of them. Their Craft names *are* them, and a lot more vivid than John, James, Jane, or Heather.

Glitter is Glitter because she wears purple lamé to work. She's an NYC probation officer, which means Civil Service, vested with a pension, and just *try* to fire her for violation of dress code. She gets a lot more fun out of life than she would if she worked somewhere they approved of her. She also carries the world's only—thank god—purple-rhinestone-hilted *athame*.

The Cat looks like one—a brown tabby, say, with all those fingerprint-swirls of black through her fur. It's caused by interlocking dye jobs that make her the sole support of Lady Clairol. The Cat goes to City College. She's been going for years. Her hobby is Making Things Work—the kazoo doorbell was her creation. She's been trying to get me to let her record a tape for my answering machine, but I've heard the one she did for Dorje.

Sundance's name comes from a long, elaborate, and mostly forgotten joke about mad dogs and Englishmen. You'd say he was painfully normal—except for the fact that his wife left him and took the kids when he went into the broom closet. Beaner is from Brahmin stock—the pahk ya cah in Hahvahd Yahd kind. Gay as a cavalier and a tenor for the Light Opera of Manhattan. His father's somebody in the foreign service and according to Beaner can't make up his mind which is worse: a Pooh-Bah who's a Witch or A Son Of His singing on the public stage.

The kazoo played *Ode to Joy* again. Dorje got the door this time—Glitter and the food arrived together. I flopped down on Belle's emotional rescue couch and stretched out.

And try as I might, I couldn't stop thinking about that other coven. Miriam's coven, the one she'd tithed to in blood and bone and tears, the coven that seemed set up to be a mockery of everything I knew the Craft to be.

Survivor's guilt, they call it.

I got back to my apartment late—or early, depending on your point of view. The ritual had gone well, and I'd talked out some of what I felt about Miriam. We all agreed that it was Too Bad she'd gotten involved with rough trade, but that it was Not My Fault, no matter what I'd bought her. I received a stern lecture on borrowing trouble—"Why bother?" said Dorje. "You get so much of it free."—or not borrowing trouble, as the case might be. Plans for the open circle tomorrow night were set. The Cat promised to put it on the NYC Pagan BBS—that's computer bulletin board, for those of us not quite technoliterate.

When I got in I found my answering machine light was flashing with what turned out to be half a dozen disconnects. This is an annoying but unavoidable complication of having one of the damn things, and I didn't want to listen to it have seizures all night. I turned it off and the phone bell down low, and went to bed.

A long time later I woke up from a vague unpleasant dream of a dentist doing root-canal work to a muted rhythmic bleating. It was still dark outside. After about a dozen rings I identified the sound as my phone.

After about six more rings I realized it wasn't going to stop, and that somebody must want to reach me pretty badly. My bedside clock said 3:45 A.M. I groped over to the phone.

"Hello?"

"Miriam doesn't need your help. Call off the ritual, Witch-bitch, or somebody's going to put your eyes out."

He hung up and I hit the light switch and sat there in a small pool of halogen wishing I still smoked. Anything. Useless adrenaline made the inside of my mouth metallic. I replayed the call in my mind.

Hate. Enough of it to up my heart rate. And not the same voice that had called Miriam's apartment and been so stunned when someone answered.

I got up and walked, to keep my mind from feeding its memory of the call until it tried to open up a link between me and my caller. I put on the tea-water. I opened a beer. I wrote down the date and time and text of the phone call and drank my beer and my tea and watched the clock tick over numerals to 4:38 A.M.

The caller was the same one responsible for all those hang-ups. I was morally certain of this on the basis of no evidence. He wanted me to call off the memorial service for Miriam, as if I could. And he didn't like me or my eyes, which was just too bad for him.

But there was one little thing that was just too bad for me, and it kept me awake until six A.M. when I could reasonably go into the studio early.

He knew who I was, he knew I was a Witch, and he'd called me at home.

But my number's unlisted.

Friday the 22nd had started out just dandy and got better. I was in the studio about seven A.M. Around ten the phone rang.

"It's for you!" Ray yelled in my direction. He held the phone as if he intended to fling it to the floor. No personal calls on studio time allowed, so anybody calling me had to be stupid or the bearer of bad news.

I went over and picked up the phone.

"May I help you?"

"Bast?" Lace again. My stomach tied itself into knots.

"Uh, Lace, is this an emergency?" Oh please, Goddess, let it not be.

Lace took a deep breath. "There's been somebody in Miriam's apartment, Bast. I think you better see."

So in the end I had to thank my midnight caller for allowing me to put in all those early-morning hours at Houston Graphics so I could take a nice long lunch hour. I spent the subway ride north practicing my paranoia.

Lace has my home number. So do about a dozen other people who know me as Bast-the-Witch. Houston Graphics has it, for emergencies, whatever a design studio emergency might be, written right next to the name they use on my paychecks.

It's on the business cards identifying it as the number for High Tor Graphics, which is the name under which I do my freelance work. None of those clients know me as Bast. In point of cold hard fact, there's nothing anywhere to connect High Tor Graphics with Bast.

I'd be willing to bet my last pentacle that nobody I knew in the Craft would hand over my number to any stranger asking for Bast's phone number, and my midnight caller was as strange as they come.

So where had he gotten it? And what possible objection could he have to an entirely benign Neopagan funeral ritual for Miriam Seabrook?

And exactly how up close and personal did he intend to get?

Lace was standing in the doorway to Miriam's apartment when I got there.

"Did you lock the goddamn door?" she demanded as soon as she saw me.

Lace had worked through her fear very nicely, thank you, and was now on her way to furious.

"No, I'm the village idiot. Of course I locked it."

"The hell you did." It came out "hail," from somewhere south of what author Florence King calls the "Smith & Wesson Line." "You just take a looky here."

She backed up and let me in. I looked around the living room, saw what I didn't expect to see, and sat down on the couch. Fast.

Miriam's apartment had been thoroughly tossed. Books thrown all over the floor, records out of their jackets, tapes unwound, stomped, and thrown about. Pillows slashed. Curtains pulled down. All the pieces of Miriam's altar swept off the bookcase top and smashed. I was glad I'd taken the little Goddess home with me.

But Miriam's real expensive sound system, her one brand-new and high-ticket purchase, was still sitting right where I'd left it.

"You left the goddamn door open, Bast!" Lace said again.

I'd locked it, but when she's like this Lace punches people who contradict her.

"Was the door locked when you got here?" I asked.

"Sure it was. I— Oh." Lace looked around the room and back at me. "It was locked," she said. Anger drained out of her like water down the bathtub drain, leaving someone I could talk to.

"And we had the only keys. Right?"

Lace wasn't sure. The building super, I knew, had one, and Miriam might have given out others. But I couldn't think of anyone who wouldn't just have taken things away.

"Okay," I said. "Let's look around." Lace wandered into the living room, scuffing through the wreckage. I went into the kitchen.

True, the place was a mess, but not as bad as if it had been tossed by thrill-burglars (who locked up after themselves?). For instance, the plates weren't broken—although everything had been taken out of the cupboards and the refrigerator door had been left open. Somebody had been looking for something.

The bedroom was the worst.

The mattress was off the box spring. Both the bedside lamps were smashed—which was pure temper. All the drawers were torn out of the dresser. The closet had been emptied. The two foot-lockers that I'd gone through so carefully on Saturday were tipped up on end, their contents flung around the room.

"I thought I better come up and look at it today, so we could get the stuff out by the end of the month." Lace came in behind me and was standing looking around, as much stricken as angry. "It was *locked.*"

Somebody had indeed been looking for something.

"Lace, whatever happened to Miriam's *athame?* Her ritual knife?" I added, just in case Lace was being too Dianic this week to remember what they were called.

Lace took another step into the room. Something beneath the papers went crunch under her boots. She bent down and picked up part of a porcelain plate. It had brown smudges where Miriam used to burn cone incense on it.

"They took it."

It took me a minute to realize this was a question.

"No. I went through everything when I was here. I found the rest of her tools, but I didn't find her knife. Did she leave it with you?" It was a stupid question, but sometimes lovers do stupid things.

Lace shrugged irritably. "Forged iron's patriarchal, anyway."

Maybe it is, but we live in a sexually dimorphic universe and play by the House rules. "Sure, but have you seen her knife?" And I'd rather have my will symbolized by a dagger than a shrub.

"No, I haven't seen her goddamn *altecocker* knife! And what I want to know is, who came in here and tore this place up?"

"And what were they looking for?" I added.

Lace turned around, mad again and reminding me uncomfortably of a buffalo about to charge. One of the nasty African ones. Lace is frequently silly, and ludicrous, and lives in her own private Idaho, but she is not stupid. As science fiction's patron saint John W. Campbell was so fond of saying: "thinks as well as a man but not like one."

"What *were* they looking for, Bast?" Lace said dangerously.

"I don't know." But I did. The Khazar book. Miriam's diaries. Her necklace.

"And who are they?" Lace added.

"I'm not sure," I said.

Lace's face got that flat intent look it does just before she brains some other dyke with a full beer bottle.

"I'm *not*," I insisted. "I'm trying to find out—you remember I asked you who she was with when she died?"

Inflection is all. I wasn't asking Lace who'd been at the apartment, nor yet who Miriam had been romantically involved with. "Who are you with?" in the Community has just one meaning: What coven are you in?

"You think those *Baklava* people came here and did this? *Pagans* wouldn't do this!"

Oh, my people. For some of us it is still Woodstock time, with the Neopagan Community replacing the counterculture. And we are all of one ethos, and would never prey upon one another.

Even among hippies this idea lasted about fifteen minutes, but Lace would rather believe this hadn't happened at all than that it had been done by a fellow Goddess-worshiper.

"It has to have been somebody else. And I'm going to find them. And when I do . . ." Lace promised.

Any Gardnerian knows better. The infighting that's gone on in our branch of the Craft since the sainted Gerald Gardner died makes us look like a bunch of Protestants.

"Sure," I said for Lace's benefit. "But you know, if she was working with them, maybe her group'd know who it could be. And when I find out for sure, I'll tell you."

Lace made a noise like a downshifting truck.

"I promise," I said hastily. "Lace, there isn't any more we can do. We aren't even supposed to be in here. What do you want to do—call the police?"

It took me two hours to settle Lace down and stop her going door-to-door with a baseball bat. By then she'd called some of her friends to come over and help with the cleaning and scavenging, and Miriam's place was full of well-adjusted women with large muscles.

I went back to the studio. I had no trouble getting sympathy over my story of a friend whose apartment had been tossed. It's as common as having your apartment searched by the KGB used to be. In the old days. In Russia.

Russia. Khazar Trad. And a bunch of people starting to look a lot more organized, motivated, and twisted than any Pagans I'd ever seen outside of bad fiction.

A bunch of people who were looking for *me*.

4

By seven o'clock Friday night I was a nervous wreck and desperately in need of at least five of the six beers I'd refused to let myself have. For one, it isn't a good idea to ride the subway while impaired because to survive in Fun City requires constant alertness. For the other, it's a damn poor idea to walk into a circle under any influence other than magic. It's disrespectful to the Gods, and it could leave you with your psyche in a mangle.

How mangled had Miriam's psyche gotten? I shoved the thought aside. No matter what had happened, the Community was going to do right by her tonight.

Bellflower's place was jammed. Sundance took one look at me and handed me the beer he'd just opened.

"You could use it," he said. He had to raise his voice to be heard over the dull roar of three dozen people yammering at once.

"Thanks," I yelled back. I made the beer go away and shook my head when he offered me a refill. Somebody started playing with Belle's sound system and an old Leigh Ann Hussey tape added "The Goddess Done Left Me" to the general noise level.

"I'm sorry about Miriam," Sundance said.

"People die," I snapped back, sharper than I'd intended. "Yeah, well, it's harder on Lace," I emended.

"I think I saw her here," Sundance said, and about then Glitter and The Cat saw me and carried me off.

* * *

"I remember Miriam. She was a good person. She always took time to help you out."

The speaker was a man, someone I didn't know. Since this was an open circle we were meeting in street clothes. He had on a tie-dyed T-shirt silk-screened with roses and skulls. He passed the talking-stick to the woman on his right.

"I remember Sunshrike. One time we invited another coven for Sabbat, and Sunshrike made twelve dozen oatmeal raisin cookies. She cleaned up after, too."

There were about forty people jammed into Belle's living room, making a wobbly oval circle-by-courtesy that filled the living room, the foyer, and wandered into the kitchen. Belle had cast the circle in her best ecumenical style and used the Neopagan Crossing ritual that almost everyone would know, the one that starts: "We are here to say farewell to a friend who must travel far." Then she started the talking-stick around. When it got to you, you said good-bye.

I'd put myself opposite the altar. The stick had a ways to go before it reached me. I wondered what I'd say.

I also wondered if any of the people here had called me up real early this morning. Or had a key to Miriam's apartment.

But I still couldn't figure out a *reason.* It's true that we're none of us angels, and a lot of people hiding behind some fancy Neopagan or New Age handle are as thoroughly bad-hat as they come. But they're almost always mundanes looking for the money to be made off gulling the marks—not believers themselves.

Maybe the Neopagans learned from the mistakes of the previous winners in the World Religion Sweepstakes. Maybe a collection of religious practices exalting *laissez-faire* and everybody finding his own path to divinity just can't spark the moral indignation needed for a pogrom. My personal favorite belief is that we're just too disorganized.

But the cold fact is that I've *never* heard of a real case of intramural lawlessness in the Craft or the Community on purely doctrinal grounds. Name-calling and tiffs, yes. Head-tripping like what Miriam had recorded, yes. But never any real-for-true Pagan-to-Pagan police blotter stuff.

And while my hate call early this morning could be business as usual in the peace-love-and–rock'n'roll Pagan Community, the person-or-people who'd ransacked Miriam's apartment and left behind everything of resale value wasn't.

But my conviction that all the weirdness that had happened was directly related to Miriam's last religious affiliation barely convinced even me, and I'd known all these people intimately for years. As an actual accusation to bring in the mundane courts, it was hopeless.

The person on my right bumped me and handed me the talking-stick.

"I knew Miriam Seabrook. She was a friend. I hope she finds what she's looking for. Good-bye, Sunshrike." I passed the stick to the left.

Everybody hung around after the circle was over. A lot of people had brought cookies or chips or soda and I'd chipped in $5.00 to the Changing general fund for more. The gathering wasn't solemn like a mundane funeral—more like a wake is supposed to be, I'd guess. Most people here hadn't known Miriam very well, and most of them were still young and flaky enough to think that their death would never come.

If the Craft has any failings at all as a religion, it's that it doesn't really do a very good job of taking people through the absolute gut-crunching worst that Life can do. The Lady's mercy was a consolation to me, but I'd be damned hesitant about offering the joys of the Summerland to a mother whose child had just been killed by a drunk driver. People tend to forget that the Craft is the newest religion, as well as the oldest. Maybe it's just that the human race has gotten arrogant enough that the phrase "It's God's will, it's for the best," isn't good enough anymore. Maybe it's never been good enough and we're just admitting it now.

Or maybe the Lady shows Her true face now, as ever, only to those who can manage their lives without a convenient god to blame.

I don't know. Ask me in fifty years when the Craft starts building churches.

Lace came over to me with Tollah; Carrie must be minding the Revel. Lace's eyes were red and she hugged me, and we ended up hanging out in a back bedroom at Belle's with a couple other of Miriam's particular friends for a few hours telling each other the ten stupidest things Miriam had ever done.

"There was this one time—you've got to hear this, Lace; I bet she never told you," a woman named Andre was saying, "when me and Miriam and a bunch of that coven from Fort Lee went out to one of the old Pan-Pagan Festivals in Indiana. And for the main circle they had these big thirty-gallon water-cooler jugs up on top of pillars and they'd dumped this chemical in them to make them glow. So the next time I turn around she's walking up to one to get a drink out of it, right?—you know the stuff's poisonous?—and when I stopped her she said she thought it was just water and they were glowing because of the power we raised in circle!"

"Magic Power of Witchcraft," several of us said in ragged chorus. It's one of those old Community jokes: There's a difference in believing in the power of the Lady and thinking you're Samantha of "Bewitched."

Had Miriam ever found it out?

The Crossing ritual had settled my mind, despite my usual misgivings about the Craft as a full-service religion. Miriam was now beyond any earthly hele or ill, and we had done what we could to speed her safe on her way. Having done that, I had the emotional distance to sort things out in my mind.

Unfortunately, I didn't like what I found.

Item: Last Friday, the day she died, Miriam called me. Upset. Very upset. She had to see me. I knew Miriam frequently but not intimately. Since then I'd had cause to wonder how well Miriam thought she knew *me*.

Item: Some time after her call Miriam Seabrook, age thirty-two, lay down and died. Literally.

Item: From all the written evidence, Miriam was into a pretty bad-hat form of Neopaganism. I thought about the phone call I'd intercepted at her apartment and decided it didn't prove anything at all.

Item: In the wee small hours of this very Friday morning, somebody phoned me up to try to stop tonight's ritual and to tell me with menaces that "Miriam didn't need my help." So far, this was my only grounds for thinking that any of this had to do with Miriam's new religion.

Item: Somewhere between last Saturday and this afternoon, somebody entered Miriam's apartment with a key. They turned the place inside out looking for something, but didn't take anything of mundane value that they found. Oh, yes—and they locked up when they left.

Item: Miriam's *athame* was missing—at least, it hadn't been there when *I* searched the place.

These were all terrific facts. It was just too bad they didn't add up to much.

Miriam had been scared before she died. True, her coven had probably been head-tripping her, but did I trust Miriam to be scared only for a good reason? No. Did I see any connection between Miriam's phone call and her death? No.

Did I want to find out more about the Khazar Trad and whether it was them Miriam was scared of?

You figure it out.

I was one of the last people to leave Belle's. It was about three in the morning and we were down to coven and one or two hangers-on—the kind of people who leave any party about ten minutes after the host has gone to bed. Lace had left a couple hours ago, probably to cruise some of the dyke bars in the East Village and find something to stuff in the big empty of never being able to share a joke with Miriam again.

Belle wanted me to stay the night, but Beaner and The Cat already were—and besides, there's something about wandering the city at this hour. It's one of life's riskier pleasures, but if you haven't got a taste for risky pleasures, why live here?

I hit the street. It was empty. The air had that peculiar softness it acquires, regardless of the season, after three o'clock in the morning. The sky would be showing light by the time I got home, probably, and the predawn breeze was already up.

Spanish Harlem moves farther north and west every year; most of the shops down on Dyckman are bilingual. But even they had given up and gone to sleep. It was just me, and the long wall of High Bridge Park on my right. My boots made sharp quiet sounds on sidewalk the color of old pewter.

There is beauty in the city's artificial stone. But there's a lot more harm. To the Environment, people call it, as if it's nothing to do with them. As if, if the Environment were all gone, there would still be someplace to live.

Illiteracy has a lot to answer for. Environment is just a long word for where-you-are.

I heard footsteps on the street behind me. Probably somebody leaving Belle's after me, wanting to catch up. I slowed down and made the automatic, ever-so-subtle, look-over-the-shoulder gesture.

Nobody. So I picked it up again, heading down the hill.

Footsteps. And now that they'd stopped and hid once I was very interested in them, so I stopped dead and looked outright, because maiden modesty kills more New Yorkers every year than AIDS.

Nobody.

Or was that a flutter of movement from somebody ducking into something just out of my line of sight?

Why find out for sure?

So I crossed the street and didn't hear any more footsteps.

The Dyckman/200th Street Station is the next-to-last stop on the A line. It is down one of those bad old twisty subway stops, and no matter how many "Off-Hour Waiting Area" signs the MTA puts up, nobody is going to wait in them for fear of missing their train. Waiting in them wouldn't make you any safer, anyway.

The station has a long flight down, then a landing with a right angle to another half flight of stairs. Then you're down at token-booth level (closed, at this hour). From the bottom of the stairs you can't see the top.

The platform is on the same level as the booth, cut off from it by a combination of tile walls and a big iron fence with a set of old-fashioned wooden turnstiles. You can't see the whole platform from the token booth area, which can be unnerving.

The station extends the width of Broadway and there are accesses from both sides. You can walk across Broadway from below if you're of a mind to, and go up the stairs at the other end, or you can pay your fare, go through the turnstiles, and have your choice of uptown and downtown trains.

I'd just reached the right-turn landing and was starting down into the station when I heard footsteps behind me, skipping down the stairs. I did one of the basic Directed Imaging exercises real fast—"Visualize a cloudbank. Now wrap it around you so that you're wearing a cloak of mist. Nothing can reach you through this cloak"—and hurried out onto the platform. If the footsteps were following me I wasn't sure I could get across the station and up the other stairs before they saw me—and even if I did it wouldn't be a lot of help.

For once I beat the fare—I didn't want the person following to hear the turnstile go clunk. I got out of line-of-sight and stood in the corner by the pass-under to the uptown trains wearing my cloudbank and pretending I was uninteresting so hard my teeth hurt. I felt the wind on my face that meant a train was moving in the tunnel, and concentrated on making it come here fast.

I heard the footsteps outside the token booth. I couldn't be seen except from the platform itself—I wondered if he was a scofflaw, too, or would think it worth paying a dollar-plus to make sure I wasn't here.

The footsteps crossed the area in front of the token booth, then started up the steps on the other side.

The train pulled into the station. I lunged into it before the doors finished opening and crouched low between the seats pretending I wasn't there. If my shadow got on the train at all he could hopscotch cars at the next station and find me.

The doors closed and the train began to move. I saw someone run down the steps to the platform, but it could have been anyone.

Anyone at all.

So much for Friday.

The trouble was that all of this could be coincidence, or my nerves (which I'd used to think were good), or something real—either sacred or mundane.

And I had no way of finding out which, you should pardon the expression.

In fiction it's different. The detective goes around asking questions, stirring everyone up—and he gets answers. Even Kinsey Millhone gets answers.

If I tried that, everyone including my best friends would shut up like a clam.

We've lived with secrecy for too long. In 1963 when the Craft came over from England and the only kind of Witch there was, was Gardnerian, we hid. Nineteen sixty-three was before the Summer of Love. People advocating love and peace and trust were slightly to the left of UFO cultists on the Cultural Weirdness Scale. We learned to be secret to keep from losing our jobs and our kids and our credit ratings.

After the Glorious October of '79, when Margot Adler published *Drawing Down the Moon* and Starhawk published *The Spiral Dance* and Wicca and Neopaganism became boring instead of threatening, the habit of secrecy remained—even though by now the only ones asking questions were our own.

Oh, some secrets should be kept, and some should be revealed at the right time, but the simple fact is that keeping secrets and saying "I Can't Tell You" is *fun* for those of us who are full-grown in body only, and they have no intention of giving it up. The only way to get answers is to convince your listener you already know them.

The way to find out exactly how Miriam Seabrook died wasn't by asking questions.

Saturday. Miriam's directions would have been easier to follow if she hadn't left out every other one. Fortunately, I figured out from the street names that I was going to Queens, or I never would have known to take the uptown train.

I wasn't followed, this time.

I had no idea if I was going to the Khazar covenstead, or if I could even find it from Miriam's directions or recognize it when I had. And even if I could do all those things, what was I going to do then?

I replayed Miriam's last phone message in my mind. Whatever its cause, her fear was genuine.

And she'd called *me.* Why?

Think about it. She had a lover and she had a coven. If the problem was in the Real World, she'd have called Lace, not me, as Lace, believe it or not, is very good at dealing with other people's problems. If her problem was magical-with-a-*K*, she'd have called someone in her coven, right?

The only reason I could think of for her to call me was if the problem *was* her coven. Which brought me back to Square One, and, as it might be, Miriam's deathbed request.

Help her. And if she was dead, find out why.

Most of the "subway" lines in Queens are elevated, and any time I go there it gives me the feeling I've wandered through a space-warp into Chicago—rows and rows of tenements built before World War II interspersed with the occasional McDonald's sign.

I counted stops until I reached the right one and got off, looking for Miriam's landmarks. It was dark under the tracks, and Manhattan felt about a million miles away. I located the bridal salon and the taverna and started walking.

Why was I doing this? I wasn't the Occult Police. Even if Miriam's covenleader was the original bad hat there was nothing I could do. I couldn't prove it to the mundane authorities, and nobody *ever* gets thrown out of the Craft. Not even Geordie Angel, who runs that fraud mail-order Christian Wicca course from a post-office box in Idaho and who, at the last Neopagan event he attended, slugged a friend of mine in the face. In front of a dozen witnesses, and of course no one even thought to charge him with assault.

Nobody cares. This is the essential meaning of entropy. And if nobody cared, then what I was doing was pointless, wasn't it?

Or was I just cruising to become a legend in my own mind, like all those well-known subway vigilantes?

I turned down a street that had a Gulf station on the right and a deli on the left and a laundromat at the end—according to Miriam's directions, the place she'd gone was on the right side of the street.

No restaurants. That meant she'd been invited into a private home, which is a little unusual on a first meeting.

It's unusual because there are a lot of kinks out there. I'd told Miriam and told her, and in the end I guessed it hadn't helped at all.

Miriam hadn't written the building number or the street name down, of course—the directions said something about "third door, seventh floor." Third door—or building—was the only one on the street that looked as if it could have that many floors. I went into the lobby.

The names on the buzzers for the seventh floor were either missing or seemed to date from when the building was new. No clue there as to which door Miriam had disappeared behind, but all the same I wanted to get out of there.

It was June and I'd never been here before, but I had a sudden flash of how the street would look in winter—cold and dead and sterile. Or worse, how it would look once everyone was gone, and the houses were all burnt-out grafitti-covered shells.

I did not run all the way back to the subway stop. I did *not*.

While I was waiting for the subway back to normalcy I wrote down the address I'd just been to. I felt creepy, as if I'd just burgled a funeral home or wandered into one of those strange rites only found in Thomas Tryon novels. I needed a good dose of Earth-plane reality, and I knew just where to get it.

Chanters Revel is decorous and politically correct. It is a credit to the fistful of Dianic, Feminist, and Goddess-oriented traditions it serves. Aphrodisia lets questions of religion pass it by—it's an herb store, period, and has no affiliations to shake a stick at. Weiser's, East-West Books, and Star Magic are all massively disinterested in what their clientele is into.

The Serpent's Truth is wildly partisan and unashamedly trashy.

They say it's in the Village, and they lie—as Edna St. Vincent Millay once similarly said in connection with Vassar and the Hudson River. The Official New York Northern Cutoff Point for Greenwich Village is Eighth Street (except in the minds of real estate salesmen), and The Snake is almost a dozen blocks north of that, up where the real estate's cheap—or was, back when anything in New York was cheap.

The Snake shares its street with the back of a parking garage, an S&M bar, a commercial photofinishing lab, a sleazy Greek coffee shop, and a store whose plate-glass window says "Novelties"— and lies. You can recognize The Snake by its Beyond Tacky neon sign. To be fair, the sign was there before The Snake was, and is almost certainly the reason for the store's name.

In the long decades of its career, the sign has lost all of the neon tubing that went to make up whatever name the previous business had. All that's left now is a neon picture of a walking stick with a bright green snake wrapped around it. When the sign's lit, the snake coils up and down the stick and flicks its tongue in and out. It fits, somehow.

Today the front window contained a crystal ball on a light-up stand, a selection of grimoires and magic wands, some ritual swords (stamped out of pot metal and liable to bend), and a dressmaker's dummy with a full set of Genuine Wizard's Robes on it, including a long pointy hat with silver stars that I coveted unreasonably. The store has double narrow doors, meant to both be open, but as usual only one was, and the six-foot-high Day-Glo Technicolor Mighty Wurlitzer jukebox containing every record Elvis ever made blocked the other half. Once you made it past that obstacle you were confronted by an eight-foot-high plaster statue of the Goat of Mendes and a jewelry case full of pentacles, bat earrings, and pendants made out of glass eyes. Some of them had made their way into my wardrobe in days gone by. The whole shop was Tourist City.

The Snake is not, and never has been, good press for the Community. It gets dished a lot. Just about all you can say in its defense is that it's been around a long time (it opened sometime in the early sixties), it provides a highly visible intake port for people looking for the Craft or something like it, and it has done less harm to more people than televangelism.

It is also definitely a more interesting place to be than the Revel. I slid in past the jukebox. When I'm especially unlucky, I get to the shop when Tris has decided to play it—the thing has speakers that'd make Metallica blush with envy.

There was the usual haze of frankincense up near the ceiling, and the whole back wall was filled by the lighted glass cabinet Tris (the owner) had just put in dedicated to the orisha-and-floorwash crowd. Between the floorwashes and the jewelry case were the books: Wicca on the right, Magick on the left, Rosicrucianism and what-have-you down the middle. There were also herbs, thunderstones, herbal smudges, do-it-yourself voodoo-doll kits, candleholders in the shape of gargoyles, wishing mirrors, scrying glasses, stained-glass pentacles, salt-and-water bowls, and polyester acetate wizard robes like the one in the window.

To say the stock is overcrowded is an understatement. The place is a retail designer's nightmare. If Tris (it's short for Trismegistus, actually) ever cleans this place he'll find the Lost Ark of the Covenant in the storeroom. Guaranteed.

Julian was at his usual post, behind the cash register. The checkout is on a built-up platform that raises it about eighteen inches off the floor. Julian resembled a scrivener in a Herman Melville story.

When the jukebox is running I deduct ten points from my Karma Batting Average. When Julian's behind the desk it's a plus ten. It was with a moderate amount of difficulty that I reined in my libido. Ah, if only . . .

Not that Julian's to everybody's taste: Unless your fancy runs to pale, tubercular intellectuals with lank black hair you won't have much use for him. Julian is, among other things, a Ceremonial Magician. I've heard it said that he's the only person ever to have actually done the entire Abra-Melin Ritual, which takes a year to perform and requires you to own your own lakeside cottage.

His sexual preferences, if any, are a mystery to the entire Community, which is good as it keeps me (barely) from acting like an utter fool in his presence, further encouraged in this laudable aim only by his utter indifference to me except as a source of Visa receipts. It would be a lot more comfortable if I could reciprocate said indifference, but there's precious little hope of that. Maybe it's those silly little glasses.

"Hi, Julian, got a minute?" I asked. I wasn't being overfamiliar; he may have a last name, but I've never heard it. And on this occasion I had a perfectly legitimate reason for engaging him in a conversation unrelated to spending money.

Julian peered down at me and glare turned his glasses white.

Sigh. He was, as usual, wearing a Roman collar (which he may be entitled to, for all I know), a secondhand hammertail coat, and those tiny oval clerk's glasses. I have always admired Julian's fashion statements. They make no concession to the twentieth century, which is why he makes such an admirable manager for The Snake.

"Oh hi, Bast," Julian said vaguely. "Your books are in."

This is Julian's standard greeting to me. When I tell him, as I do, that I haven't ordered any books, he either tries to convince me that I have (in an amnesiac moment) or that I would have if I'd heard of them.

This was a hands-down case of the second category.

The book he unearthed was a facsimile copy of John Dee's *Talismantic Intelligencer,* which is not, as you may think from the title, a small-town occult newspaper. I'd drooled over it when it came up in the Weiser's catalog a few years back but couldn't afford it. Limited edition, gold-stamped slipcase, bound-in ribbon bookmark, hand-sewn signatures, and guaranteed not to fit any bookcase I owned.

"They reprinted," Julian said. I pulled out my Visa.

"I'd kind of like your opinion on something." I stepped up onto the raised platform of the checkout cubbyhole while Julian rummaged around under his desk for the charge slips. "Ever seen anything like this?"

I dug the Khazar book out of my purse and waved it at him.

Julian came up—without the slips—and grabbed the book. I'd come to him not for slavish hormonal reasons but because Julian is that unpredictable—and rare—commodity, a scholar. The history of magic is his specialty.

"Nice work. Yours?" Julian flipped through it and came back to the icon.

"No. I got it from a friend. I was wondering about the Trad."

"Looks Slavic," Julian said. "Very ceremonial." He paged through it again and stopped to read. He could probably read the Russian too, damn him. "Sort of an ecological version of Rasputin," he said and handed it back to me.

"Rasputin—the guy who murdered the little princes in the tower?" I asked, just to be provoking.

Julian adjusted his little glasses and regarded me disapprovingly. "Grigory Efimovitch, popularly known as Rasputin, or "The Dissolute," magical healer and spiritual advisor to the court of the

last Tsar of Russia—that's Nicholas the Second, if you're counting. He was thought to be able to cure the *Tsarevitch*'s hemophil-
iac attacks by prayer and the laying on of hands. His major
contribution to religious thought is the doctrine of 'sinning in
order for God to have something to forgive.'"

"God: That's Adonai Elohim, right?"

Julian actually smiled; the two years I'd spent studying Kab-
balah weren't wasted. "But what *is* this?" I asked. "What's it *for*?"

"It's a prayer book," Julian repeated patiently. "A devotional—
for raising magical power by prayer. You Witches don't go in much
for that sort of thing."

"I've raised some power in my time, Julian," I pointed out. Wiccan and pseudo-Wiccan groups just don't go in for prayer as an
end in itself.

"But then you used it yourself. This is obviously a . . . Think
of it as a funnel. A link. The power is poured into the godform
shown in the book—probably an artificial elemental of some sort—
and then siphoned off later. At least it could be, if that was what
they were doing," said Julian the ever-cautious.

Craft slang for people who siphon and store energy is "vampire."

"So it's not a Wiccan thing," I said, very casual. "My friend said
it was a new Trad. Too bad; someone should do something with
Russian Paganism." Why, I don't know—it's just one of those
things a person says to fill up a gap in the conversation.

"You can't tell from this whether they're Witches or not. Poly-
theists, certainly, but most of this is rewarmed Golden Dawn, the
usual mishmash; the only thing really original is the ecological nihilism. There's this guy in Queens doing a Russian Wicca coven.
Very into secrecy. Very high church. Calls his group *Baba Yaga*.
You could ask him about this—if you're interested, I could let him
know."

Baba Yaga. Or, as Lace might hear it, *Baklava.*

Bingo.

"Do you know anything about them?"

Julian frowned. "No. Like I said, they're very secretive. I don't
think they'll even talk to you unless you're vouched for. If this is
theirs, that friend of yours might be able to get you in."

"And they're C.M.?" I prodded.

"If they are, nobody knows them." Which meant that Julian
didn't know them, and Julian knew every serious practitioner of
ritual magic on the Eastern seaboard.

The name *Baba Yaga* was tickling something in the back of my mind, and I wasn't sure what.

"Cindy might know," Julian added, trying to be helpful.

"Yeah," I said. "Thanks."

He bagged my book and I decided to take his advice. I went off to see if Cindy was home.

I should have remembered that Julian is never helpful.

5

L ife in the Community often resembles the peripateisis of the Edwardian novel. You go here, you visit, you go there, you visit. It isn't so much caused by the Community as by the City.

This is New York in June, which means intermittently hot, verging on beastly. Most of the people I know live in a tiny apartment or fraction thereof that either doesn't have an air conditioner or has one that the landlord won't let them run. Add to this the fact that anybody who *is* home isn't answering the phone for one of the following reasons:

A) It's hooked up to the fax/modem
B) He's too paranoid to answer it
C) There isn't one because his roommate stole it

and you have the reason why members of the Community spend their weekends wandering from deli to bookstore to apartment to coffee shop, hoping against hope that one of them will be air-conditioned.

Cindy is the first person who realized all of this, and, in a dazzling bid for popularity, bought a commercial air conditioner and stayed home.

Actually, that's only half the truth. Cindy has a typesetting and design service called Incendiary (her last name is Airey—at least it is now) that she runs out of the same loft she lives in. She specializes in catalogs—like Tree of Wisdom, The Snake's mail-order service, or Witchwife, the occult jewelers.

Cindy's street-level front door is one of those industrial-strength gray riveted things. Saturdays she keeps it propped open with a brick. Once you drag the door open you're confronted with a long narrow flight of stairs that goes up to Cindy's third-floor loft and no place else. There is no light bulb because the ceiling of the staircase—and the stairs are narrow—is about thirty feet away. I have always wondered how she got two thousand pounds of Computronic typesetter up them.

I trudged to the top of the stairs. On Saturdays the door at the top of the stairs is unlocked, too.

Cindy is about five foot two and looks like what God could have made out of me if She'd (1) had money and (2) meant me to go through life as a French maid in a bedroom farce. We both have black hair and blue eyes, but where Cindy looks mysterious and elfin, damn her, people always ask me if I have a headache. She's neither Neopagan nor Craft, and she runs the closest thing to a salon New York has seen since Edith Wharton stopped writing. I pushed open her living room door.

Cindy has a table made from one of those twelve-foot doors scavenged from some old East Side mansion. On Saturdays it's covered with food, with a tea urn at one end and coffee at the other. Nobody has ever been able to figure out why she does this.

You would think, with a free and semipublic spread, the place would be jammed, but it isn't. People who don't fit in hardly ever come back twice. I think Cindy changes them into toads.

(This is a joke. The only documented case of mantic theriomorphism on record is Aleister Crowley's turning a friend of his into a camel on one of their Near East walking trips, and Crowley lied.)

I came in and got tea. Cindy was sitting on a pile of pillows surrounded by her intimates. She looked like a punk Germaine de Stael.

I've never really been able to figure out whether I'm "in" Cindy's crowd. I think I'm the only Witch who hangs out at Cindy's, but I'm not sure about that either.

Another thing you learn to live with in New York is uncertainty.

I found a seat and sat. The conversation turned on the usual topics: bands I didn't know, books I hadn't read, scandals where I couldn't name any of the players. I fared slightly better when talk entered the World of Publishing: There the talk was all about who was (a) printing or (b) designing what magical book and what (c) lawsuits or (d) supernatural manifestations were attendant on that. Eventually I worked my way into an eddy in the conversation.

"I've really started getting interested in Russia, lately. You know, the pre-Christian magical system there?"

Neglect to substitute the codephrase "Pre-Christian religion" for "Paganism" in circles like these and you may be forced to listen for up to half an hour to someone telling you that Pagans do not exist. I've also heard that said about gremlins.

"Do you know anybody into that?" I kept saying, and eventually I struck paydirt.

"His name's Ruslan."

The speaker looked vaguely familiar and I finally placed him—he'd come to the Crossing circle last night. Fortunately for my peace of mind he'd left almost immediately afterward—hours before I had. He couldn't be my midnight tailer.

"He's into stuff like that."

"The guy up in Queens?" I said. *Baba Yaga?*"

"Yeah." My informant relaxed, having fallen for the oldest trick in the book—the one about pretending you know more than you do. Convinced I already knew everything he was telling me, my new friend Damien told how Ruslan had moved into the area (New York Metropagan Community) and started working Russian. "Very shamanic," he said—which probably meant drugs used in Circle. Damien had only gone as far as the one visit, since what they wanted—"that secrecy shit and all"—was "too heavy" for him.

Cindy'd heard of *Baba Yaga,* too, and nailed down the reference for me.

"It's named after that evil sorceress who has a hut that walks around on chicken feet: Baba Yaga. The one who eats children. Like in *Fantasia.*"

The things people think are in a harmless little movie never cease to amaze me. The same people who take their kids to see *Batman Returns* think the "Night on Bald Mountain" sequence from a fifty-year-old Disney film is corrupting our young.

Besides, I saw *Fantasia* again on its last release. There's no chicken feet in it anywhere.

I stayed another couple of hours at Cindy's but I didn't get anything else at all useful, if you don't count a couple of leads on who might need some freelance layout work done for them by someone who doesn't freak out at the sight of a pentacle.

But I had enough to annoy me. There was a coven in Queens that had been running for about a year. It was named after a black Witch in a Russian fairy tale, who was intimately connected with chicken feet a little bigger than the one Miriam had been wearing around her neck. Its leader's name was Ruslan, and it was a good bet he was the leader of the group that Miriam had been working with when she died.

6

So here it was Monday again, and just about ten days since Miriam died. As an avenging angel I was a bust.

Belle'd called me Sunday night. The usual thing—how was I, how were things, was I still going unreasonably apeshit over Miriam's death.

I told her death was a part of the Great Cycle of Rebirth. I did not tell her about any death threats I may have received, or that there might be a black coven in Queens murdering people. It sounded stupid even to me, and Belle is so *laissez-faire* she makes Ayn Rand look like a Commie. If I told her everything I knew about the *Baba Yaga*s Belle'd want to invite them to Circle.

So she talked and I didn't, and she reminded me that Changing was meeting again this Friday and would I be sure to be there?

Belle only makes these special quality-time phone calls to people she suspects may be in need of them. I did not like the feeling of being considered needy. I was supposed to be "over" Miriam by now—that much was plain.

But now it was Monday and I had a cup of truly awful coffee at my elbow and a razor blade between my fingers and a spread in front of me where the repro was in so many pieces that it resembled a ticker-tape collage. And Miriam wouldn't go away.

The ancient Greeks (who, as the Discordian saying goes, were in the sorry position of not being able to borrow any of their philosophy from the ancient Greeks) made dramatic hay from the idea

SPEAK DAGGERS TO HER   75

that the blood of the murdered cries out for action on the part of the survivors—a literal, decibel-measurable crying that literally had to be done something about or nobody would get any sleep.

I envied the ancient Greeks. They at least had a murder or two in hand. I didn't have anything, except a line on some probably unpleasant people that my backbrain was trying to work out a way to meet.

I put in a long day at Houston Graphics/The Bookie Joint, first trying to jack up the old paycheck, then on a freelance piece of my own. It was after eight but still light when I left the studio.

It was the end of June, but the worst of the summer heat was still to come. It was pleasant enough that I decided to walk instead of taking the subway.

I often wonder, when I'm trying not to think about other things, if the citizens of Atlantis ever had any more idea that they were living at the pinnacle of civilization than the average New Yorker has. New York has been called "the only city" and "the new Atlantis" in about equal measure. Maybe it is: so big, complex, and information-packed that when people have really evolved to fit it they won't really be like other people anymore.

And then again, maybe sometime all the city services will go on strike at once and we won't have to worry about evolving any more.

My answering machine was flashing when I got home around nine: brilliant self-referential paragraphs of vermilion Morse that told me *lots* of people wanted to talk to me. I cranked up the volume and hit "Play."

Sometimes my capacity for self-abuse frightens me.

Lace, who left her name but no message. Somebody for High Tor Graphics (me), who left a message but no name. A couple of hang-ups, faithfully recorded. Someone trying to sell me the Sunday *New York Times* (an automated random-dialer). Tollah, calling from the Revel, and could I please read Tarot down at the shop on Saturday because their regular reader was having a crisis? More hang-ups. It's a good thing answering machines don't get bored.

Pay dirt.

The tone, then: "My name is Ruslan. I believe we have a number of friends and interests in common. I do hope you'll call me.

My number is—" he rattled off a string of digits in 718, which is, among other things, Queens.

Nothing is ever gained by hasty action. I went and found the cassette I'd recorded Miriam's last message onto and added Ruslan's. I wrote down the phone number and tucked the cassette away again. I took the little Khazar missal out of my purse and looked at it.

There's a kind of phone book called the CrissCross Directory. Most libraries carry the one for their area. Instead of the usual alphabetic listings of Ma-Bell-as-was, all the phone numbers of your area are listed in numerical order, followed by who has them and where.

So if you have a phone number, you can get a name and address. If I took this phone number down to the New York Public on Forty-second Street, I'd bet more than a nickel it would go to the address in Queens I'd visited Saturday.

Bast, Girl Detective.

I hesitated between coffee and a beer and settled for tea. While I was waiting for the teabag to commit hygroscopia, I got out Miriam's last occult diary and turned to where I'd been using it to make notes on things Khazar. Under my notes on what Julian had said and what I'd heard at Cindy's, I added my first impressions of Brother Ruslan.

"I believe we have a number of friends and interests in common."

Ruslan had what is inaccurately referred to as a "white" voice— i.e., one that has been educated out of ethnic and regional identifiers. Not as common in New York as you might think; it'll soon be a thing of the past, but you can still frequently tell the borough, and sometimes the religion, of New Yorkers through vowels alone.

"I do hope you'll call me."

Yes, an educated voice. Maybe overeducated—just a little bit trying-too-hard to be upper-crust. *Look how very important and refined I am.*

It was familiar. Not the voice itself, but the *kind* of voice. I sat and drank my tea and stared out my only window while the light slid down toward *l'heure bleu.*

It was a professional voice. Doctor, lawyer, tax accountant, one of those fields that attracts bullies and sadists and emotional basket cases who have about as much compassion as a paper cup. An "I can do whatever I want, and not only are you helpless to stop me, if you don't pretend to trust me I am going to stick it to you even worse" voice.

Paranoid ravings aside, during the course of your schooling most professions slap a thin veneer of whitespeak over the vowels you were born with, and most professionals pretend to an infallibility that God Herself couldn't cop to once they get out into the world.

Guesses.

Was it the same voice as whoever called me the night before the Crossing circle? I thought about it hard and honestly and decided I'd never be sure. It wasn't impossible, though.

And if the mystery caller wasn't Ruslan, it was a safe bet the caller knew Ruslan and had handed over my unlisted phone number. Which Ruslan had chosen to call now.

I felt like the heroine around Chapter Seven of a horror novel, at the point where she dimly suspects she's the victim of several interlocking conspiracies, but doesn't know who's in them or how they fit together. Why should Ruslan call at all? Why now? What did he know—and what did he think I knew?

A professional voice. Doctor, lawyer, accountant . . . priest.

There was no help for it. I picked up the phone.

Ring, ring, ring . . .

"Hello?" The same voice, but a little more rough-edged.

"I'm returning Ruslan's call," I said and waited.

"Oh hey, *Karen*," Ruslan blossomed into polished talk-show sincerity. "*Hi.* How ya *do*ing?"

I thought over which of my many personae to plug in to keep him talking. I decided on Pathetically Grateful, which someone with a voice like that would want everyone to be.

"*Hi*," I emoted. "I'm so *glad* you *called*."

Dead silence, while both of us listened to the conversational ball roll under the sofa. Columbo never has this problem.

"Well, I Knew you were trying to reach us. I was meditating, and I just . . . Heard you. I can always tell when someone's ready to Find us. So I called."

It was pure snake oil, delivered in the hushed pluralistic undertone of a mortician with a tapeworm. The next thing he'd do would be to remind me that my number was unlisted, so I could marvel at how he'd called anyway.

"Karen? Don't be afraid," he said reverently.

Pathetically Grateful took the bit in her teeth, which was a good thing, as left to my own personality I'd simply have hung up.

"Oh, no!" I agreed. "It's just that this . . ." I trailed off. I hoped he knew what I meant. I didn't.

"Miriam told me about you and how much you were into things like this—and I bet she told you a little about us, too."

It was a minute before I recognized the tone: Rogueishly Playful, with just a hint of "We're all boys / girls / little - green - furry - things - from - Alpha-Centauri here together."

I hated him. It was pure, primal, instinctive. It was also getting in my way.

"Miriam?" I said blankly.

There was a pause. It was a lot harder to string total strangers along into making Damning Confessions on the telephone than it looked in the books. "I mean, I *knew* Miriam. . . ." I added.

"Life and Death are in the Hands of the Gods," Ruslan intoned, tabling the question of what Miriam had or hadn't told me.

"I don't know what Miriam could have told you about me. I know she's been with a lot of groups. I'm in a group now, but I'm really looking for someone to study with who's more *shamanic*," I babbled on. And may Goddess have mercy on me if Belle ever found out what thumping lies I was telling.

"Perhaps Miriam mentioned the sort of things we do," Ruslan said. Fishing again, I realized.

"I'm really into *northern* things," I said, ignoring the hint. "Look, do you think it would be possible for me to visit your group? Are you open?"

Language is a wonderful thing. A translation into English of what I'd said so far in Paganspeak would go like this: *I'm interested in working with a magical group that uses drugs and related physical discipline to produce altered states of consciousness, but I'm not interested in anything Native American or related to Ceremonial Magic. Is your group currently accepting new members, and do I sound interesting/safe enough to you for you to let me come and see if I want to join you?*

"Some people think we're a little hierarchical," Ruslan said. (If you aren't willing to follow orders, forget it.)

"I think I'm ready for that. It's important to me to be with a group that's serious." (Just try me.) "I think I was meant to find you." (Remember who called whom.)

"I think you're right, Karen. Why don't you come over on Wednesday, around seven? You know where it is, don't you?"

Subtle as a truck.

"Well," I said coyly, "I don't know *exactly* . . . Somebody told me you were in Queens?" (You and I are both creatures of great occult power, of course, and I will admit I could find you by following your psychic emanations as long as you don't ask me to prove it.)

Finally Ruslan gave up trying to get me to admit Miriam had told me anything and reeled off a set of directions that sounded just like the ones she'd written down. Probably he did this a lot.

"We'll go out to dinner, and afterward maybe you can stay for the Circle." (Providing we like what we see, of course.)

"I'm looking forward to it," I said.

I hung up and stared at the phone for a long time.

My name is Bast.

That was the name Miriam had known me by. As far as I knew, she'd never heard of Karen.

Just who had supplied the information about Karen Hightower to Ruslan?

7

Seventy percent of all reported UFO sightings occur on a Wednesday. This particular Wednesday I was sitting on an uptown subway with no air-conditioning getting ready to meet Baba Yaga. I was being careful—at least I thought I was.

There was a letter in my apartment. I'd debated between addressing it to Belle or to Miriam's sister—neither of whom would do anything, I realized, so I addressed it to Belle, she should live and be well. At least I wouldn't have to tell her what all the words meant.

First impressions count for as much in the Community as anywhere. I didn't know if Ruslan knew anything at all about me (then why had he called?), but I didn't want to look either too amateurish or too professional. I left off all my funky in-group "kick me" jewelry and wore silver rings in the holes in my ears and my lesbian clusterfuck necklace around my neck—the one that you have to stare at for quite a long time before you realize it's entirely made up of women being nude and naughty. Black silk T. Black dress pants that (I fondly believed) made me look like a slumming runway model. My one set of really upscale footwear—a pair of black suede boots I'd blown an entire freelance commission's pay on at Bloomie's on sale.

I'd brought cash and tokens to cover the evening and left my purse at home, along with everything else that would tell Ruslan who I was and how much money I made. Was I a slumming yuppie? An upscaling waitress? Did I spend more time in the New York Public Library than he did? He wouldn't be able to tell by looking.

Never tell me the early Christians did not have these problems. After all, they used to worship naked, too.

Ruslan met me at the subway stop.

"*Karen,*" he said. "So good to see you. Ruslan." This last in case I hadn't noticed the immense aura of magical power around him.

Ruslan was about average height, maybe an inch shorter, say five-ten. My boots had two-inch heels, which made me about as tall as he was. He didn't like it. He had that light hair that's neither brown nor blond, and pale blue eyes, and the kind of build that isn't quite fat but makes you think of something prize and pampered and well fed with ribbons on its halter. He was wearing an open-collared white dress shirt with jeans; he had a sterling silver belt buckle of a wolf biting the moon with a lot of Cyrillic around it. The buckle looked expensive and custom.

His hands were short and blunt, almost like paws. I shook one of them.

"And this is my lady, Ludmilla."

"We're so pleased to meet you, Karen."

Ludmilla looked like someone had jammed her head between two books and squeezed—a piranha caught halfway through a transformation into a guppy. Pale bulging eyes and hair barely dark enough to be called brown. She wore it parted ruler-straight down the middle of her head and hanging down. She couldn't be old enough to have worn it that way as a teenager. Or maybe she could. It was hard to tell.

Ludmilla was wearing one of those expensive organic dresses— Laura Ashley or something like it—makeup, nylons, heels, and a suspicious lump on her left breast that might be a chicken foot stuffed into her bra. Her voice had a nasal out-of-town rasp I couldn't immediately place.

"I'm happy to be here," I said. Ruslan clapped me on the shoulder. I felt like I'd joined Rotary.

"I know this great restaurant," Ruslan said.

The restaurant turned out to be Turkish, or Armenian, or at least dark. The waiters all knew my hosts, which was how I found out that Ludmilla was Mrs. Ruslan, which implied that Ruslan had a first name somewhere. He kept calling me "Karen" at frequent intervals, like someone who has been too long in the thrall of Norman Vincent Peale.

Ruslan ordered for all three of us in the tone that's all smiles until you contradict it.

The food was good.

And I realized I was going to have to confess. *Everyone* confesses when they meet someone new. The story of their life. When they knew they were different. Trying to find God in all the places the approved sources say to, and finally deciding the sources are cruel or crazy because they tell you to go stand in this building where a bunch of men reel off centuries of rote words and they tell you this is God, this is religion, this is all there is of the not-human that interests itself in Man.

The Firesign Theatre had an album once: *Everything You Know Is Wrong.* Once you've found that out, been lied to that comprehensively, you look at everything a little more closely, trying to find out what other lies all the blind ones around you are accepting. And there're lots of blind ones and they're all happy and content and you're not and it gets damned lonely.

So when you find someone else who maybe, *maybe,* knows what it's like to wake up one day and realize everyone else is playing Let's Pretend, you talk.

I couldn't quite bring myself to do that. I fenced in the inarticulate *patois* of the nineties, that dialect where if the other person doesn't already know what you're saying he'll never find out by listening.

"Well, I came to New York a few years ago, you know, searching? I don't know if you *know.* And I never was really comfortable with a lot of the stuff people were into, you know, when I *found out.* They seemed, well, like they weren't taking what they were into *seriously?*" I poked at my something-with-lamb-and-lemon.

"Most people don't," Ruslan intoned. I'd learned by now that he had two speeds—jovial and oracular. Jovial was like being French-kissed by a bulldozer. Oracular made me want to turn atheist. "Even those who should know better don't realize that they are meddling with living archetypes of immense power."

And there are things that man was not meant to know, I finished silently. And I thought about being someone with that desperate need for belonging and validation and knowing I wasn't just alone and making things up—and finding Ruslan.

"I didn't think anyone else understood," I said.

"It isn't especially easy," he admitted. "A great man once said that the first thing one must give up in order to study magic is the fear of insanity."

"Dessert?" said our waiter.

Apparently I could be trusted to order that by myself. I had the baklava and Ludmilla had the galactobourkia. The waiter looked at Ruslan.

"Now, Love," Ludmilla said. Ruslan shook his head. The waiter departed.

"I have to watch what I eat," he said. A little defensively, I thought.

"Ruslan has these *shamanic trances,*" Ludmilla explained proudly.

A fact that you may have forgotten if you live in one of the major population centers is that women's liberation, The Revolution, has not yet been universal. It seemed that Ludmilla Ruslan adhered to the older, purer doctrine — that of full-time cheering section for the man of her choice.

This is not a good way to be. If it's unilateral, it's degrading. If it's reciprocal, it's nauseating.

Think about it. If you had "shamanic trances," would *you* tell the world?

I turned back to Ruslan. "You go into trance?" I said, hoping I looked fascinated.

He smiled. Of course he'd wanted to be asked. Another thing an old-fashioned girl is good for is providing a straight line.

"Started when I was a boy. I was pretty severely diabetic, so I used to be sick a lot of the time. And when I'd go into coma I'd have these *experiences.* Nothing like them in the literature. And strange things would happen when I woke up. So I started trying to understand them, and I realized that the shock to my system was actually projecting my astral self into the shamanic dreamtime."

I looked politely impressed. It might even be true. I'd heard weirder things from people who were perfectly sincere about it. The religious urge itself is bizarre enough; after that it's all quibbling. The question was not "Is the story intrinsically unbelievable?" but, "Does *Ruslan* believe it?"

Or was he lying, and if so, why?

"I realized it was important for me to learn all that I could about the dreamtime, so I could learn to guide others." Ruslan smiled. Ludmilla looked proud.

I had a sudden snapshot image, vivid as a cliché: the Russian steppes, flat as the plains of Kansas and a thousand times wider, salt-white with ice under a sky as blue as midnight. Chiaroscuro moon and fat white stars unwinking in the airless vault.

Ruslan's dreamtime, as offered to his acolytes.

"Yes," I said.

On the walk back from the restaurant to the house I delivered to myself a stern mental lecture on not being a self-abnegating romantic jackass. Ruslan had a good line of patter, and he wasn't exactly the first to decide that post-Bomb America is a culture romancing oblivion. People have always worshiped what scared them, on the plausible theory that if they were nice enough to it, it would go away. The gods of agriculture and husbandry are the gods of famine. The gods of love are the gods of rejection.

What was it Julian had called Ruslan's theme? Ecological nihilism? The flirtation with the ultimate terror—extinction.

So Ruslan had a good line of patter. Fine. If that was all he had, that was fine, too. Miriam hadn't killed herself; I wasn't here because I thought he'd talked her into suicide.

I was here because Miriam had asked me to help. And because if she were still alive, I'd be here, gathering my own facts in order to be fair.

We went back to the apartment, so I guessed I'd passed the initial interview and would get to see an actual episode of Russian Shamanic Wicca. Even though I was nine-tenths certain that Nothing Was Going To Happen I had damp palms and a dry mouth standing there in front of the door while Ruslan dragged out his keys. Suppose they dragged me inside and cut me up with a chain saw? Suppose his whole group was waiting inside with sterling silver icepicks? Suppose—

I'm sure the Lone Ranger never felt this way.

Ruslan opened the door, and the only thing waiting for me was a cloud of stale Russian Church incense. Ruslan's apartment smelled just like Miriam's apartment. Ludmilla turned on the lights.

"Why don't I just go and make some tea—people ought to be arriving in about half an hour."

Ludmilla bustled off across the living room. I looked around.

I don't know every practicing Neopagan in America, but I've been in a lot of living rooms, in New York and out. Rich, poor, and in between, they all have a certain family resemblance that comes of being decorated by a bunch of people coming from the same microculture, with the same assumptions about the world.

Ruslan's didn't.

It wasn't just that there weren't Sierra Club posters on the wall, or that there *were* large pictures of the Sacred Heart of Jesus. It was something subtler. A sense of priority.

It was a big apartment—big by New York standards, meaning that it had a separate kitchen, through the doorway to which I could hear Ludmilla bashing the tea things about. There were doors leading off both sides of the living room; two bedrooms, probably.

The living room furniture was stylish and modern and new-but-not-good. Vinyl couch, glass-and-brass tables—Monkey Ward's copies of *Architectural Digest* originals. Abstract geometric rugs in earth tones, from the same source. No books in sight. The only honest things in the room were the paintings.

There were twelve of them, about eighteen by twenty-four, done on wood in Russian lacquerwork style and hung without frames. They were done by the same artist who had done Miriam's missal.

They were not nice. But I wondered, as I looked at them, if I would have disliked them so much if I didn't already dislike Ruslan.

"What do you think?"

"They're very well done."

"Thank you. My own work." That much was an honest reaction. "Of course, I'm not a professional. A number of people have said I should do more, and of course I've exhibited, but it would take too much time away from my real work." A line of patter so standard I could parse it in my sleep.

"They're beautiful." I felt something warmer was called for, even if I do always get irritated with myself when I lie. They weren't beautiful—not even with the romantic Gothic "terrible beauty" of an advancing lava flow. They were just *there*, inimical as a beaker of cyanide.

I stepped closer to the pictures.

"I paint in blood," Ruslan said behind me. I turned around and caught the sadistic good-ol'-boy gleam in his eye. He expected me to be freaked out. That was why he'd told me. To watch me squirm and then apologize for squirming.

"Yours?" I asked politely.

His face went completely blank for a moment; then he laughed and I saw him abandon his cat-and-mouse game for the moment. When he spoke again it was almost a non sequitur.

"I'm very drawn to the Russian archetypes. The Khazar people were a vital and important Pagan culture that flourished in the Black Sea area around the second millennium B.C.E. When Christianity was introduced by the ruling classes as a means of disenfranchising the indigenous Pagan tribes, they embedded the vital images of Khazar religion in their own mythology. I'm trying to reclaim them so that the eastern Slavic peoples can once again practice their native tradition," Ruslan orated.

We were back on track with Pagan Indoctrination Lecture #4-B. Nobody wants to be the one to start something, especially a religion. There are two ways of handling this: Either say you are actually reviving a religion that fell into disuse longer ago than anybody can remember (that's how Judaism started; read your Bible), or say you are reforming the one that's already there (Christianity, which started as Reform Judaism; and Protestantism, which began as Reform Catholicism).

Even in Wicca someone is always unearthing a Book of Shadows that belonged to his great-grandmother, which is always exactly like most of the others that have been published, the first of which can be documented as having been written circa 1953.

"I've always been fascinated with Old Russia," I said, turning my back on the pictures painted in blood. I was saved from parading my ignorance by Ludmilla's arrival with a big tolework tray: tall glasses full of black tea; sugar lumps and cherry preserves; right out of Chekhov. The *folklorico-manqué* clashed just a trifle with the Levittown *moderne.*

"Sugar or jam?" chirped Ludmilla brightly, dropping a big glop of cherries into her glass. The glass rested in a little brass basketwork holder with a ring-shaped handle down near the bottom. It looked more like a candleholder than anything else, and like a perfect way for Bast to slop boiling tea on herself.

"Sugar," I said. "Is there milk?" I was deliberately not picking up on their cues for in-group bonding, and I could see it was putting Ruslan just a little off balance.

"We're going to have to teach you to drink tea like a Khazar!" he said in a hearty-sinister voice, but in all fairness I would have found a discussion of the weather sinister by then.

"Now, Love," Ludmilla said. "There's milk in the refrigerator, Karen; I'll—"

"Oh, I can get it." I was already standing, and the buzzer buzzed, so Ludmilla went to let whoever-it-was in and I went off to the kitchen.

I did not poke around, but I kept my eyes open. When I opened the refrigerator I saw a lineup of little bottles in the egg-holders in the door that nobody uses for eggs. Insulin. The name on the prescription label was Michael Ruslan.

One thing verified. He *was* a diabetic.

I heard voices in the living room. I came back with the milk and poured it in my tea and made meaningless friendly noises at the two men and a woman who'd come in. Max, Norris, and Starfawn, if I heard the mumbles right.

"And what's your name?" Starfawn said. She was small, round, and young—younger than any of the rest of us by a good ten years. Twenty-two, maybe.

"Jadis," I said firmly, before Ruslan could introduce me. "That's my magical name," I added. I thought it would be a good idea to establish my alias early on, and I didn't think I'd have trouble sounding plausible to a woman who had chosen to be known to her gods as Starfawn.

"Hey, right on," said either Max or Norris.

"It's a good strong name," said Ruslan.

It should be—I'd stolen it from the witch-queen of *Narnia*. Ludmilla took the milk carton back into the kitchen. I looked down at my tea. The milk had settled about a half inch below the surface, like a ball of taffy dropped in ice water.

There was a short awkward time after that. Ludmilla brought out more tea. A couple more people arrived—I was glad not to see anybody I knew—and the talk skittered nervously around Baba Yaga secrets; things they couldn't discuss in front of an outsider.

It was probably mostly entirely harmless stuff. If it had been any normal coven I would have known that for sure—it would have been about magical healings, divinations, the usual small talk of a busy extended family. Here I didn't know what to think.

Ruslan ran the conversation. He didn't say much once the company arrived, but the others had a tendency to look at him before they spoke and several times he corrected their opinions.

Starfawn was the one edited most often.

"Are we going to do anything else about S—" she began.

"Secrecy builds power," Ruslan said, looking pointedly at me. "Jadis hasn't taken an oath, Starfawn."

Starfawn's cheeks went pink and she looked away.

"That's quite all right," I said. Do anything else about who? S. Sunshrike? *Miriam?*"

Whether they could do it or not, simply thinking about dragging someone back from the Summerland was so unethical my teeth hurt. But they hadn't wanted her to reach it, had they? They'd wanted her to wander through the outer dark forever.

"Oh, what a cute necklace!" Starfawn squealed, fastening her gaze on my chest full of intertwined sterling *frottagistes.*

They might be clowns, but nasty ones.

Eventually everyone was there—ten people, including me—and we got down to the serious business of the evening. There were no coed dressing or undressing rooms; in fact, Baba Yaga worked robed, and I was shuttled off to the bedroom with Starfawn, Ludmilla, and two other women to dress.

I kept my eyes open, just as I had in the kitchen. The bedroom had the same distressing air of mundanity that the living room had had. The only thing even remotely out of the ordinary was the neat pile of boxes in the corner. I took a closer look. The boxes were still sealed, bedight with "Fragile" and "Flammable" stickers, and had been shipped to Michael Ruslan at Clean-O-Rama, somewhere in Queens.

People's day jobs are lousy for the soul of true Romance. Here he was, Ruslan the Great, freelance prince of darkness; by day a mild-mannered laundromat owner. Sure.

"*Here* you are, Karen," Ludmilla sang out. She was holding a bundle of white muslin out toward me.

I stripped down to my Jockey for Hers and put it on. The fabric was scratchy and had a harsh chemical smell that I was determined to ignore. Mothballs? It had a white drawstring sash, and when I looked in the mirror I saw an overaged refugee from Santa Lucia Night.

Everyone else had on black robes. I remembered Miriam's robe with its careful embroidery. I'd thought about bringing it, but I was glad now that I hadn't gotten cute. The black robes were enlivened by varying degrees of ornamentation, and when the ladies were all suited up the bedroom looked like a cross between a medievalist event and a Roman Catholic reunion.

Ludmilla's black velvet robe was accented by cuffs, cummerbund, and stola in some gaudy, glittery, patterned material. She had a string of antique amber beads around her neck I would gladly have committed several illegal acts to own, and her chicken foot was proudly displayed on its heavy silver chain. It was shriveled and yellow and looked like a depraved saint's relic.

To top everything off, Lady Ludmilla wore a weird little round hat on her head that made her resemble an escapee from a demented Victorian nursing school.

Status, wealth, and temporal power—all the things you're supposed to leave outside the circle. Not because they're evil. Because they get in the way. Maybe they didn't get in the way of whatever sort of ritual Ruslan's coven was used to.

When all five of us were tricked out in what the well-dressed Khazar—and sacrificial victim—will wear, we went back into the living room. I was glad I'd had the chance to see Ludmilla in all her glory first, because then when I saw Ruslan I didn't even blink.

They say that the "Reverend" Montague Summers used to dress up in full Roman Catholic regalia to attend afternoon tea—which is a case of costume inappropriate to the occasion, but not as much so as wearing the same drag to a Wiccan covenmeet.

Well, not quite the same. Ruslan had on the alb, the stola, and the embroidered gauntlets, and the hat that looks like a folded napkin, but there were no Christian symbols on them, just a lot of moons and stars and wolves painstakingly hand-embroidered by somebody else. He had on a long necklace of black beads that might very well have been jet.

He also wore a bird-footed pendant. I wasn't sure what bird had donated it—it was a little too small for an ostrich, though. He had a whatever the Baba Yaga call their *athames* sheathed at his waist.

He opened the door to the other bedroom and led us all into the temple.

If you're going to get picky about it, a temple is a permanent structure dedicated to the working of magic-with-a-*K*. Magicians have them. Pagans don't.

Oh, the *asatruer* in your life will have his *fane*, and the *santerio* his *axe*, but a coven is an *organization*, not a place. The place where it meets is the covenstead, but that's only a special name for a place, not a special place. Wherever a coven meets it builds its Circle, and when the meeting is over and the Circle is broken, there's nothing left behind to indicate anything extraordinary ever occurred there.

This was not the case with Ruslan's Khazar temple, which looked as if it owed more of its inspiration to the Russian Catholic Church than it did to the precepts of Gerald Gardner.

Julian's words about "the usual mishmash" came back to me again. The floor was painted with a full-dress Solomon's Seal after Francis Barrett's *The Magus*. It was done in four colors of deck paint and must have taken hours. The walls were painted in the elemental colors (Golden Dawn attribution) and hung with large painted satin banners with the Four Tools on them. There were four large candleholders at the cardinal points, each of which held a faintly oatmeal-colored candle weighing easily five pounds. Assorted icons, oil lamps, and ritual paraphernalia were hung from the hooks on the walls, giving the place something of the look of the Serpent's Truth's broom closet. The altar was set up in the center of the circle, and everything (still, so far) looked normal.

At least to me. It had been years since I'd given a thought to walking into a situation like this with a group of more-or-less total strangers. I'd made my decision a long time ago, when I started chasing deity the way Harvard MBAs chase money.

Ludmilla lit the lamps on the walls and the lamps on the altar. I heard the subway rumble by outside as Ruslan shut and locked the door. That made me a little nervous, but it was his empowerment symbol, and a door locked from the side you're on can be got through easily. Ruslan proceeded to open the closet, and I could see packages of supplies, neatly labeled, inside.

Ludmilla made another pass around the room and lit the quarter-candles. I was standing next to the northern one; it smelled spicy and sweet as it burned. My skin under the robe itched.

Ruslan turned away from the closet and walked toward me.

"I thought you might like to borrow an *athame*, Kar—*Jadis*. We keep this one as a spare."

The smile was enough warning, but there wasn't anything I could do. He held it out and I took it.

It had about a six-inch blade, and the pommel was amber. An Ironshadow blade—there was his signature near the quillons. The edge of the pommel was rough and shiny where someone had taken a Dremel-tool and sanded Miriam's name off.

It felt like cold and death and pain and dying alone.

My stomach convulsed around my Lamb Surprise and tea and I swallowed hard, but Ruslan had already turned away from me. This was one reaction he didn't need to see to savor.

"Brothers and sisters of the Khazar, tonight we meet in worship of the Old Gods. With us is Jadis, a seeker, and out of respect to her, we will engage in worship only this evening."

He turned back to me. "I have to ask you to respect our privacy, and ask you not to reveal anything you may see or hear tonight." He stared at me, his eyes as bright and horrid as if they were blue glass, and I clutched Miriam's *athame,* my gift to her, the one thing she would never have given willingly to anyone else.

I must have said something and it must have sounded normal. Ruslan went over to the altar and he and Ludmilla began the ritual.

The fondness of the Gardnerian tradition for incense is a standing joke in the Community, but the Baba Yagas went us one better that night. Ten minutes into the ritual the room was actually foggy, with a sharp, cloying smell I could taste. It reminded me vaguely of winter woolies, and closets, and things like that, and I found myself swaying back and forth just like everyone else. My eyes watered. I wondered if what the Khazars were burning on their charcoal was DEA-legal.

By the time they got around to passing the wine cup—what Belle always calls Sacred Cookies and Milk Time—I had a pounding headache. My mouth and throat were cottony and dry. We were all sitting on the floor with people swaying back and forth to that unheard music which is sweeter. Wolves and winter wind howled in the background, courtesy of a sound-system The Cat would have coveted.

All my energy was going into keeping the ritual from reaching me at the deep-mind level where it could fuck me up for years— that, and keeping from parting Ruslan's hair with one of his pretentious High Church candlesticks. If I'd wanted to go to Mass I would have stayed a nun.

My sinuses had given up long ago, and by now my eyes were watering so badly that Baba Yaga Her Own Self could have shown up and I wouldn't have been any the wiser. Despite my best efforts at insulating myself from what *Baba Yaga* and Ruslan were doing I had that unsettled, hair-prickling feeling of just-before-a-storm, and my skin felt like it was on inside out and backwards.

I trust my feelings. When the cup reached me I didn't drink.

Oh, I tilted it back, all right, but I kept my mouth tight shut and I was glad I had. The candles lit up some oily beads of non-wine liquid floating on the surface, and I got a caustic breath of something that cleared my sinuses and made my head ring. I held my breath and lowered the cup, and the person next to me took it away from me. I took a deep breath of camphor smoke and tried to stay upright. *Camphor,* I realized with a sense of how foggy I was. The candles were scented with camphor. Why?

The sense of something waiting got stronger. Again, there was no need of occult power to guess why. Most people don't realize how much of their information about other people is based on reading nonverbal cues. Their conscious mind offers it to them in the form of "feelings" or "hunches," and they promptly discount it as being irrational.

I didn't.

"It is usual, when one of us has gone to live in the dreamtime forever, to release the last of their ties to the earth-plane," Ruslan said as soon as the cup had gone all the way around the room once. "But we haven't been able to do this for Sunshrike. Can you help us, Jadis? Karen?"

My head felt like it weighed a thousand pounds and was stuffed with white phosphorus. I had just enough brains left to realize I was blitzed and to be very, very careful of what I said.

"Can I help you," I repeated thickly. I was starting to realize how much earth-plane trouble I was in, and how unequipped I was to deal with it.

"Miriam had some things that belong to us. They're too dangerous to leave around loose. Weren't you in her apartment after she died?"

My thoughts turned into little heraldic salamanders, each orange and burning and with a pinpoint of sapphire brilliance lodged in its skull. Take that stone from the salamander and become impervious to fire—or use it to make the Philosopher's Stone, which turns lead into gold and makes men immortal.

I hadn't been in this condition for *years.*

"Karen? I know you were in Miriam's apartment after she died." Ruslan, standing there calm and magisterial. And why not? He was above the worst of the smoke, and I'd bet he hadn't had any of the wine. Everyone else in the room looked like bleary-eyed opium eaters, including Ludmilla.

"Won't you help us?"

Actually, I was willing to tell him anything to make him go away. I had an unshakable conviction that he'd know if I didn't tell the truth.

But, damn it, I was High Priestess and Witch. And Ruslan wasn't. I summoned up all my pride, if nothing else.

"Miriam's apartment was burglarized," I said carefully. My tongue felt like a cucumber. Bad, bad violation of Craft ethics to use drugs in a Circle without making sure everyone knew in advance and could consent.

But they hadn't wanted me to know and to consent. They'd wanted to get me to where they could put the boot in. And I'd walked in just like Mary's little lamb.

I'd made two mistakes that I wasn't ever going to make again. I should have yelled a lot longer and louder when Mr. Michael Ruslan called up my unlisted number with my legal name.

And I should never have assumed that "covener" meant "law abiding."

"Miriam was talking about leaving. She was talking about showing those things to a friend of hers. That's against the oath. If someone took those things, they took Miriam's oath, too, and the Babayar will find them wherever they are."

"Hunt them down," said Starfawn, slurrily.

I wanted to confess. I was going to confess, I was almost sure of it, and then I was going to kill him.

Goddess Who art bound to me by oaths and love, strengthen me now —

Someone started to chant; a short sharp line with a lot of plosives. The rest joined in; a conditioned response as automatic as the "amen" at the end of a hymn. Ruslan smiled at me. The wolves on the "Environments" tape howled. In that room Ruslan's Babayar was as real as gravity, and I clenched my teeth to keep from making any noise at all.

"If you hear of anyone who might have Miriam's things, I'd really appreciate it," Ruslan said again.

We were back to reality. I was standing in Ruslan's living room, dressed in my own clothes. The clock showed 12:45 A.M., and people were standing around getting ready to leave.

My nose ran and my lungs hurt, and my (hand wash only silk) shirt was already soaked through with sweat. I had a putrid headache and was too miserable to be self-righteous or even to pitch my voice very loud. In addition, I wasn't sure where the last four hours had gone and I had the vague feeling of impending doom that comes from having made a serious mistake that you don't quite realize yet. I mumbled something.

"They're dangerous in the wrong hands. Miriam was trying to leave, and look what happened to her."

Even if it was fevered intuition, there was no mistaking his meaning. I stared at Ruslan. He smiled.

"Miriam wouldn't have died if she'd kept her oath. But you know that, Karen. Secrecy builds power. And power can be very dangerous when it turns against you. I think Miriam knows that now. Don't you?"

Someone opened the door to the apartment. I went through it without looking back.

8

This was not how it was supposed to go. I was supposed to be sure there was a murder and not know who did it. But I wasn't sure there had been a murder—and I had somebody confessing to it. Hell, *bragging* about it.

It was raining as I left the Ruslans' apartment, the peculiarly unpleasant thin warm summer-in-the-city stuff. I could feel the smog-in-solution coating my skin and ensuring that everything I had on would have to be dry-cleaned.

I felt that special light-headed gratitude that comes from having had a brush with death or root canal and surviving. I didn't even worry about being mugged on the platform as I waited for the downtown train. It was after midnight; the sky had that weird greenish underglow that comes from reflecting a lot of light. New York, the city that never sleeps.

And now I had my fact, my real-for-true undeniable fact. The fact I'd wanted, angled for, and gone out on a limb to get. Miriam's death was neither accidental nor coincidental. Michael Ruslan of the *Baba Yaga* Coven, Khazar Tradition, had motive and opportunity and swore he'd put them together and killed Miriam Seabrook.

With sorcery.

My train got there and I got in. The New York Transit Authority had kindly arranged for it to be air-conditioned to a level capable of dealing with the thermal output of its peak ridership, thereby guaranteeing that the after-midnight travelers had a good chance of catching pneumonia. It did nothing to improve my headache.

I shared my car with a couple of members of what is tactfully called these days the underclass—fat, dark, weary ladies wearing white and talking together in Spanish. Too close to poverty and reality to live in a world where people did things like Ruslan's guest-bedroom cathedral. The money he'd spent on the incense was a week's groceries in their world.

It's called innocence, and the distinction between it and ignorance is fast dying out.

Three stops later—at the first Manhattan stop—one of the joys of MTA ridership boarded. He was tall, white, and barefoot and wearing corrugated cardboard placards front and back. His head was wrapped in purple cellophane and he wore one of those bouncy antenna headbands that'd been hot a few years back. I couldn't read his sandwich boards. He carried a saxophone. As soon as the train was in motion and he had a captive audience, he started to play it.

Pontius Pilate wanted to know what truth was. If he'd just waited twenty centuries he could have given up on that one and started asking about sanity.

And how was the Sax Man different from Ruslan? Or for that matter, from me?

I got off the train near Rocky Center and walked over to an all-night coffee shop I knew. It had stopped raining by then and the streets were all black glass, shining and as deserted as Manhattan ever gets.

It was only when I saw the lights and people at the Cosmic Coffee Shop that I realized how badly I wanted both. I was shook all the way down to the prerational level that good ritual is designed to touch. And whatever else was true, the Baba Yagas knew how to make a ritual.

Of course, so had the Nazis.

I slid into a booth with the same sense of relief a player of Tag-You're-It feels reaching home.

I had coffee. I had white wine. I had scrambled eggs and home fries and I wanted a cigarette desperately, even though I'd only ever been an occasional smoker and that not for years. I bought a little metal box of Excedrin from behind the counter and took them all with a second glass of wine, and finally I was able to put down the feeling that a Stephen King Nightmare From The Id was waiting to drag me off into the fifth dimension.

Fact: Ruslan had said that *Baba Yaga* had killed Miriam for oathbreaking. But black magic wasn't illegal, even if it worked. Was it? I didn't think there was a jury in the world that would convict Ruslan of Miriam's death, even if he'd been serious. Plain and fancy bragging is a long-standing tradition in the Community, after all. *"Look what I healed, invoked, divined."* This was just bragging of a darker sort.

But in my heart I knew it wasn't. If intention counted, Ruslan had killed Miriam Seabrook.

The next question I had to ask myself was, *Had* he killed Miriam? Effective *malificarum* is rare in the world today—it's so much harder than calling your lawyer, and about as healthy for you as smoking crack.

It comes down in the end to what you believe. If you think, down in the dark night of your soul, that a person can die on command, and that another person can give them that command, then Ruslan *could* be guilty.

If the human mind can raise stigmata or cause hot coals not to burn, surely it can stop the human heart?

Can, not *had.* Ruslan *could* be guilty. *He* thought he was. But what if he was firing blanks?

And what if he wasn't?

The Roman Catholic Church used to distinguish between intending to do something wicked and actually getting around to it. They were both sins, of course, but there was a difference in degree. I sat in the diner and drank lots of coffee and thought deep philosophical thoughts about the exact moment at which a crime has been committed.

If there was an ecclesiastical court for the Craft, Ruslan was definitely guilty on a number of counts.

He was (I was pretty sure) using drugs in ritual without the prior informed consent of all participants.

He was engaged in invasive, coercive magic—what we used to call, in less enlightened days, Black Magic. Whether he had any success at it or not, he had "attempted to compass the death of the said Miriam Seabrook by nigromantic operations."

Fine. But it wasn't a civil crime—at least I didn't think there were any laws against *malificarum* on the books in the State of New

York. The closest there were (and a real pain in the ass to people like Tollah and Tris) were the Gypsy Laws, which are designed to protect the moron in the street against fraud enacted by the palm-and-tea-leaf reading brethren.

Guilty or not, Ruslan had committed no temporal crime.

The question was, just how good was he at committing spiritual ones?

The jury was out on that one, but I took the proper precautions around the apartment anyway when I finally got there: from salt and iron to a blue candles ritual. By eight A.M. I had my apartment swept and garnished and psychically sealed, in as valid and practical a defense as Ruslan's could be an assault.

My wards were designed, as all good ethical magical systems are, to be purely passive; they would draw their energy from being attacked. If Ruslan wanted to take the trouble to hoodoo me, I wanted to make sure he got back what he sent, doubled and re-doubled in spades.

Needless to say, it was not a night for sleeping.

But it was a day for earning a living, so later Thursday morning I washed the vervain and lemongrass and golden seal off in my dinky claustrophobic shower and got dressed and went down to the studio. My subconscious still had that overfed and undigested feel to it that meant it was just itching to bring things to my attention if left alone. I felt that I'd be happy to leave it alone for an equinoctial precession or two, along with Ruslan's nasty-minded godplayers and all the rest.

Because there was nothing I could do. And that was the unkindest truth of all.

Having missed a night's sleep didn't bother me—yet. But it would if I didn't make it up, and I had coven tomorrow night. So when I got into work that Thursday I told Raymond I'd be in late on Friday, planning to leave early and catch up on lost sleep, and then like a right jerk stayed overtime instead.

It was late. Everyone else was gone. It was nice and quiet and still light out, actually my favorite time of day to be here.

The phone rang.

You would think that the first thing on my mind would be all the nasty phone calls I'd gotten lately, but my subconscious was too busy with other stuff to bother making my life miserable. I answered the phone without a qualm in my heart.

"Bookie-Joint-can-I-help-you?"

"It's Lace. I tried your apartment and there wasn't anybody there, so I thought . . ."

I resisted the flip and cowardly urge to ask her if somebody else was dead. "How are you?" I said instead.

"Oh, not too good. Tollah says you're coming down to read at the Revel on Saturday. Maybe you'd like to go out to dinner afterward. Shop'll pay."

This is not quite as magnanimous of Tollah as it might appear. I don't read Tarot for her very often, because while she splits the take fifty-fifty with her usual fortune-teller, I have an ethics problem with taking money for magic—so when I read, Tollah scoops the lot. Her conscience bothers her enough to feed me.

"Yeah, sure," I said, wondering why she called, and knowing why. There was a Miriam-sized hole in Lace's life, and I'd known Miriam, too. Lifelong relationships have been formed on less.

"Have you heard anything? About the autopsy, or . . . anything?" Lace said.

Autopsy.

Brain-fever struck, so hard I almost hung up on her. *CAMPHOR* I wrote in large letters on the top of my board and underlined it three times. Camphor in the candles. Ether (or something) in the cup. Drugs.

Poisons.

"Hello?" said Lace, after a minute. "Hello? Bast?"

"I'm here." The patter of little feet that was my subconscious doing a tap dance of joy at finally getting my attention was deafening. "No, I haven't heard anything more about the autopsy."

"What about the *Baklava* people?" Lace asked with unerring precision.

"I just talked to them," I admitted, wondering how I was going to edit my experience to keep Lace from going after Ruslan with a baseball bat.

And I *was* going to keep her from doing that, because as much as I wanted justice, I wanted even more not to be responsible even slightly for some kind of "Commie Satanist from Mars" story in the *New York Post,* with Lace stuck in the middle of it. We're edging up on the millennium, and newspapers have always had a bit of trouble distinguishing between "Neopagan" and "Nut."

"Look. I really can't talk right now. But I'll tell you all about it on Saturday, okay? Really, they're mostly harmless."

So's a rattlesnake.

I spent another ten minutes soothing Lace down before I could hang up, and then I flew on wings of song to one of the bookshelves where the fruits of Houston Graphics' labors are stored.

A studio like Houston, which handles (let's face it) the leftovers and bits-and-pieces that fall through the cracks of the big studios and the publishers' in-house art departments, does a little of everything. We've mechanicaled pornography, haute fantasy, how-to books, technical manuals, medical textbooks, and everything else under the sun—including the monster *World Encyclopedia of Wine* (all nine hundred pages) that comes in for a complete patch-and-fit job every time somebody comes up with a new way to spell Chablis.

And usually the publisher sends us a couple copies of the book when it comes off press, which explains why the walls at Houston Graphics resemble a library gone wrong.

When you stare at something day after day you can hardly help reading it, which is why I know as much about diagnostic approaches to cardiopulmonary resuscitation as I do. And I'd read something, sometime, about camphor. And ether.

The book was called *A Poison Dictionary*. It was one of those helpful reference books wherein a technical subject is demythologized for the layman, and the consensus at Houston was that it was written so Middle America would be able to off troublesome spouses and children with ease. It was a trade paperback with a (you should pardon the expression) poison-green cover and an alphabetical list of "over 1,000 common household substances" that could be fatal.

Some of them were very weird. I mean, aspirin? *Coffee?*

And Vicks VapoRub (used incorrectly, of course, as the entry was very careful to point out). Or to put it another way, *camphor.*

If it doesn't kill you, said the book, camphor induces, along with your headache, excitement, dizziness, and irrational behavior—though the book didn't mention what it considered irrational behavior. I made a note of the page number and kept on looking, because the candles hadn't killed Miriam.

The wine had.

Consider what you want out of life if you're some kind of charlatan working the occult circuit. You probably don't believe in magic, but you want your followers to believe in you, and you want to be sure they are docile, biddable, and experience Real Occult Manifestations they can brag to their friends about.

In the Middle Ages, it was easy. The so-called Witches' Flying Ointment used a combination of belladonna (nightshade, water parsley), bufotenin (toad sweat), digitalis (foxglove), and aconite (wolfsbane) to achieve these useful effects. As compounded from medieval recipes and tested by modern researchers (some people will do anything for a government grant), W.F.O. produces the sensation of flying, a feeling of exhilaration—and a set of three-ring hallucinations that may have accounted for most of the more lurid depositions people like Spengler and Kramer collected during the witch trials. Oh, people believed they'd been to the Sabbat, all right—with that particular chemical cocktail coursing through their blood, how could they not?

But this is now. And if you wanted to get the same effects in the modern coven, those particular ingredients were pretty hard to come by.

But ether wasn't. Or chloroform.

Especially if your day job involved a Clean-O-Rama—or any other place that might handle dry cleaning. The boxes in the bedroom suddenly made a horrible kind of sense. Both ether and chloroform are used in dry cleaning. Anybody with a plausible excuse and a credit card can get his hands on them quite easily.

Chloroform. A mildly caustic gaseous anesthetic, I read in *A Poison Dictionary,* liquid when chilled, gaseous at slightly above room temperature. It would burn your mouth if you drank it, but mixed with the sacramental wine you probably wouldn't notice much. A whiff would give you a dizzy, floaty, out-of-body feeling—add that to the camphor in the candles and the hypnostasis of the ritual and you would be sure that in Russian Orthodox Wicca you had found something with more bang for your buck than spending Sunday morning down at the First Methodist Bar & Grill.

Ingest enough chloroform over a period of time and it would kill you. Cirrhosis. Necrosis. Your liver stops working and you die. Without warning. Real fast. Alone, in a locked room, miles away from your killer.

My hands were shaking so hard I dropped the book. I crawled under my table to get it and rang my head on the underside of my board. Getting out seemed like too much trouble so I just sat there, reading over the entry again.

Chloroform causes liver failure. And there had been chloroform or its next-door neighbor in the wine. Ruslan had put it there.

Motive, opportunity, and access to tools. There was a real-world cause of Miriam's death—and if I could prove it, I could nail Ruslan with manslaughter, voluntary or in-.

But if he used that stuff on a regular basis, why wasn't everyone in Ruslan's coven dead?

The dictionary—admittedly not the most reliable source in the universe—cited repeated doses—or overdoses—as cause of death-by-chloroform. Maybe other people *had* died. Maybe the police were closing in even now, their dragnet drawing ever tighter around *Baba Yaga* and its High Priest.

Or maybe Miriam had just come up unlucky.

But would she have been quite so unlucky, I wondered, if *Baba Yaga* hadn't been working magic to cause her death?

I took the book with me when I left the studio. Ray wouldn't miss it, and I wanted to think—about it and everything else in the world.

Miriam Seabrook was dead. And Ruslan was at one and the same time a vicious and merciless committer of premeditated murder and an irresponsible goof who thought it was cute to slip people drugs without their knowing.

Just about everybody my age either knows someone it happened to or had it happen to them: the LSD in the orange juice, the hashish in the brownies, the magic mushrooms in the scrambled eggs. Back in the sixties, when drugs were supposed to be powerful and liberating and upscale things, these were harmless pranks—at least people said so.

But heroin moved out of the ghetto and cocaine moved into the marketplace and about the time your local pusher's daily special was something that would kill you before it addicted you, drugs stopped being cute.

But some of us were still hanging on to all of the sixties we could. And maybe Ruslan was one of them and still thought of drugs in the same breath as "recreational." I'd said I didn't mind working shamanic when I spoke to him on the phone—that might be taken for informed consent of a sort. And Miriam had gone back freely for months—surely she'd known what he was using?

I tried to sell myself on that all the way home and failed. Okay, Ruslan used chemicals in his rituals out of a countercultural sense of giddy irresponsibility—but he'd been very responsible when he set his coven to kill Miriam by magic. He'd said right out that he wanted her dead and had done his best to make her that way.

And she *was* dead. How he'd killed her didn't matter—or, I admitted, *if* he'd killed her. He'd wanted to. He'd tried to. He would have been just as guilty of *malificarum* if Miriam were still alive.

Morality is even more indigestible than ethics. By the time I made it up five flights of stairs I was sick of the whole thing. I solved the problem that evening by getting drunk on Slivovitz boilermakers.

Never do that.

9

Friday was the kind of day that gives reincarnation a bad name. I mean, who'd want to do something like this *twice?*

I woke up hungover and with a bad case of attitude that it wasn't hard to pinpoint the cause of. Anger. Frustration. I'd turned over a rock and a whole nest of moral culpability was lying there wriggling, and the only thing I could think to do was put the rock back down.

I gave Bellflower an excerpt from my troubles that night.

"I went up and saw the people Miriam was working with on Wednesday."

Belle and I were drinking tea in her kitchen. Belle's kitchen is four feet wide and was painted gas-chamber green sometime in the 1950s. It's furnished in early Gift Of The Garbage Goddess — curbside salvage — and contains a large number of nonworking appliances that the landlord refuses to remove, as well as Washington Heights' only four-quart teapot.

Nobody else was here yet — I'd left work early in addition to arriving late; the weekly paycheck was going to be on the slim side. Belle was eating fried bananas and *raita* from the Indian place that delivers and I was poking at my chicken curry and feeling morose.

"And?" Belle said.

"And," I said, "they are coercive, nonconsensual, and doing drugs — well, chemicals. There's this stuff in the candles that I'm pretty sure is camphor, and stuff in the wine—"

"So why did you go there?" Belle asked in her best voice of sanity. I stared at her.

"To find out what they were doing."

"And now you know. And you won't go back there, right?"

I looked at her. "You're getting at something, aren't you?"

Belle dipped a banana in yogurt. "You told me that they were pretty secretive, didn't you?"

"Yeah." I'd told her just about what Julian had told me, and left out the invitational phone call from Ruslan.

"And so it's not like they were running something open. Probably they let you come to their meeting because you were a friend of Miriam's."

"Yeah. Right. And then they told me they put a deathspell on Miriam for trying to leave the coven."

That finally got Belle's attention. "Are you serious?"

"I swear it by the Goddess, Belle. They had her *athame,* the one I gave her, and they said they killed her because she broke her oath to them."

Belle regarded me critically, although not as though she was about to leap up and go for the police.

"Well, no wonder she called you, if that was the kind of head trip they were putting on her. People like that make me so mad—and that kind of power-tripping, you just *know* it's built on secrecy and disinformation. And it's so stupid—the Craft isn't about coercion and fear, it's about knowledge and empowerment."

"Somebody's empowerment, anyway," I said. I'd pushed one of Belle's buttons and got one of the standard fifteen-second screeds; she does a lot of public-awareness outreach. "It doesn't matter what the Craft's 'about' when somebody's using it for something else."

Belle sighed. "I thought we'd got over this Witch-war stuff. These are the nineties—this mystification and blind-faith Ancient Atlantean Magus stuff doesn't do anybody any good."

"It sure didn't do Miriam any good," I snapped.

Belle got the expression on her face that she gets when she's trying to be open-minded and not say anything to contradict somebody else's value system.

"Look, Bast. We all know about negative magic. There is no excuse for it. It's wrong. But it's out there, and everybody deals with it in their own way. It can't hurt you unless you open yourself to it. You just have to stay grounded in the earth-plane."

The day I discovered that all Witches don't believe in magic was a great shock to me. It was also long enough ago that I was no longer surprised that Belle, who is my friend and I love her, could say in one breath that the Magic Power of Witchcraft could reverse everything from cancer to tooth decay and in the next that black magic can't kill. Personally, I have always believed that the tail goes with the dog.

"Belle, these people are into power-tripping and weirdness and black magic. When somebody tells you they've killed somebody, what do you do?"

The bell for the downstairs door rang and Belle pushed the buzzer to unlock it. When she looked back at me her mind was made up.

"I really don't know what to tell you, Bast. If you're looking for a villain you'll find one, and you could let this take over your life. But Miriam's dead and you're not—and what could you do, anyway? There isn't some central validating agency that decides who's a real Witch and who isn't. Different traditions have different value systems. You can't just stand here and say this is right because I like it and this is wrong because I don't like it, because those are not judgments based on objective criteria."

"Murder?" I suggested.

Belle smiled sadly at me. "Everybody has their own way of dealing with the truth," she said. "How are you going to prove that something Ruslan did magically was the real cause of Miriam's death?"

I couldn't. Because I didn't *know* that Miriam had died of liver failure, and even if the autopsy proved it, *I* couldn't prove to the satisfaction of the police or anyone else that Ruslan had given her the chloroform that (maybe) caused it.

And Belle was right. Even though he'd confessed to doing something that was wrong by Gardnerian tenets, it was undoubtedly right by Khazar rules—and there was no Neopagan ecclesiastical court to bring him up on charges in front of, anyway.

No temporal authority. No spiritual authority. Nobody with any clout to call Michael Ruslan a bad boy.

Part of me hoped, cravenly, that Ruslan had been well and truly frightened by Miriam's death. That it had been the tonic dose of reality he needed to stop dicking around in his syncretic dream-time and either grow up or get out of the Community.

Because down at the back of my mind was the knowledge that

anyone who isn't a white Protestant Christian from a mainstream denomination is getting his or her religious freedom eroded every time the Supreme Court meets, and a nice big case of witchcraft murder could give all of us—Witches, Neopagans, Goddess-worshipers, and even the Iron Johnnies—more attention from bureaucrats and name-takers than most of us could possibly stand.

Paranoia. Right up Lace's alley. Don't even think of going after Ruslan because it would rock the boat into broad daylight.

My public position had always been that John Q. Mundane did not give a damn about what the rest of us worshiped as long as we didn't do it on Wall Street and scare the insider traders. And I still thought that. Mostly.

So I wanted Ruslan quietly brought to justice—but I'd settle for him just drying up and blowing away.

As of Friday night, I still believed he might do that.

On Saturdays the Revel opens at noon. I put on my New York blacks and lots of my funkiest jewelry and half a dozen rings and the beaded belt pouch that holds my cards and another one for my keys and subway tokens so I wouldn't have a purse to watch and went.

Everything looked different, and it didn't make me feel any better to know it was just me. Everybody else was the same; just as admirable or as contemptible as they'd ever been. They'd never been saints. They weren't quislings now, no matter what Ruslan had done or thought he'd done.

Maybe I was burnt out. Maybe I should gafiate—Get Away From It All. Take up a quiet life of secularity and stop worrying about questions to which the twentieth century has thrown away the answers in a body; questions like morals and ethics and fault and responsibility. Justice. Restitution.

Revenge.

I actually stopped at a liquor store on the way to the Revel and bought a half-pint of brandy. It was a cheap, obvious, and useless escape, and the eagerness with which I went after it scared me enough to keep me from opening the bottle.

But I'd still bought it.

I got to the Revel about ten-thirty. Tollah saw me and opened up for me.

"Oh, Bast, blessed be! You're a real lifesaver—Mischia had to go out to Crown Point for a wedding—her brother—and she thought it was Sunday or next week or something and if it was next week I could've told everybody this week that we weren't doing it next week but you see—"

"Just remember me in your will."

Tollah looked nervous, and for the life of me I couldn't figure out why. I recollected the paper bag I was holding and handed it to her. "Here. Contributions to the community chest."

She saw what was in it and gave me a funny look. I went over and sat down at the table set up in the corner for the Tarot reader.

It was one of those collapsible card tables, and it was draped in a purple pall embroidered with Ur and Geb and Nut and all those Egyptian guys. I'd seen it a dozen times, but this was the first time I'd ever looked at the corner with the signature painstakingly embroidered in genuine J. R. R. Tolkien Elvish. It wasn't too hard to make out the transliteration. Sunshrike.

Miriam.

Damn her anyway. If I'd been her worst enemy she couldn't have done worse by me than opening up this Khazar can of worms in my face.

There were little blue card-outlines embroidered into the cloth in the Celtic Cross pattern, not that I needed the *aide de memoire.* I got out my deck and began to shuffle.

People always ask me if I "believe" in Tarot cards. It's pretty easy to do: I own five decks of them. What they mean, of course, is "Do you believe that Tarot cards can tell the future?" and the answer to that is yes—and no.

You can tell the future. If you wear a white cashmere sweater-dress to an important lunch, there is an eighty percent chance that you will spill shrimp cocktail or something else with tomato sauce on it—if only because you're so worried about spilling something that you go all awkward. You *know* this, but you're unlikely to act on the information, even if your mother, your roommate, and your best friend all tell you so.

But if the cards tell you so—and mind, tell you what you already know—you're more likely to accept and act upon the advice, wear bottle-green wool gabardine, and avoid serious grief and dry-cleaning bills. Tarot is a way of sorting out what's bothering you and getting advice from the best-informed source—you—in a way that you're likely to listen to.

So I lay out your cards and tell you all the things your mind is busy sweeping under the rug so it can get on with its business of complicating your life. As for where *I* get the information—well, go figure. But I'm right more often than I'm wrong.

There is something exciting about working with the cards. The more you work to match your knowledge and skill to the seemingly random spill, to understand this one of the seventy-eight-to-the-thirteenth-power possible combinations of symbols and positions and what it means for the woman sitting opposite you, the more you become conscious of reporting only the high points of a river, and the more you become aware of the unchanging subtext of that river; the eternal dialogue with sundered self. I saw the cards and listened to the river, and that took all my concentration. My own problems lost their importance.

It's a lot like jogging.

My first client of the day came over and sat down. I handed her the cards and watched her shuffle and cut. She had no trouble shuffling seventy-eight outsized cards. Probably she read Tarot herself, but there's the "who shaves the barber" paradox: Tarot readers can't generally read for themselves. You lie to yourself. You might as well watch television.

I didn't ask her what she'd come to find out. That comes later, after you see what the cards say.

She handed me the deck back. As I took them they sprayed out of our hands, cards going everywhere. One of them flipped over. The Chariot.

Or as some people call it, the Fool's Paradise. I scooped the cards all back together and began laying them out.

I try to keep omens in their proper perspective.

Carrie brought me a tofu pita and a soda at about two. Traffic had been brisk; there were still about half a dozen women waiting for readings. Lace was behind the counter, with her hair all hennaed, oiled, and spiked out, looking like dangerous sculpture.

Sometimes, despite all your best shuffling, the same cards will turn up over and over again from reading to reading. This can be interpreted in many ways—from poor manual dexterity skills to the possibility that the people being read for are somehow linked. One of the common interpretations of the phenomenon is that the recurring cards are messages meant for the reader.

I'd been seeing a lot of The Chariot today. A young man crowned in glory, his chariot canopied in stars, rides forth from the walled city he has conquered. You have to look at the card for a few seconds before you see that the animals that pull the chariot have neither reins nor bridles. It's the Captain James T. Kirk card, the card of leaping before looking, of burned bridges and uncovered asses. The card of thinking you know what's going on when you don't.

As a message to the reader, it was ambiguous.

Lace saw me see her and waved: black leather fingerless gloves with spikes across the knuckles. I looked down at my rings and necklaces. We were all in our best identity war paint today, dripping with symbols of being who we wished to seem.

And who was Bast—*Lady* Bast, High Priestess of the Wicca?

"When a man's partner is killed, he's supposed to do something about it. It doesn't make any difference what you thought of him. He was your partner and you're supposed to do something about it."

But I wasn't Sam Spade. I wasn't even the Queen of the Witches. Miriam wasn't my partner. And Ruslan hadn't broken any laws.

I took a bite of the pita and opened the soda and went back to telling other people how the cards said they should run their lives.

The Chariot. Willful stupidity. Fool's Paradise, as in "Living In A—"

What was I missing? If anything?

And what should I do about it?

About five o'clock I looked up and there wasn't anybody standing around waiting. I wrapped up my cards and stuffed them back in my belt pouch. I stretched, and wiggled my fingers, and stood up, and generally indicated that the cartomancer was done for the day.

Lace came over and folded up the cloth, and the card table, and the chairs, and I leaned against the jewelry case and hung out. The Revel was open until nine, but sometime sooner than that some assortment of us would be going out to dinner, and eventually I was going to have to talk to Lace.

I still felt as if I'd lost my last pair of rose-colored glasses. I didn't like it. It meant thinking about too many things—and if the goal of modern life is satisfaction, ratiocination was taking me further from it every minute. So life is unfair, people are amoral jerks, we're all going to die, and as a race humanity is too stupid to put out the fire in a burning house. Life is the business of forgetting all that, and the sooner I could get on with life, the better.

* * *

I made a good stab at forgetting any number of things at dinner. It was about seven by the time that got underway, what with closing the shop up and everything, and by the time everything had jelled it was Lace, Tollah, me, and three other women who had accrued during the wait. Tollah and Lace knew them and I didn't. We went to a new cheap Thai place a few blocks away and stuffed ourselves on things cooked with coriander and coconut milk. I had several beers, since it was courtesy of the Revel.

Lace kept giving me meaningful looks and I kept willfully ignoring them. If I didn't have to talk about *Baba Yaga*, I didn't have to think about *Baba Yaga*. I knew I was being hard on Lace, but on the other hand, if she knew what I knew, she too would have to sit here deciding between life in prison and impotence. Maybe I was acting out of charity.

Lace nailed me during a lull in the conversation. "You are holding out on me, you damn vanilla bitch."

I glanced around. Tollah had her back to us, talking to the three women. I gathered that they were Dianic Gaians, and I hoped nobody would tell me what that was.

"Will you for gods' sake lighten up? You want me to do my John Barrymore imitation or something?" I sotto voced at her.

John Barrymore was one of the most talented drunks ever produced by the great Barrymore line, and when he died his friends stole his body from the funeral home and used it to scare the shit out of Errol Flynn. I wondered if I would ever have friends like that. If I did, I hoped I would outlive them.

"You said you'd tell me tonight what happened Wednesday. So it's tonight," Lace insisted.

"I can't do it here," I insisted right back.

Lace grabbed my wrist with a hand that resembled one of those devices you use to shape sheet metal. If I hadn't had my Third Degree bracelet on she would have crippled me.

"You can damn well tell me here if she had a lover!"

There were tears in Lace's eyes, and I realized that all the Khazar Trad meant to her was the people who had taken Miriam away from her. She'd like to think they were rotten, but I didn't think that even Lace's wildest imaginings were wild enough to match the truth I'd uncovered.

I thought I knew what she'd do if she knew what I knew. And what the Real World would do to her. I didn't want that to happen.

"It wasn't like that." Out of the corner of my eye I saw Tollah take an interest in our conversation. "She was leaving them, okay? No lover."

Eventually the party broke up. Lace and I walked Tollah back to the Revel.

"So you want to invite me over to your place for a beer?" I asked, when Tollah was inside.

"Cheap bitch," said Lace, and threw an arm around my shoulders.

I knew that Lace shared a two-bedroom apartment with three other like-minded women way up north near Columbia, but I'd never been there until tonight. Sliced four ways the rent was bearable—just. Lace and one of the others had the bedrooms, and the other two shared the converted dining room.

I would bet good money there isn't a single dining room in all of New York City being used actually for dining, outside of a few Park Avenue atavisms. In Manhattan you spell dining room "extra bedroom."

"They're out," said Lace comprehensively as we got inside.

The living room was furnished in that bizarre accretion of furniture gathered by women who have always been roommates—i.e., have lived their lives in a succession of bedrooms in houses or apartments that they don't themselves rent. A lifestyle like that doesn't run to couches or coffee tables, and even when where you're living now has room for one you don't buy it, because where you're living next might not, and then you'd have to leave it behind with people you (may) have grown to hate.

The living room of Lace's modern urban commune contained six chairs of wildly differing ethnology—from overstuffed Conran's upholstered in black polished cotton to a rather nice Biedermeier rocker—two mismatched bookcases and a salvage-it-yourself table that had been painted in gaudy Peewee Herman colors. There was a fake Tiffany lamp and one in Star Trek *moderne.* The walls were the same way—it was like living with a multiple personality affective disorder case where all the personalities got equal say in the decoration.

Lace got both of us "lite" American beers from the kitchen. She opened hers, and sat down, and *waited* at me.

"Okay," I said. I'd had all dinner to make up my mind and Lace herself to tell me what tack to take. "Her coven leader called me up last week and invited me to a Circle."

And then I lied. Oh, I got all the facts right—at least the ones I told. But I'd never told Lace about Miriam's magical diaries or my midnight phone calls, and I didn't tell her now.

Nor did I tell her about the poison Ruslan was feeding to his coveners or the fact that he'd boasted of working toward Miriam's death. I didn't tell her how he made my skin crawl, or how on sober reflection I was willing to bet that Starfawn was his next victim; a new wannabe Witch to Trilby-ize. Lace didn't need to know all that. Lace didn't *want* to know all that. Lace wanted to know that Miriam had loved her till she died, and that I could tell her without lying.

"So . . . they were sort of *mondo* weird, and I'm pretty sure that Miriam had gotten fed up with them and that they were trying to scare her into staying when she called me. They're not exactly lily-white magically, if you know what I mean. So when she died . . . I guess she'd talked about me, and they wanted to find out if she'd talked *to* me."

"She wouldn't even talk to *me*," grumbled Lace.

"They have a secrecy riff that makes the Gardnerian oath look like the Freedom of Information Act."

Lace laughed, a little gruffly, and raised her beer can.

"Well, here's to all goddamn dumb femmes and dykes. Screw 'em all."

Which seemed, as an epitaph, good enough for anyone, really.

IO

L ace invited me to stay the night. It wasn't even a pass, really, but I turned it down all the same. I wanted to go home and pull my covers up over my head and sleep forever or at least until Sunday afternoon, and maybe when I woke up I'd be my old cheerful self again. I had a doom-laden feeling, as if I'd forgotten something terribly important, and I could not imagine what it was.

I found out.

There was no way I could have mundanely known what was waiting for me five flights up when I walked into my home lobby. I told myself stories of imaginary muggers lying in wait in the doorway, but there weren't any. I assured myself that all my neighbors had been smoking crack and fighting, which accounted for the vibes in the air, but that wasn't it either.

My apartment's down the end of a hall, and of course the hallway lights don't work. I stepped in the blood before I saw it.

In New York the apartment doors are metal. Someone had thoughtfully affixed a wooden board to mine. It looked as if something might be painted on it, but I couldn't be sure, because somebody had also nailed a cat to the board, and then cut the cat open and nailed its ribs to the board, and then stuck everything that was left inside full of razors.

I thought I saw it move, but it couldn't have. It could *not* have—it had been dead for hours and most of the blood on the floor was dry.

I backed up. And then I was sure that was a dreadful mistake, too, because I felt my back hair prickle the way it does when there's someone behind you.

But there wasn't. The hall was empty, yet full of presence, and I had the conviction that the moment I'd taken my eyes off it the cat had begun to pull itself free from the board, and once it was free it would come for me, full of razors.

I looked back at it quickly. Had it moved? Had they done that to it while it was *still alive?*

There were big nails through the eye sockets, holding the head to the board.

"I'll put your eyes out, Witch-bitch." I heard the words from the phone call I'd gotten the day after Miriam died as clearly as if someone was saying them now. *Baba Yaga.*

Reason told me there was no threat, only horror, in the hallway. Intuition assured me the danger was urgent.

I could not enter my apartment any more than I could have done that to an animal—alive or dead—myself. But someone had done it. And they meant to do it to me. The sense of someone in the hallway with me was strong, and none of the mind-tricks I knew would make it go away.

But I could make myself go away. I pulled in my perception, my imagination, my intellect—all the things your mind can use against you. I would not think, I would not feel, I would not imagine. When all of that was gone I forced myself back down the stairs.

I got to the lobby, and instead of going out the front I went down another half-flight and went out the back. There's a sort of a courtyard and a long roofed alleyway leading to the street behind. I went down it without hesitation, even though it was pitch dark. Then I was out on the street again, feeling things swirling around inside me like the demons in Pandora's box and over everything the raw sense of someone—some*thing*—that had been cheated.

I wanted to go back up those stairs. I wanted it desperately. I could see myself unlocking the door and going inside. I tried to see myself locking the door again and making myself safe, but I couldn't bring that image into focus. I'd go in, and leave the door unlocked behind me. Then I'd drink—I wanted a drink; I'd been drinking beer all evening and I wanted something to keep me from sobering up.

And anyone who wanted could come up the stairs and get at me. Anyone who knew I was there to find. Anyone who'd made sure I'd be there.

I was cold sober now. And I wasn't going back. I pushed back against the insistent images, not letting myself feed them. I was a Child of the Goddess; if the Wicca was for anything, it was for a time like this. I was the Goddess, and She was me, and into that charmed circle of light no blackness could penetrate.

I reached Broadway and flagged a cab. I didn't dare take the subway. There was too much *possibility* in the subway.

It was July first, and eighty-five degrees at 1:30 A.M. My teeth were chattering uncontrollably.

One of Lace's roommates let me in. I'd banged on the door until somebody answered, and when she finally took the chains off the door and opened it I barged in past her like she was furniture. Everybody was up by then; when Lace saw me she just put her arms around me.

I must have looked like a rape victim. The other two kept asking if I could identify . . . someone. My perceptions jump-cut with the discontinuity of shock; one minute one of them would be there, and when I tried to answer she'd be gone, coming back with tea or brandy or a wet washcloth.

It was a reaction way out of proportion to that common urban inconvenience of coming home and finding a dead cat nailed to your door. But it was perfectly in line with a reaction to a murder attempt. Because that was what it had been.

A deathspell for a Witch.

One of the charming old European folk customs thankfully not perpetuated in the Community at large today is that of taking a sheep or pig's heart and pricking it full of pins, nails, glass, and anything similar you might have lying about—like razor blades. This is guaranteed to be certain death for the Witches in your neighborhood—once you've got the thing ready, you take it and bury it under the doorstoop of the Witch you most particularly dislike.

They'd nailed it to mine. *Baba Yaga.*

I'd been innocent beyond permission to think Ruslan didn't know exactly who I was. He'd known about Changing's Crossing Circle. He'd known enough to call me and try to stop it. Yet when I went to his circle, not one comment about Changing or my Craft affiliations. I'd assumed he didn't know.

Now I knew better. He knew. He just didn't care. He'd had me out to Queens to look me over, and like a mindless sacrificial goat I'd gone. Now he'd made up his mind what to do, and he was doing it. I was not even bothering to be fair and open-minded and pretend that somebody else in little old New York might be trotting out the old *malificarum* to torture cats to death and nail them to my door. There wasn't anybody else.

Just Ruslan—and his Khazar coven that had gotten a taste for blood, murder, and vendetta, and wanted the thrill of hunting down another victim, even if they had to manufacture one themselves.

Eventually I looked around the Real World. The others had gone; it was just Lace and me, and she was holding my hands. Eventually I realized I was the one holding her hands, and let go.

"I didn't tell you quite everything about *Baba Yaga*," I said. My throat ached as if I'd been screaming.

I guess I was lucky; if I'd been in any better shape Lace would've decked me sure. As it was, she heard me out and put me to bed.

I'd been wrong about Lace. Vendettas weren't her style. She accepted absolutely the idea that Ruslan had murdered Miriam, no question, but she also accepted that there was nothing she could do about it. The great Anti-Pagan and Lesbian Conspiracy would ensure that justice could not be done. She was bitter, but fatalistic.

She also loaned me the money later that day to go shopping for what I needed and then came back with me to my apartment, on a bright and reasonably sunny morning in the later twentieth century when the idea of worshiping gods was as unbelievable as the concept that someone would try to kill someone else with magic.

The *thing* was still on the door. In the morning sunlight with Lace at my back it was gross but not terrifying, all its potential for harm leached away.

Maybe.

Lace and I levered the board off the door and slid it into the garbage bag we'd brought, and poured a mixture of Lysol and Uncrossing Floorwash over the door and the floor and mopped everything up with paper towels until my end of the hall was cleaner than it had been in years. I couldn't get the residue of the carpet tape used to mount the board off the door, but I guessed I was going to have to settle. Only when everything was neat and tidy and I'd blessed the whole door frame with patchouli and blue chalk did I unlock my door.

Everything inside was serene. The sun illuminated a solid bar of dust motes on its way to the sink. I felt like I'd gotten a stay of execution.

"Tea?" I said to Lace.

"Beer," said Lace firmly. She picked up the bag full of dead cat and bloody paper towels. "You want I should toss this for you?"

"No," I said. It went against all of my training and self-preservation instincts to just throw a major spell-component out with the trash to go on wreaking havoc, but I would not take it into the apartment to give it a really good psychic eradication. "We can't just leave something like that lying around ungrounded."

So I brought newspapers and tape and a box out into the hall and wrapped what had been on my door in a nice neat package. Later that day I dropped it off at a place that accepts UPS packages even on Sunday.

I came back from that alone and let myself in to my apartment again. This time it was evening, and the place had the overbaked scent of someplace that had been shut up for a whole summer's day. I wished Ruslan much joy of his package when he opened it, one to four days from now.

Miriam's little Goddess of the Games glimmered down at me from her place on my altar. I smiled up at her and lit some incense and paused, like a mirror, for reflection.

I had been the victim of a magical attack.

Credulity stretched. Oh, they were a major topic of conversation among newbies and wannabes at Pagan festivals. Everyone was almost certain they'd been the victim of one. It was a good explanation for everything from a case of herpes to being fired, and so flattering to be the center of attention of an emissary from the Unseen World. Even I, once and a long time ago, had Almost Certainly created a magical child that haunted me for some weeks knocking books off shelves until I got bored with it.

Eventually you grow up, find out how the laws of magic actually work, and stop making an ass of yourself in public. Because real gen-u-wine ducks-in-a-row Black Workings are just about as rare as actual persecution of Witches. Rarer.

But not, I'd just found out, nonexistent.

I could not walk away from this now. I could not wring my hands and say that I could not build a temporal case, and so no spiritual measures need be taken. Not anymore.

I'd been given the chance, on which I'd rather have took a miss, of gazing on the naked face of capital-E Evil, the thing which, as Hannah Arendt more or less says, does things just because it can. And I could not do nothing.

Caring is what separates good from evil, not the motions you make with your body. A lot of the motions are identical in the gray area that the moderns say proves that there is neither Good nor Evil. Dion Fortune said that Evil is only misapplied Good, which was a brave thing to say in the time where she was living, but she never lived to see the worst aftermath of the War To End War.

If we have a soul, a better nature, any altruism at all, Evil is its autism. Evil is Evil, proving that even tautologies can be true.

And now I had to do something about it, without doing something Evil myself, because if I looked at it and called it by its True Name and then walked away, it had me. You aren't born with a soul. You purchase it in installments. And I'd just been handed the bill for the next one.

Hubris. What a lovely convenient thing a label is. Better than a straitjacket for pulling all your energy into fighting it.

Ruslan was doing evil. Ruslan had to be stopped. But he had committed no provable crime against the people of the City and State of New York. And there was no central authority in the Community that could or would stop him.

I was the only one who knew the truth.

Heady stuff, that. Bast, Lone Ranger of the Wicca. A free ride to megalomaniac paranoia.

Truth, we are taught, does not come from consensus, but from knowledge. The knowledge was there, but somehow I didn't think Ruslan would hold still while I trotted a jury of his peers past his questionable ethical practices.

And even if everyone in the Community believed me, what would they do? Anything?

Ha. I'd already heard Belle's vote. "We are not qualified to sit in judgment. . . ."

Yet I could not do nothing. And that was the bone in the throat—I had to do something. Something legal, and more to the point, moral.

I curled up in a chair where I could see Miriam's little Goddess, pulled out one of my sketchbooks, and began to think.

It took me a week to get what I wanted, but most of that was because the typesetter was so damn slow—closed for the Fourth, and other light holidays. During that period Ruslan was blessedly silent, package or no.

Lace phoned me a couple of times, but we didn't have much to say to each other. I hung out around the Revel a bit, but I really didn't fit into their feminism-and-granola Paganism any more than I did with the Serpent's Truth's heavy-metal high sorcery.

Where did I belong? My own High Priestess thought I was over-reacting, and Belle was pretty much middle-of-the-road as Witches went. If I didn't belong in Wicca, what was left?

I wouldn't worry about that now. I belonged to the Goddess at least—that's one good thing about *gnosis.* And I thought that what I was doing was right.

And whether it was right or not, it was still what I was doing.

I picked up the type Friday noon, and stayed late at the studio mechanicaling it up. When I was done it was a poster—a hand-bill, really—8 1/2 × 11, easy to reproduce at any city copy shop, full of big black letters.

WARNING: There is a Black Coven operating out of Queens. They call themselves Baba Yaga and claim to practice a Khazar (Russian) Wiccan tradition. These people perform black magick and use dangerous (illegal) drugs in their rituals without the consent of the participants. They have already been responsible for the death of one woman who was trying to leave them. If you were a friend of or knew Sunshrike, avoid these people and warn your friends.

The wording had been what took me the most time to get right. I hadn't mentioned Ruslan's name, or added my own to the poster. I had tried to make it something that would have no effect in the mundane world—I could not imagine these posters causing Ruslan to lose his Real World job or make the police come looking for him. All I wanted was to neutralize Ruslan in the same arena where he and *Baba Yaga* were trying to kill me, not to raise the stakes.

And that is the difference between Good and Evil, and the reason Good never wins.

That night I took the mechanical home and cast a spell of my own—an intention, really—that the poster it made should shine such a bright light that the shadows people needed to work evil would no longer exist. The next day—Saturday—I took it to the Eighth Street Copy Shop and ordered twenty-five hundred copies.

* * *

Saturday night at 8:30 I went down to the Revel, hoping Lace was there. In spite of the weather (hot but clear) I was wearing an extra-extra-large army surplus parka, which I keep for wearing to Pagan Festivals because nothing in its sad shabby life is ever going to make any difference to it again. I had reinforced its immense pockets with duct tape; they contained fifteen-hundred flyers, a staple gun and two boxes of staples, and a dozen glue sticks. I looked like a mugger waiting to happen.

I waddled into the store. Mischia, having got her brother safely married, was sitting behind the card table finishing up a late customer. A coffee can full of bills sat at her elbow. Lace looked up from the cash register. The henna was black now, and so were her fingernails. She looked like a punk vampire whose mother'd had a heavy date with a Mack truck.

"Hi, Lace—doing anything tonight?" I said in my best Donna Reed voice.

"Keeping you out of Bellevue, maybe. Shit, Bast, what's with you?"

I went over to where Mischia wouldn't hear us. "I just joined the Occult Police," I told Lace.

"I'm telling you because I figured you'd guess."

It was an hour later; we were outside the Revel and Tollah was locking up inside. She hadn't raised an eyebrow over the arctic parka in July. I wondered how strange people thought I was.

I handed Lace a flyer. It was hard to stand there while she read it and wait for her to laugh. I was doing this because I *had* to; the same way you have to move your hand out of a candle flame. I didn't think she'd agree with me.

"And you're going to put these up all over town?" Lace said, poker-faced.

"You will have noticed my name's not on them."

"Yeah, sure. That's really going to confuse the hell out of people, Bast."

"But they can't prove anything. Just like I can't prove that *Baba Yaga* poisoned Miriam and nailed a cat to my door."

Lace laughed then. Maybe the irony of it amused her, or maybe she was just tickled at the thought that I was never going to laugh at her Conspiracy paranoia again.

"Sure. Okay. Where do we start?"

*   *   *

If you take a map of New York and turn it so that Battery Park is
at the bottom and Spuyten Duyvil is at the top (the name has nothing to do with the devil; it's Dutch for *whirlpool*), Chanter's Revel
is the occult shop nearest the bottom. So we started there and
worked our way uptown.

I stapled flyers to fences and glued them to lampposts. I slid
them through the mail slots of the stores we visited. I hit up bookstores, bars, *botanicas,* and any other likely looking funky New Age
place I saw. I think there are "Post No Bills" regulations still on
the books in Manhattan; Lace kept lookout and we were careful
to make sure nobody saw me actually doing anything. It was a
clear night; eventually Goddess Luna made it up over the buildings to shine down on the Batman and Robin of the Neopagan
Community.

I glued several flyers to the windows of The Snake. I didn't do
that anywhere else, because glue stick is hell to remove and I had
no grudge against the owners of the walls I was decorating, but I
suspected Julian of knowing more about Ruslan than he'd told me.
Petty, I know.

When I'd done a street, I could look back down and see my
handbills: lemon yellow, orange orange, and raspberry red. The
fluorescent copier paper had cost extra, but it'd been well worth
it. Nobody could miss them.

Eventually we ran out. I had another thousand at home, and
the original, so I could make more any time I wanted to, but what
I'd been carrying had pretty well plastered the Village. The only
occult shop I'd missed was Mirror Mirror, which is pretty chichi
and New Age—and way over on the West Side, besides.

The full moon was sliding off toward the east—that made it a
little after midnight. I felt an incredible sense of euphoria; whether
it was the presence of the Goddess or the rush that comes from
making mischief, I didn't bother to examine.

"Buy you a midnight snack?" I said to Lace.

"I figure you owe me, Caped Crusader."

I avoided my usual haunts on Sunday, so as not to be seen too
obviously smirking. The sense of well-being I'd lucked into on Saturday continued; it's wonderful to bask in approval, even if it's only
yours.

I coasted uptown and spent the day window-shopping on the

Upper East Side and thinking that if I got my hands on enough of the right pieces of Art Nouveau I could convince Neopagans everywhere that the Victorians were a Goddess-worshiping matriarchy. I entertained once more the unlikely dream of Owning My Own Occult Shop, which I never will because more than fifty percent of all businesses go bankrupt in the first year and I'm too smart to get into things with a failure factor that high.

I tell myself.

I splurged on a sushi dinner — one last time, since with taxis and cleaning supplies and all (not to mention the book I'd bought at The Snake in the middle of all this) I was going to have to put in serious hours at the Bookie Joint to stay on the profits side of the ledger. But that gnawing feeling of being a helpless consentor to what *Baba Yaga* had done to Miriam was gone.

I felt up enough to make a pass by Cindy's on the way home, but the salon had closed up shop. I saw a couple of my posters on the buildings nearby. They looked like I felt. Cheery.

My answering machine was taking a message as I walked in. Belle wanted me to call her. She'd wanted me to call her, I found, at eleven, one, and three P.M. also.

And her all the way up at the top of the island, and this such a secret between us. I tried to wipe the smirk off my face and failed.

There was also a message from Lace to tell me she'd gotten Tollah to post a copy of the flyer inside the shop. I looked at the pile I had left. Maybe she'd like some to hand out, too.

II

You would think that Martin Luther had never nailed ninety-five theses to anything—or that there weren't handbills all over the city telling people everything from the date of the Apocalypse to the Queen of England's sexual habits. Why should they make such a fuss about one more?

Belle nailed me at the studio Monday.

"Bast? I really think we ought to talk about this," she said as soon as I picked up the phone.

"I'm not really somewhere I can talk," I said, not even bothering to deny I knew what "this" was.

I was safe because it was true: Ray doesn't object to my religion (if he's noticed it), but he does object to tying up Houston Graphics' one phone line for anything other than Houston Graphics business.

"I had no idea you were so upset about Miriam," she said. "I know you can't talk now, but will you come over tonight? I really feel bad about not having been more there for you."

"If I can," I hedged. "Look, I'll call you later."

But I didn't go to Belle's later. I went down to The Snake.

The Snake opens every day at noon and remains open until ten or midnight, depending on the will of Tris, Julian, and the gods. When I got there around seven, the usual house-party atmosphere prevailed. There were leather boys with rosy crosses tattooed on their

pecs hobnobbing with *brujas* wearing every piece of jewelry known
to medical science and enough mascara to equip a Tammy Faye
Bakker impersonator. There were people for whom the sixties
hadn't ended and those who were already living in the Age of Horus.
It was pure sleaze. I felt instantly at home and wondered why.

There was a copy of my flyer on the bulletin board, and I definitely hadn't put it there. Lace hadn't either—she'll cross the
threshold of The Snake about the same time she goes into St. Pat's.
I slithered past the bulletin board and down one of the aisles,
where I picked up a book by a Brit anthropologist who got herself
inducted into an English coven. She concluded that belief in magic
causes belief in magic, provided the believer wants to believe.

Well, hell, *I* knew that. Belief is what makes it work. In theory
unbelief should work the same way, but the mind is a divided
camp at the best of times. You can eradicate reason from your
mind much easier than you can banish superstition. In the end,
the reality of magic has to be decided by each person for himself,
with full knowledge of the consequences.

Magical theory has never been popular with the masses.

I worked my way around past Atlantis and the Rosicrucians to
the front desk. Julian was behind the cash register, presiding
over his little kingdom. When he saw me he blinked, as if he
couldn't believe his eyes.

"Bast—I was hoping you'd come by."

Not convincing. And Julian was always convincing. Right then
little warning bells started to go off in my head.

"You've got a book for me, Julian?" What was it really? He
couldn't be picking this inopportune a time to discover an interest in girls.

I was standing between the bulletin board and the cash register; behind me two gays were discussing the Baba Yaga flyer in
the patented New York Gay Male Accent.

"Remember how a couple weeks ago you were in with that
Russian thing?" Julian said, ignoring what I'd just said. Behind
me the conversation turned on the imperialistic judgmentalism of
whoever had prepared the flyer. "Do you still have it?"

That was the moment at which I knew what I hadn't even suspected, but I shoved the knowledge down in order to concentrate
on what I was saying. I tried desperately to remember what I'd told
Julian about the Khazar missal. "Maybe," I said.

"Burn it," Julian said flatly.

I stared at him, looking like a moron and for once not even caring. Because I'd been right when I pasted all those flyers on The
Snake's windows—Julian *did* know more than he was telling.

Julian was the one who'd sold me out to Ruslan.

What was the sum total of my relationship with Julian? Charge
slips. And what was on those charge slips? Nothing much: just
my (mundane) name, address, and phone number. And Julian
knew me as Bast.

Julian was the link.

I opened my mouth to say something, but then someone came
up to the register and Julian turned away as if he'd never spoken.

"Oh, hey, *Jadis!*" I turned around and stared straight at Starfawn.

Know that your sins will find you out an astute student of
human nature said once. Starfawn was standing right in front of
the sign and could hardly fail to notice it—assuming she could
read.

"It's so neat to see you again. I guess you're feeling okay?" She
was good, but she couldn't quite suppress her smirk when she
said that. Starfawn of *Baba Yaga* had every reason to hope I wasn't
feeling okay.

"I was hoping you'd maybe come back, 'cause you left so fast
the last time I really didn't get a chance to talk to you, but Rus
said he hadn't heard from you." Her eyes were flat and innocent
and brown, completely untroubled. I revised my opinion. Not a
Trilby. A little lamprey, hungry for blood.

She looked up at my flyer and dismissed it with a shrug of one
bare shoulder. "Somebody's in real trouble for that—but hey, whoever isn't for us is against us, you know?"

I'd heard that somewhere before. Maybe Starfawn thought it
was original.

"Who do you suppose could have done something like that?" I
said with an increasing sense of unreality.

She smiled; a blinding set of full dental caps. "Well, you know,
Bast, honey, Rus is going to find out."

She sashayed right out the door before I realized she'd called
me by name. I looked at Julian. He was staring down at me with
the blank expression usually worn by the better class of Puritan
Witch-burners.

"Bye," he said.

* * *

I spent the rest of the evening bludgeoning my feelings about Julian into something I could live with. Every time I started to rationalize his involvement I couldn't decide whether I was being transactional and open-minded or selling out for a pretty face.

He'd given Ruslan my legal name and unlisted phone number. Good guess: He was the only one who could make the connection between Karen and Bast who also might know Ruslan.

On the other hand, he'd advised me to burn the missal. Unsolicited advice, and one of the very few non-mercantile-based conversations I'd ever had with Julian.

Did that mean he repented his wicked ways and thought I was cute, or just that he was playing both ends against the middle to achieve balance, like a good Ceremonial Magician?

By the time I woke up Tuesday morning I decided it probably didn't matter.

But I resolved to make future transactions at The Snake cash only.

Of course the (rumored) authorship of the "Trumpet's Blast Against the Monstrous Regiment of Khazar Wiccans" (to coin a title) didn't stay a secret. For one thing, I had to talk to Belle eventually, even though she had to come all the way down to my apartment to catch me. She asked me point-blank if I'd done it, and then I got a long lecture on tolerance, responsibility, understanding, and Not Making Waves.

She kept reminding me that I didn't have any proof Ruslan was involved in Miriam's death—a confession was apparently no more proof than it would have been in a mundane criminal case.

I hadn't mentioned the cat. I think I was afraid of what I'd do if I did and heard what I thought I would.

"You really don't have any right to go publicizing something like that in that fashion. It isn't constructive, you know, and we all have to tolerate each other, not condemn. If you want to invite Ruslan to a Circle in order to talk things over . . ."

"I am going to Circle with that sonovabitch motherfuck about the time hell freezes over," I interrupted. "Are you listening to me, Belle? Are you listening to *yourself*? For ten years you've told me that magic works—changes in environment in conformation with will, remember? Well, I believed you, and now when I tell you that there is someone out there using his will like an AK-47, you tell me I'm not being constructive! If it works, it can kill—and that's against all the ethics you taught me, too! Ethics, Belle! Ruslan used black magic against Miriam—he used it against me—he admitted it—"

"Oh, Bast, I think you're taking things way out of context," Belle said, exasperated.

I took a deep breath. "All I want to know is, do you believe all this stuff about ethics and love and magic that you've been pushing at me all these years, or are you just another fucking mundane?"

"I don't think you're being terribly reasonable about this," Belle said in a tight little voice.

"I don't think I'm *going* to be reasonable about this," I said, which pretty well killed that conversation. I didn't offer to walk her to the subway when she left.

Some of the other members of Changing called too, once they'd seen the flyer and heard my name attached to it. The Cat took it as a personal affront that I'd used print media instead of an electronic BBS. Glitter thought I should have hired some of her clients to beat Ruslan up. Everyone was bewildered at my introduction of a real toad into their imaginary garden.

Okay, so magic-with-a-*K* is a crock of shit. Mental masturbation for the masses. Self-delusion. This is not the point. The point is that Ruslan, under the guise of practicing Wicca, violated a number of its central tenets—the Rules. No more enforceable or admirable than the rules in a game of Monopoly, if you like, but start breaking them and soon what you've got left isn't any kind of game at all.

Whether Ruslan was more than a little responsible for the real live death of an actual human being probably doesn't matter either. He'd *tried* to be. And unless my flyer drove him out of the Community, he was going to go on being responsible, until he made a big enough mess to interest the temporal authorities, because nobody in the Community was going to say a word against him.

A central regulating authority is not the answer. There have always been con men and charlatans in the religion business, bilking their followers to build their Towers of Power and their Crystal Cathedrals. There always will be. The only answer is to eliminate followers, but it's lonely when you don't follow the herd.

Maybe there isn't any answer.

Changing's first July meeting was on Friday the 13th. I didn't go. I had my own ritual to conduct.

I'd snagged a nice sturdy box from a trash heap and covered it with wrapping paper. Now I dumped in some potpourri and frankincense and a protection amulet or two, a procedure that always reminds me vaguely of kindergarten arts and crafts time, although I've managed to come to terms with it. And when I had the box looking pretty and inviting and strong in a way that made sense to my unconscious mind, I dumped in all that was left in the world of Miriam Seabrook, including the tapes of the phone messages I'd had from her and Ruslan. Eventually someone would be having a bonfire somewhere and I could burn the lot.

I hesitated a long time over the Khazar missal. Burn it, Julian had said—and while a part of me thought that was a good idea, and something I could manage right now, I couldn't quite bring myself to do it. So I wrapped it in red silk and tucked it into the box along with all the rest.

Then it was all hidden away under my bed. Over and done with, I thought. All that was left was for me to try and make sense of what had happened.

I'd managed to construct a sort of timetable.

Sometime in March of this year: Miriam meets Ruslan and joins *Baba Yaga*, taking their oaths of secrecy. At first she's pleased with it. She drops old friends and separates the ones she can't drop completely (like Lace) from her new friends. She starts making her very own Khazar missal, and Ruslan paints her portrait into the icon inside the front cover—with her own blood—just as he has for every new Khazar.

But then things go sour. Maybe it's common sense asserting itself. Maybe the things they're asking her to do finally outweigh the sense of being part of a glorious conspiracy. At any rate, sometime around the beginning of June she tells them she's through with them—or maybe just hints that she's dissatisfied. And Ruslan tells her "once in, never out." He has her *athame*. He tells the coven to do a deathspell. Maybe he tells Miriam. Maybe he doesn't. But Miriam, very conveniently, dies.

I didn't know Ruslan well enough to know if he expected his magic to work. Whether he got what he expected or not, the results frightened him—especially when he realized that Miriam had died with all her Khazar material in her possession.

Miriam's missal was the thing that bound her into *Baba Yaga*. Maybe it was an occult funnel, like Julian said. Or maybe Ruslan only thought it was. But the thought of losing control over it made

Ruslan crazy enough to commit an actual crime: tossing Miriam's apartment to look for it. He probably didn't have to break in — Ruslan struck me as the kind of power-tripper who ended up with keys to his coveners' apartments.

Was that how he'd gotten Miriam's *athame?* Or had he made her give it to him? I couldn't imagine her doing that — but I could imagine her fear on coming home and finding it gone. Was that the thing that had finally made her call me?

I'd never know.

But I did know that three days after he trashed her apartment Ruslan phoned me to invite me over to his place. Miriam might have mentioned me — or Julian might have told him I'd showed up at The Snake brandishing the missal. I tried to imagine Julian as a member of Baba Yaga and failed, fortunately for my sense of *amour propre.* No matter how much ceremony Baba Yaga layered on, they'd still be too Pagan for him.

Which was beside the point. The point was Ruslan, and his telephone soliciting of Yours Truly, part-time moron. Ruslan was still looking for the missal and hoped I had it — in fact, he'd made some pretty heavy-handed threats about what would happen to me if I didn't hand it over. But I didn't, and so, not having gotten it, he summoned up *Baba Yaga* to . . .

Kill me? Scare me? Search my apartment? Make me go running back to him with it clutched in my hot little hand, begging him to make the bogeyman go away?

I didn't know. And I hadn't done any of those things, which was more to the point. Instead, I'd turned the full glare of Community attention on him and made him the current hot topic of gossip. A sensible person would pull in his horns and walk away, but I wasn't sure if Ruslan was one.

And the worst of it was, Ruslan might not be sure either.

12

New York headed into the depths of July. Not as bad as August, when the streets melt, but enough to make me wish I had the money and the organization to afford an air conditioner at home.

Nothing happened.

Oh, I could feel Belle's hurt feelings from one hundred and ninety blocks away, and I spent a serious amount of ritual time making sure my "personal space" was magically clean. Ruslan and I believed in magic, even if the rest of the world didn't.

Some people bootlegged the flyer. I saw some copies I hadn't made in places I hadn't put them. I'd used up the rest of mine strewing them around the city in places you wouldn't normally expect to see things like that, like Rockefeller Center.

But the consensus (or the general consensus of opinion, as our semiliterate friends on the telly would have it) was "judge not, lest ye be judged"—a homily that had never slowed the Christians down any.

And I was perfectly willing to let the gods judge me. It was my peers that bothered me.

Friday night. Coincidentally the twenty-somethingeth anniversary of the Apollo 11 landing, which had had no effect on life as we know it. Lace had called to invite me special to the Revel's TGIF circle. I was doing the politic thing and staying home. I did not want to be patron saint of the first annual anti-masculinist Dianic Wicca *jihad.* Down at the Revel they'd taken the anti-Khazar manifesto to heart; Ruslan was a perfect *bête noir* for them, being a male Ceremonial Magician who had caused the death of a (sort of) lesbian while practicing god-centered Neopaganism.

I'd seen this before, with the scapegoat of the moment. They'd blow him up to mythic proportions, then get tired of their game and wander off, leaving behind a certified Craft legend.

Nor did I want to replace Miriam in Lace's affections. We'd developed the pressure-cooked emotional bond that comes from being victims of the same trauma, and it was probably better for both of us if natural attrition took its course. In addition to any number of other good reasons for becoming polite strangers again, I wouldn't make Lace any happier than Miriam had.

I was actually considering calling Rachel Seabrook to see if she'd ever gotten any autopsy reports when the phone rang.

"Jello?" I chirped.

"This is Ruslan."

There are times when your power of improvisation deserts you. For some reason I'd never expected to hear from him again. I didn't have a script ready.

"I suppose you think you're very clever," he said, in the tone that daddies everywhere use to begin the scold of the erring nymphet. That saved me; I've never been any daddy's girl and I'm way too old for nymphethood.

"Hello, Michael, it's nice to hear from you." Hearing his first name stopped him for a minute; I'd hoped it would.

"I don't think you'll think so when you hear what I have to say, Karen. I'm calling on the advice of my lawyer about those flyers of yours. You didn't think I knew about them, did you?"

Why not? Aside from their being the hot topic of the last two weeks, I'd even posted some on the Double-R line. He'd probably ridden to work in the same car with them.

"My lawyer thinks he can make a pretty good case for libel, here, but I'm not a vindictive man. If you'll just make some good-faith reparations—"

"What exactly is it that you want?" The song and dance about the lawyer was bullshit; if he had one he wouldn't be talking to me now.

"Look, I know you're kind of overwrought. You know what I mean. But I think I can cut you a little slack. Just give me back the stuff you stole from Miriam's apartment and we can both just walk away."

Oh, he was cool. Nothing I said was going to jar him loose from his preplanned script.

"You know, *Jadis*, a lot worse things than lawyers could happen if you don't. I warned you. The gods of the Khazar are real, and they are not mocked."

"I think that the Khazar gods are getting a little too much help these days," I said. It was pure inspiration, in the literal sense; I had the same feeling of right and proper action I'd had when I posted all those flyers.

"Did you know they're autopsying Miriam Seabrook? Suspicious accidental death. You should have used Mogen David in your fucking Dixie cup, Mikey. There's somebody down in the Manhattan County Coroner's office slicing her liver up with a microtome right now—and when they're done they're going to find your signature all over it. Murder. Plain real-world murder that even the mundanes can believe in."

"Bullshit," said Ruslan.

I laughed. "I've got Miriam's Khazar book and a nice long letter full of names and addresses. Do I have to prove anything—or do they just have to look?"

"Miriam Seabrook died of heart failure!" Ruslan said. *"Baba Yaga—"*

"Ever hear of chemical footprints, jerkball? The traces a drug leaves in the user's body? What's in the wine, Mikey? Something good?"

There was a pause, and the next time he spoke I had difficulty recognizing it as the same voice.

"You cowan *bitch. I am going to bury you."*

The bottom dropped out of reality and I clutched the phone. My heart was hammering as if I'd stared into the open throat of a Hell I professed not to believe in.

I'd gotten his attention, all right. I'd finally made him mad.

I stood there wondering if I dared to hang up, knowing he knew where I lived. Then he laughed. It was a friendly, confident sound that wasn't quite sane anymore.

"You know, you really do have some things that belong to me, Karen. Why don't you give them back?"

You always read in these spatterpunk effusions about terror on top of terror, and despite the bouncing heads and flying entrails, the fear never seems plausible. Maybe you can't get down on paper or film about how *real* terror is what you do to yourself with the knowledge of what the other person can do, and probably will do, when there is nothing at all that you can do to affect his actions.

Why don't you give them back? Because if you don't, some night you'll wake up and I'll be standing there, and I will do things to you that you don't even want to begin to imagine.

If I didn't give Miriam's things to him he'd be mad. Bottom line.

"I'll trade you. Then we're quits." I am not brave, and I wasn't then. It was an atavistic certainty that running from the nightmare would only make it attack that made me say it—that, and the hunch that somewhere on this path lay the only way out.

"*You* want something from *us?* Well, this is unusual." Oh yes, he was willing to string this out now. His *daimon* was riding him, just as mine was me.

"Miriam's *athame.* For the Khazar prayer book."

"I'll be right over."

"It isn't here," I said with quick desperation. Ruslan laughed. "Be reasonable—it's packed up and hidden to mail to the cops— why would I keep it here?—if I died, nobody'd find it."

"You'd be surprised. You know, I don't think you know as much about magic as you claim to, Karen."

"I know I have your book." I wanted to boast about the counterspells I could cast on it, the banishings I could do to make it only a decorated piece of board. But I didn't.

"And you're going to give it to me. And your letter." Perversely, the fact that he believed in that made me feel better. Ruslan of *Baba Yaga* was not omnipotent.

"Tomorrow night. Nine-thirty. St. Mark's Place. Bring Miriam's *athame.* I'll trade you."

"Aren't you going to ask me to come alone?" Ruslan sounded amused. In control.

I hung up on him.

Now I had one more definite fact: Even while he was deluding and drugging his coveners, Ruslan believed what he was telling them. He believed there was magic in the Khazar icons he painted, and the more he failed to get Miriam's back, the more important it became to him, until it became an obsession.

An obsession that I'd played right up to by telling him that the Khazar book could tie him into a murder investigation.

Arguably the stupidest thing I'd ever done.

About an hour later, when I stopped shaking, I realized what had been in the back of my mind when I'd done it. There was no Seabrook murder case. There might not even be an autopsy; New York's a busy town.

But even at nine P.M. there would be people all over St. Mark's Place when I met Ruslan. If I wanted to see some justice done, I had to make a civil pothook on which the temporal courts could hang him.

Frame him? Not quite. I'd just given Ruslan a real good motive to shut me up. It shouldn't be all that hard to get him to assault me. And then I could swear a charge out against him.

If the Goddess was on my side, if magic was afoot in the world, if this was a good idea . . .

If it wasn't, I could just spend the rest of my life looking over my shoulder.

I needed witnesses.

"Hello, Glitter? This is Bast. I need you to do something for me."

Glitter had been one of my partisans during the late unpleasantness with Changing. She was sorry I'd missed coven, glad to hear from me, eager to think everything was going to be fine now. I felt a little guilty drafting her for the role of Sancho Panza. I could have gotten Lace much more easily, but I could never have gotten her to testify afterward.

But Glitter was not only a Probation Officer for the City of New York, she was perfectly willing to come down to St. Mark's Place and meet me. I had a plausible excuse. St. Mark's Cinema is one of the last revival houses in the city, but it's no place to go alone unless you're Arnold Schwarzenegger.

"I've got to give some stuff to somebody, but he should be there about nine-fifteen. Then we can go and get some Chinese and probably hit the ten o'clock show, okay?"

She said the playbill was *The Women* and *Idiot's Delight.* Gable tap dances. With any luck, I'd be on my way to the hospital instead, with an assault charge against Michael Ruslan in my pocket.

The more I thought about it, the worse I felt about lying-by-omission to Glitter. I could tell myself that the end justified the means, but it never does. Neither does the means justify the end.

Ethics. Promises. The seduction of vendetta.

Goddess, let me get through Saturday night alive and I'll reform. Promise.

*   *   *

Saturday. The sun was still high when I started my preparations for meeting Ruslan—not that you could see it. The sky was an overcast pewter and the air was hazy. I pulled down my shade, lit my candles, and made every other preparation to get ready for tonight.

I had settled the temporal side of the matter; if Ruslan was obliging enough to break the law in a provable fashion, I would have him prosecuted for it.

That left the spiritual. And what I owed Miriam. Justice.

To call upon the gods for justice in a proper framework of magical ethics, justice alone must be the goal. Not "I win"/"You lose." How can you be sure who will win, if anybody? Maybe *both* of you are wrong. To ask for justice with magic you must care that there is an outcome without caring what it is—the sublime disinterest of the jurist.

That was what I wanted. I would bring Ruslan face-to-face with moral superiority—not mine, because I might not be—and there would be judgment, in which I would take no part.

Magical judgment for magical crimes. Everything else had been leading up to this. And tonight, when what I had set in motion stopped, it would be over for all time.

I watched the candles burn before the Goddess of the Games, and tried to empty myself of hopes for the outcome.

13

There are some odd anomalous nights when the weather goes completely mad. I can never remember whether it's cold air/warm ground or warm air/cold ground that makes fog, but sometimes—even in polluted, overindustrial cities—the conditions are still right.

It wasn't a very heavy fog, but it turned the street lamps into soft balls of golden light and made the geography of the next street over just a little uncertain. There was the lightest of warm misty rains falling; enough to make the air glitter. If the need arose, I could wrap the air around me like a cape. Or walk on it.

And if I fell, that was because there was need for that too, in the glittering patternless design that stretched farther and farther the longer I looked. I was part of that design; I could see the steps that had been laid out for me before I was born, and dance their pattern willfully and foreknowing.

And that I never suspected Ruslan was smart enough to anticipate me, that was foreordained, too.

Below Eighth Street the aseptic grid of Upper Manhattan gives way to a tangle of streets that intersect in any way they please. The *place* in St. Mark's Place where I was meeting Glitter—and Ruslan—was a mostly triangular traffic island built nearly flush with the surrounding asphalt and put there in the hope of unknotting the chaos of five intersecting streets. It contained a lamp-post and a god-awful piece of cubist modern sculpture, but was in plain sight of stores, pedestrians, and suicidal motorists driving *en pointe* in the lemming ballet. The fog made things especially chancy.

I achieved the little plaza. Barely. I checked my watch.

I'd told Glitter nine-fifteen. I'd told Ruslan nine-thirty. But it was nine o'clock when I got to St. Mark's Square, and Ruslan was waiting for me.

He stepped out from behind the sculpture, and at first I didn't recognize him. He was wearing a trench coat; he looked like a rumpled, pudgy Bogart, but he wasn't funny.

"Give it to me," he said. No, not funny at all.

I stared at him. I had brought the presence of the Goddess with me; I felt Her as an infinite peace. Even so, I'd been expecting something more confrontational, with rhetoric.

"The book," Ruslan said. He didn't look like someone carrying an *athame,* either. I *knew* he didn't have it, but I said my lines like I was supposed to.

"We trade."

He pulled something out of his pocket, but it wasn't Miriam's *athame.* It was a gun.

I stared at it stupidly. *Cold iron breaks all magic,* I thought, just as if this were a fairy tale and the gun wasn't real. Traffic whipped by scant feet away. It might have been on the dark side of the moon for all the useful help it was.

"Give it to me," Ruslan said. He smiled, and for an instant we were both in on the joke. Both of us knew what was to come. Neither of us was fooled. We had consented to this mystery play a long, long time ago.

I pulled a red silk bag out of my jacket. I was wearing the same one I'd worn the night I posted the flyers, but I was only carrying one thing now. I turned the bag upside down and shook the contents out on the ground.

It was the front cover of the missal; I'd burned the rest of it that afternoon. The wood was soft; when push came to crunch I'd been able to split it into nine pieces with my *boline* and tie each piece up with hand-dyed red wool yarn and twigs of American mountain ash.

"Rowan tree and red thread." Proof against all sorcery. I'd knotted feathers into the cords, and blue glass beads, and a little sil-

ver pentacle—binding, purifying, breaking the power of the Khazar coven over Miriam forever. There was nothing they could do to her—or her spirit—now.

Ruslan giggled, and even in my self-induced trance state I thought it was a bizarre reaction. He waved the gun as if he didn't care who saw it. The fog made haloes around everything.

He looked at me with a weird crinkled little smile on his face. He was sweating; the light reflected off each moving drop as it slid down his cheeks.

Then he looked into my eyes for the first time. I felt a chill shock of kinship even as I realized how far gone he was.

Gone. "A journey to that far country from which no man returns." Meaningless tag-ends of poetry beat through me, and the passage of the cars on the street seemed to take on an intentional rhythm.

Ruslan's smile died like a burnt-out lightbulb. He brought the gun down and settled himself into the brace familiar from a hundred TV shows. I realized that he was going to shoot me now, and that the act wouldn't touch him at all.

The Goddess folded Her wings around me and I stood waiting for some cue to move. There was a letter addressed to the police—it was on my desk at work along with the rest of the Khazar material. Maybe this was the way justice would be served.

Then Ruslan broke stance and stepped backward off the curb—getting ready to run; getting a better angle. I don't know.

There was an impact, soft and heavy at once, like dropping a stone onto a lawn. The gun in his hand vanished like a magician's trick, leaving me blinking after it.

That was when I saw the car. It swerved wildly out, and then speeded up. I never saw what color it was. I don't know if the driver was even quite sure he'd hit somebody.

Ruslan tottered on his feet for a minute, face thrown back into the mist. Long enough for me to believe he was fine and we'd go on to Act Two. Then he fell and rolled into the gutter at my feet, just like in the movies.

The presence of the Goddess—or just ritually induced euphoria—was gone. Shock made me cold. I knew—good Samaritan, good citizen—that having witnessed a hit-and-run accident, my duty was to summon the authorities.

Ruslan was moving, trying to get up. I knelt down beside him, but I couldn't have said a word if there was money in it for me.

His eyelids fluttered. His face was sickly pale, and he didn't seem to be able to move his right arm. There was no blood; only a smear of dirt on the trench coat to indicate impact.

He opened and closed his mouth, but I didn't hear anything. I leaned closer, too stunned to be afraid. There was a rank fruity smell on his breath, and I remembered all those little bottles in the refrigerator in Queens. Michael Ruslan was a diabetic, and by the time the ambulance came and took him to Bellevue Emergency and figured that out, it might be too late for insulin to do any good.

I looked around. No one was paying attention. Nobody in New York pays any attention to anybody else. A lot of people sleep in gutters in New York. Ruslan could be just one more.

My mind raced with the chill hyperlexia of shock. I thought about a gray cat, fur brown with blood. Nails through its eyes and its mouth and stomach filled with broken razor blades.

I thought about Miriam, alone and afraid. Calling me for help, and dying before I could give it. Hoping even at the end that things could turn out right.

I thought about the Goddess's justice. *Her* justice, not mine.

"Emergency? I need an ambulance. A man has been hit by a car at St. Mark's Place. He's hurt and unconscious. He's a diabetic. I think he's in shock."

The operator said something while I was hanging up. Probably asking who I was.

I'm nobody, who are you?

Are you nobody too?

When I got back to the Square at nine-thirty there was no sign of anyone, including Ruslan. So I went home. There was a message on my machine from Glitter, telling me she had some emergency overtime and couldn't make it.

Gable isn't that good a dancer, anyway.

Ruslan died on the way to the hospital. So I heard. There's a death certificate on file in the county courthouse, and the name and address matches. I looked it up.

Did Miriam Seabrook die of black magic or just liver failure? Does the intent of the person who sincerely wanted her dead not matter just because his tools weren't good enough—if they weren't?

SPEAK DAGGERS TO HER   141

And was I right—never mind effective—to do what I did?

You have your version of the truth and I have mine. I know what killed Miriam. And I know why Ruslan died.

A week later I went up to the apartment in Queens; it was vacant. I told the super a bunch of lies about being from the City Housing Commission; it was enough to make him tell me Ludmilla Ruslan had left suddenly. No warning, no forwarding address.

On the way home I stopped into The Snake. It was fuller than usual. Next Wednesday was August first—Lammas—so last-minute shoppers were stocking up on candles and incense.

I wondered where I'd be celebrating it. Belle hadn't called. I hadn't had the nerve to call her. I wondered if she knew about Ruslan yet.

Julian spoke to me before I'd quite got in the door.

"Bast? I've got your book for you."

I would have ignored him except for the fact that he wasn't up on his throne. He'd come down to floor level to be sure of stopping me. And he was actually making eye contact.

So I followed him back to the cash register, still determined to refuse whatever he came up with, but the package he handed me was too small and lumpy to be a book. It was wrapped in brown paper, and squished with the feel of layered newspaper when I took it. I felt the hard shape of the blade even through the newspaper, but I tore it open to be sure.

Miriam's *athame.* I looked at Julian. He looked past me, meaningfully.

I turned to where he was looking and saw Starfawn. She saw me see her and ran like hell.

Last week I sent a sympathy card to Rachel Seabrook. I didn't put my return address, but I signed the name she'd know. Sometimes I wonder what she did with Miriam's ashes.

BOOK OF
MOONS

I

It was a Saturday in the middle of April and I was at the studio, making up for lost time at my day job by working overtime. I was short because last month I'd gone up to Rites of Spring, the Boston-area Pagan festival, and so had been out of the studio for more than a week.

Going to festivals affects everyone in different ways. It made me want to have a cleaner, larger, more upmarket apartment.

It made Belle want to have a similar festival here.

I suspected I was going to be asked to organize things, and I suspected I'd agree, because Belle and I were just now putting the icing on a patch-job of our friendship. It had been badly strained by the events of last summer and Belle's friendship was not something I was eager to lose, any more than I particularly wanted to leave Changing, which is my coven and Belle's.

The difference between us is that Lady Bellflower is Changing's High Priestess and I'm just another spear-carrying urban Witch. My name—my real name—is Bast, and you can stop doing that Elizabeth Montgomery impersonation right now.

Religion, Threat or Menace, is shaping up to be the hot issue of the nineties, as anyone who's studied the history of centuries ending in zero could predict. This time, however, the lines seem to be drawn not between this sect and that, but between those who believe in Deity—*any* deity, God or Goddess—and those who think that religion belongs in the past tense.

Wicca, the Religion of Witchcraft, the Old Religion, the Craft of the Wise, or whatever you want to call it, may be the new religion that sociologists and millenialists have been predicting since the 1950s—a life-affirming, politically correct, empowering, individuated, and nonsexist map to gnosis—or merely another post-Bomb, ante-millennial flash in the pan.

Personally my money's on the First Church of *Star Trek,* which has motivated more people in its various revivals than have ever heard of Wicca. This is why television is the religion of the masses, and religion is the television of the few, the proud, the freelance graphic artists.

Like me.

This particular Saturday I'd volunteered to take a rush job that Mikey Pontifex, our fearless owner, had dumped on Ray Lawrence (Houston Graphics' art director) at a quarter to five yesterday. The client needed it Monday morning by ten. Surprise.

Rush jobs with stupid deadlines are what Houston survives on, so it wasn't a question of whether we'd do it, but who'd get stuck with it. Ray has a wife and kid he likes to see occasionally. So guess who volunteered?

Besides, if I wasn't working, what would I do to keep out of trouble?

The phone rang.

"Bookie-Joint-Can-I-Help-You?" I sang into the mouthpiece, because Houston Graphics is only open from nine to five weekdays. After hours the studio is taken over by freelance graphic artists and other urban elves and, like much of New York, travels under an assumed name.

"Bast, is that you?" It was Glitter, a friend as well as being one of my coven mates.

"Sure," I said recklessly.

"It's gone," Glitter said agitatedly. "I've looked everywhere for it, and Goddess knows I didn't loan it to anyone; why would I loan it to anyone? And you've seen my apartment, Bast—I can't have overlooked it."

Glitter's apartment is bigger than mine, but not by much.

"*What* is gone?" I demanded, hideous possibilities suggesting themselves.

"My book," Glitter said, as if I should already know. "My Book of Shadows. It's *gone.*"

I tactfully stifled the urge to laugh, if only for sheer relief. "It's a mitzvah," I said. "Be happy." Which might have seemed callous, until you considered what Glitter's book looked like.

"Bast!" Glitter wailed in my ear.

I wasn't really worried yet. Dark forces stealing your Book of Shadows—BoS for short—is right up there with being under psychic attack by a black coven and being haunted by poltergeists as things that Do Not Happen In Real Life.

And besides, outside her day job, Glitter is not the world's most organized person.

"Did you look under your mattress?" I said.

There was a deep breath at the other end of the line. "I've looked everywhere. I've looked. I *have* looked."

"Okay," I said soothingly. "Have you told Belle?" Belle, being Glitter's High Priestess and mine, should logically be the first one approached with these little miseries.

"I called you first. Can't you do something?" Glitter said. "*You* know."

Whether it is because I have the misfortune to be a tall, blue-eyed, thirtysomething brunette who looks as if she has all the answers, or simply because I was born to stand in the wrong place at the wrong time, I am the sort of person whom people like Glitter ask to "do something."

Or it may be because last summer (if you believe the Magic Power of Witchcraft crowd—the ones who believe life is an episode of the *X-Files*) I single-handedly banished a black magician from the Community with the force of my immense Wiccan power.

He *was* a black magician. But he was hit by a car.

"I'm supposed to meet Beaner and go down to Lothlorien," I told Glitter. "But I'll come up after that, okay? I'll look for it for you."

I heard Glitter take a deep breath. "Okay, Bast. But it isn't *here.*"

After promising to stop at the Chinese place on the corner and pick up two quarts of shrimp fried rice on my way, I hung up. I stared sightlessly at myriad tiny veluxes of women in girdles. What I was working on, if I could believe the copy I'd run up in the front matter, was a source catalogue for fifties re-creationalists. The *nineteen*-fifties, you are to understand.

Next to that, *my* lifestyle almost looked mainstream.

I tried to believe that my recent phone call was some sort of a joke, but I couldn't convince myself that Glitter hadn't sounded serious. Still, I continued to hope she was mistaken.

A Book of Shadows is part logbook, part recipe book, part liturgy, and part magical diary. Every Witch makes her own out of material both handed down and self-created. It's a very personal thing, but on the other hand it wouldn't be that hard for Glitter to re-create the contents, even if she didn't have the help I knew that Belle would give her for the asking. The rituals in it are supposed to be secret, but that hasn't kept a number of different versions of the BoS from being published at one time or another, from *The Grimoire of Lady Sheba* on down through Raymond Buckland's numerous "Create Your Own" handbooks.

There wasn't much more I could do now, either about Glitter's Book or women in girdles. I tidied my area, took Friday's paycheck out of my purse, wrote "Karen Hightower" on the back with my Mars Technograph Number One, slipped it into an envelope for deposit to Chemical, and went to meet Beaner.

Houston Graphics is located (thanks to a long lease) in what used to be cheap commercial space in beautiful downtown New York where Broadway meets Lafayette—and for that matter, Houston.

It's still commercial, but it's no longer cheap. A few blocks south the nabe remains authentically tacky in all its antique sweatshop glory, but around here the creeping Disneyfication of New York goes on.

You could call it urban growth, but from here it looks a lot more like a war; a war not against a government, but against an era. And, as in any war, there are casualties.

In the Age of Fable, around the time I was learning to walk, New York was a city of bookstores. There were the great uptown temples of Brentano's and Scribner's, the lesser chapels like Shakespeare & Co. and Gotham Book Mart, and no one had ever heard of a national chain or a shopping mall.

Downtown was the Land of Cockaigne: used, secondhand, antique—call them what you like, they were bookstores where you might, indeed, find anything. Stores where you would certainly find something. Sweet-smelling catacombs filled with second chances for authors not fey enough to grab the brass ring of literary immortality the first time out.

Economics and the rising price of real estate were the Modred in this particular Camelot, and like all good destroyers, they moved from the weak to the strong. Today the Strand, at Broadway and Twelfth, is the last faded standard-bearer of the thousand shining emporia that once were threaded like pearls on Broadway's shining silver cord. Scribner's, though landmarked, isn't a bookstore anymore.

In the war against the written word, the logoclasts are winning.

It was raining when I got outside—that April rain with the subversive undertone of warmth that insists spring is just around the corner. I detoured to the ChemBank on the corner and sent my paycheck to join the other deposits. My boots splashed through puddles. A taxi cut close through the intersection, soaking me to my denimed knees. I caught up with Beaner under an awning near a coffee pushcart at Grand.

He tossed his Styrofoam espresso cup in the trash when he saw me and flung out his arms. He looked expensive and well kept, both of which he is.

"Bast! *Dah*-ling! You look *mah*-velous!" He also does the best Fernando Lamas imitation this side of Billy Crystal.

"Yeah. So do you." I hugged him. "How's it going?"

"We start full rehearsals next week." The rain had moderated itself to heavy mist. Beaner took my arm and we headed downtown.

From him I don't mind it. He tells me it's genetic. Beaner was born in Boston with a silver swizzle stick in his mouth to a family that is genteelly horrified at the path his life has taken.

His family doesn't mind that he's gay. They don't care if he's a Witch. What gives them fits is that A Son of Theirs is performing on the *public stage*. Which is another way of saying that Beaner is an operatic tenor and he does it for money.

This year he was abandoning LOOM temporarily—the Light Opera of Manhattan, if you're from out of town—for the Archival Opera Consortium, which was doing something by Donizetti called *Maria Stuarda*.

Which was why we were going to Lothlorien, a specialty bookstore (Things Celtic) that had survived Manhattan's misobiblic carnage through some oversight of the gods of urban renewal.

"And?" I said, because with Beaner the first sentence is never the whole story.

"Dearie, it's the usual. The soprano has a teeny substance abuse problem and a large attitude problem. Ken is a dear thing, but if we follow his blocking we'll all be impaled on pikes at the first exit. And then there's That Woman."

He shuddered dramatically and I laughed.

"That woman?" I asked, as I was meant to. "What woman?"

"Her," Beaner said. The distaste in his voice was suddenly real, not theatrical. "Mary. They're all raving Mariolators. I should have expected it, but if I have to hear one more person singing—you should pardon the expression—the praises of that round-heeled, dim-witted—"

"Mary? Bloody Mary Tudor?" I floundered.

Beaner stopped and patted my arm. "Mary *Stuart*. You should get out more, Bast, dear—and read some history that doesn't have Witches in it."

The rain had stopped and the sidewalks were fairly clear this far down. We began walking again. My elbow was left to its own devices.

"Mary Stuart." I sorted through my vast exposure to PBS mini-series and horrible movies that nevertheless contain the shining presence of Timothy Dalton. "Mary, Queen of Scots. Elizabeth's—"

"Cousin," Beaner interrupted, before I could say the wrong thing again. "Born 8 December, 1542, in Scotland, and a week later Papa died and she was Queen. Henry (that's the Eighth) wanted her for Edward, which would have been just perfect for England, but of course the Scots, oddly enough, did not wish to be an English province. So the adorable tot was smuggled off to France in 1548 and married Francis, heir to the French throne, in 1558. It must have been one hell of a Sweet Sixteen party. Widowed at the age of seventeen and went back to Scotland the same year—1560—where she ruled with such enormous ability that she was forced to run for her life eight years later," Beaner said. Venomously.

Maybe he was related to her travel agent.

"Anyway, she spent the next twenty years in an English prison as the centerpiece of plots formed by people who actually managed to be stupider than she was, and was executed in 1587, thank god."

I'm always impressed by people with a grasp of history that includes numbers. What I couldn't figure out was why Beaner was taking some bimbo who'd died before Boston was a city so personally.

"So she died four hundred years ago," I said.

"Four hundred eight," Beaner said promptly.

"You make it sound like she stepped out with your boyfriend last week."

"*My* boyfriends have much better taste," Beaner said, swanning it. We turned the corner and we were there.

"What the *hell?*" I said.

"Been a while, has it?" Beaner said.

Lothlorien was in one of those buildings from the eighties— that's 1880s—that aren't landmarked simply because New York can afford to squander them; a Victorian pseudo-classical riot of columns and friezes and pillars in cast terra-cotta and painted wrought iron, with skylights, pressed-tin ceilings, leaded glass, and strange rotundas.

But urban elves had indeed been busy while Bast was off having a life. The building's Victorian detailing, formerly a dirty green, was now picked out in *trés chic* colors of biscuit, terra-cotta, and teal. Brasswork glittered. Windows gleamed. There was a FOR LEASE sign in an upper window.

"Good-bye Lothlorien," Beaner said gloomily. "The new owners are jumping Ilona's rent."

I skittered across the street, Beaner in pursuit, and rushed inside. Lothlorien was still there, for the moment. I released a breath I hadn't known I was holding.

Lothlorien Books inhabits a space that is sixty by ninety, with eighteen-foot ceilings. Around three sides are built-in shelves that go almost all the way up, with a ladder that slides along rollers and tracks for reaching the shelves and their contents.

It takes a visitor some time to realize how large the place actually is because every available space is crammed with books, both in single spies and in battalions. Lothlorien's specialty, as intimated, is Things Celtic: new and used, antique and rare, paperback and hardcover.

I inhaled the smell of books. There was a tape playing over the sound system, something wailing and fey; Lothlorien had recently started carrying tapes. Clannad, Phoenyx, The Chieftains. Things Celtic.

"Ilona!" Beaner caroled, stepping around me toward the counter. The subject of his salutation came ducking out from behind the curtain leading into the back room.

Ilona Saunders is an expatriate Brit, and the closest thing to a Grand Old Dame that the New York Wiccan and Pagan Community can boast. She's been running Lothlorien for at least forty years at the same location and has come to HallowFest every year for the last ten, despite all of which, she is tactful to the point that for all anyone knows she may not be a Pagan at all. She was wearing a print shirtwaist and a shawl held in place by a Celticwork brooch and looked like everyone's kindly old white-haired nanny.

"Can I help—? Oh, it's you, dear. Come for your tapes? I was just brewing up. Would either of you care for a cup of tea?"

We both declined, and Ilona vanished behind the curtain again. I looked around. "Tapes?" Beaner hadn't told me what his special order was.

"*Maria Stuarda,*" Beaner explained. "The Edinburgh Opera Received Version. One must do something."

Beaner leaned on the counter. I wandered around, looking at the new books. There were chairs for browsers, and most of the new stock was displayed on two vast oaken library tables in the center of the shop. I picked up a half dozen music tapes and a slipcased reproduction of *The Book of Kells* that I couldn't really afford.

"Here we are," Ilona said, coming out carrying a cup decorated with elaborate Celtic designs in stained-glass colors. She sat down behind the counter. I approached. On a shelf about eye level, an enormous brindled cat the color of the wood blinked green eyes at me.

"You look cheerful," Beaner said. "How's the moving going?"

"I've decided not to move," Ilona said firmly. "I shall buy the building and stay. What a pity I didn't think of it when Mr. Moskowitz was alive, but one doesn't, you know."

I glanced at Beaner. He looked bland, which meant he was stunned, and reasonably enough. To buy the building Lothlorien was in would cost a quarter million, minimum. How could a business like Lothlorien come up with that kind of financing?

"Come into money?" asked Beaner.

Ilona sighed. "Not precisely. I've decided to sell . . . Well, I suppose you'd call it an old family heirloom." She laughed a little sadly. "I admit it was hard to make up my mind, but I found I couldn't really bear to leave." She sipped her tea. "But you'll be wanting your order. Ned!" she called.

The cat blinked, slowly. The tape deck wailed about blood-red roses in someone's black silk hair. A person—probably Ned—appeared, descending the ladder that reached to the ceiling.

"Bring the special order for Mr. Challoner, will you, dear?" Ilona said, and Ned vanished in the direction of the back room. I formed a brief impression of dark hair and bulkiness.

"I don't know what I'd do without Ned," Ilona said. "I can't afford to pay him much—and if I'd sold up, where would he be?"

A silence fell. The next cut on the tape started; drums first, then an eerie tangle of unaccompanied voices.

"From the hag and hungry goblin / That into rags would rend ye," the singers wailed. *"All the spirits that stand by the Naked Man / In the Book of Moons defend ye—"*

"That woman again," Beaner said aggrievedly. "I'm being *haunted.*"

Fiddle and pennywhistle and drums that would make a dead man dance joined the singers.

"Mary, Queen of Scots?" I said. I couldn't see what she had to do with Mad Maudlin and Tom Rynosseros and the rest of Bedlam's bonnie boys.

"Oh, you know her?" Ilona said, as eagerly as if we'd just discovered a mutual friend.

"We've just met," I said.

" 'Tom O'Bedlam's a political ballad," Beaner said. "Sixteenth century."

Reasonable. Say something vicious, and, after enough time has passed, it becomes harmless art, suitable for children. Most of Mother Goose started out as political character assassination. Mary, Mary, quite contrary, how does your garden grow?

"And not a very nice one, either," Ilona said, just as if Beaner were making perfect sense. "Calling her a Bedlamite. Poor dear Mary—all she ever wanted was what was hers by right."

Ned came out of the back room with a glossy box that was probably Beaner's opera.

"Unfortunately," Beaner said waspishly, "what she thought was hers already belonged to other people."

I was looking at Ilona; Beaner wasn't. So I saw her face go very still, the way a polite person's will when she has been mortally offended.

Beaner drew breath for another volley. I bumped into him, stepping on his foot, and set my purchases down on the counter. "Can you ring this up for me?" I said brightly.

"I can't take you anywhere," I said to Beaner. He sighed.

"My god, my god, I am heartily sorry for having offended Holy Mary Stuart, martyr of the True Religion, and never mind that since her son James the Sixth became James the First of England her cause was hardly lost. How was I to know that dear Ilona was

one of *Them?* She's always seemed so sensible." Despite all the
fluttering, I could tell that Beaner was flustered. He hates being
unintentionally rude.

We walked uptown in the gathering dusk. The buildings were
a mix of antique sweatshops, weird marginal industrial supply
outlets, and newly remodeled buildings waiting for an influx of
Pretty People. Probably they were owned by the same development
corporation that currently owned Lothlorien's building and hoped
to turn Lothlorien's space into a combination open-plan boutique
and coffee bar, perhaps laying in a little neon around the plate-
glass window to give the place just the right *soupçon* of cognitive
dissonance.

Well, Ilona had scotched—pardon the reference—that notion.
"Things Celtic, remember?" I said. Beaner shrugged, his opera
under his arm.

"That reminds me," I said, to change the subject. "Have you
seen Glitter's book?"

"Yes," Beaner camped, "isn't it *dreadful?*"

"It's missing," I said. He raised an eyebrow. "She says," I added.

"*How* could you miss it?" he demanded plaintively. He had a
point. Glitter's Book of Shadows measures twelve by eighteen and
is covered in purple metallic fabric decorated with sequins, rhinestones, and chrome studs.

"Anyway, I'm going to go up and help her look for it. You want
to come?"

Beaner shuddered delicately. "Mary has any number of faults—
but she is not fuchsia. Pass."

"Coward."

"Granted."

We parted at West Fourth, Beaner to a hot date with a dead
queen and me to Glitter's.

Glitter lives on Dyckman near Broadway, almost as far uptown as
Belle. The neighborhood was okay when she moved in to it a few
years ago, but there have been so many "incidents" on her block
since that everyone's nagging her to move. Even I am nagging her,
which, when you consider where I live, will tell you how bad Glitter's neighborhood is.

She shrugs it off. I suppose you have a different view of things
if you're a probation officer for the City of New York, which Glitter happens to be.

I picked up two quarts of shrimp fried rice at the Cuban-

Chinese place on the corner and a six-pack of *cerveza fria* at the deli next door. Cold beer in hand, I headed for Glitter's building.

You can tell it used to be what New Yorkers call "a good building": marble steps, terrazzo floor. But it was a good building sometime around 1920—now it's just tatty. I buzzed Glitter's door first for courtesy, but her bell's been broken since she moved in, so I punched buttons at random and announced myself until someone let me in. Who knows?—maybe I knew them.

The building is six stories. Glitter is the top right front. There is a purple glitter star painted on her door that her fellow denizens have not yet been able to efface. I shifted my burden to get a hand free and knocked.

When Glitter answered the door I saw she'd been crying. I rearranged my mental picture of events: if not objectively serious (jury still out on that one), then serious to Glitter.

"Come in," she said forlornly.

"I brought beer."

"Yuch."

We sidled around each other in the narrow hall. Glitter locked the door. Rather than change places again, I preceded her into the apartment.

Kitchen downstage left. Bathroom on the right. Closet. At the end of the hall two tiny connecting rooms, about eight by ten each. Glitter uses the one overlooking the street for her bedroom, holding the opinion that when the world ends she wants to know it at the time.

I set the Chinese down on her kidney-shaped Lucite coffee table. Most of Glitter's furniture is transparent. She says she doesn't want anything interfering with the "full effect."

Glitter herself is part of the "full effect," so maybe she's got a point.

When I first met Glitter she wore large purple-tinted glasses, which have since been replaced with contacts that turn her eyes the color of drowned violets pickled in Welch's grape juice. She has her hair Cellophaned with Wild Orchid on an average of once a month, and there are very few items in her wardrobe that are not purple, or glittery, or both. Sometimes I wonder what her clients make of her.

"Glass?" she asked. I shook my head, extracted a Tsingtao from my six-pack, removed the cap, and drank.

"I'll get them," Glitter said, and bore the rest of the bottles off to her refrigerator. I looked around.

The walls—up to the strip of molding about eight feet up—were sponge-finished in fuchsia, purple, aqua, and just a hint of gold, all applied with the reckless disregard of the Manhattanite who knows she isn't going to get her security deposit back no matter what. The living room window shades were some paisley fabric, and the windows themselves were liberally swagged with cheap fringed gold shawls.

The three bookcases and the coffee table were all Lucite, as in transparent.

There used to be a Gothic Cabinet Craft–type place downtown on Broadway back in the early Eighties where you could get anything you wanted custom-built out of Lucite (including chests of drawers, but whose underwear is that decorative?). Glitter had patronized the establishment heavily.

I sat down on a throw pillow. Glitter came back with plates and chopsticks. I told her about Lothlorien's not-closing.

I was glad to see how much it cheered her up, but then I'd known it would. The rituals she designs for Changing have frequently been labeled the Celtic Twilight Zone. Like most people whose milk-tongue was Yiddish, the glottal stops of Gaelic are as nothing to her.

"Heirloom? What kind of heirloom?" Glitter wanted to know.

"An expensive one, I guess, if she's going to buy the building. She didn't say, and I could hardly ask, what with Beaner putting his foot in it big-time over Mary, Queen of Scots."

I watched Glitter closely for any signs of rabid partisanship, but she just snorted and helped herself to more rice.

After we finished eating, and I had another beer, we searched the entire apartment together. I did it because Glitter expected me to, and because to not do it would have been to call Glitter a deliberate liar. I was sure we'd turn it up in one of those out-of-the-way places that Glitter stashes things because they're so convenient.

But we didn't. It wasn't there. Not in the bedroom. Not on her altar, not under the bed, not stuffed behind the fabric swags concealing a horrible home-grown stucco job by the last tenant. Not in the bathroom. I even looked under the clawfoot tub. Not in the kitchen, although for a moment I entertained the theory that the roaches had decided to take up Wicca and stolen it. Not in the closet, although we did find a gorgeous pair of red silk stiletto-heeled pumps that Glitter couldn't remember buying and that were too narrow for me.

Not here. Not there. Not anywhere.

I sat back down in the living room on my pillow. Glitter swept her caftan around her and sat down opposite me.

Looking anxious. Looking as if she expected me to do something.

"When was the last time you saw it?" I asked, giving up.

"This is—what? Saturday? Then Wednesday, because Dorje came over to copy the *Hymn to the Shopping Goddess* I wrote for when he goes to look for a new kitchen table," Glitter said.

One trouble our mainstream apologists have with Wicca is that parody is alive and well and living in the Craft. It's hard for the ethnography set to take us seriously when they're being told about New York Metropagan "Insta-traditions" like Etaoin Shrdlu rituals (useful if you're doing desktop publishing) and hymns to the Shopping Goddess (great for the urban scavenger). They forget that every liturgy was once written down for the first time, and that even Christianity used to have parody rituals and sacred clowns.

"Okay," I said carefully. "Is there any chance he took it with him?"

"Been there, done that," Glitter said. "I *called* him, Bast. He doesn't have it. It was here when he left."

Wednesday night. "Did anyone—"

"Break in? With my locks? And only steal my BoS?" Glitter jeered. I had to admit that she had a point. Despite the neighborhood she lives in, Glitter is careful about who knows she lives there and how easy it is to get into her apartment. If any of her current or former multiple-felony-committing Probation Department clients ever managed to follow her home things could get messy.

"I thought maybe you could do a reading," Glitter said diffidently. "I got a new deck. I haven't used it yet."

"Sure," I said, since all magic aside, if a tarot reading would make Glitter feel better there was no reason for me not to do one. And besides, it wasn't as if I was going to charge her for it.

She came back with the reissue of the Coleman-Waite deck from the original plates that U.S. Games (the world's largest printer of tarot cards) came out with last spring. She set it down on the table and sat down across from me.

I shifted my pillow closer to the table and picked up the box. There is a great deal of ritual associated with reading the tarot cards, such as each reader having her own deck, wrapping the cards in red silk, and never letting someone else read with your cards. Even if you don't believe in magic, these rules focus your attention on the cards. You can't get serious help from something you take lightly.

Isn't paradox wonderful?

I broke the seal on the box and spilled the cards out. New decks are usually in order: first the Major Arcana, zero to twenty-one, then the fourteen cards of each of the four suits in numerical order, ending up with Page, Knight, Queen, King. I cut and shuffled and cut again until I was pretty sure that all the cards were completely mixed, then I set the deck down in front of Glitter and she cut it into three piles.

I prepared to do the reading that Glitter had asked for, based on the rules of divination as I knew them. What did both of us already know about Glitter's book that the cards would enable us to see?

Tarot, as I have said before, is a symbol system that allows the unconscious and the conscious mind to communicate with each other—a language of symbol, invented to communicate something that has no language. Since many Witches believe that the unconscious mind is bound neither by time nor distance, it follows that it already "knows" the answers to most of the questions you may ask.

But—just like using your home computer—the art lies in getting it to cooperate.

I turned up the first card. A cloaked figure in a gray landscape, mourning over three spilled cups, oblivious to the two full cups behind him. Or her. The Five of Cups. Traditionally the card of not knowing what you've got, of swearing that your life is over when you still have *beaucoup* resources.

"Well, this much seems clear," I said to Glitter, holding up the card to her. She grimaced.

Like I said, on some level you already know everything you're going to find out in the average tarot reading. But the fact that Glitter could reconstruct her book from Belle's—as I interpreted the Five of Cups—was not a large amount of comfort when she didn't know how hers had vanished.

I laid out the rest of the cards. Wands: intuition, travel, the element of fire. Cups: emotion and the unconscious; water. Swords: logic, intellect, and the daylight mind; angels and aerials. Pentacles: money, possessions, time, the Left-Hand Path, ruler of the things of Earth.

Overall, gibberish; a message I might be too close to Glitter to understand. I read tarot best when I have no stake in the outcome of the reading, and I didn't seem to be able to fall into that disinterested mode tonight.

I added cards and added cards until the entire tabletop was covered and I had the subtle but distinct impression that the cards were laughing at me (in fact there's one deck—Morgan's tarot—that has a card titled precisely that: *The Universe Is Laughing at You*).

I pulled the cards together and put the deck away. I looked at Glitter and shrugged.

"Call Belle," Glitter and I said in chorus.

Glitter unearthed her phone from a pile of cushions and dialed. In a few moments I was listening to a one-sided conversation— Glitter telling Belle she'd somehow sort of managed to slightly but permanently misplace her Book of Shadows, and could she make an appointment to copy a replacement out of Belle's?

Meanwhile, I considered my options vis-à-vis Glitter's information.

The book was not here. Fact. Dorje didn't have it. Fact. Glitter was telling the truth, as far as she knew it. Fact.

What did that leave? Nothing that made sense. Either someone had broken in without trace and stolen it and nothing else . . .

Or Glitter had lost it without knowing she had.

I considered that, looking around the room. It was not inside the apartment, but if she'd balanced it on an open window ledge and then bumped it, it *could* have fallen out, in which case it was gone forever.

But that was the only mundane, real-world possibility I could come up with, and it seemed a little far-fetched even for a charter member of the Conspiracy to Prevent Conspiracies, which I am.

"She wants to talk to you," Glitter said, waving a Louis XVI–style telephone receiver at me and derailing my train of thought.

"It's Belle," Bellflower told me, unnecessarily. "Look, are you busy tomorrow night? I've got a candidate for Changing I want you to meet."

"Who referred her?" I asked. This was business as usual here on the New Aquarian Frontier. Belle usually called either Glitter or me to sit in when she was thinking of admitting someone new to Changing and wanted a second opinion, and usually me because I'm more or less out of the broom closet—unlike, say, Glitter, who might actually get into trouble if her religious affiliations (as opposed to her clothes sense) came to the attention of the City of New York.

At least as long as the *New York Post* spells "Wiccan" S-A-T-A-N-I-S-T.

"Him, not her," Belle said. "His name is Edward Skelton. He's been going to the Snake's Open Circles for a while. I talked to him on the phone Tuesday. He seems—" Belle shrugged eloquently down the phone line.

I knew what she meant. What can you tell about somebody's honest responses to the One True Polytheism (as some of us jestingly call it) from a few minutes on the phone and everybody on their best behavior?

And attendance at the city's most notorious occult bookstore's Open Pagan Circles might or might not be a recommendation, actually.

"Okay. When?" I said.

"Well, he wanted to get together on Wednesday, but Daffydd had night classes all last week and Edward works late hours three nights a week, so really the only time we could all get together soon was tomorrow."

"Sunday?" I mentally rearranged my notions of free time and sleeping late. But I wouldn't mind seeing Daffydd again.

Daffydd has another name when Columbia signs his paychecks. He's Belle's and Changing's on-and-off High Priest. She must be serious about this one if she was ringing him in, too. That, or she wanted backup for something else.

I had a hunch what it was, too. Beltane—May Day in the mundane world—was in two weeks, so if Belle wanted me to help her organize a Beltane festival, she was going to have to tap me for it soon. Like Sunday.

"Okay, Sunday's fine. Hunan Balcony down on 116th?" I said, guessing.

The Balcony is one of Belle's favorite neutral meeting spots, being right on the "A" line and not too far from Columbia.

"Sure. Seven o'clock." Belle hesitated, but if she wanted to talk about Glitter she certainly couldn't do it with her standing next to me. We said our good-byes instead.

I hung up. I looked at Glitter. "New candidate," I said.

"That Skelton guy?" she said. I nodded. She shrugged. I didn't think anything of it at the time.

2

I finished the Nifty Fifties catalog up around noon Sunday and had a whole afternoon to kill before my dinner date appearance in my official capacity as judgment-caller and name-taker of the Wicca. I'd even dressed for the occasion, all in Urban Black: boots, jeans, turtleneck on one of its last outings before being packed away for the summer.

I wasn't alone in the studio, even if it was Sunday. Seiko was there, working on a project of her own. Seiko dresses like an all-night viewer of the S/M Shopping Channel, but the one time I dropped a few names from that area of reality I got nothing but a blank look. I can't think of any reason she'd feign ignorance while wearing all that leather, so I'm forced to the conclusion that Seiko wears chains and studs and leather because she *likes* wearing chains and studs and leather, and not for reasons of recreational athletics.

For what it's worth, Seiko is also the one who brought the Teenage Mutant Ninja lime Jello-O mold containing the secret ingredient of two bottles of vodka to the studio Christmas party last year. Ray recited all the verses of "Christmas Day in the Workhouse" and Mikey Pontifex actually smiled. It was a memorable occasion.

I packed up all thirty boards of the catalog with the desktop page-for-page front and back matter (the catalog would run about fifty pages once a printer was done with it) and left it on Ray's desk so he could give it the Houston Graphics seal of approval when he got in tomorrow morning. I threw my used razor blades into the coffee can full of similar razor blades that I keep beside my desk and washed out my Number Triple Zero Mars Technograph and filled the reservoir with ammonia so that it would continue being a Number Triple Zero Mars Technograph pen and not, say, a cute and useless piece of modern sculpture, and even washed out my coffee cup.

Wasting time. If these were delaying tactics, my subconscious had a lousy sense of timing: the only appointment I could conceive of not wanting to go to was five hours in the future. I had all of Sunday afternoon before me. April in New York. The day was soggy and cool; raining again. You'll love New York, the ad campaign says. I put on my hat and coat and went out.

This hat was the latest in a series of hats: wide-brimmed black leather suggesting that I might be the biggest attitude case east of the Pecos. I like hats, but I never seem to be able to strike up a permanent relationship with one. But I keep hoping.

I didn't want to go home. Belle was off taping a week's worth of little recorded squibs for WBAI, and I felt too anticipatorily broke to want to spend money loitering in any of the innumerable cafés the Big Empty has to offer.

I had, in short, that rootless, disconnected feeling that comes of knowing there is a place you want to go, which for some reason you can't go to.

And as Katharine Hepburn always used to say, "Human nature, Mr. Alnut, is what we are put on this earth to rise above." So I squared mental shoulders (try it sometime) and headed for the Snake.

The Snake—also known as the Serpent's Truth—is on the northernmost fringe of the Village, on a street that'd be a dead-end street if it weren't between Broadway and Sixth.

The Snake is, was, and always will be the kind of occult bookstore that makes the professional god-botherers' eyes light up in greedy anticipation. It is trashy, vulgar, tacky, and unabashedly commercial, with some of the highest markups for the sleaziest merchandise known to man or beast.

It also boasts a neon-purple industrial-strength chrome jukebox that contains every 45 that Elvis ever recorded. It is just too bad that among my many failings I can count an inability to listen to rockabilly in any form. Trismegistus, who owns both the

Snake and the jukebox, knows this. He also maintains a Nietz-schean faith in the perfectibility of humankind.

This is why, when he saw me coming up the street this partic-ular afternoon, he dropped six quarters into the Mighty Wurlitzer's gaping neon violet maw and kicked the side. Elvis began telling me and everyone else within a two-block radius that he'd found a new place to dwell, with enough wof and yabber thrown in to make me hope that the speakers would explode.

Despite this encouragement, I persevered.

"Hi," I said to Tris, who, since he was loitering negligently against the jukebox, was also blocking my way into the Snake. Tris is not much seen in the Snake during the week, though where he goes and what he does no one knows. He keeps informed, though, and occasionally, in a truly heartwarming upswing of amateur standing over commercial instinct, Tris will ban someone from set-ting foot within the Snake's hallowed precincts for social crimes unspecified. I wondered if I'd somehow made it onto his blacklist.

"Howdy," Tris said after a moment, moving to let me by. I was reassured. I glanced downward and saw what I expected to.

The Boots. To be exact, bright red leather cowboy boots with snakeskin insets. Trismegistus, need it be said, has never been west of the Hudson in all his five decades, and has never been seen in any other footwear.

I rely for a certain amount of my mental equilibrium on inter-mittent sightings of the Boots, and in weaker moments have been known to fantasize the making of a perverse Nashville music video starring Moira Shearer and those boots.

Possibly my sense of humor is too obscure.

Having sidled into the Snake at last, I ran headfirst into a pal-pable wall of Three Kings incense, which effectively insulated my sinuses from any other scent in the store. There was some slightly-older-than-New-Age tape dueling with Elvis over the antique sound system in the hope of encouraging the purchase of its brothers, and the narrow aisle that runs down one wall of this re-tail designer's nightmare and up the other was stuffed full of reg-ulars, for whom a weekly pilgrimage to the Snake takes the place of a more conventional religious observance.

I inserted myself into their midst, a process not unlike that of a salmon's heading upstream to spawn. Safely wedged in among them, I looked back over my shoulder in the direction of the ele-vated platform that holds the cash register and felt a perverse jolt.

Julian was there. He was, as usual, wearing a Roman collar, a (probably) secondhand hammertail coat, and those tiny oval clerk's glasses. In my boots with two-inch heels I am about half an inch taller than he is, and I outweigh him by at least ten pounds. Makes a girl feel safe at night, superior strength does.

Julian, I hasten to add, had every right to be where he was, since he was the manager of the Serpent's Truth — aka the Snake — the man who ordered the books, the candles, the gen-U-wine Magus-Brand purple polyester acetate satin wizard robes, those commodities the sale of which kept the Snake in the black.

He was also the man who'd given my legal name and unlisted phone number to someone I would really have preferred not to have them.

This would have been a relatively minor crime, in the greater cosmic New York Metropolitan scheme of things, except for the fact that I had lusted after Julian and his tubercular seraphim good looks in unrequited silence for years, and to have him take just enough notice of me to sell me down the river was a betrayal on the supernaturally disproportionate order of the ones you experience in junior high.

Old scars are the rawest.

It was another reason I'd been avoiding the Snake. And the lowering grown-up consciousness that Julian had no idea what I'd managed to do to my psychic landscape with his (actually marginal) assistance did not make me feel one whit better, thank you very much.

So I buried myself in rapt contemplation of the Snake's antique herb collection, displayed in equally antique flint-glass jars all down the right-hand wall of the shop, and worked my way along the aisle, past the congested knot of browsers in front of the "Witchcraft and Women's Mysteries" section. The herbs had been new sometime around 1957. I didn't know about the jars.

Eventually I made it all the way down to Theosophy and Ancient Atlantis, which meant I was about as far from Julian as it was possible to get without going into the Snake's backroom ritual space. It also meant I was in a prime position to cruise the back-wall display of Santeria accessories.

I have no earthly need for a two-foot-high plaster polychrome statue of Saint Barbara (patroness of artillerymen and demolitions experts, a.k.a. the orisha Chango), but there's always the possibility I can talk myself into one someday. Besides, I was low on Uncrossing Floorwash and jar candles.

"I *trusted* you!"

Theatrical venom delivered in an undertone is always inter-esting. I opened my ears and turned sideways, as if my attention had suddenly been riveted by a four-volume boxed set of *The Se-cret Doctrine* and *Isis Unveiled.*

The dialogue was coming from the space in front of the Sante-ria supplies. It's the largest open space in the shop—when Tris has someone here reading cards this is where the reader sets up her table.

"—*gave* it to you in good faith—" The speaker was doing a good job of keeping her voice down while filleting somebody fast and fu-rious. I turned a little more and reached for one of the books.

"Xharina—" A man's voice this time. I almost dropped the book. I did look up. Xharina. Definitely Xharina.

Xharina—sometimes known as Xharina, Princess of Pain—is what you might call an ornament of the Community. Xharina runs an otherwise all-male coven in Brooklyn, and is a very dec-orative addition to any Pagan Festival, although not a real good advertisement for the Community at large.

I don't know what her day job is, and I don't want to know. I just wish I had the money she spends on boots, let alone the price of something like the laced-in little number she was wearing today, which looked like it had started life as a Victorian riding habit be-fore it got its sleeves removed in order to display Xharina's full-glove tats to an admiring world.

At the moment the Princess looked like she wished she had the riding crop that went with the outfit. She was glaring up at the leatherboy who was probably one of her coveners—and, judging from the color of her complexion, wasn't going to be for much longer.

"I gave it to you to copy," she said in a low dangerous tone. "What do you mean, 'It's gone'?"

This was even more interesting than the admittedly interest-ing sight of Xharina. I could think of few things that one person would hand another to copy and get that bent out of shape at the loss of besides a Book of Shadows.

On the other hand, the boyfriend could have come up with a better place to tell her than the center ring at Gossip Central.

I sneaked another look around the end of Madame Blavatsky. Xharina was breathing in the jerky fashion of somebody who couldn't quite get enough air, and her Max Factor Sno-Pake was clearly outlined by the deep maroon of an approaching coronary.

"I just— I kept it safe, Xharina. I'd never—" The leatherboy's New York Nocturnal complexion was currently turning that shade of greenish white that is nearly impossible to fake.

"Just get it back," Xharina said. She turned her back on him and plowed through a knot of tourists as if they didn't exist.

More food for the legend.

She was moving too fast for me to catch her, and I wasn't sure what I'd say to her, anyway. I knew what she'd say, though, because it was what *I'd* say if some semistranger came up and asked *me* if my BoS'd gone for a walk.

Just like Glitter's.

I picked up a pamphlet on the Rollright Stones and tried to herd my wandering brain cells into some kind of order.

If I was placing the correct interpretation on what I'd just heard, Xharina had loaned her book to young Heather in Leather, from whose custody it had vanished.

It was, of course, possible that he'd gotten careless and lost it. It was also possible that the Pope would be marching in the gay rights parade come June.

Nothing else I did that afternoon was nearly as interesting.

I got to the Hunan Balcony on 116th a little before seven o'clock and spotted Edward Skelton instantly. He had that desperately eager air that was too intense for even the best blind date you ever wanted to go on, because Edward Skelton's blind date wasn't any mere corporeal bimbo, but Revealed Truth Herself.

He was also, I was pretty sure, Ned, the clerk at Lothlorien.

I needed a beer. I pushed open the door and headed for the PLEASE WAIT HERE TO BE SEATED sign.

Edward lunged to his feet instantly as I came in. It could have been the immense aura of witchy power that surrounded me, or, then again, it could have been the fact that you could smell the incense on my clothes from three feet away.

"Um, excuse me, are you . . ." he said, pushy and tentative all at once.

I felt an instant flare of irritation, and suppressed it because this is an awkward situation for anyone and he didn't need me to slam-dunk him on top of it.

"Reservation for a party of four," I said to the hostess who showed up about then, "under Flowers."

I turned back to Edward as the hostess began gathering up

menus. "I think we're both waiting for Bellflower," I said with
as much pleasant neutrality as I could muster. "Why don't you
come on?"

We sat down. I ordered a Tsingtao. Edward looked surprised
and ordered a Coke. I hoped he wasn't a better-living-through-
dietary-fascism type, but even if he was, it wouldn't have much effect on either my life or the possibility of his inclusion in Changing.

He was here because he was looking for a coven to join, and
because he'd either met someone who'd referred him to Belle or
because of her show on WBAI. They'd talked on the phone a couple of times, and now Belle'd decided to let it go a step further. If
Belle and Daffydd liked what they saw tonight, he'd be invited to
one of Changing Coven's open meetings.

It's not much of an intake process, but it's all we have. You can't
quantify sincerity—and sincerity alone isn't a virtue, anyway. The
Craft, like all religions, deals in intangibles.

With that much settled, I took the opportunity to make a detailed survey of Edward Skelton, Wiccan-wannabe.

He looked like he was within hailing distance of thirty, but high
or low I couldn't quite peg. I already knew that he was taller than
I was. He had one of Per Aurum's medium pentacles on a leather
cord around his neck and one of those big steel watches on his
wrist that does everything but send a fax. A CZ stud in one ear.
His hair was the darkest possible brown, a spiky buzz-cut that reminded me of porcupine quills or feathers, and his eyes were one
of those extraordinary color combinations that hazel sometimes
produces: a vivid green star around the pupil, the rest of the iris
light brown with a dark rim.

But even with that promising beginning, something wasn't
quite right. To this crucial meeting he had chosen to wear a white
polyester short-sleeved shirt over a light green T bearing a design
I couldn't quite make out through the translucent shirt. Blue
jeans, dirty sneakers (when, as everyone knows, the current fashion is for dirty *work boots* instead). With that kind of fashion sense
he was probably straight, not that it mattered to Belle, Changing,
or me.

What mattered was that I didn't like him.

It was irrational; a telegram from the unconscious mind, swift
and final.

We don't always get these flashes when they'd do us any good.
Usually they arrive when they're an active social embarrassment,

since, having made my mind up about Edward in the first five seconds of seeing him, I was reduced to playing devil's advocate to my better self for the rest of the evening, toting up items for the plus side of the ledger.

Our drinks came. I resisted the urge to order a second beer immediately. My day hadn't been *that* bad, and my night wouldn't be either.

"So. Have you known Bellflower long?" Edward said. "I'm Edward Skelton. Ned."

"Yeah," I said. "We've met."

"You were at the bookstore," Ned said, pleased with himself for remembering. I nodded, and was instantly irritated with myself for being so condescending.

Ned began to talk. He turned out to be one of those people who show up somewhere full of questions and then engage in a non-stop monologue about themselves. This was an unfair assessment, and I wrestled with my better nature while I consumed the first of what would be not-too-many Tsingtaos and learned that Ned was the youngest of four and the only boy, came from upstate New York, and had come to the City in the face of massive parental disapproval.

"They wanted me to be a doctor—my dad's a doctor—but I couldn't really see going through all that when what I wanted to do was write." He sipped his Coke. "I'm a writer, really."

In Manhattan we spell this word *unemployed*.

"Anything published?" I asked, although I could guess the answer.

Ned shrugged, embarrassed. "A couple of things. You know, like in magazines? Small press."

About then Daffydd and Belle arrived.

Daffydd is tall and spare and favors tweed jackets with black turtlenecks, giving him a passing resemblance to a member of a road show company of *Bell, Book, and Candle.* Other than a pentacle ring and his HP bracelet he looks absolutely mundane and very reassuring.

Daffydd's interest in the Craft is—to put it tactfully—mild; his association with Changing is primarily in the nature of a favor to Belle, whose friend he has been since her student days twenty-something years ago. The reason for his involvement is that Craft law—from the olden days around 1957, when there was only one Craft and it was Gardnerian—once mandated that all covens be organized in perfect pairs, just like Noah's Ark.

Magically speaking, it makes sense, but magical theory has never been popular with the masses. These days women outnumber men on the New Aquarian Frontier by about five to one, and the Noah's ark theory of Wicca has gone the way of the hula hoop and casual sex. Meanwhile, Belle and Daffydd go on like an old-time married couple, and Daffydd comes to coven about as often as most people go to church.

Introductions all round. Ned and Daffydd shook hands, then we arranged ourselves again and contemplated the menu. Daffydd ordered a Miller Draft. I had another Tsingtao. Daffydd and I did a little catching up—not much, as Ned wouldn't know any of the people and it wasn't polite to underline how much of an outsider he was.

Belle did bring up the subject of the picnic, though, which was Ned's cue to realize that I was not an outsider like himself, but one who had already attained Ned's desired goal. He shot me a look of betrayal.

"Not very big," Belle was saying. "I thought we'd start small. We can get High Bridge Park—"

"I know a lot of people you could get to come," Ned burst in, friendly and tactless as a Labrador puppy.

Belle looked at him, wanting to include him but taken a little aback. "We can put up flyers in the bookstores," she said, pitching it as if she were answering him. To me: "I'll call you next week."

"It sounds pretty exciting," Ned said heartily to the table at large. I winced, remembering a time when I would have greeted news of a gathering where I could meet actual Witches with the same maladroit glee.

"I hope you'll come," Belle said. "I'm sure Bast will post it down at the Snake."

"Is Bast your Witch name?" Ned asked me. I thought of telling him my parents were rogue Egyptologists and decided against it. "Yes," I said, and left it at that.

Eventually we got down to the fortune cookies and vanilla Häagen-Dazs with fresh ginger.

Ned waited—first with confidence, then with increasing apprehension—for the invitation that didn't come.

We settled the check.

Ned waited, waited, waited . . .

"I'll call you next week, all right, Ned?" Bellflower said.

"Sure." He smiled, covering his disappointment. "Or I'll call you."

He went to retrieve a jacket, and then went out the door.

Was it only my overheated and guilty imagination that told me how rigidly Ned Skelton schooled himself not to look back, not to linger, not to look in our direction?

"My place?" said Daffydd to Belle.

"Sure. Coming, Bast?" Belle asked me.

"Sure." I followed Daffydd and Belle out onto Broadway.

I hate this part. I hate having this much power over someone else's happiness, and I hate the possibility that because I'm tired, because I'm irritated, I'll use that power without thinking and leave welts on someone else's psyche that a lifetime can't erase.

This is why non-judgmentalism is so very popular. Because judging and choosing and making decisions means saying yes to one possibility and no to all the others. To do that is to take back all the responsibility that Society encourages you to give away.

Real freedom scares most people to death.

Daffydd has a little apartment on the top floor of one of those former stately homes that line Riverside all through the hundred-teens. His two rooms are decorated in English Docent Classic and contain more material than Belle's eight rooms and my one put together. Every possible wall is covered in bookshelves. Rolled maps, esoteric fan-tods, and books too big to be conventionally shelved jut from the shelves at all angles. You move through Daffydd's space at your peril.

We arrived. Belle took the hassock, I took the chair that went with it—both upholstered in villainous nappy mauve wool. Daffydd went into the kitchen and came back with three glasses and a bottle with a cork. He extracted the cork and poured, and sat down in a foldable wooden contraption that would have looked perfectly at home in Alexander the Great's RV. He looked at Belle. Belle looked solemn.

Apparently none of us had thought Edward Skelton was right for Changing.

Belle looked at me. I shrugged and pretended I was fascinated by my drink. It was a sweet dessert thing, the kind Belle likes. And me too, come to that. Wine snobbery is not among my virtues.

Neither, apparently, was acceptance. I sat there and disliked myself.

"I don't know if Ned Skelton would really be comfortable in a traditional Wiccan group," Daffydd said, when it became plain that nobody else was going to say anything.

To call Belle's coven "traditional" is just plain inaccurate, but after a moment I thought I saw what Daffydd meant.

I looked up and saw that both of them were looking at me.

"Traditional meaning Goddess-oriented," I said. Daffydd smiled and raised his glass in salute.

"Hmm," Belle said, thinking it over. Lady Bellflower of the Wicca does not believe in magic, and doesn't trust hunches. "You think he might be uncomfortable with what we do in Changing," she said, trying it on for size.

At least half of the Craft traditions—and all the Gardnerian-descended ones—venerate the perfect balance of male and female energies, as symbolized by the God and Goddess. But to senses blunted by centuries of anthrocentrism, equal time often looks like preferential treatment—which is why, inaccurately, Wiccans are referred to as Goddess-worshipers, as if She had no consort.

I thought over what Daffydd had said. Ned Skelton didn't fit. He just didn't, for reasons I couldn't articulate. Saying he wouldn't like our rituals was as good a polite excuse as any for following a prompting that none of us could put into words.

"He's been working cyber-Welsh down at the Snake," my better self said, unasked.

Lorelli Lee is the Snake's general-purpose Pagan priestess. She works a different godform every Saturday; if Ned had been going any length of time he'd already been exposed to old-fashioned God/Goddess polarity as well as to rituals featuring Gaia Parthenogenete, Herne the Biker, Triple Hecate, and Gilgamesh/Enki.

Belle looked a little surprised. I could see her inclining toward inviting Ned to an Open Circle with Changing so that everyone could meet him and I wished I'd kept my mouth shut.

"The picnic will give him a good chance to meet a lot of people," Daffydd said, coming to my rescue.

"Works for me," I said. Yeah. Maybe Xharina'd have an opening.

"That sounds good." Belle looked relieved, and that settled Edward Skelton's fate.

Not for Changing. For someone, but not for us.

Thinking about Xharina made me think about missing Books of Shadows. Belle already knew about Glitter's bereavement. A second loss—of which I wasn't even certain—could be only coincidence.

And Belle didn't believe in Witch Wars, didn't believe in Pagan-on-Pagan lawlessness, didn't believe in the High Gothic silliness that so many of us love to indulge in, with secret passwords and coded recognition signals.

Secrecy is second only to conspiracy as a cheap euphoric decorator accent for Reality.

"Bast?" said Daffydd. I realized I was staring off into space.

"I was just thinking. About Mary, Queen of Scots," I added quickly, grabbing the first name that popped into my head so that Belle wouldn't think I was still wasting any brain cells on Ned.

"Why the sudden interest?" Daffydd asked, leaning forward.

"Well," I said, "Beaner's singing in that opera."

"And probably filled your head with all sorts of nonsense," Daffydd said disapprovingly. Which meant he was, as Beaner would say, one of *Them.* "Interested in more unbiased information?"

Daffydd's day job is something in the soft sciences at Columbia, which means a lot of people send him free books. In a stunning conflation of resources and inclination, Daffydd's great passion in life is loaning books to people.

"Oh, sure," I said innocently. Hadn't Beaner said I should read more history?

Daffydd went off. He came back with a book. "Here," he said, handing it to me. "This should give you the basics."

Yeah. To start a fight with my closest friends and selected strangers over someone who'd been dead for four centuries. Oh, yeah—and eight years. I glanced at it. Academic press; small, heavy, acid-free paper. Blue buckram binding (the optimal meld of economics and respectability) with title-name-and-publisher stamped in gold (Optima 24-point for the title; Times Roman 18-point for the author's name; publisher in 12-point Caslon Antique plus stamp-blurred colophon) on the spine. It might even have come through Houston Graphics—we do a lot of academic press work.

"Call me if you have any questions," Daffydd said as I flipped through *Mary Stuart: A Rose in the Shadows* by Olivia Wexford Hunt. "History can be a little daunting when you're dropped into the middle of it, but it's just—history." Daffydd shrugged. I recollected that he's also a member of the Richard the Third Society; possibly Daffydd's interests lie in being spin doctor for dead royals in need.

The talk turned to the picnic and Belle's hopes for it.

Despite all of us being stuffed onto one island and/or five boroughs, the New York Metropagan Community is really fragmented. Some of us only meet at festivals far outside the city. Getting us together where we lived sounded like a better idea the more Belle pitched it—but then, Belle can talk almost anyone into almost anything.

We finished the wine. I agreed to coordinate Beltane Ecumenipicnic I. Daffydd insisted I take a cab home. He was probably more concerned about Mary than about me.

I live across Bowery (which used to be a high-rent district about 150 years ago) in the usual sort of crumbling Middle European prewar monocultural neighborhood that developers love to target. My landlord would love them to target it, too: my building's one of those *prix fixe* renter's dreams.

I had to pay three months' key money to get in, and my apartment strongly resembles a coffin—being ten feet wide and something more than twice that long with a fifteen-foot ceiling—but I've never regretted it, not with my rent being what it is.

I paid off the cab and went up five flights and opened three locks and I was home. I dumped my hat, jacket, and bag on my old-enough-to-be-an-antique-but-not kitchen table and went to check my answering machine. It used to be the only techno-toy I had, but at Yule I blew myself to a "portable" boom box with two cassette decks and a CD player. I doubt if I'll go any farther into consumer electronics, though—anything more would probably blow the building's wiring.

Even though it was well after midnight, I wasn't sleepy. I put on the water for tea, scaring the roaches half to death, and decided to take a look at Daffydd's book. The only other thing I had on my To Be Read pile was a romance by Pat Califia, anyway.

The water boiled. I made tea. I put Ned Skelton and peripatetic Books of Shadows out of my mind in favor of the musical question of what made someone four centuries dead hot news?

The basic facts Beaner had given me were correct. Mary Stuart, Queen of Scotland. Raised in the French court, the Manhattan of its day. Married at sixteen, widowed at seventeen. Superfluous to her de Medici mother-in-law (Mary wasn't in the succession for the French throne), she was packed off home to Scotland—away from glamour, away from sophistication, away from the meeting of like minds.

As far as I could tell, Mary did not handle being formerly important well. She was still a queen, but in Scotland she was a queen surrounded by people who were not at, who could not aspire to be at, the center of the world.

Every transplanted New Yorker—even those leaving voluntarily and for the best of reasons—knows the regret of leaving Avalon, Atlantis, the Hesperian garden that is the biggest and most golden apple of them all, and Mary Stuart was no exception. Her life was spent attempting to regain that same orient and enchanted sense of place that living at the center of the world had given her.

Looked at that way, Mary Stuart's life had a sort of grisly relevance to modern times. If there's something you want, something you think you need to have to survive as the person you think you are, what price is too high to pay for it?

Compared to her cool Apollonian cousin to the south—Elizabeth the First, England's virgin queen of cities—Mary does not come off particularly well in the historical accounts. As Beaner said, a moron who failed Interpersonal Politics 101.

But as a woman who had been at the hub of her century's Manhattan glitterati circle and would do anything to regain that place, I understood her. She wanted the only important thing, and its gift was in the hands of others. Like Ned Skelton, she was desperate, obsessed—not to return to France, but to transcend France, by making her own island kingdom even more glorious.

Surrounded by incomprehension of what she was, maybe even knowing that what she wanted more than anything she could never have, but driven desperately to try for it . . .

That woman I knew.

Maybe too well for my peace of mind.

The sun was finally coming up when I turned out my lights.

3

I spent the next three weeks playing amanuensis to Belle's Beltane picnic, which grew from a New York–only event that maybe sixty people would attend to a happening welcoming every Pagan in New York, New Jersey, and parts of Connecticut.

Setting this up required more than just a phone call.

Belle got the permit to assemble from the Parks Department, and Dorje arranged the one-day liquor license so that we could legally bring kegs into High Bridge Park. The Cat posted our picnic on the appropriate computer bulletin boards, and I posted flyers in all the right places.

So much for the easy part.

What was slightly less easy was keeping any kind of track of *who* was coming, *what* (and how much) they were bringing for the potluck (and telling them over and over to *label* what they were bringing, to keep from accidentally poisoning someone with food allergies), and deciding who was in and who was out of the opening and closing rituals that Belle was working on.

Every time we got the cast list settled, something came up.

Either somebody couldn't invoke the East because Belle assigns the element of Water to the East on the fairly reasonable logic of there being an entire ocean in that direction, or they couldn't participate in a ritual where edged metal was used (even though we weren't using any).

Or they couldn't participate in a ritual where edged metal

wasn't being used, since the one thing everybody found to pick on was the fact that Belle was being real nonnegotiable about letting people flash their *athames* in a public place. An *athame* is the purely ceremonial knife used by most Wiccans and Pagans in their religious rituals, and a knife is a knife is a real button-pusher, especially if John Q. Mundane sees sixty people in weird clothes waving them.

I wished it would only be sixty. *New York* magazine reports there are over ten thousand practicing Witches in Manhattan.

I hoped they weren't all coming.

But if they were, I bet they were all bringing potato salad.

In between bouts of damage control on the Ecumenipicnic came my stints at Houston Graphics. Ray'd liked the catalog, Mikey'd liked the catalog, even the customer'd liked the catalog, and it looked like a coffee-table book on the same theme was in the pipeline.

Despite which, it looked like being a bad summer for Houston— bad in the sense that the big jobs that kept the studio staff fully employed just didn't seem to be out there.

And that wasn't good.

Winter is Houston's traditional slack time, but every publisher going still does a Fall/Winter list. Fall/Winter pubdates mean that raw manuscript is turned into what you take to the printer from May through August—peak season for in-house art departments and places like Houston Graphics.

Not this year. And that meant lean times ahead.

There are other things I could do to pay the rent besides courting planned obsolescence. I could read tarot cards for money— good money in that, so I'm told, and working conditions no more uncertain than these. Only I have a small ethics problem with taking money for magic, and in my book, reading tarot is working magic.

I could go to work in an occult bookstore, but when all is said and done that's just retail sales, and even less job security than I had now. Not that I hadn't done it, but it was more in the nature of a hobby and I wanted to keep it that way.

I could hustle harder for freelance design work, I suppose, or pack up my portfolio and try to get a job at Chiat/Day or someplace like it. But the media in its wisdom has finally coined a term for us just-post-Woodstock folk (that's Woodstock *I*), and it's *slackers*. I'd hate to disappoint them.

Or maybe I'm just waiting for a sign to appear in the heavens. And while I was waiting, it became April 30.

Beltane Eve is one of the Eight Great Sabbats in the Wheel of the Year and one of the two biggies, Samhain (Halloween to you) being the other. Changing would end tonight's Beltane ritual by turning out at dawn to watch a Morris side that was dancing its traditional greeting to the spring around 5:30 A.M. in Riverside Park. In addition to no sleep, that meant doing on Saturday everything that we possibly could about Sunday.

So we did.

Saturday at noon I opened the unlocked door to Belle's apartment.

"Don't do that!" Beaner shrieked.

The smell of baking bread hit me in a wave. I shut the door quickly before the draft could affect conditions in the kitchen.

"How can I—? Oh, it's you," Beaner said. He was wrapped in a white apron and looked like a demented alchemist.

"I love you too," I said, setting my overnight bag on the floor.

"We're having the last one for dinner. *This* one had better be perfect," Beaner said, meaning the bread. He went back into the kitchen. He'd be singing Leicester (*i.e.*, Robin Dudley) sometime this month, but what he was doing right now was baking a four-foot-long challah in the shape of the May Bride and Groom in Belle's kitchen (not to mention in Belle's oven, a harrowing achievement). I wished him luck.

I looked around. Ominous atonal wails came from the living room, where The Cat was checking out her portable sound system and tapes, including the background music for the rituals.

"Hi," I said, walking in. The Cat waved absently. The sun through Belle's curtainless windows haloed her Lady Clairol'd mop, a mass of interlocking dye jobs about the same color as the fur on Ilona's tabby cat—which is, of course, one of the reasons The Cat has the name she does.

"Sundance wants you. When he gets here," she said.

"Which is?"

"RSN," The Cat said. Real Soon Now. She went back to work.

Sundance arrived forty-five minutes later (traffic on the Long Island Expressway) and the two of us took Sundance's car to Queens to fill it with cased soda and kegged beer, his and my and Glitter's contribution to the picnic, as none of the three of us is any too domestic. Sundance is one of our few coveners with wheels—a consequence of having a job out on the Island—which is why a large portion of his contribution was cartage and haulage.

Glitter's book had never resurfaced. She'd recently purchased a new blank book, covered in lavender snakeskin, that she was filling in. I hadn't told her my suspicions that she was not alone in experiencing an unlicensed withdrawal from her private library. Glitter has enough problems in her life.

Sundance and I got back from the drinks run and I joined several other coveners up at the site of tomorrow's picnic, where we raked and cleared it (a process involving rubber gloves and tongs) and filled three large trash bags with other people's site garbage. I'd be guilt-free for weeks as a result of this burst of civic spirit.

Around the time it got too dark to work we went back down to Belle's to see who'd joined us in the interim. Everybody tries hard to make it for Beltane, and it was a weekend day to boot; we'd probably have a full house.

There was a large pot of vegetarian chili adding its scent to the baked bread when Dorje and Topper and Coral and I came in. Topper and Coral are married and will probably be the next to hive off from Changing; their presence today was a direct result of having been able to leave the kids with Coral's sister overnight.

"Who else?" I asked Belle. She was on the phone, but hung up as I came in.

"Ronin called—he'll be here after ten because he has to take Jeffrey back to his mother. Glitter's picking up some cookies and should be here in about an hour. Sallix had to cover for somebody in the emergency room today so she'll be here when she gets off shift."

"Actaeon?" Topper asked. They have motorcycles in common.

Belle shrugged. Actaeon usually shows up but never calls.

"Daffydd," she offered, as if he were the alternative entree.

"Hey, we'll all be here," said Coral. Being a mother, she can count.

"Lucky thirteen," I said. It felt good.

My coven—I think I'll keep them.

Five o'clock in the morning is *cold*, whether it's May 1 or not. We'd changed mostly back into inconspicuous street clothes to go out—although in Glitter's case that meant a purple lamé *hapi* coat—and, lightly garlanded, headed down to Riverside Park to watch something called the Seely Side.

Morris dancing is one of the Great English Mysteries, like cricket and warm beer. It dates back to the Middle Ages, and has been variously identified with Moors, or Moriscos (for Moorish dances), the Conversos, or recursant Jews, and the *sidhe,* the Fair Folk. There are eight men to a Morris "side" (although no one knows why it's called a side, unless it's a corruption of the Gaelic *ceilidhe,* or blessed).

This side was wearing white and green clothing, black hats with red and pink flowers, and came with a piper and drummer. Each dancer carried what looked like an ax handle without the ax and had belled garters tied just below the knee.

In addition to the thirteen members of Changing who'd come to watch, there were about a dozen other people gathered in the park, every one of us bundled up against the ice-cold breeze off the Hudson. Across the river, the rising sun gilded the topless towers of Fort Lee, New Jersey.

I think the dancers were a little surprised at the turnout—they weren't there to give a performance, after all; they were there simply because they were Morris dancers, and Morris dancers dance on May Day. While everyone agrees that Morris dancing is *some* sort of Pagano-folkloric manifestation, no one can agree on what sort, and your average Morris side is likely to be about as Pagan as, say, Fred Astaire.

So they danced as the sun came up. Clack of batons and ruffle of drum, skirl of the pipe over all, and the thump of the dancers' feet on the grass, a stubborn survival of ancient folkways in the teeth of rationality.

At one of the breaks I went over to put a dollar in the piper's hat.

"Hey, um, Bast?" someone said behind me.

It was Ned Skelton.

He looked less like a fashion victim than he had at dinner, which might simply be the effect of the knee-length green wool cloak he was wearing today. He smiled hopefully.

"Hi, Ned."

He stopped to put money into the piper's hat—a ten; Ned must be feeling flush—and the two of us stepped back to give others the chance to be generous.

"So," Ned said. "How've you been?"

"Coming to the picnic today?" I said to change the subject. He was presuming an intimacy that didn't really exist between us, and it made me skittish.

"Yeah," he said, and looked suddenly sly. "I figure it'll be a good place to tell everyone the news."

My line was: "Gee, Ned, what news?", but I'd been up as close to all night as made no nevermind, and I wasn't in the mood to play more-occult-than-thou games with someone I was still having to try very hard not to dislike.

"Oh, good," I said.

"Wait till you hear," Ned said. "This is really going to change some people's minds about some things, *that's* for sure."

Terrific.

"I'm really looking forward to it," I said, in a tone of voice that indicated that grouting the bathroom tile would be more fun. I saw it get through to him and I felt instantly guilty.

"Well . . . see you there," he mumbled, ambling off.

I might have gone after him. Apologized. Something. But just then the Morris dancers' piper and drummer started up again, making conversation impossible.

So I walked away. An hour later I'd forgotten all about it.

The morning fulfilled its promise and became what the local weathermongers call "one of the ten best days of the year" (of which, fortunately, there are far more than ten): bright, blue, and mild. Considering how many weather spells had been worked on its behalf I suppose it would hardly have dared to be anything else.

After breakfast, those of us who could stay for the picnic (as opposed to coming back for it later) started shifting things up the hill to the park; giving the area one last raking; hanging banners. Actaeon brought up his bike (as in Harley) so he could keep an eye on it, New York being particularly hard on those who wish to retain ownership of two-wheeled vehicles.

I noticed Belle's eye on me in the fashion that indicates that she wants a quiet word. As my conscience was currently clear, I drifted over to where she was.

Belle was dressed for the picnic in one of her Public Awareness Outreach ritual robes, the ones she wears when she's being an "official" Witch in the mundane world. It was tie-dyed in purple and pink and painted all over in gold pentacles, and made Belle look the way it was supposed to, which was harmless, accessible, and nonthreatening. The robe was cinched at the middle with a gold glitter sash and she was carrying a wand stuck through that: a carved rowan twig with a faceted crystal suncatcher set in the tip. She looked like the advance man for Glinda the Good.

" 'Scuze me, ma'am, can you tell me the way to the Witches' Picnic?" Belle ingenuoused.

"First star on the right and straight on till morning. Mind the teddy bears. They're having their picnic today too," I ingenuoused back.

I leaned against the tree. It was only eleven, and the official starting time for the Ecumenipicnic was one, but people were already starting to show up, heading for the folks wearing the green armbands that identified them as members of the host coven. I pulled mine out of my pocket and slipped it on.

"I saw you talking to Ned Skelton this morning," Belle said.

"Yeah. He's coming today."

With a "big surprise" for a cross-section of New York society that did not, on the whole, count charity among the virtues, I suddenly remembered. Maybe I could get to him first, talk him out of whatever public display he was planning.

"You know, Bast, you've been Third for quite a while now," Belle began.

I tried not to goggle at her. I knew what was coming. I just hadn't expected it this soon, certainly not at the picnic, and most of all I couldn't imagine what Ned had to do with it.

You see, there are three levels of training in most Wiccan systems, and when you've completed the third—or, as we call it, taken the third-degree initiation—you have the right to go forth, teach, and train others as you were taught.

Some people—Belle included—feel that this is an obligation, not a right. Unfortunately I've never been a great believer in doing things just because you can.

If I'm perfectly honest, the thought of that kind of responsibility scares me. It's not just that power corrupts. It's that power magnifies your every action, until nothing doesn't count. Nobody's behavior can be flawless under those circumstances. And I can't stand the idea of making mistakes with people's lives.

It's possible that some people might call me a perfectionist.

"And—?" I prompted.

"Well, you know that Daffydd and I didn't think that Ned was right for Changing, but *you* seemed to like him. You might consider training him as a working partner," Belle said delicately.

Witches, as previously mentioned, often come in pairs. And certainly if I hived off and began my own coven I'd need a teaching partner—and, in the traditional Gardnerian system, a male one. And it isn't that unusual to find someone you like and train them.

But *Ned?*

No, no, and no.

"I, um, actually was more concerned with being fair than—" I stopped, because the fact that my knee-jerk assessment of Ned Skelton was that he was a smug, self-obsessed little prick was not something I was proud of.

"Well, think about it," Belle said. "You know I don't want to push anyone into anything . . ."

"But you think I'm in a comfortable rut," I said.

Belle grinned. "Something like that. It doesn't have to be Ned. Think about it."

I made noncommittal noises. You don't tell your HPS and best friend she's being ridiculous, especially when you suspect she may be right.

But *Ned . . . ?*

There were somewhere between seventy-five and a zillion people in the park by one o'clock when Belle did the opening ritual. Since there was no way of counting them as they came in, there was no way to tell how many there actually were, but the park looked well populated.

Since this gathering was both ecumenical and a picnic, the ritual Belle had put together didn't bother with most of the formal Circle-casting ceremonial that a good half of us probably used at home. Instead it was more like a more elaborate form of the grace said at a Rotary luncheon.

Belle made the introductory invocation, thanking unspecified gods for their blessing of and attendance at our party, and we started around the Circle, invoking the Four Elements.

Tollah from Chanter's Revel did Water in the East, departing from Belle's "only a suggestion" script with a prayer to the whales cribbed from T. S. Eliot. In the North, a priest from the New York Odinist Temple called forth the blessings of Earth on the Children of Men, which also wasn't the way Belle'd written it and which drew a few PC scowls from the feminists among us.

Xharina was doing South.

She was a last-minute addition, since Reisha, who'd been supposed to do Fire, hadn't shown up by showtime. Since Belle's point was to show us how well we all worked together despite our varying convictions over which Elemental went in which Quarter and similar canonical conflicts, it would look bad if the opening

ritual consisted solely of members of Changing. Hence the drafting of Xharina.

And since there was no chance for rehearsal, only the fact that
everybody involved had lots of experience made it come off as well
as it had.

So far.

Xharina stepped up to the plate. She was wearing what were
probably—for Xharina—sensible shoes, with only a two-inch heel
and a wide ankle strap. She also wore a black leather hobble skirt
that had straps and buckles all the way down the back like a designer straitjacket. It was high-waisted, and above the waist she
was wearing a black high-necked Gunne Sax blouse with big leg-
of-mutton sleeves that covered her tattoos. She had on a cartwheel
hat that must have measured three feet across, and she looked
like a demented Gibson Girl.

But she rattled off her lines letter-perfect the way Belle'd written them and in a voice that rang the back rows without even trying. I wondered if she was something professional in the dramatic
arts, as so many of us are. Not that it was any of my business.
But maybe Beaner'd know.

A man named Nighthawk added a prayer for a successful space
platform to his Air invocation in the West, and we were almost
done.

Next, Beaner's *challah* made its procession to where Belle and
Lord Amyntor, High Priest of a Minoan trad coven somewhere
downtown, were standing, and the gathered Ecumenipicnickers
chanted to invest it with intention. And then we *were* done, and
settled down to break bread.

While the loaf was passing, I wandered over to where Xharina
was standing with what looked like two of her coveners (denim and
leather), looking as if she wasn't certain that coming here had been
a good idea.

"Hi. I'm Bast, from Changing. Thanks for helping us out."

"Sure. I'm a quick study; it wasn't that hard." She smiled; it
made her look younger. "This isn't quite our usual scene."

"You mean chlorophyll, shrubbery, all that?"

She shrugged. "Yeah, I guess. Sunlight's awfully bright, isn't
it?" she added with an exaggerated wince. "Um, maybe you can
help; we brought stuff for the potluck but it's down in the van. I
wasn't sure when we should bring it up."

Or if you were going to stay, I added mentally. There's nothing so conservative as the radical who has already rebelled, and as I've said, charity is not generally among the Community's virtues.

"Now's good," I said. The dismembered *challah* reached us and we each took a chunk, the two leatherboys looking to their mistress to make sure this was *comme il faut*. Neither of them was the one from the Snake, and I wondered what'd happened to him.

People were still getting here. The picnic was growing and spreading over most of the hilltop, and out of the corner of my eye I could see Sundance and Actaeon wrestling one of the kegs into place.

"If it's something heavy, I know an easier way up the hill," I said to Xharina.

The four of us—the guys answered to Cain and Lasher—went back down the hill to where a black van was waiting in front of a fire hydrant. The legend "Hoodoo Lunchbox" was airbrushed on the side, along with a phone number and a flaming guitar.

The man waiting with the van was costumed in Early Biker Slut: mirror shades, bandanna tied sweatband-style around the forehead, low-riding Levis, and no shirt under the open leather jacket. A Marlboro dangled from his lower lip. I was in love.

"Jesus, Xhar, I thought you'd gone out for a pizza," he said.

"Life is pain," Xharina answered, and all four of them laughed. "This is Arioch," she said, introducing him to me. "Arioch has a driver's license," she said, in the tone indicating it was another family joke.

"Printed it myself." Arioch grinned, and ground his cigarette into a brown smear on the sidewalk before popping the van's side door open.

Cain and Lasher horsed out two big Coleman ice chests and headed back up the route I'd shown them. Arioch slammed the door.

"Guess I'd better go park somewhere legal. See y'all next Christmas," he said.

"Pain is truth," Xharina said, and Arioch waved amiably.

The van rumbled to life, emitting a gust of blue smoke from its tailpipe, and wabbled off in search of parking. Xharina and I started back up the hill. On the way down she'd unbuckled her skirt so she could walk, and every step exposed her legs halfway up the thigh.

"So, um, I hear that Ned's going to join Changing," she said.

We'd stopped to rest halfway up, but within sight of the revels. Someone had a tank full of helium and was assembling a lighter-than-air balloon garland.

"Well, he's pretty interested in finding a group," I said cautiously. Unfounded rumor travels fast, and I was very curious indeed to hear how the next sentence was going to go.

"He worked with us for a while last year," Xharina said, in the cautious tone with which nice people impart bad news. She made a face, hesitated on the edge of the plunge, and drew back. "I hope he works out for you."

She pushed herself to her feet, waved apologetically, and strode off to find her coveners and rebuckle her skirt.

What the hell?

So Ned had more experience than Belle'd thought, or at least more than she'd told me. As a factoid, it sat there in a nonrelevant lump. So he did. So what?

Nothing to do with me, nothing to do with me, nothing to do with me, I thought, chanting my mantra. I wished I'd remembered to mention Ned's surprise to Xharina. Maybe she'd know what it was.

When I got back up to the top of the hill the party was pretty well rolling. More people had arrived, food was being passed. Xharina was going to be popular—the ice chests contained two five-gallon drums of ice cream, kept rock hard in dry ice that smoked upon exposure to air like the proverbial witches' cauldron.

"Yo! *Bast!*" shouted a familiar voice.

Lace forged through the crowd, beer bottle in one hand, someone else's wrist in the other.

Lace is short for Lacey, which is Lace's honest-to-Goddess legal middle name. Lace works down at Chanter's Revel, which is the Wiccan, eco-feminist bookstore voted Most Likely To Be At The Opposite End Of The Pagano-Political Spectrum From The Snake—which makes it particularly odd that Lace, herself, is strictly a studs-and-leather dyke-type.

Of course, she *is* a vegetarian.

"Hey, girl, where you been keeping yourself? Isn't this a hoot?" Lace waved her Bud longneck at the immediate vicinity. "I got someone here I'd like you to meet."

The wrist in Lace's hand proved to be attached to a corporate-looking lass wearing a mint-green polo shirt and deeply impeccable khaki gabardine slacks. Her hair was cut in one of those expensive and severe earlobe-length designs. Her ears were pierced (once) and contained chaste gold knots. She was wearing pale pink lipstick and a smudge of taupe eyeshadow. In short, Gentle Reader, she was normal.

"This is Sandra," Lace said happily. "Sandra's a lawyer. Sandra, this is Bast."

Somewhere in the vicinity of this time last year Lace's lover had died, and it looked like Lace was ready to love again. I was glad of that, even if this particular relationship appeared to be doomed.

"I'm so pleased to meet you, Bast," Sandra said. She had one of those well-bred accentless dictions that was nearly a cliché. "Georgina has told me so much about you." She extricated her wrist from Lace's grip and held out her other hand.

Georgina is Lace's front name. Sandra and I shook hands.

"I hope it wasn't accurate," I said.

I valiantly resisted the temptation to ask her what her position was on Mary, Queen of Scots. Sandra looked polite but wary, as if at any moment I might do something horribly artistic.

"I hope you enjoy the picnic, Sandra," I said, with what would probably pass for sincerity. "Lace, it's good to see you again; I like the new color."

Lace's hair was bright cobalt blue. I saw Sandra dart a look of faint resignation at it. "But I'd better go see if Belle needs any help," I finished, before I said something stupid.

"See you," Lace said, happily oblivious. "C'mon, Sandy, let's go get something to eat."

I went off in the other direction, feeling as if I'd just avoided booking passage on the *Lusitania.* Why do people who already know it isn't going to work always find each other and try? I could not imagine Sandra and Lace even making it through the ninety-day trial period.

Of course, I might be wrong.

"Hey, Bast!" Glitter. She'd gone home this morning to change for the picnic, and the effect was blinding. "Seen Ilona yet?"

It took a moment to shift mental gears. Ilona. Lothlorien Books.

"She coming?" Odd. Not quite her scene, to quote the *patois* of my youth.

"She's supposed to be. I talked to her yesterday. She's bringing someone with her. Nephew."

"Who?" It was hard to imagine Ilona Saunders related to anyone.

"New partner in Lothlorien, she said," Glitter amplified. "Because she's buying the building. Don't know his name. She wants to introduce him 'round."

"I'll look for her—them," I said.

"Sure. Boy, did you see what Xharina was wearing? I'd never have the nerve." Glitter rolled her eyes and waved her glitter-lace batwing sleeves. Everything is relative.

I went off and collected a beer, a tofu burger, and a handful of oatmeal walnut chocolate chip cookies sprinkled with silver star-shaped jimmies certified edible. Nothing like a balanced diet, and this was certainly nothing like one.

And then I saw Ned coming up the hill.

He was wearing a black T-shirt blazoned with "The Goddess Is Alive, Magic Is Afoot!" in silver and carrying a white bakery box big enough to be holding a couple of pounds of cookies. I waved to attract his attention. He came over.

"Welcome to the Ecumenipicnic," I said. "I can show you where to put what you brought."

He looked hopeful and . . . not young exactly, but curiously un-aged. As if he hadn't yet done much with his life, although he must be my age.

"Sure," Ned said. "Is everybody here?"

I felt ghostly warning bells go off at the question. One of the few points of etiquette nearly everyone in the Community observes is a healthful lack of curiosity about each other. People looking that hard for personal information are usually planning to use it, and not in any way you'd like, either.

"Well," I said cautiously, "we don't know exactly who's coming, and of course people show up and leave whenever."

Ned nodded sagely, as if I'd answered his question.

I herded him in the direction of one of the two picnic tables up here, which served as a sort of central depot for everybody's potluck offerings. Ned continued to explain as he walked.

"I want everybody to be here when I make my announcement," he continued with happy officiousness. He set his box on the table and opened it. Bakery cookies, as I'd suspected.

I felt a pang of alarm, and not at the cookies.

"Ned, could I have a word with you?" I said carefully.

He let me lead him off to an area that, if not uninhabited, was at least out of the main traffic pattern.

"Do you think you could tell me what you're planning to announce?" I asked.

Ned stared at me, his expression gradually changing from suspicion, to pleasure, to cunning.

"So you want an advance preview?" he said archly.

As opposed to the usual sort of preview?

"Well," I said, being driven, as Lord Peter Wimsey says in *Busman's Honeymoon,* to the inestimable vulgarity of reminding him who I was, "it *is* my coven putting the event on, so I'm one of the people responsible for making it run smoothly. So I sort of need to know." I gestured to the green armband.

"Oh." To my surprised relief, Ned seemed to think this was reasonable. "Well. You know the Book of Shadows?"

For one stomach-turning moment I thought he was confessing to stealing Glitter's, and then I realized he was speaking generally. I nodded, although it had to be a rhetorical question.

"Let me tell you a story," Ned said. He leaned toward me like he was trying to sell me cheap real estate. "No. Let me ask you a question. You're a Witch. You know that they're saying that guy made it all up; that Wicca isn't a real religion and all. What if I could *prove* that the Craft was hundreds of years old? No, *thousands.*"

I suppressed an impulsive rejoinder along the lines of having taken a religious vow never to buy any beachfront property in Florida, or bridges, or antique Books of Shadows guaranteed to have been passed down from ancient Atlantis.

"What if you could?" I said pacifically.

Ned frowned. I hadn't given him the answer he was expecting.

Oh, I won't say that it didn't matter passionately to any number of Witches, just that I wasn't one of them. If the sainted Gerald B. Gardner, founder of the feast, had been able to impeccably document his antecedents in his lifetime he might have done so or he might not, but the fact remains he didn't, nor has anyone who came after produced Wiccan documents that can be dated earlier than the late thirties, including that guy on the Left Coast who had the bad taste to publish the ones Gardner *did* leave.

And I was just cynical enough to think that any "proof" that surfaced after this long was proof that had been faked when there'd finally be money in it, New Age having become big business once everyone'd caught millennial fever.

"So you don't believe me?" Ned said, starting to look sulky.

"I thought it was a hypothetical question: What if you *could* prove it?" I said. Oh Goddess, don't let this be Ned's big announcement. I could choreograph the fights that would break out from here, and none of them would improve Ned Skelton's standard of living.

"Well, I *can* prove it. I've got an original Book of Shadows—a *real* one, an old one from before Gardner! I've got the real Book of Shadows—and I didn't have to be initiated to get it," he added smirking.

"Okay," I said. "So you've got a Book of Shadows." I wanted to tell him that I didn't care, but I doubted he wanted to hear it.

"You don't believe me!" Ned accused. "You don't think I've got it. But I do. It's called *The Book of Moons.*"

Ned watched me sideways, to see what impact this revelation had on me. The answer was none in particular, except that something called *The Book of Moons* sounded familiar.

Ned monologued on. Having gotten him started, I now realized, it would be almost impossible to shut him up.

"Now everyone will know all your nasty little secrets. I'm going to have it published. I wasn't going to. Books of Shadows aren't supposed to be published; you keep them secret so the rituals won't fall into unauthorized hands and lose their power. Everybody says Gardner made it all up, but I knew that wasn't true, because the Craft is thousands of years old, only there's no way to prove that it's real, because the rituals are supposed to stay secret. Except now I have the proof. And it's where you and everyone else can't get their hands on it and suppress it, and—"

I sighed.

"Ned," I said.

He stopped. He looked at me.

"Listen to me. I don't know you all that well, but I've been in the Craft a lot longer than you have and I don't wish you any harm. If you get up on a rock here at this picnic today and make an announcement like that, people are not going to be impressed. They're going to laugh at you. It doesn't matter whether you're telling the truth or not."

Ned goggled at me like I'd just kicked his puppy. "That isn't true," he finally managed to say. His ears turned red, like the ears of laboratory mice.

"Yes it is," I said. "Talk to some people privately. Talk to Lorelli Lee; you know her, the priestess at the Snake? Nobody will believe you. And the way to convince them isn't—"

"But it's true!" Ned interrupted indignantly. "It's real. It's the spellbook that used to belong to Mary Stuart—the queen. She was a Witch, see, and this is her book."

That settled it. I was being haunted.

"You have the Book of Shadows of Mary, Queen of Scots," I said, just to be sure I had it right.

Ned nodded. He rocked back on his heels. The smirk had returned.

"And where did you get it?"

"I—bought it," Ned said, hesitating a little over the obvious lie. I did my futile best to hold on to my temper. Why does every newbie feel compelled to reinvent the wheel?

When love and all the world were young (1963 or so), there was a "tradition" of setting oneself up in the Craft not through a process of training and initiation, but through theft of someone else's ritual book. The person with the stolen book then covered his tracks by inventing a provenance for his version of the Craft that backdated it to somewhere around ancient Atlantis, a pretty good example of one-upmanship in a religion that can only reliably document its roots back to, say, 1947, if you really stretch a point.

This form of spiritual cattle-rustling fell out of fashion after about fifteen years, when everybody suddenly decided it was much more chic to be creating a new religion than to be curator of a survival. And at any rate, how you got your BoS stopped being a big deal with the widespread dissemination of xerographic technology and the computer disk. But here was Ned, trotting out that old chestnut about somehow acquiring a legitimate antique Book of Shadows just as if no one had ever heard it before.

"You must think we're all pretty damn stupid around here," I said to Ned in my most courteous tones. "The only cliché older than that is saying that your grandmother initiated you into a secret family tradition. Nobody is going to believe you, Ned. I promise."

He stared at me, slowly going red. Probably nobody he'd ever spoken to had been so blunt. We in the Community tend to avoid confrontation, as a rule. We don't argue. We just go away.

"If you want to be a Witch, okay, you're a Witch," I went on. "Now all you—"

"You can't threaten me!" Ned blustered. "You don't know what you're talking about—and you're wrong, too!" He stalked off, ears flaming.

I sighed. I hadn't handled that particularly well, but maybe I'd at least bullied him into shutting up. I didn't particularly give a damn—and besides, he'd thank me for it someday, providing he stayed in the Community.

And if he didn't, he'd be even less my problem than he was now.

Or so I thought at the time. As it turned out, I was wrong straight across the board.

4

I walked—or stalked—back through the picnickers, heading for the beer. I wondered what Beaner would do if I told him that Mary Stuart was Queen of the Witches. Or Daffydd, who could at least tell me whether she'd been mixed up with sorcery according to Official History.

Her cousin Elizabeth had been. Lizzie's court sorcerer was that learned Rosicrucian Doctor John Dee, who worked with that highly suspect Irishman, Ned Kelley. Most historians agree that Dee, no matter what else you may say of him, was devout and sincere—and managed to survive the experience of casting a horoscope for both a reigning queen and the princess in waiting.

Ned Kelley (not the Aussie Bushranger of similar name popularized by Mick Jagger, trust me) is another story entirely. Profane, irreverent, and Irish, he was constantly implicated in shady deals and criminal acts, escaping prosecution due to his Court connections. Kelley's claim to fame and Dee's patronage is that he is alleged to have been a medium: he saw, so he said, angels in a "shew stone," or speculum, that he had given Dee directions on how to build. Evidence suggests Kelley was not entirely fraudulent, at least not all the time: Dee's creation of the glorious and abstruse system of Enochian Invocation from the stuff of Kelley's visions is the jewel in the crown of Elizabethan sorcery.

I doubted that Ned Kelley (who vanishes from history as mysteriously as he appears) had ever felt left out and awkward and socially maladroit.

Or had been on the outside wanting in. Or back in. Like Ned Skelton. Like Mary. Who, according to our Ned, was a Witch, with a genuine Book of Shadows that had somehow managed to escape the notice of her inquisitors and jailers at the Fotheringay Resort for Inconvenient Queens.

Damn Ned, anyway; the woman was dead four hundred years and change and I couldn't escape the spookily persistent feeling that she was someone I'd spoken to this morning—that she was someone I could still advise. *I know how you feel. I know how you hurt. But there's no cure; there's never any cure once they've shut the door. You can't trust other people for your happiness, Mary— people are just too damn fickle.*

But no. And if not Mary, how much more so not Ned? Their problem was exactly the same: If there's something you think you need to have to survive as the person you think you are, what price is too high to pay for it?

Is any price too high?

I tried to put all webby ethical brain-twisters out of my mind, and succeeded reasonably well with all the distraction on offer. I even talked myself into a reasonably good mood, or at least a better one. What with one thing and another I knew most of the people here; I wandered through, collecting greetings and invitations and information about this, that, and the other gathering. Reaffirming old friendships, laying groundwork for new ones.

And I heard tales. Tales that slowly, oh so slowly, started to frighten me.

Otterleaf was a Gardnerian High Priestess who ran a training coven in Astoria. She was trying to figure out how to get in touch with her Queen, who'd moved to Arizona, because she couldn't find her Black Book and needed to get a new copy.

Crystal had braided her hair with knots of ribbon and had painted both cheeks with rainbows for the picnic, but despite the Sparkle Plenty affectations she was a pragmatic Faery Trad of the Victor Anderson stripe (Victor being another of the Grand Old Men of the Craft) who ran Starholt Coven and the Cyberfae BBS. She was sure her book must be around *somewhere,* although she hadn't seen it for the last month.

Lord Amyntor, the Minoan HP from downtown who'd opened the picnic with Belle (he had "friend of the family" status because Beaner'd dated him for a while last year) was talking about the *new* book he was putting together to replace his old one.

Now that I knew what I was listening for, the undercurrent was everywhere: not outright admission, but an uneasy sort of "here comes the hangman" humor. Having your book stolen had become a black joke that everyone understood.

As in: "And then there was this funny-mentalist who was so dumb he burned a *blank* Book of Shadows."

Glitter's wasn't an isolated incident. It was the leading edge of a plague.

But no one was fingering anybody for thief. We—the Community at large—had no suspects. None. And that was odd in a bunch famous both for getting its exercise jumping to conclusions and for having an Official Summer Feud each year to wile away the time till Hallows.

I looked around. I saw people with bubble pipes, people with balloons, people with flutes and guitars and celtic harps (live music later), and people carrying hula hoops and ferrets. There were people wearing chain mail and wearing chiffon and wearing full Klingon battle dress and wearing baseball caps with stuffed antlers attached.

Party clothes. Persona clothes, for people who had found a safe space in which to wear their inner child on the outside for a while. I wondered if the person with the ever-growing BoS collection was here. I wondered if all the BoS's had been stolen by the same person. I wondered if all the ones that were missing had been stolen. I wondered if I was losing my grip on probability.

Who would steal Books of Shadows? Who, and why—and, dammit, *how?* These people were New Yorkers; their doors had *good* locks.

Belle waved to me, from a kaffeklatsch of other New York–area covenleaders. Ah, Bast, play your cards right and this time next year you too can be among them.

Although after our last conversation, Ned probably wouldn't join a coven of mine if I asked him. Not that I was going to.

Where had Ned gotten the "Mary, Queen of Scots" Book of Shadows? Stolen? Or self-created out of the mass of public material? And why choose Mary for his fall guy? She wasn't exactly the most plausible candidate.

Echo answereth not.

I wandered, cataloguing the people I knew who weren't here. No Cindy, no Julian—none of the downtown Ceremonial Magic crowd who thought of Pagans as Bridge and Tunnel People. No Santeros, or representatives of any of the other tropic-zone religions: Huna, Voudoun, Candomblé, Brujeria. Only the one Odinist.

No Ilona, with or without partner. I wondered if she'd changed her mind about coming. I couldn't see Ned at the moment, which was a blessing. I had what Ned wanted, and there was no way on earth for me to give it to him, no matter whether I wanted to or not.

Was Ned Ilona's new partner? Now *there* was a daunting thought. Fortunately I didn't shop there much.

I hove in sight of the beer. Beaner was standing next to the keg with someone I hadn't seen in too long.

"Niceness!" she trilled, in a voice only bats and dogs could hear. "Niceness is all!" She and Beaner broke into an impromptu duet à la Eddy and McDonald of "Ah, Sweet Mystery of Life."

"Hi, Maidjene," I said. She turned around and mimed a heart attack brought on by ecstasy.

Maidjene is a coloratura soprano. She has brown hair, brown eyes, and is the sort of person of whom people say, "Oh, what a pretty *face* she has." Maidjene is the founder of the Niceness Wicca tradition, in which she parodies Craft politics—a routine that has a small but appreciative audience. She'd come to today's picnic in her alternate Pagan *persona,* the Niceness Fairy, and every exposed body surface was covered in multicolored glitter and sequins.

She was wearing a size-60 fuchsia polyester nightgown and marabou peignoir over her T-shirt and overalls and carried a Lucite wand topped with an enormous glitter-encrusted star. More fairy dust flaked off every time she waved it.

I refilled my beer and she got a Coke and we found a place to sit and play "How long has it been," Maidjene interrupting herself every once in a while to bless passersby with "Concentrated Essence of Nice." In between these minidramas, she confessed that she and her husband were, as she put it, "giving up."

Larry, Maidjene's oh-so-mundane husband, had been a staple of Community folklore for years. Maidjene had gotten religion after they'd married, and Larry had not been pleased.

"And now, one day I come in and the basket's gone through my things and helped himself to a big chunk of my notes."

"Well, damn," I said. I wondered if Maidjene was out on bail. "What happened?"

"Well, he denied it and I told him he could deny his ass out the door and into a hotel." She pronounced it midsouthern fashion: *ho*tel; Maidjene and Larry are both originally from someplace in Tornado Alley. Kentucky, I think. "May the Nice be with you!"

"And then?" I asked, fascinated. Even if it was some floating Book of Shadows bandit and not Larry responsible for the theft, his eviction couldn't happen to a nicer newt. He'd made a pass at me, the one HallowFest he'd come to, on the expressed theory that Witches believed in casual sex.

"Lawyers are talking, he's in the hotel down to Route 17, and I had to go back to my Queen for my real book. But *fortunately* the whole Nice liturgy was published in *Enchanté* last year, so I've got that. And by the way, you hear Lark might be coming back East this fall maybe even in time for HallowFest? Selene says he said— Nice Makes Right!—that last quake did for him and he's not staying anywhere that the four seasons are Drought, Riot, Fire, and Quake—Niceness Rules!"

HallowFest is the big Pagan festival held in upstate New York every October—four days of fun and frolic in the mud and freezing rain. I go every year.

"We'll have to have a welcome home party for him," I said. I'd known Lark pretty close to very well a few years back. I wondered if he was coming back unattached.

"And let me say this about that," Maidjene went on, in her trademark nonstop rattle, "if you're looking for a working partner— Niceness Upon You!—you'd be one helluva lot better off with Lark even if he's commitment shy—which we *don't* know for sure, and he may have changed—than with Fast Eddie Skelton if you ask me and even if you don't." Even Maidjene had to stop after that one and pause for breath.

"You know him?" I said, surprised. Maidjene lives in the occult wilds of northern New Jersey. A long way for Ned to travel.

"Whooo-eee!" Maidjene shook her head, shedding sequins. "Had him in an Open Circle. *Once.* I tell you, you want somebody joggling your elbow, you call in Fast Eddie—Have a *Nice* Day! He not only knows what you're doing, he's got a better way to do it— Niceness Rules! Wah!"

"It sounds to me like he's been around," I said.

"You want to know how far, you ask Reisha. Or Lorelli Lee. Everybody knows him. Nobody likes him. He's pushy," the Niceness Fairy said, wrinkling her nose.

Belle must have known all this. There was no way she could not. Okay, so she did, and didn't tell me in the name of impartiality.

But while it was true that people could not-click for reasons having nothing to do with whether or not they were good people, if Ned had as much experience in the Community as Maidjene said and was still acting as jerkishly as he had today, the odds were against his being one of the innocent ones.

Maidjene saw someone else she wanted to talk to, and I gravitated to the edge of the party, where you could look down the hill and see the real world. Reality, as the saying goes, is a nice place to visit, but I wouldn't want to live there. Not what passes in this modern day for Reality, anyway.

I watched the escape of a fugitive balloon, my mind full of things I hadn't yet mashed down to thinkable-size portions. Behind me, The Cat's sound system slid lower in volume and then cut out, and in the sudden silence I could hear musicians tuning up: flute, guitars, and harp.

"Hey, everybody—hey!"

I winced. Ned. And, from the sound of things, not 100 percent sober.

I turned around and walked back into the picnic. There was a clearing-within-the-clearing that provided seating by way of two stumps and a big rock. The Cat's tape deck was there. So were two bemused Crafters with guitars, a man wearing satyr horns and carrying a silver flute and a tin pennywhistle, and a woman in medieval clothes with a harp.

And Ned. Just as if he were following a script I'd handed him titled "How to Make of Yourself a Permanent Stupid Joke and Outsider in the New York Pagan Community." He was standing on the rock, plastic cup of beer in hand, face flushed, obviously ready to make his announcement.

I felt the stunned horror that you feel watching an accident slowly happening right in front of you. You don't want to believe in it, but it's right there, and there's nothing you can do to stop it. I wasn't even angry at Ned at the moment. You aren't angry at the car that's stalled in the path of the oncoming train.

"Ned!" I yelled. Maybe I could stop him.

He swung around toward me. He sneered.

"*She* doesn't want me to tell you!" he shouted, which got him even more attention and me a lot of stares.

"She doesn't want me to tell you because she wants to suppress it! But I don't believe in secrecy!" Ned ranted on. A few people cheered. I saw The Cat crossing left behind him, heading for the tape deck. Probably on orders from Belle.

"I have a genuine Witch's Book of Shadows—a real one. It's

hundreds of years old and has all the true authentic *old* spells and rituals, and I—"

Someone laughed. The flutist played a derisive skirl. And whatever Ned had to say next was drowned out by jeers, catcalls, and people producing various bombastic takes on the rest of his speech. Ned looked stunned. He'd finally seen the train.

I'd told him. We've heard it all before. And though many of us would desperately love to trace our religion in identifiable form back across thirty centuries, it's still a joke. There've been too many disappointments.

For a moment more, Ned tried to shout over his audience. Then he just stared—angry, humiliated, betrayed. I thought he might be going to cry.

The Cat flipped a switch, and "Corn Rigs and Barley Rigs" (she'd sampled it off a tape of *The Wicker Man*) filled the space. Nearly everyone there knew the song, and some of them started singing. The harpist began improvising against it.

Ned jumped down off the rock and ran. A couple of people tried to stop him, but he jerked past them. I was on the opposite side of the crowd from him; even if I thought I could do any good, there wasn't any way to get to him.

The Cat said something to one of the guitarists, who nodded and began fitting himself into the music. The Cat took her sound levels down, and after a ragged few beats the tune was being carried live by two guitars, a pennywhistle, and a harp. Someone started to sing a set of words—not Bobby Burns's originals, but our own invention. The people within earshot quieted down to hear them.

I hurt for Ned Skelton, legend in the making. He could manage to live this down if he could pretend he'd been making a joke.

But he hadn't been, and I knew it. I think nearly everyone there knew it.

He'd been serious. And he'd brought his seriousness to people who he thought would understand. And we'd laughed at him. And he'd never understand why, not in any way that would help him heal, though it's really very simple.

When it hurts too much, you laugh.

There was nothing I could do for Ned, and the picnic seemed to be under control. I wanted to get the preceding scene out of my mind and looked around for something that would help me do it.

That's when I saw him. The stranger.

He was standing at the edge of the clearing. He was wearing a sportcoat and an open shirt with his neatly pressed khakis and oxblood loafers, and the reason he looked out of place wasn't really his clothes, although they were part of it.

Although it's not quite PC to say so, it's also unfortunately true that the men who belong in the Community actively dis-belong elsewhere. They've made a choice, conscious or otherwise, to drift from the normative centerline of Western culture, and the first place that drift appears, as the poet says, is as a sweet disorder in the dress. Even Daffydd exhibits this subtle sartorial mark of Cain. Studded leather or slogan T-shirts, there's a concrete fashion subtext there for the discerning eye.

This spectator radiated none of these cues. His haircut was a thing of expensive beauty, of the sort rarely seen above Seventy-second Street. And, confronted with the spectacle of a woodland clearing full of Us, he was not in the least discomfited.

No one else had much noticed him yet. I headed toward him, bracing myself for everything from an evangel interested in the state of my soul to a reporter to an innocent bystander looking for a lost dog.

"Hi," he said when I approached. "Is this the Witches Picnic?" The accent was English, pure BBC Received.

He was around my age, with light brown hair and eyes the color of expensive Scotch.

"Yes," I said cautiously.

"Is it okay if I stay?" he asked. "It isn't a private party, is it? Oh, I'm Stuart Hepburn." He held out his hand.

His Englishness shouldn't have made any difference, but it did. I shifted mental gears and shook the hand. It was innocent of rings. He wore a very well-bred and expensive watch on a black leather strap.

"Hello, Stuart," I said. "My name is Bast. What can we do for you?"

"Well, I saw the poster for the event and thought I'd take a dekko. I'm interested in learning more about . . . Wicca?"

He pronounced the name as if he weren't quite sure he was pronouncing it right, but he hadn't boggled at mine. I smiled. He smiled.

"Sure," I said. "There're a lot of people here who can answer your questions. Would you like a beer?"

We sauntered back toward the food. I was steering Stuart in Daffydd's direction because Daffydd is erudite and respectable and makes the Craft seem like nothing more than an enthusiastic exercise in reconstructive anthropology. But when I got close enough to hear what he was saying, I was sorry I had.

"Look. If Henry hadn't forsaken the Catholic Church, none of this would have happened," Daffydd said. "Mary was the logical heir, the rightful heir—"

Oh god. Not her again.

"Yes, and if she *had* got her hands on England we'd all be speaking Spanish today," Beaner shot back with passionate inaccuracy.

"*¿Y eso te molesta?*" Ronin said, and those who could follow the Spanish laughed.

"The point is—" Beaner said.

"The point is, even though the Great Divorce was driven far more by the need for the dissolution of the monasteries and the reappropriation of capital by the Crown—" Daffydd said.

Stuart put a hand on my arm.

"Before we go any farther, there's something you ought to know," he said, nodding toward Daffydd and Beaner.

My heart sank. *Uh-oh,* I thought. *Here it comes.*

"I'm the rightful king of Scotland," Stuart said gravely.

I stared at him. The corner of his mouth quirked upward in mockery. "Hepburn," he explained. "The Earls of Bothwell. If you go back far enough."

Thanks to my recent reading I was ready for him, although I was beginning to sympathize with Beaner's desire to scream when That Woman was mentioned.

"James Hepburn, Earl of Bothwell, Mary's third husband," I said. And related to the Bothwell that'd tried to assassinate James the First by magic, leading to the Berwick Witch Trials, one of the most famous cases in the history of the subject.

"Or as we prefer to think of her, Bothwell's second wife," Stuart said solemnly. He smiled again, encouragingly. I breathed an inward sigh of relief and decided conditionally to like him.

He was crazy, all right. But he seemed to be crazy like us.

"Are you married?" Stuart asked me a few minutes later. It took me a moment to recognize the question for what it was: mundane world small talk.

"I used to be, but I got out of the habit," I volleyed back glibly. It's true, actually.

Just within hearing the historical debate raged on, with Belle hovering nervously around the edges. Sandra had joined it, as a voluble partisan of Elizabeth the First, Christendom's most puissant prince (her words). I sympathized with Lace's bewildered expression. I have enough trouble staying afloat in one century at a time.

"And what's your interest in the Craft?" I said to Stuart, steering him away from the new English Civil War.

"Well, I admit that I'm coming to it from an historical perspective," he answered. "I understand that the witchcult can trace its roots fairly far back."

"Oh, more or less," I said. It's true enough. There's material in the BoS that appears nearly word for word in a manuscript dating from the early 1300s, which is no proof of antiquity for either the book as a whole or our religion.

"I don't suppose you'd like to tell me all about it?" Stuart said. I glanced at him. He flashed me a charming smile. I wished I'd worn more upscale clothes.

"Mmmn," I said, not committing myself to anything. Sheer force of habit. "Your best bet is to do some reading. Talk to people. There're a lot of books on the subject; you could do worse than hit up some of the occult bookstores and look at what's in print."

I gave him some titles and some addresses, and the talk turned general. He was over here visiting. He was in business for himself and could set his own schedule. He was interested in Wicca and was looking for someone he could talk to about it.

He hinted that it wouldn't be all that unpleasant to see me again. I made it as clear as I could manage that I didn't think it would be any hardship without quite coming out and saying so. Explicit declarations would have to wait until I had a better idea of his agenda.

Like rock stars, doctors, and movie producers, Witches have to resign themselves to the fact that there will be people who don't love them for themselves alone, but for what they can get out of them, from social introductions to magical initiations to free spells cast on their loved ones. I wasn't quite sure how to peg Stuart yet, and keeping my distance until I found out who he knew and who knew him couldn't hurt.

Eventually we went amiably in our separate directions, me

wondering if Stuart was what I needed to take my mind off Julian and Stuart thinking whatever Stuart was thinking. I honestly thought I'd never see him again.

This was not my day for being right.

The Closing Ritual went off smoothly at around six o'clock, when most Ecumenipicnickers (we'd drawn over two hundred people, Belle thought, and I thought she was being conservative) were still here but thinking about leaving. Xharina had collected her troops and her ice chests and left about four, saying she hoped to see me again at HallowFest. I hoped she'd heard enough about missing books to make her give her covener another chance, but I doubted if I'd ever know.

The closing ritual was essentially the opening ritual in reverse, where we thanked the Powers that Were for attending and seeing to it that nobody was beaten up, struck by lightning, or afflicted with food poisoning.

The speaking parts were cast entirely from Changing, both so that other people wouldn't feel obliged to stick around and to give Changing—which was, after all, responsible for all this—the chance to shine, now that all the politicking had been done. Once the ritual was over there wouldn't be much else in the way of site aftercare, Pagans making a you-should-pardon-the-expression religion of leaving their campsites cleaner than they found them. At least when someone else was looking.

Topper and Coral were Priest and Priestess, standing in the center with their kids Jamie and Heather, who would someday be able to boast, like many of their generation, that they were hereditary Witches, raised in the faith of their foremothers—and finally, after all the lies and unprovable asseverations, it would be true. If their parents weren't arrested first.

Ah, political correctness, the gentle art of minding somebody else's business.

It had been a long day, but fortunately I could do this particular set of closings practically in my sleep, even if I couldn't enunciate as clearly as Xharina. I kissed my hand to the Lion in the South and passed the metaphysical ball to West, North, East again, and home.

And the First Annual Beltane Ecumenipicnic was over.

Of course, Belle was already talking about *next* year.

5

Most people get particularly stupid just after pulling off something large. It's the letdown of having worked real hard and now it's over and you're left chock-full of energy and intention with nothing to apply them to.

The moral is, don't do anything when you're tired, when you're rattled, when you're pumped full of adrenaline.

It's just too bad that nobody ever takes their own good advice.

What I did take advantage of was that seniority which hath its privileges to show up around eleven at Houston Graphics, which meant that Ray was waving a phone at me before I quite got the door open.

Most of us didn't start life intending to end up at Houston Graphics, and Ray is no particular exception. He used to be a dancer—Jazz Ballet of Harlem and a bunch of Broadway shows—until something happened. When Ray wears shorts to work you can see the scars the surgery left; big black S-shaped marks on the inside and the outside of his knee.

So Ray took up graphic design. Mikey Pontifex owns the business, but Ray runs it. And keeps us all happy. More or less.

"No, she just walked in," Ray explained to the phone. "Yo, Kitty—it's for you."

Ray Lawrence also has a differently abled sense of humor.

"Hello?" I said cautiously into the phone. Unless America has declared war on Manhattan, *nobody* calls me at work between nine and five.

"Bast?" Glitter. Her breathing was jerky, as if she'd been running.

"Yes?" I waited for the punch line.

"Ilona's dead. Someone killed her."

No, not running. Crying.

I looked at Ray, who was waiting, with the full force of his personality, for his phone back. I wished Mikey would put in a second line.

"Where are you?" I said. "Let me call you back."

Glitter was at work. I gave Ray back his phone.

"I'll be right back," I said, heading for the door.

"Nice of you to stop by," Ray said. Such a wit.

I hoofed it downstairs to the deli next door, which has in addition to other amenities, a phone. I ordered a *caffe latte* and called Glitter back. By that time she was crying so hard I had difficulty in making out what she was saying.

Ilona was dead. Sometime Saturday. The landlord had found the body. There'd been a break-in and she'd died.

"How did you find out?"

"Maura told me." Maura is a cop who frequently arrests the people who later become Glitter's clients. "She knew I knew her, and she— And they— It isn't *fair!*" Glitter wailed.

Life is pain, I remembered Xharina saying to Arioch. Yeah. And pain hurts.

I stayed on with Glitter for several quarters' worth of phone time while my coffee grew cold and undrinkable. There was nothing to do, nothing for anyone to do but the police and the coroner. Ilona's death was just another point on the curve plotting the urban evolution toward the apocalypse.

I got back upstairs forty minutes later. The phone rang as I came in. Ray picked it up. "Houston Graphics."

There was a pause.

"It's for you," Ray said to me.

Thank the good Goddess that Mikey wasn't there. I took the phone from Ray.

"Yes?"

"Is this, um, Bast?" The caller sounded like an anemic bassoon.

"Yes?" Who the hell was it? No one's voice I recognized.

"I got your number out of the phone book. Remember, you said where you worked? I hope it's okay to call you," the voice went on forlornly.

No, it wasn't. Ray was staring at me with a fixed non-expression.

"Is there something I can do for you?" I said to the phone in carefully correct accents.

"This is Ned Skelton," the forlorn voice said. Now I recognized it—and I remembered that I had indeed mentioned Houston Graphics' name, somewhere during that dinner two weeks ago.

"Ilona's dead," Ned told me. "I came to work this morning, there was a police notice on the door, and I went down to the station like it said and—"

I'd completely forgotten that Ned worked for Ilona. There was no way I could cut him off without being cruel. I semaphored apologies at Ray. He turned back to the job he was working on with ostentatious disinterest.

"I have to see you," Ned said desperately. "Please!"

I started to tell him okay, but he must have heard it as a refusal. Maybe Ned Skelton was used to hearing a lot of refusals.

"No!" he said. "You don't understand. It's not for me. I've heard a lot about you. I'm sorry, I'm sorry, I never meant— At the party. You were right. At the picnic. It was wrong. It's a sacred trust, you can't just— Everybody says you're fair. You have to— I need you to— It's just a *box*. That's all it is, I *swear* it. Just a box, just for a few days. Oh, please, *please*—"

Despite the ease with which we bandy the word about, most people have never heard someone actually beg. Ned was begging now, and I found myself willing to promise almost anything to make him stop.

"Yes. Okay, Ned. I'll do it. It's all right," I soothed.

I wasn't quite sure what I'd agreed to. Something about a box for a few days. At this point I didn't really care.

"I'll do it," I repeated. Ray gave me a funny look.

There was a brief silence. Over the open line I could hear the faint sounds of Ned trying to be quiet.

"Can I bring it over now?" he said at last. My jaws ached in sympathy with the effort he was making to hold on to his self-control.

"Yes," I said. I asked him where he was. He told me: uptown, on the West Side. I gave him directions. He said it would be about an hour and a half. I told him we could go have lunch.

I handed the phone back to Ray.

"Finished with your social life?" Ray said.

"And the horse you rode in on," I told him sweetly. "His boss was murdered Saturday night."

"Bummer," Ray said, accepting my apology. He was specing a job, and I looked over his shoulder to see what it was. Ned and his box would be here about one-thirty, but meanwhile I was out of work.

"You can have this when it comes back," Ray said, laying the typesheet down on the copy and making obscure notes in the margin. Designers make good money—Ray was one of the few Houston Graphics inmates making a living wage.

"Great," I said. But not that great because it would be at least two weeks and maybe three before StereoType got the raw type back to us, and what was I going to do in the meantime?

"So you got anything for me now?" I said.

"You think you deserve work, after tying up the phone all morning?" Ray asked.

I didn't dignify that with a reply.

"Couple'a binding dies," he said, relenting.

I went over to the shelves where incoming and outgoing jobs are stacked and found the jobs. The type had already been set; it was paper-clipped to each mock-up.

Even though book cover design has long since been supplanted by book jacket design, book spines—like the one on *Mary: A Rose Among the Shadows*—are still stamped with title and author and publisher's logo. The way the stamp looks is up to places like Houston.

There were six of them; ten hours' work if I dogged it unspeakably. I took them back to my board and got to work.

One of the better fringe benefits of this business is that jobs are frequently no-brainers. While I filled my pen and cut and ruled my board and kerned (adjusted the spacing between the letters by hand) the waxed repro into place I had plenty of time to think about things I didn't want to think about.

Ned. Ilona. Mary, Queen of Scots. Stuart Hepburn. Urban violence. Passion and free-range stupidity. And what would happen to Lothlorien now? Would Ilona's partner take it over?

If it wasn't unfair, you wouldn't know it was Life.

Fortunately Royce got into work before Ned did, which put a little glamour into my day. It was 12:40 by the clock on the wall, and it was instantly obvious what had taken Royce so long.

This was a Dress Day.

Royce was wearing a little brown frock with white polka dots, a saucy brown straw cocktail hat with a scrap of a veil, full maquillage, and white gloves. The shoes were modern—brown ankle-strap Capezios—but everything else was vintage.

Royce collects. It's a good thing he's skinny, or he'd never find retro clothing to fit him.

He saluted Ray and waved to me and went over to his desk. Nobody said anything—Tyrell'd used to, but he'd stopped.

Beaner camps, on the reasonable presumption that performing artists are obliged to provide street theater, but Royce has never queened it in my presence. He's always the same person no matter what he's wearing; it's just that sometimes he's wearing dresses: a warrior in the cause of *laissez-faire.* I smiled to myself and went back to work.

Ned arrived more or less on schedule. I'd finished one die and started a second. I wasn't in a lot of hurry. When I'm not working, I'm not earning.

He was carrying a stuffed knapsack (what male New Yorkers carry because purses are for sissies). I went over to the door when I saw him.

"Come on in," I said.

He stared in all directions when I let him into the studio. It's just one big room, not quite square, with a rectangle-shaped bite out of our space near the door to make room for restrooms for this floor of the building. In the corner thus created stands the stat camera, blue and hulking and requiring disassembly for cleaning by Royce every Tuesday morning. We're supposed to kick back a dollar a stat to the studio if we use the machine for our own projects, but nobody ever does.

The rest of the room contains Mikey's desk, Ray's light table, innumerable metal bookshelves filled with past successes, and a bunch of four-foot-high free-standing partitions sheltering light tables and stools, set at right angles down the middle to give everyone a little storage area and the illusion of a private work space.

"This your place?" Ned said.

I looked him over carefully. Ned Skelton had the particularly brittle, sharp-edged look of someone who'd had a severe shock and was currently refusing to admit it. A confrontation with mortality, even if it's only someone else's, tends to have that effect. There were dark soot-bruise smudges under his eyes and his skin looked over-scrubbed. He was wearing jeans and a work shirt and was doing a complex impersonation of someone who was just fine.

"I work here," I admitted.

"They know you're—you know?" he asked, lowering his voice conspiratorially.

An odd question, on the face of it.

"They wouldn't care if they did know," I said, which is true. Both Mikey and Ray are remarkably uninterested in anything that doesn't make them money.

"What would happen if somebody told them?" Ned persisted.

I gave him a sharp look, wondering if agreeing to help him had been a mistake.

"Nothing would happen, Ned," I said with a sigh, "because nobody cares. Now, where's this package?"

He dragged it out of the knapsack, which deflated conspicuously. The package was a brown cardboard box, about thirteen by twenty, and eight inches deep. The box had probably originally been used to ship books in and was almost completely cocooned in monofilament-reinforced strapping tape, as if Ned were afraid something inside might get out.

He held it out to me in a fashion suggesting it was a large box of chocolates I should be pleased to receive. Ray, Seiko, Eloi, and Royce watched with interest.

I took it. It was heavy—two or three pounds—and solid. I wondered what was in it. I was afraid I knew.

But *how?* That was always the question: *How?*

"Just for a few days, okay?" Ned said.

"Sure," I said. I shook it gently. Nothing shifted.

"Be careful," Ned said warily. "Don't open it."

"Let's go get lunch." I stuffed the package into the storage shelf in my carrel next to *The Casablanca Cookbook.*

Around the corner from the deli there's a restaurant that ought to be more upscale than it is considering how convenient it is to New York University and CBGB's. It has a fine selection of imported beers, and the only decent thing on the menu is the burgers.

I ordered a burger. I warned Ned. He ordered cheesecake and a Coke.

"So what are you going to do now?" I asked. Now that your former employer's been murdered, I meant. I didn't wonder why Ilona was dead. This is New York. There's hardly ever a "why."

Ned shrugged. "I'm okay. I've got another job. It was only part-time. Lothlorien."

I'd thought we were going to talk about Sunday and other things, like the possibility the box Ned had handed me contained the fictional *Book of Moons* that he'd been raving about at the picnic. We were not, it developed, going to talk. Ned's discovery of Ilona's death seemed to have shoved Sunday's picnic so far into history for him that bringing it up would be as relevant as discussing the siege of Troy.

But I couldn't leave it alone.

"About Sunday, Ned—"

"They're all wrong. And they're going to be sorry. It really *is* old," he said. "And it's real Wicca. Margaret Murray was right."

He said it as if it were the only thing he had left to hold on to. It might be.

Dr. Margaret Murray was a nice, respectable Egyptologist until the day she got the notion that the medieval witch-trial records should be taken literally. She wrote three books of progressively less mainstream scholarship: *The Witch-Cult in Western Europe, The God of the Witches,* and *The Divine King in England,* in which she links more of the English nobility to Wicca than any writer until Katharine Kurtz—and swears that Wicca is a religion stretching in unbroken practice back to the caves at Lascaux.

"Why are they going to be sorry, Ned?" I asked in my best imitation of Belle's psychiatrist voice.

Ned's eyes slid away from mine and he flushed. "They just will," he mumbled. "You're— Look, you're not *mad* at me, are you?" he blurted out.

It was not a question one adult should ask another. It contains too much acknowledgment of subservience, of emotional comfort that depends on someone else's whim. But Ned Skelton was—still—looking for someone else to provide that. Looking for someone else to give him what he thought he needed: power.

As the ad campaign for the *Godfather* movies reminds us, power cannot be given, only taken. The great flaw in the Western mind-set is the conviction that power must always be taken from someone else.

We all have power. It can't be given to us. And when we take it, we take it *for* ourselves, not *from* anyone. This is the great mystery.

The secret is that there is no secret.

"No, Ned. I'm not mad at you."

Not yet, anyway. But I could get that way.

"What's in the box?" I added.

And why leave it with me?

He winced as if I'd slapped him and gazed pleadingly at me with those hangdog hazel eyes. "Could I . . . Could I tell you next week?" he asked. Humbly. "I will. I promise. I'll tell you next week, if you'll just keep it for me now. Please?"

I couldn't stand it.

"Sure," I said gently. "It's all right." I'd make a lousy dominatrix.

I hunted around and found one of my cards that has my business name—High Tor Graphics, Freelance Design Work—and my legal name—Karen Hightower—and nothing else on it. I wrote the studio number down. "It's better to call me after five, though."

Lunch straggled painfully to its end. I paid my check. Ned paid his. We went to the door.

"You won't open it, will you?" Ned asked. "You promise?"

The chill I felt then was entirely the product of my own overactive imagination. While I suspected that if I opened Ned's box I'd be unhappily surprised, I couldn't pin my conscious mind down to the form the surprise would take.

"Why did you want *me* to hold it?" I asked, unable to resist any longer.

"Everyone says you—" Ned hesitated and actually shuffled his feet. I was filled with agonizing curiosity about "everybody."

"They say you'll keep your word."

A Witch's word is law. Belle had told me that during my training. It doesn't mean what it sounds as if it does. What it means is that oathbreakers make lousy magicians, and what you say, you'd better do.

"I won't open it until I see you again," I promised. "Call me soon, okay?"

"Sure," Ned said.

Later I'd say to myself that some part of him already knew what was going to happen, but hindsight's always twenty-twenty.

I was back in the studio by three. Seiko'd left, which left me, Chantal, Royce, and Eloi—and Ray, of course. I applied myself to the binding dies, and by the time it was five o'clock I'd finished three of them.

I decided to save the rest for tomorrow. Maybe there'd be more work then, depending on the calls Mikey'd made today.

I left Ned's package on the shelf. It was just as safe there as it'd be at home, and this way I didn't have to lug it around.

I grabbed my hat and headed out.

When unsettling things happen, people seek solace in normalcy. I headed for the Snake.

When I got there, Elvis was blessedly silent and the store was reasonably empty. I had the section marked "Witchcraft and Women's Mysteries" completely to myself. It had been restocked recently.

The Grimoire of Lady Sheba by Lady Sheba. *The Complete Book of Witchcraft* by Raymond Buckland. *A Book of Pagan Rituals,* Herman Slater, ed. *Mastering Witchcraft* by Paul Huson. *A Witch's Bible* by Janet and Stewart Farrar. The book alleging to be Gerald Gardner's unpublished notebooks, which almost certainly wasn't.

And that was just the top rack.

In short, more published, legally accessible books of Wiccan and Pagan rituals than any one person could possibly need.

So who was stealing the homegrown ones? And why? And—and this was what was driving me crazy—*how?*

If I could only figure out "how" I'd be willing to suspect Ned of it, since my gothic imagination couldn't think of any better contents for the box he'd left with me. I freely admitted this, in the privacy of my own brain.

Unfortunately for my future as a lurid fiction writer, I couldn't make all the pieces fit.

"Why" would be simple: revenge.

But after that, things started falling apart, starting with "How" and ending with "And Then What."

Skip, for the moment, how Ned, my villain-elect, got into all those apartments without leaving a trace, and where did that leave you?

Nowhere. Because someone who knew the Community well enough to know where to go to steal all those books wouldn't have pulled a dumb stunt like that hoaxical announcement at the picnic.

Or would they?

And, that aside, even if I was willing to jump to the conclusion that there was a stolen BoS—or half a dozen of them—in the box Ned had left with me (though unfounded suspicion was no grounds for breaking a promise), I couldn't come up with a reason for his leaving them with me.

Why me?

Nothing made sense. Whichever way I tried the frame, it fell apart.

"Hey, Bast," someone said from over my shoulder. A voice I recognized.

It was Lorelli Lee.

Lorelli Lee is one of those people who reassures me that looking straight is still an option here on the New Aquarian Frontier. She is of average height and weight and build. She has mouse-blond hair that she wears in one of those shoulder-length styles that would be invisible in any office in the country, a not unreasonable number of holes punched in each ear, and vision-correcting glasses that do not suggest that she is the visiting shootist from any one of a number of left-wing military organizations.

She wears skirts. She has been known to wear them with co-ordinating jackets. She maintains a lucrative and responsible accounting practice, standing between a number of fringy small-business owners and freelance service providers (such as Yours Truly) and the unveiled wrath of the IRS.

"Ilona Saunders died, did you know?" I said. "Over the weekend."

"No!" Lorelli's protest was the automatic one of someone who didn't know the other person particularly well.

"Saturday night," I said. Which explained her absence from the picnic, now that I thought about it. "And—"

"Hi, Bast," Julian said, appearing not quite in a puff of smoke. "I was hoping you'd come in. Per Aurum's just sent us their spring shipment, but I haven't gotten around to getting it out."

He looked, as usual, like a dissolute priest. It is rumored that he attended seminary somewhere and left before taking his vows, but I try to ignore rumors.

"You want to tag them and check off the manifest for me? Off the books," he added.

With the way things were going at work I could use a second job, but I didn't want to put my non-relationship with Julian on such a mercantile basis.

"Store credit—wholesale," I counteroffered, and Julian actually smiled.

"Deal," he said, and held out his hand. We shook on it.
It was the first time I'd ever touched Julian.

And that was how I wound up sitting in the Snake's secret temple at six o'clock at night with seventy-five hundred dollars' worth of wholesale jewelry plus manifest.

I always derive an immense furtive kick every time I go back here, although the Snake's "clandestine" temple is probably the best known secret in the entire Community. The rack that holds the robes (back right, next to the figurine candles) swings out to reveal the hallway that leads to the bathroom at one end (important urban survival information) and the temple at the other. I'd sorted through the boxes waiting in the hallway until I found the one from Per Aurum, collected the box and everything else I needed, and gone back into the temple to work.

The Snake's temple (and lecture hall) is actually the back third or so of the shop footage. The walls are painted matte black, and someone—probably Tris—has installed enough track lighting to qualify the place as a theater of the absurd.

At the moment two floods—one blue, one purple—were focused on the built-to-spec altar that was still set up from the O.T.O.'s weekly Wednesday ritual. I sat down on the bottom step of the altar and ripped the box open, being careful not to cut into any paperwork that might be on top, assuming Per Aurum'd remembered to send it.

I found the invoice. Good. I looked it over. No surprises.

Notwithstanding that their name translates from the Latin as "By (means of) Gold," most of what I unpacked in the Per Aurum shipment was silver.

Item: Thirty-six plain pentacles, the interwoven star in a circle that no self-respecting Neopagan would be without; a dozen each of small, medium, and large. The mainstay of the Snake's business, even in these troubled times.

Item: Two dozen medium pentacles set with assorted stones: lapis, amethyst, hematite.

I counted them and stacked them in neat piles, each one in its slippery self-seal bag, and checked them off on the invoice. After I had everything logged in, I could price them for sale, a simple matter of multiplying the wholesale cost by 300 percent—a process called triple keystoning.

I said the Snake's merchandise was overpriced.

I continued my explorations. A dozen pentacle rings, sterling. A dozen moon and star rings, ditto.

Six Art Nouveau Moon-Goddess or maybe Fairy Queen stickpins. Or maybe they were angels; angels were a hot property just now, for people who liked the idea of a twenty-four-hour feathered yenta in their lives.

Pentacle earrings, pairs. A dozen—no, the manifest said a dozen and a half. I hunted through slippery plastic packets to find the other six pair.

"How're you doing?" Lorelli asked, coming through the secret door. She was carrying a pizza box and a couple of containers of coffee. I looked down at what I held in my hand and tried to decide whether this was a Celtic pendant or a Norse pendant.

"Norse or Celtic?" I replied, holding it up. She studied it for a minute.

"Norse. They're gold with pewter accents. The Celtic ones are pewter with gold accents."

Lorelli sat down on the step next to me, careful not to dislodge the small piles of jewelry, and set down the box. "They're both regular," she said of the coffees, which in New York means cream, no sugar. I took one.

"Thanks," I said.

"Dinnertime, anyway," Lorelli said. "I made Julian buy."

I took a slice of pizza.

"You said Ilona'd died?" Lorelli said, taking up the conversation where it'd been left.

The talk drifted around Lothlorien's demise, Ilona's death, and mutual acquaintance. I filled Lorelli in on the details of the picnic.

"And it's funny," I added, not really thinking about what I was saying, "but everyone seems to be missing Books of Shadows."

Lorelli choked, and sprayed a mouthful of coffee halfway across the room.

"Really?" she said, when she could speak. "Because mine's gone, too."

"I keep wondering if I just misplaced it," Lorelli said, in the tone of one trying an unworkable theory on for size anyway. "It was in my office with the account books. It looks pretty much like them. But then it was gone."

I began removing silver pentacles from their bags. I wrote control numbers and grossly inflated prices on tiny white tags and started threading them through the bail at the top of each one.

"When?" I asked, seeing what a direct question would get me.

"I'd wanted to use something in it for last Saturday. So, a week ago Thursday I missed it."

That would be around the twenty-eighth of April, about two weeks after Glitter lost hers. I bet if I could get real answers out of people, I'd find that practically everyone's book had vanished sometime in April.

Why?

Lorelli took a pen and a sheet of sticky dots and began pricing the Celtic pendants.

"Somebody broke in?" I suggested.

"I keep the room locked, there's a gate on the window, the front door is locked." Lorelli recited the list in a singsong monotone, as if it were something she'd gone over and over. Probably she had. "I don't have a group meet at my house, I'm not all that out, cyber-Welsh is a self-created trad." She stopped, shrugging. "I can replace just about all of it," she added.

"Sure," I said. I finished tagging the small pentacles.

Her head was down, bent over the sheet of labels. Colored lights turned her skin and hair a ghastly, ghostly color.

Translated from the Paganspeak, Lorelli did not have either a study group or a coven meeting at her house, she was not "in your face" about her religion to the outside world, and since cyber-Welsh was a self-created Neopagan tradition, that meant she'd assembled it herself from public—and published—material, so she didn't *have* any hidden unpublished secrets to steal.

Locked, she'd said, doors and windows both. If either'd been forced, she would have said. So it was another "walks-through-walls" reasonless theft.

If it was a theft at all—but Lorelli seemed both reliable and organized.

"You know, I must just have misplaced it, you know?" Lorelli said wistfully.

I knew.

I finished marking up the shipment and went and told Julian he owed me sixteen dollars of store credit. On the way out I ran into Stuart Hepburn.

"Well, hello there," Stuart said. He smiled. I smiled. He still looked well favored and aggressively normal.

"I see you're taking my advice," I said.

"This is quite a place," Stuart said, looking around.

To call the Snake "quite a place" is like calling Versailles a little villa in the country. I admired Stuart's English reticence.

"I work here sometimes," I said. "Can I show you around?"

I showed him the Witchcraft section and made some recom-
mendations. Stuart poked through some of the Books of Shadows
but didn't seem to find what he was looking for.

"But none of these is really old," he said.

"The really old stuff is in the case behind the counter," I told
him, "But you won't find any Books of Shadows there. Just grimoires."

The talk turned personal. Stuart asked if he could see me. I for-
bore to mention that he was looking right at me, since that wasn't
what he meant.

I wondered, perversely, if Julian could see us back here and if
he was jealous.

Not a chance.

I said yes. I gave Stuart the card with my home number on it.
He said he'd call tomorrow or Wednesday, since he had some
business appointments that weren't too definite yet. He left.

I wondered if I could successfully get through a date without
making too big a fool of myself, which at least made a nice change
from everything else I'd been wondering about lately.

I got home around nine, unlocked and relocked my door, got myself a beer and a shot, and realized with regret that it was again
approaching the time of year during which even a large fan in my
only window would not render my apartment inhabitable. I picked
up *Mary Stuart: A Rose in the Shadows* and popped a cassette containing, among other light classics, "Tom O'Bedlam" into my newest electronic toy. When I hit "play" it was the middle of the song.

"With a host of furious fancies / Whereof I am commander—"

Beaner'd said it was a political ballad about Mary, Queen of
Scots. The lyrics were printed on the lyric sheet folded into the cassette box, and made about as much sense three hundred years
after the fact as the jokes on "Laugh-In" do after a slightly shorter
period. Gibberish.

*"The punk I scorn and the cutpurse sworn / And the roaring
boys' bravado—"*

The past is a foreign country; they do things differently there.

Thus the beginning of another perfect week in the Attitude
Capital of the World.

6

T uesday was normal until a quarter after five.

I was at Houston that late because High Tor Graphics, my freelance business, had picked up some work: a complete series of invoices and tracking forms for a company calling itself "Sopht-Wear."

The Cat could have run them up in an hour on a CAD-CAM system.

I glared at the pile of technology in the corner of the studio. Last year Mikey'd bought a low-end CAD-CAM system for the studio, intending to obsolete all of us (the hand-drawing of charts and graphs is a good third of the studio workload). Fortunately for job security he had not internalized the knowledge that the hardware would have fits when the temperature spiked over eighty degrees.

Since my place of employment, Houston Graphics, maintains its fingerhold on solvency by not squandering money on useless inessentials like air-conditioning (or heat in the winter), the temperature in the studio is well over eighty much of the year between June and September.

Eventually Mikey'd decided the system he'd bought was simply unreliable, and none of us had any intention of enlightening him. I think a commercial air-conditioner would blow every fuse in the building anyway.

The phone rang.

"Bookie-Joint-Can-I-Help-You?" I rattled off on one lungful, because Mikey only owns the place until five. Since he doesn't want the studio phone answered after five, we answer it that way. Most of life's problems can be worked out with a little creativity.

"This is Ned," Ned said. I shot a not-quite-willed glance down at Ned's package. "I need help."

Ten minutes later I hung up the phone. I'd promised to be there as soon as I could.

Ned had indeed been a Skelton of his word. Though his apartment had been burgled Monday night, he had waited to call me about it until after five P.M. Tuesday.

Nothing was taken. I'd asked. And Ned had spent today doing the right things, so far as filing reports and buying new locks went. What he'd wanted had been a subtler form of help.

Ned wanted his apartment blessed, so that the energy the burglar had brought—call it the stamp of his personality, for lack of a more precise term—could be removed. A psychic cleansing, to go with the physical tidying up.

There was no doubt that I'd go, although he didn't know it. The last time someone'd asked me for help, I'd been too late.

I went home and packed my Danish bookbag with what Belle calls my Traveling Priestess Kit: *athame,* charged water, incense, sea salt, and a few other things. Then I hit the subway. Ned had given me directions. They weren't too hard to follow, but the destination they led to was a bit of a surprise.

Fast Eddie Skelton, part-time bookstore clerk, lived on West End Avenue on the lower Upper West Side (above Lincoln Center, below Columbia), at an address where apartments rented for more than I made in an average month. I found Ned's building without much trouble.

There was an ambulance and a cop car in front of it, flashing red and amber keep-aways at a small huddle of licensed gawkers.

I saw them from across the street: the cops, the wagon, the crowd. It was unseasonably hot, but I felt cold down to my fingernails.

Coincidence. It's coincidence, it's coincidence, it's—

I stayed where I was, as if to move would be to participate in this hideously routine street theater. It was someone else. Of course it was. How could it be Ned? He was young, healthy, and I'd spoken to him on the phone no more than an hour ago.

The two EMTs with the gurney came out of Ned's building. It

had a dark plastic mummy-bag on it, zipped-up shut the way there is when there's a dead body inside. They loaded it into the ambulance, and slammed the doors, and got inside, and drove away.

A few minutes later the cop came out and got into his cop car and did the same. Just another of our forty daily homicides here in Baghdad on the Hudson.

I was certain of what I'd find when I went into the building. Certain the way you are in nightmares, outside of logic. That ought to mean I didn't need to go, to see for myself, but a few minutes later, when the crowd had diffused, I went in anyway, telling myself I was wrong.

I had the spooky hopeless feeling you have in tragedies, knowing you're going to say your lines and it isn't going to change the outcome. Insisting, meanwhile, that everything was fine, that Ned and I were going to go out for drinks.

The lobby was a study in genteelly-diminished elegance: gilded egg-and-dart molding, elaborate ceiling fixtures, a fireplace that might even have worked once. Ned's apartment was first-floor front.

There was a notice on the door, and bright yellow tape. Not a surprise. Never a surprise—didn't you know that Witches can see the future? I gulped and gulped, swallowing hard, even though I knew what the notice said because I'd seen one before, at the last place I'd gotten to too late.

I tried the door and banged on it anyway, reaching through the tape that told me this was a crime scene, this was a murder.

"Hey, lady! Cut it out!"

I jumped. Guiltily.

The speaker was the tenant of the apartment across the lobby. He teetered on the verge of looking like a Brooklyn truck driver, glaring at me. He was probably an expensive lawyer.

"If you're looking for the super, he's gone. The police took him out in a bag." He seemed to derive an immense personal satisfaction from being able to say that.

"Super?" I said blankly.

The man frowned, thought about slamming his door, and decided not to. "Someone shot him, lady," he said. Then he did shut the door, but quietly.

I turned around and looked. There is a futile and useless push-bell beside most New York apartment doors. This one had a little white sign over it that said "Super—1A." Ned's apartment. Ned's other job.

I thought about knocking again and didn't have the stomach for it. Besides, there was no one in there to hear, was there? Someone had shot him.

Shot him dead. Ned is dead. First he said and now he's dead. Ned is dead, dead is Ned. Did someone shoot him through the head?

I felt faint, and cold, and unwilling to face facts. I didn't want to think about this. Ned had called for help and I'd come too late. Again.

I didn't want to unleash the yammering guilt-monster that said this was all my fault, and I didn't want to face the fact that I ought to call the police and tell them that I'd spoken to Ned and when.

Would Ned still be alive if I'd taken a taxi instead of the subway?

Would I be dead?

I wanted to go home.

But I didn't go home. I went back to the studio. I even took a taxi.

I was terribly unhappy, as if I'd missed the only chance I would ever have to meet someone that I could have loved if we had only met. But I didn't and hadn't and wouldn't have loved Ned Skelton. Who, between 5:15 and 6:35, had been permanently cut from this eon's performance of the Traveling Reality Roadshow.

I wished I'd taken a taxi to his apartment.

All the way back to the studio the wheels kept repeating the same sentence: *Ned is dead, Ned is dead, Ned is dead . . .*

I'd been too late again.

I got back to the studio around seven-thirty; it was just starting to get dark. The building was still open. If you're there after eleven you're there for the night; the super puts the outside shutters down then.

I was shaking so hard I dropped the keys three times before I could let myself into the studio. There was nobody here, just me and the rats and the roaches. I flipped on all the lights, even going around and turning on the tensor lamp at each workstation. I wanted light, lots of light.

Ned is dead.

Something didn't make sense. It wasn't just the reasonless guilt. *Something didn't make sense.* That was why I was afraid. Irrationality is the greatest terror of all.

But I didn't know what it was that didn't make sense. It was something lurking down among the unexamined assumptions in the dark unconscious, and I was here, on the surface of my daylight mind.

Ned was dead.

The box. Was it why he had been murdered?

"I won't open it until I see you again," I'd promised. Well, now I had.

I went to my carrel and picked up the package he'd left with me. Still heavy, still thoroughly sealed. I grabbed a mat knife, knowing I was probably going to slice myself with it. I did; the tape was tougher than I expected and the knife got away. The razor point slid a narrow red line down my left wrist—lengthwise, the way the ancient Romans used to like to open their veins. It didn't bleed much.

I finally got the package open.

"Fuck. Fuck you, Ned Skelton. Fuck you, you son of a bitch," I said hoarsely.

It was Glitter's book.

It was Glitter's book and more. Two and three and four and five and a sheaf of printout in a data binder that had Lorelli Lee's name and address on it (six) and a slim handmade book of red leather embossed with a bull's head (seven) and another one swathed in bubble wrap that I could see had a binding chipping and cracked with age (eight).

I counted. Eight.

I got up. I walked around the studio. I made a list of the phone calls I was going to make and decided not to make them. I made a new pot of coffee. If the phone had rung I think my heart would have stopped right then, but it didn't.

And then the coffee was ready and I poured it and stared into my cup and prayed to the Goddess very hard, notifying Her that I was willing to trade any amount of three A.M. craziness and anxiety attacks for the next two years for the ability to think clearly now.

And after a while my mind stopped sprinting around my brain like a nervous gerbil and I was able to pull the timeless disinterest around myself that good magic comes from.

You can say that the Goddess answered my prayers or that She gave me the strength to answer them myself; it doesn't matter. What did matter was that I was ready to make some preliminary decisions on what I would do with the contents of that box.

I went back to Ned's box of stolen secrets.

* * *

What are the Gods worth on the open market? What price a hot-line to gnosis, or a designer-direct package of Revealed Truth? Can a person *need* religion, and, granting that, did the intensity of Edward Skelton's self-perceived need legitimize his theft?

No. Ned's thefts were neither legitimate nor excused. I understood the desperation that could lead to what we must politely term temporary moral confusion, but it still wasn't right, or even necessary. It was just a fact that I had to work with, because Ned was beyond being able to do so.

Who was stealing Books of Shadows? Ned Skelton.

I'd always had "why." And now I had "how," didn't I? Because working at Lothlorien had been Ned's part-time second job. And now I knew what his first job was.

Ned was a building superintendent. A nice white English-speaking strong young man to service the upscale needs of upscale tenants on the Upper West Side. And because the upscale tenants had upscale toys they also had upscale locks. State-of-the-locksmith's-art, and Ned had very nice master keys to fit them. He could come and go anywhere, invisible in a work shirt and pants and jangling bunch of keys.

And now he'd never do it again.

Now it was my problem.

I liked to think that he'd realized that stealing Books of Shadows wouldn't take him where he wanted to be, that he'd been working himself up to returning them. It didn't make the position he'd put me in any easier, though. I was the one who was going to have to return them, dodging awkward questions of how I'd gotten them. If I could.

I went through the books again more carefully.

Here was Glitter's, unmistakable. I could find her and give it back. No problem, except maybe with the explanation. And Lorelli's, ditto — in fact, I had her home address; I could mail it to her anonymously and explain later.

The red book belonged to Lord Amyntor (how not, with all those bull's heads?). I didn't know his real name, but Belle might. Beaner certainly did, and where to find him, too.

That left five. One was Gardnerian, Otterleaf's. One was Xharina's. One was Crystal of Starholt's — she had a heavy hand with rubber stamps involving fairies. One book belonged, apparently, to "Diana–27," someone I'd never heard of, even at the picnic.

I was able to put names to all these books so easily because
one of the things a Witch puts into a Book of Shadows is her own
Craft name: the name she takes when she decides to become a
Witch. The name she's known by in Circle. The first page of my
BoS, for example, says "The Book of Shadows of Lady Bast of
Changing Coven." It wasn't much as a real-world address went,
but it did mean that with a little asking around I could get these
back to their rightful owners.

And none of them, my mind informed me with irritating inclu-
siveness, could possibly be the Mary, Queen of Scots, grimoire that
Ned had been puffing off at the Ecumenipicnic.

But the box wasn't empty yet. I reached in for the last item, the
one so carefully wrapped, when none of the others were.

One old book, about twelve inches square. I eased it out of the
bubble wrap. The cover was dark brown leather, cracked and
showing tan where the glazed surface had flaked away. The spine
was hubbed and channeled; old-style bookmaking from when
books were sewn, not glued.

I picked it up. It was lighter than it looked. I opened it carefully.

The pages were real vellum, which is to say lambskin scraped
until it's thin and soft and white as paper. Age had turned the
pages tea-colored, their edges toast-colored and chipping.

I steadied it with one hand and opened the book carefully to
the first page.

Marie, it said. And *Le Livre des Lunes*.

The Library of the Moon? No, my French was better than that.
The *Book* of Moons.

Not a Gardnerian book. Nor Alexandrian, or any other this-
century Wiccan tradition. It didn't even have the "family resemblance" that my book did to Lord Amyntor's.

I turned a few pages. They were covered with antique writing,
head to foot and gutter to margin. The script was long and loop-
ing, pale and brown with age, insanely regular even though the
pages weren't ruled. The words and sentences ran together until
the page blurred into an even, unreadable pattern. The noodle
script was broken by a string of symbols that looked vaguely like
a Celestial script called "Crossing the River," familiar to me from
hours spent with Francis Barrett and other nineteenth-century
mages.

Despite my best efforts, the edges of the pages crumbled at my touch. I turned carefully to the last page. The writing stopped abruptly a few lines in. The rest of the page was filled with a signature, faded to brown after all these years but written large in defiance:

Marie the Queen, by the grace of God Queen of England, Scotland, and Ireland.

I closed the book and set it back in the box.

The Book of Moons.

My life had suddenly turned into cheap pulp fiction. This called for another cup of coffee at the very least. I got it and drank it and retreated to the far end of the studio.

I drank my coffee. I wished I still smoked.

The Book of Moons of "Marie la Reine"—Mary, Queen of Scots. Maybe real, or maybe just a forgery, but *old;* you could smell it rotting away every time you opened it; a more intense, concentrated version of the pervasive odor at Lothlorien Books.

Which did not exist anymore, because Ilona had been murdered during a burglary.

And Ned, who had worked there, had also been burgled—a fitting karmic commentary on his covert agenda—and murdered—which was not.

No, wait. That wasn't quite right. Ned had been burgled—at least, he'd told me he had—Monday night. But he was murdered *Tuesday* night.

Why the twenty-four-hour delay?

I gave up on self-restraint. I went over to Eloi's carrel and picked up the pack of Camels I'd remembered seeing there, making a note to buy him a full pack in penance for looting. I lit one up and sucked the smoke in deep and then coughed and coughed while my eyes and nose ran and little blue stars crawled across my visual field and I felt giddy and slack-muscled and knew that somewhere Nicotina the Tobacco Goddess was laughing at me.

I threw the cigarette away, soaking it carefully first. Chastened, I returned to my coffee. Everything tasted of salt, smoke, and metal. The brief flirtation with uncontrolled substances hadn't done anything but waste what little energy I had left.

I walked back to my desk. Slowly.

Houston wraps each of its jobs in brown paper before it sends them out. I carried seven of the books to the front of the studio. I typed out seven red-and-white labels, centering the names neatly. I wrapped each book separately in a thick, generous allotment of butcher's paper, sealed each with brown package tape, and put the nice red-and-white label on the outside. I took them back to my desk and made a cute little ziggurat of them, Glitter's on the bottom, Amyntor's on the top. Then I walked around the studio some more, barely refraining from wringing my hands.

Because Ned did not have, could not have what he'd thought he had and what I thought I'd seen. Mary, Queen of Scots, wasn't a Witch. She just *wasn't.*

How do you know? A serpentine inner voice asked me.

"I just do," I said out loud. Besides, whether she was Queen of Scotland or Queen of the May, the Witch she would have been would have been so different from the kind I was that we probably wouldn't recognize each other's rituals in a darkened room.

So, nu?

My heart was racing. Caffeine, nicotine, fear.

I went back to my desk. I opened the book again somewhere in the middle. Halfway down the crowded page there were some letters written larger. *Por Atirer en Bas La Lune.* The antique French puzzled me for some minutes, but I finally figured it out. Translated into modern and English it read:

"For Drawing Down the Moon."

The page crumbled where I held it and my fingers made a darker print on the vellum. I closed the book without trying to read any more.

Drawing down the moon. The title of a book by Margot Adler about twentieth-century Witches. The central mystery of our mystery. Say Mass and you're a priest. Draw down the moon and you're a Witch.

And everyone who'd worked at Lothlorien was dead.

I looked at my watch. It was ten-thirty; too late to bother most of the people I knew. And I didn't want to do that anyway, until I got things straight in my head.

Ned. Ilona. *The Book of Moons. Marie, la Reine de Caledonii.*

I cast my mind back over that damned book Daffydd had loaned me, chock-full of historical facts about the universe's favorite sixteenth-century queen. Okay, just suppose what I had here was what Ned thought it was. Mary Queen of Scots grimoire. No, not grimoire — Book of Shadows. *The Book of Moons* of Marie the Witch.

Just like in the ballad. Tom O'Bedlam. *The Book of Moons.*

Okay. Suppose Mary *was* an initiated Witch. Just suppose.

Where would it have been done? Scotland is a traditional haven of the Craft: Margaret Murray found scads of examples of "surviving folk belief" there in the Scots witch trial records, and even Gerald Gardner had a Scots nursemaid from whom (some say) he learned his Wicca-craeften.

And James the Sixth of Scotland (aka James the First of England) — Mary's son — was one of the most relentless anti-Witch propagandists that history records, his philippics opening the door to that sanctimonious butcher Matthew Hopkins, self-styled Witchfinder General of all England, and the bloodiest witch-hunts ever enacted on English soil.

A case of adolescent rebellion?

My mother the Witch?

Was I actually taking this *seriously?*

Why had the Berwick witches (one of Dr. Murray's prize exhibits, whose capture led to one of the most famous witch trials in history) followed the Earl of Bothwell in his plan to kill James the king? Because it would put someone sympathetic to their religion on the joint thrones of England and Scotland?

I thought about it. It was a tempting possibility. But no, if I was going to play fair with the historical facts as I knew them, Mary could not have been initiated in Scotland — she left when she was six and didn't come back until she was eighteen, and after that Knox and Moray and that lot would certainly have seized the excuse of her paganism not just to boot her out, but to *burn* her.

Not in Scotland.

In France, then. At a French court whose entire sixteenth-century existence was owed to the intercession of one of Dr. Murray's other prime candidates for Wiccanhood: Joan of Arc. *La Pucelle,* Joan the Maid. Joan the Witch. Saint Joan. Who heard voices. Who followed orders. Who collaborated in her judicial murder, to the utter confusion of friends and foes alike, at the order of — some say — the head of her coven. Some say.

If there *had* been a living French Craft tradition, it could have made the jump to the French court from the French folk, then.

I stared at *The Book of Moons.*

My speculation had now reached the outermost orbit of the supermarket press and I knew it, but I couldn't stop. Fanciful history was more palatable than factual murder.

The French court. A royal coven, headed by Catherine de Medici, perhaps, or by Dianne de Valois, the king's mistress, who raised Mary as her own daughter. What would be more reasonable, if there was a coven, than that Mary should be inducted into it?

Almost anything.

In which case, where had the book in front of me come from? A top-flight modern forgery of a sixteenth-century holograph document—which *The Book of Moons* was—took more skill than poor Ned had possessed.

So maybe it was real. Maybe. Could be. Might be.

When she returned to Scotland, Mary's lack of zeal for the Catholic faith was one of the things that made her political position so difficult. Was her indifference to the Catholic Church and her acknowledgment of the Protestants due to the fact that she herself adhered to a third faith, that of the Wicca? Not a member of the Old Religion, as Catholicism was beginning to be called, but of the Oldest Religion?

And, banished from France, had Mary been banished from her coven as well?

And if there was a royal French coven, and she was separated from it, then Mary spent her life trying to reclaim not merely temporal glory, but spiritual.

Ridiculous. Impossible. There was no proof of the existence of organized Wicca before 1947–53, when Gardner began publishing.

I stared at the book in front of me and thought hard.

Gerald Gardner ingested all three of Murray's published revelations and on the basis of Murray's discredited scholarship proclaimed that the practice of the Craft went back centuries—at least, that's the way his critics say it happened. And once the Craft developed a more broad-based demographic, people with credible scholarly training attempted to climb the Wiccan family tree and found nothing before Gardner. From all the evidence they have been able to gather, what we know as Wicca began with Gerald Gardner.

What would they give for concrete real-world proof that it did not? That it was, in fact, a centuries-old religion?

I shook my head, driving the cobwebs out. If this was real, if it involved Mary, it was much bigger than that. If she could drive people like Daffydd and Beaner crazy after four hundred years of being dead when she was just an unlucky Catholic queen, imagine what her being a Witch would do.

I looked at *The Book of Moons*. Where had it come from—and

228 Bell, Book, and Murder

what was I going to do with it? It wasn't mine to dispose of. It wasn't Ned's either, it was safe to say, but whose was it?

Whoever the book belonged to, I didn't have to worry about it tonight. I was so tired I could hardly keep my eyes open, and almost anything I did would be sure to be wrong.

So I wrapped it up the way I had the other eight, typed "Book of Moons" on the label, and put it with the rest of my new collection of purloined Books of Shadows. At least this way I wouldn't lose it.

Then I locked up the studio and walked home, a habit I'm going to pay for some night, I know.

But not this one.

7

Having been so reasonable and prudent, I didn't get much sleep after all.

I lay in bed and stared at the ceiling and thought about Ned and *The Book of Moons*. I thought about what intervention I could have made in Ned's life to have given it a different outcome. I wondered if he'd be alive if I'd taken a taxi, if I'd listened to him more, if I'd encouraged Belle to take him into Changing.

And I knew I wouldn't have done those things. I hadn't had any telegram from the future telling me what Ned would turn rejection into—and if I had, what then? This was the dark side of the possession of power: knowing the pain it caused people like Ned, who somehow, by some standard, weren't good enough.

Pain that could, in the end, kill.

If the Craft is all smoke and mirrors—if it is merely the recreation of ignoble minds—then there is no justification for all of the pain that it causes.

But if instead it is not a faith, but a practicum inspired by gnosis and observation of the noumenal world, then the pain is, if not justified, in some sense pardonable. Pardonable because mere comfort cannot be the human animal's highest good. If it is, Nature, daughter of the Goddess, is made unnatural, since She has overfitted Her creatures for this world.

These were not comfortable thoughts to spend the night with. But comfort, as I have said, is not the goal.

And in that much we had made Ned a part of the Craft after all, because he had found no comfort with us.

Seven A.M. I thought about calling in dead, but I needed the hours. Besides, the books were at the studio. I had to return them before something else happened to them. So I dragged myself out of bed and took a shower, drank three cups of coffee, dug out and emptied the Danish Bookbag, and went.

It was still cool on the street, cooler—in fact—than it was indoors. I stopped at the deli and bought replacement cigarettes for Eloi and coffee for me and went up to the studio.

"You left the coffeepot on last night," Ray said when I came in.

I groaned and looked around for Mikey.

"He isn't here yet. I put it to soak," Ray said, relenting. "You look like hell. You got those dies done yet?"

"Soon," I said. "Patience is a virtue," I added.

Ray sneered. He's very good at it.

I went and washed out the coffeepot in the sink by the stat camera. I went back and made fresh coffee. Royce and Seiko were here, but most of the carrels were empty: no work, so no Angela and Tyrell and Eloi and Chantal.

I took four Excedrin for that run-down feeling and put extra sugar in my coffee from the deli. Then, feeling nauseated and slightly buzzed, I finished the jobs for Ray and meticulously cleaned my area. I made two brief phone calls on the studio phone: Glitter was in, Belle was not. Around noon I put the binding die mechanicals on Ray's desk.

"You got anything else for me?" I said.

"Go home. Sleep. You look horrible," Ray said. "I'll see you tomorrow."

Which meant he didn't.

"Yeah," I said. I bundled seven wrapped parcels into the bookbag and left.

It is an amazing truth of the universe that people always feel better the moment they leave work. For example, I almost felt as though I'd managed to get some sleep. I took the 6 downtown and got off at the City Hall station.

Glitter works in the big building on Court Street. The lobby is black and white marble, and in addition to bearing a generic resemblance to postwar buildings of a certain age, has always struck me as being a facade of tidiness slapped over some of the bleaker functioning of our society. Magical thinking: if you don't see it, it isn't there.

I gave my destination to a guard and took an elevator and gave my name to another guard who called into the back to see if I was expected. Glitter came out and conducted me into her office.

The place where Glitter does her probation officering for the City of New York is a glass-walled cubicle with a glass door, WPA vintage. It's about eight by ten, and where it isn't glass it is painted gas-chamber green. It contains two file cabinets, two chairs, a coatrack, and a desk, also green. The cubicle walls do not go all the way up to the ceiling. The back wall, above the height of the cubicle, is a dark brown-black and covered with exposed ductwork. The blackness does go all the way up.

"So, you want to go to lunch?" Glitter said. She was wearing tiers and layers of hand-painted lavender-rose chiffon, spangled with fugitive rhinestones. Her pumps were a violent purple.

I took a deep breath. "I got something back for you, but I don't want to talk about it yet, okay?"

I handed her the package. She knew what it was the moment she touched it, but tore at it until she'd opened a corner of the wrapping just to be sure. Purple lamé showed.

"It's my book," Glitter said in an airless voice. She stared at me, open-mouthed, and then at the neat burden of similar parcels in my bag. She sat down behind her desk, clutching her book. After a moment she collected herself and put it into her bottom drawer.

"Ned Skelton got whacked last night," she said. "Maura told me, 'cause I knew him. He'd come to my place a couple times. With Ilona, you know? He wanted to join a group. I was the one who told Belle about him."

I waited. I couldn't see where this conversation was going. *Whacked?*

"It was a very professional job," Glitter went on. "Close up and a little gun. .22 or .25, they think. Right at the back of the head."

I didn't think I wanted to hear this.

"And we all heard Ned at the picnic," Glitter said, talking to the top of her desk. She threw up her hands. "Oh my god, I can't do this!"

I finally saw where the conversation was going. I sat down, feeling as if she'd punched me.

"You think Ned stole your book." Which, as a matter of fact, he had, but never mind. "You think I killed him to get it back?" This was far stupider and more unfair. My voice rose indignantly.

"No, no, no." Glitter waved her hands very fast. "Just took something from the crime scene where you maybe were. That's all. For Goddess's sake, Bast, I don't think you'd *kill* somebody!"

Probably hung heavy in the air. Sometimes I wonder what my enemies think of me, considering the opinions my friends have.

"Glitter, you are a wonderful human being, but—go. Write novels," I said. "Have a rich, full, emotional life."

I could have explained it all—the package Ned asked me to hold (for the receipt of which I, comfortingly, had witnesses), the phone call, the ruined city and fair Helen dead, but I didn't want to tell her about any part of last night. Glitter is an officer of the court, and while she is flexible about most things, she isn't about some things. If I actually had to talk to the police, I wanted to do it on my own initiative.

She sat back. "Sorry," she muttered. "It's this job. You look for reasons. And there aren't any. But where—"

"I can't tell you that," I said. I wasn't sure why. Damage control. Or maybe I was trying to gear myself up for a career of outlawry.

"So, lunch?" Glitter said finally, after I hadn't said anything for a while.

I shrugged, a woman of few words and many gestures. "Some things to do," I said. "I'll see you later."

She walked me out. There were the tenderings of explanations in my future—I could see that—but just now, the way I had last night, I was buying time.

I wasn't quite sure why. But I knew there were things I had to do before the reckoning came.

There's one place where all the lines of communication in the Community cross: the Snake—or rather, the Snake's manager. Julian.

Julian is a ritual magician, a scholar of magic and its history, and one of the more closemouthed people alive. This does not mean that he does not hear things. As if to Rick's Café Americain, everybody eventually comes to the Snake.

And Julian would know whose books these were and how to return them. If I was lucky, he'd even leave my name out of it.

I got up to the Snake around one o'clock and was glad to see the store was open — the Snake's hours tend to be rather whimsical. I passed under the neon sign, slid around the blessedly silent Elvis jukebox (it was blocking the doorway even more than usual), and walked in. As far as the naked eye could see, the place was deserted.

The shop smelled resinously of burned incense; a haze of frankincense hung in the air like a set-dressing special effect. I looked around and spotted the source in front of the Snake's ecumenialtar, the one that started life as a birdbath that'd had a heavy date with *Primavera*. The shell part is usually full of pennies (this being a retail establishment) or flowers. Today it was full of hot charcoal and about half a pound of expensive resin busily transforming itself into blue smoke. I went on, past the case full of crystal balls and ancient Egyptian meteorites and genuine Lady of the Lake chalices. The Siege Perilous was deserted, and something about that nagged at me, even in my current preoccupied state.

I had the growing conviction that I was being led down the garden path, round Robin Hood's barn, and up to a conclusion I was supposed to jump to without understanding. In short, I had the feeling that my subconscious mind knew what was going on and I didn't.

I hate that.

I was halfway down the right aisle when I saw the secret bookcase swing out. I nipped around the end of the rack and surprised Julian coming out of the back room. He had an open book in one hand and looked like a pensive divine. He glanced up and saw me. The corners of his mouth quirked upward ever so slightly.

"I suppose you know why I'm here," I said, which was not what I'd meant to say.

"You've come to see our new look?" Julian said blandly.

I looked appropriately puzzled. The bag on my shoulder was getting heavier. Julian watched me not get it, and finally explained.

"Somebody tried to break into the Snake last night," he said.

Religious tolerance and the gentle art of minding one's own business being what they are, the Snake receives an average of one editorial declaration per week from people who just can't bear its existence one moment longer. More, if you count the phone threats.

These declarations range from pamphlets advocating the religion of your choice stuffed in the door, to bricks and bullets aimed at the window. The window has been replaced twice—to the best of my knowledge—in the time I've been going to the Snake.

I followed Julian up to the front of the shop.

We got to the front door. Julian pushed the jukebox back, and I saw what it had been hiding.

He'd lied.

Tried to break in was not truth in advertising.

Whoever it was that had paid the Serpent's Truth a visit last night had gotten the padlock off the outside gate and then gone after the door with a wood chisel. There were long flat gouges all down the red-over-green-over-blue-over-white paint, but those were only hesitation marks, really. Eventually whoever it was had found his angle, and there were deep, competent cuts into the door around the lock-plate exposing new white wood. It looked like performance art by Beavers With Attitude.

"The alarm went off and the service called me and then Tris, but—" Julian shrugged. "At least they didn't do too much damage."

"What did they get?" I asked, before I could stop myself. The urge to meddle is strong, even though I've never done myself any good by it yet.

"They went straight for the grimoires," Julian said.

I looked up at the locked glass case behind the cash register and Julian's Siege Perilous, where the really, *really* expensive part of the Snake's inventory is kept. Most of it is first or rare editions of occult books—like an 1801 edition of Francis Barrett's *The Magus* with marginalia, or a signed copy of *White Stains*—but sometimes a limited-run tarot deck or a piece of jewelry will be added to the collection.

It wasn't there.

I realized why the front of the shop had looked so odd to me when I came in. No cabinet.

It was on the floor, propped against the wall. The doors of the cabinet had been sheared cleanly off, leaving small whorls of pale splinters where the hinges had used to be. The shelves, usually jammed, were bare.

I would say that the contents of that one cabinet represent about fifteen to twenty-five thousand dollars of the Snake's total inventory.

"Damn," I said. "I'm sorry."

"That's life in the big city," Julian said. "Someone went on a spree. Weiser's and Mirror Mirror were hit up, too."

Weiser's, Mirror Mirror, and the Snake are all occult bookstores. They are also the only three occult bookstores in New York that have a rare books section.

"Last night," I said. Julian nodded once.

Which gave Ned Skelton the best alibi anyone ever had, not that he needed it. The BoS thefts had been done by someone who knew the Community pretty well, who laughed at locks and went through them as if they weren't there. He did not chop his way in with an ax.

It wasn't—I dredged up terminology from my leisure reading— it wasn't the same M.O., even if it had the same sort of Wonderland illogic to it as Ned's had.

For example, who would break into the Snake and not even smash anything? When Chanter's Revel, a feminist Wicca store in the East Village, got tossed last year the burglars didn't take anything, but they totaled all the merchandise they could get their hands on.

Here, they'd only stolen the rare books. Why?

It wasn't for their arcane secrets; almost everything in that case was available as cheap reprints.

It wasn't for the money; you couldn't resell those books for anything like what they'd cost retail. If it was a straightforward robbery for gain, why had they taken the books and left the gold and silver jewelry? If they had—but Julian'd said they went "straight for the grimoires," and the jewelry cases looked typically cluttered.

I wondered if the pattern was the same at Weiser's and Mirror Mirror.

"What are you going to do?" I asked Julian.

"Call the insurance company. Prove what we paid for them. Get half of it back." Julian shrugged and shoved the jukebox back into place. He looked strange in the afternoon sunlight; Julian is a creature of night and shadows.

I recalled finally that I had another purpose for being here.

"Would you do something for me?" I asked Julian. *Like help me get some stolen property back to its rightful owners.*

I knew he did this sort of thing because I'd had it done for me once. Or maybe *to* me would be more accurate.

Julian stopped looking at the door and looked at me.

"There are some packages," I said carefully, "that I would like to see get to their proper destinations. I think most of the recipients come in here."

I waited. Julian waited. Or maybe he was thinking. He turned away and stepped up to the Siege Perilous. He quirked a finger and I followed him.

The reason that the Siege Perilous is raised up is so that the person sitting at it can clearly see both aisles and most of the rest of the retail floor of the store. I regarded the empty aisles and swung my carryall up onto the table. I pulled out the books.

Julian sorted through them. He piled Xharina's and Amyntor's and Lorelli's brown-paper-wrappedbooks in one corner. He hesitated over Crystal, then piled her and Otterleaf and Diana-27 in a second pile.

"I don't know them," Julian said, which meant you'd have to go a long way to find anyone who did.

"Any clues?" I said. "Crystal works Faery in Fort Lee. Otterleaf's a Gardnerian."

His brow cleared. He retrieved Crystal's package and wrote "Doreen" on it with a large soft pencil, then added it to the first pile. I was touched at the special effort he was making for me, or possibly he felt that all those good customers and true would show their gratitude at these returns by overspending.

"You can find Otterleaf yourself," Julian said reprovingly, which was true, although it'd probably mean going to Freya.

Freya is Belle's Queen—the woman who brought her into the Craft—a very public woman from a very public family who manages to avoid most of the woo-woo associated with the public profession of Wicca and Goddess-worship by simply being far too cool for anyone to ask her stupid questions. She's also almost never home.

"Yeah, right," I said.

I put the two he hadn't ID'd—Otterleaf's and Diana-27's—back into my bag. Belle might be able to place both of them and get the books back to them, but then again she'd probably tell their recipients where she'd gotten them, Belle being incurably forthright and a rebuke to us all.

While Julian loved nothing more than mystery, and would probably delight in keeping my name out of things.

I shouldn't like that, but I do.

"Anything else?" Julian asked. He sounded like the chief devil in a Restoration farce.

Why did someone break in here after grimoires? Is it tied to Ilona's death? Here, and Weiser's, and Mirror Mirror are the only three places in the city that stock antique occult books, and who-

ever it was hit all three. How did he know? What is he after? Do you know who he is? Would you tell me if you did?

"No. Nothing," I said.

Wednesday. Two-forty-five. I made it up the stairs and behind my own locks alive, which is a triumph of a sort here in Fun City. And every year it gets harder.

Twentieth-century occult thought holds that the major population centers are a generation ahead of the rest of the world—or, what New York is now, Tulsa, Oklahoma, will be in twenty years.

Makes you long to see what 2015'll be like at Fourth Street and Sixth, doesn't it?

I tried Belle again. She was still out. Which was annoying, considering how much I wanted to talk to her.

It's not that I run to Belle with every little thing. But this was not a little thing. This was theft—crazy, extensive, and stupid. It might even be connected to murder, an explicit, real-world murder that our friends the police were even now investigating. I wanted to know what she thought, what she knew, what she'd heard.

I wanted to shove the responsibility onto someone else so that I wasn't even a psychic accessory-beside-the-fact to Ned Skelton's life. Backward, turn backward, O time in thy flight. But childhood was a long time gone.

My apartment was airless, but not yet an oven. I got the fan down from where it lives the rest of the year and propped it in the window and turned it on, facing out. Air began sliding through.

From the hag and hungry goblin, that into rags would rend ye / All the spirits that stand by the Naked Man in The Book of Moons defend ye.

I stretched out on the bed, tried to think about *The Book of Moons,* and fell asleep.

The phone woke me. It was hours later, and the temperature had dropped to where I was shivering. I hoped it was Belle calling back, but it wasn't. I picked up anyway as the caller began leaving a message.

"Hi, Stuart," I said, just as if I were a normal person.

"Hello," he said. His voice was sultry and edged, like good Scotch. "I was wondering if you'd care to have dinner with me this evening?"

Oh, Jesus, no! my mind said, while my mouth said, "Sure, Stuart, that'd be great." I regarded the phone with the horrified feeling you have when the car's front wheels leave the paving, but it transmitted my words without editorial comment.

"That's lovely, then," Stuart said. "Why don't we meet somewhere and go on from there? What about the Russian Tea Room?"

I laughed out of sheer nerves, though he couldn't know why I found the suggestion funny. "I'm off things Russian," I said, feeling all my old heterosexual diplomacy skills come raging back. My turn to curtsey, your turn to bow.

"Top of the Sixes, then?" he said.

I blinked. According to the formal Rules of Engagement that govern dating, if you decline the first suggestion made for where to go you have to accept the second one, since two refusals imply lack of interest.

But the Top of the Sixes is an authentic New York Legend located at 666 Fifth Avenue and has commanded a panoramic top-floor view of New York City for lo these many years. It is expensive. Very, very expensive. Either Stuart had been struck independently wealthy or was expecting more out of this evening than I thought he was going to get.

I mentally reviewed my wardrobe, wondering if I even owned anything I could wear there. Nothing to wear was a valid justification for negotiation.

"Sweetheart?"

"Huh? I mean sure, great. When?" Why was my mouth doing this to me?

"Perhaps an hour?"

"Oh, yeah, fine, sure," I said, with the immense suavity that characterizes my dealings with real grown-ups.

Stuart swore he was looking forward to seeing me and also to a delightful evening, which I thought was more optimism than the English are generally credited with. I put the phone down and stared at it.

I'd agreed to go out on a date to the Top of the Sixes with a man I'd barely met and hardly knew. I ran a quick sanity check and found all systems stable.

I realized that I was going to enjoy this evening. It would be the tonic antithesis of murdered booksellers, *The Book of Moons,* and all the byzantine Community politics that were beginning to grate on my nerves. It would be awkward and tense, possibly expensive, almost certainly mortifying in spots, and would leave me feeling massively incapable of coping with the innocent social interactions of our culture.

It would also be normal. Supremely normal. It was a date, a thing that everybody did—people who had never heard of the Goddess or Mary, Queen of Scots, people who had never known someone who'd been killed, people who had never been handed a dead man's legacy to return, people who owned televisions and didn't live in a coffin-shaped and coffin-sized apartment on the edge of Alphabet City.

People who owned suitable clothing for the occasion.

I got up, shoved my hair out of my eyes, and went to my closet.

I own any number of clothing items, including skirts (most in basic black), but only two dresses: the Laura Ashley print that makes me look like an escapee from a Burne-Jones painting and a lined black linen sheath that unfortunately does not make me look like Audrey Hepburn but does allow me to state truthfully that I have a dress from Sak's, even if bought on sale. I could also field an envelope clutch and shoes that matched each other and the dress.

Fine.

Half an hour later I was standing in front of my mirror smudging my eye sockets in with expensive *grisalle* powder the purchase of which (if not the use) is one of my few unjustifiable vices, realizing that I owned no jewelry that went with the dress and that if I spent much more time worrying about it I was going to be late. I left the silver studs in my back piercings and put big silver crescents in the front ones and decided I was understatedly elegant. Time to go.

Wearing a dress in my neighborhood made me feel vulnerable and out of place, as though I were somehow out of contact with the ground. I decided on yet another in a series of taxis, but they don't come down into my locality much. I walked across the Bowery and got lucky, snagging one cruising Lower Broadway. I got to Top of the Sixes a little after seven.

I did not belong here. The sense of inappropriateness was as seductive as a drug.

The first thing you see when you walk into Top of the Sixes is a wall of glass looking out over the city. Sunset turns every visible window into a mirror flashing back gold sunset light, and down below the streets are already in shadow, even though the sky is light. It's a stage set, meant for after the theater, for later evening, for someone I wasn't and didn't want to be.

But the power to be this far from my proper place was, all side issues aside, power. And, as Lord Acton said, power delights, and absolute power is absolutely delightful.

I was not in a harmless mind-set.

The wait-staff elicited the information that I was waiting for someone, which seemed, somehow, to relieve them. I was installed on a real leather end stool in front of an intimidating sweep of mirror and mahogany, where I allowed a bartender to pour me a Scotch on the rocks for seven-fifty. I set my purse on the edge of the bar and felt that someone ought to offer to light the cigarette I wasn't smoking. Ah, expectation.

I sat and read the labels on the expensive booze and admired the pretheater diners and the collection of people who thought nothing of coming to the Top of the Sixes for a drink before dinner and marveled at the infinite diversity of human society. How lovely it is to have money, as the song goes.

It was a good thing that I found so much to amuse myself with, because Stuart didn't make an appearance. Seven-thirty became eight. I ordered another drink and tried not to feel the twitch from that old bad girly-girl hardwiring: *he* boots it and it's *your* fault. Prepackaged inferiority.

But he *had* said Top of the Sixes and he *had* said seven. I sat there, giddy with disrupted sleep patterns and emotional dressage and the sublimated terror of unconnectedness. Possibly everyone else felt this way all the time. Maybe that was why they were here. Maybe that was why all of twentieth-century culture was here.

And what about Mary Stuart? my mind demanded.

I wasn't surprised to be thinking of her. It's like that old Discordian koan: "All things happen in fives, or are divisible by or are multiples of five, or are somehow directly or indirectly appropriate to five . . . depending on the ingenuity of the observer."

Mary was my five. Mary, Mary, quite contrary, who, if she *was* a Witch, knew when she went to the block that her co-religionists had abandoned her, the latest in a long series of abandonments, jiltings, and betrayals.

Speaking of which—

At eight-forty-five I decided that Stuart had either stood me up or been unavoidably delayed, and I wasn't going to invest any emotion in either possibility until I found out which it was. We are all so modern and reasonable here at the end of the millennium.

I settled the bill and got ready to go. So far the evening was living up to expectations—embarrassing and expensive. Nobody paid any attention to me, but then, nobody would. This is New York's great gift to the neurotic: anonymity.

I'm not neurotic, but I try to keep up with my friends' interests.

It was dark outside; the place looked less surreal. There are things meant to be seen only in darkness that exist, anticlimactically, in the light of day. Like Julian.

Who I was supposed to be banishing from my consciousness with this little exercise.

I returned to the elevator. It opened. I recognized Stuart before he recognized me.

"What— Good heavens, sweetheart, I didn't even see you!"

He was wearing a suit and tie, which added to my sense of unreality. I don't know people who dress like that.

"Hello, Stuart," I said. "You're late," I added.

He looked cross that I'd mentioned it and contrite all at the same time, which was amusing, but probably not amusing enough to make me continue the evening any further.

"Oh, you poor girl—you must be starved. Come on, let's go get dinner. Give me a chance to explain. There's a little place around the corner."

He took my arm. I didn't like it but I didn't object. My mistake.

The technical name for Stuart's little maneuver is bait and switch, but the consolation prize was hushed and elegant, three blocks away, and so self-effacing and dimly lit that I wasn't quite sure what its name was. The decor seemed to run to polished copper implements, leather, and wooden ducks in various states of preservation. We were ushered directly to a booth, suggesting that this was where Stuart had been heading all along. Leather menus the size of solar panels were tendered unto us. I discovered that the restaurant's name was Sandalford's and the entrées started at $22.50. Stuart asked me what I was drinking.

"Perrier with a chunk," I said, feeling it would not be a good idea to send a third Scotch to live with the other two just yet. Stuart ordered a double Bushmill's, no ice. His shirt had French cuffs and his cufflinks were gold lions' heads. Very fancy. I wondered if they were Scottish lions.

"You must think I'm a perfectly dreadful person," Stuart said charmingly, in a fashion that encouraged me to disagree.

"Not yet," I said.

I am not easily charmed. Neither am I anyone's sweetheart, baby, darling, or poor girl, which you may consider a moral failing on my part, if you like. Stuart was oh-so-subtly pushing me around—manipulating me, if you prefer—a practice of which I disapprove.

"I tried to reach you, but you'd already left," he said. Winsomely. There was something underneath the winsomeness, some dark current of self-congratulation that interested me; I'm not trophy enough that possession of me would engender it. "I was just about to pop out the door myself when *les gendarmes* appeared upon the horizon." He raised his eyebrows, inviting sympathy.

"What?" I said blankly.

"The police," Stuart amplified. He shrugged. "I'd already told them everything I know, but apparently something new had come up and things had changed." He finished his drink and called for another with a practiced flick of the finger. "I don't mind telling you, I'm quite at the end of my tether. What a horror."

"You had to talk to the police," I said, wondering if I'd heard him correctly.

"Well, of course," Stuart said. "Ilona was my aunt; they usually want to talk to the family. I'd ask you to the funeral, but I'm having the body shipped home, and—"

I was suddenly far beyond sober, in the nauseated nightmare realm of three A.M. awakenings poisoned with adrenaline, among jagged annunciations that it takes years of practice to learn not to reject.

Stuart was Ilona's nephew.

Ilona had been supposed to come to the picnic on Sunday with her nephew, her new partner.

But Stuart had come alone, with never a mention about Ilona to me or anyone else.

Why?

If she'd been alive, he would have brought her. If she couldn't come, he would have made her excuses. Ilona was a lady of the old school. She had manners. She would have sent her regrets.

If she were alive.

If she was dead, what kind of lunatic would register that fact and then go on to his next social engagement?

Ilona had died sometime Saturday night. She'd been going to bring him to the picnic; they would have met at her place or his. He must have known she was dead, all the time I was talking to him that Sunday.

What kind of lunatic . . . ?

"Bast, darling, are you all right? You look a bit illish," Stuart said.

"Bad drug reaction," I said automatically. The fresh drink arrived.

"Look, I can't go on calling you by that ridiculous name," Stuart said. "You must have a real name somewhere." He put his hand over mine and I realized he was trying to pry my purse out of my fingers. "Let's see what it is." Playfully.

"I suppose Lothlorien is yours now," I said, tightening my fingers on my purse.

"Yes, of course," Stuart said, letting go of my hand. "The will has yet to be proved, but as far as I know I'm her only relative; in fact, she'd asked me to became a partner in that bookstore of hers. I don't know what I'll do with the place. Sell the books, I expect. I suppose they're worth a bit."

"In the right market," I said. My brain was occupied with how to get out of here before I asked Stuart why he'd killed Ilona.

And Ned. The killer of one had to be the killer of the other, because he was after *The Book of Moons*.

Because it was worth a lot of money and it was an old family heirloom and Ilona had been going to sell an old family heirloom to finance Lothlorien but Ned had stolen *The Book of Moons* just like he'd stolen all the other Books of Shadows—

And I had *The Book of Moons* now.

"I know it sounds rather callous and mercenary of me to be reckoning up pounds-shillings-pence so soon, but I hadn't seen her in years, really," Stuart said.

"Excuse me," I said to Stuart. I stood up. He stood up. I fled.

The bathroom at Sandalford's is pink and extensive, with decor dropped down from another manqué: black and pink with glazed and sandblasted lilies, savagely retro and antiseptic. I looked in the mirror and saw a scared raccoon, painted and blue-eyed, teetering on the edge of cobbling together a real-world explanation for her terror, denying the fact that it was a reasonable response to the acquisition of information she could not possibly possess.

I was certain of Stuart's accountability in the murders, even while I shied away and tried to find alternative justifications for my feelings.

I was just spooked at going out on a date. Sure.

No. There was something wrong here. But if I clung to my conviction of Stuart Hepburn's homicide I'd simply talk myself out of it and walk back out onto the killing floor.

I took a deep breath and closed my eyes. What was wrong? Don't ask for specifics: magic is an analog system, not digital. I breathed deeply and sorted through my last half hour with Stuart. Something wrong. Forget murder. Cool premeditated murder was too grandiose to easily believe in.

But violence was not. There was something odd, unreasonable, unreal, forced, faked in Stuart's behavior. Something that didn't fit into the continuum of two casual meetings and the suggestion of dinner.

Stuart was setting me up.

I did not have to believe he'd killed two people to accept that warning. His character fault might be something as mundane and ugly as a taste for date rape. I didn't have to stay to find out what it was. The only question remaining was how to leave.

People die every year from the fear of looking stupid. At least when you're a Witch you have enough experience at looking stupid that you know it won't, of itself, kill you.

I walked back out to the table. Stuart stood up.

"I've already ordered," he said. "When you didn't come back, I—"

"Stuart," I said, interrupting. "This is not working out. I'm sorry about the police, but I'm leaving now. Good-bye."

He grabbed for my arm, but there was a table between us and I was expecting it. I moved fast, aceing the restaurant traffic with elite New York pedestrian chops. Stuart was tangled with waiters and explanations, unable to follow.

I reached the outside air and ran down the first subway steps I saw.

It took me a while to get out of the area and to transfer to a line going somewhere I wanted to go, and by that time it was as easy to take the Uptown A as it was to do anything else.

By now it was rising ten. So far today I'd been accused of murder by Glitter, conspired in occult psychodrama with Julian, taken a fling at being a yuppie and spent twenty dollars for two Scotches at Top of the Sixes, and almost had dinner with the real murderer.

Now that I was away from him I could go back to believing it, and the more I thought about it, the more it all made a horrible Agatha Christie kind of sense.

All it took was one leap of unproven faith: that Ilona Saunders, expatriate Brit, had *The Book of Moons,* a family heirloom, the (reluctantly chosen) sale of which was going to save Lothlorien.

Maybe she consulted with Stuart about selling it. He'd said she'd offered him a partnership. I wondered with a sudden intense yearning for knowledge what it was that Stuart did for his day job that allowed him to possess those lovely suits and gold cufflinks and familiarity with posh eateries. The proceeds from the sale of *The Book of Moons* could enhance a lifestyle like that: make it possible, or make its continuation possible.

But when the time came to show *The Book of Moons* to her nephew and new partner, Stuart Hepburn, Ilona didn't have it. Because Ned Skelton, her part-time clerk, whose other job it was to go in and out of strangers' apartments with his set of master passkeys, had branched out, entering many apartments and carefully removing from each an item that was valueless except to the Witch who had written it — or to someone who desperately wanted the moral validity that being Wiccan would give him: the Books of Shadows.

So Ned stole Ilona's book among his other thefts. *The Book of Moons.* Mary's book. The one thing that tied all of this together: the McGuffin, without which, as the saying goes, one cannot hunt tigers in Scotland.

The subway arrived at my destination. I crossed Dyckman. Belle had better be home this time.

Belle's apartment is on the fifth floor of an end building overlooking High Bridge Park, and the landlord has been intermittently trying to get her to move out for years. The place has four bedrooms, no furniture to speak of, and a door chime and sound system courtesy of The Cat, whose motto is Better Living Through Technology.

My shoes made wounded gazelle rhythms across the lobby and up five flights of stairs. The doorbell's selection this month sampled the "Mars Movement" from Holst's *The Planets* as played on the glockenspiel. I leaned on it for a while. Eventually Belle came to the peephole.

"Bast?" she said, as if there were hundreds of people out there in Fun City impersonating me.

"Yeah," I said. "I need to tell you something."

Normal people use the phone, or E-mail, or at least don't come banging on other people's doors at eleven o'clock at night unannounced. Belle is used to the differently normal. She let me in. She did not say, "What are you got up as?" because Belle's acceptance is all-encompassing.

She was wearing a yellow terry-cloth bathrobe, a garment that makes her look like an enormous baby chicken. She went to put on tea. The kitchen light was the only light in the apartment.

I wandered around the living room. There were seashells and crystals and candles on the windowsills, a "lives alone with no cats" clutter. Belle doesn't have any living room curtains, and in the dark her collection of colored suncatchers looked dull against the glass. A car swung up Riverside, and in the shine of its headlights I saw that it had started to rain.

I sat down on Belle's emotional rescue couch, the piece of furniture on which more Pagan New Yorkers have had crises than any other. The light from the kitchen made a yellowish trapezoid against the bare wood floor.

Belle came in and sat down next to me. "Glitter called me," she said.

"Ned gave me a box to hold for him," I said. "Look, do you still know that guy in the police?"

"Lieutenant Hodiac?" Belle said.

One of Belle's outreach functions is being Wicca advisor to the police. As far as I can determine, this involves going downtown and identifying pieces of jewelry and photographs of strange designs about four times a year and sorting out the difference between Wicca and rock music in the police mind.

"Whoever," I said.

"Bast, what are you—?" Belle said.

"I'm losing my last marble. Look. This is not a good day. I need to tell you a story, and then you tell me what I do with it."

"Okay," Belle said, looking worried. She went and got the tea, and some cookies that were still left over from the picnic. I took one and was about to bite it until I remembered that Ned had brought cookies that day and maybe these were those. I set it back down and sipped my tea.

"Ilona Saunders and Ned Skelton are dead," I said, as carefully specific as if I were arguing a case. "You remember what happened at the picnic; Ned's announcement and all. The next day I heard Ilona was dead, and then—the same day—Ned asked me to hold a package for him. That was Monday.

"Tuesday night around five-thirty he called and told me he'd been burgled Monday late sometime. He wanted a banishing ritual done on the place, you know? I left right away, but by the time I got there they were putting him into the ambulance. Shot dead, Glitter said today. In the back of the head with something small."

Belle put her hand over mine. I held it.

"What was in the box?" she said.

"Books. Books of Shadows. All the ones he stole. Glitter's. Everyone's. He was a building super; he had passkeys for all the standard locks. He asked me not to open it, or ask what was in it, but he was dead so I did. I've got—"

I realized that I didn't have Diana-27 and Otterleaf's books with me. "There are two of them I need your help to get back to their owners."

"And he left the box with you on Monday?" Belle said.

"What, you think he did it Tuesday after he died?" I snapped. I let go of her hand. I drank my tea and jittered.

"I'm just trying to figure out what's going on here and how I can help," Belle said soothingly.

"What's going on is I almost had dinner with the guy who clocked both him and Ilona and the reason he did it is sitting in my studio." I stood up. I wandered. I leaned against the windowsill. "I'm trying to make a straight story out of this," I complained, "and it keeps getting all tangled up."

"Just tell it any way you need to. You seem awfully upset," Belle said.

My HPS, the mistress of tactful understatement.

"He must have started doing it in April. Maybe Glitter's was the first, and then when we didn't call him to join Changing he stole all the others. Ned. I heard about it at the picnic—the missing books, I mean. *That* there were missing books," I amplified carefully. "Glitter was right all along. She didn't lose it, she didn't misplace it. Ned took it. He went up to Glitter's apartment with Ilona for dinner, and he came back and took it. They knew each other;

you gave him the look-see because Glitter asked you to. That's why you asked me to dinner instead of her—she couldn't be objective."

Belle nodded. I came back and sat down, feeling my way through the explanation.

"Ned was stealing Books of Shadows because he wanted to be a Witch and nobody'd initiate him. Apparently he'd been around the track a couple of times: Reisha, Maidjene, Xharina, Lorelli—he'd worked with plenty of people in the Community and nobody'd give him a tumble. He knew where they lived; he went in on his keys and got their books—only he didn't think of himself as a thief; he didn't take anything else. He stole their books," I repeated, "but that didn't get him what he really wanted." I held up a hand, just as if Belle were about to interrupt, which she wasn't.

"But then—I'm guessing, but it all fits—he took something out of Lothlorien. *The Book of Moons.*"

Belle frowned disbelievingly.

"Ask Beaner," I said. "The building'd been sold, her rent'd been raised, she was going to have to go, except she told us she was going to buy the building. She could afford to, she said, because she'd made up her mind to sell an old family heirloom. *The Book of Moons*—Mary, Queen of Scots's, Book of Shadows."

Damned, doomed, dazzled Mary—whose bare name, four centuries later, caused people to turn off their common sense.

"Bast," Belle said patiently, "if a major historical figure had been a Witch, we'd know. You don't believe—"

"Money," I said.

Belle looked at me.

"I have seen this book," I enunciated clearly. "It can be one of three things. It can be real, it can be a forgery of the period, or it can be a modern forgery. If it is modern, it is a good enough fake to be taken for old, which means it is worth money. Hitler-diaries money. Jack-the-Ripper diaries money—and it doesn't matter if both of those were faked; they were front-page news and million-dollar auctions. Enough to buy full-bore Manhattan real estate. Forget Mary. I don't care what *The Book of Moons* really is. It doesn't matter what it really is, when what it is, is money."

Belle sighed, and I realized then that I'd lost her. Maybe it was unfair of me to want her to believe on my bare say-so, when I'd had all the days since the picnic and the chance to hold *The Book of Moons* in my hands to help convince me.

That, and seeing Stuart's eyes.

"Maybe it sounds unlikely. But it's true."

Belle sighed. "I know *you* think of it as true," she said, trying to be kind.

That hurt. Belle looked at me and then padded off to the kitchen. She came back with a glass full of wine that looked like grape jelly and tasted (I knew from experience) like cough syrup. I set it down untasted.

Elitism is the stalking horse of American culture. Critics are automatically elitists, beginning the moment they say that something is better than something else. In our headlong rush to throw down an aristocracy that has not existed in two centuries, we avow hysterically that everything is not only as good as everything else, but *is*, in fact, everything else.

But when everything is everything, how do you define anything?

I didn't want to be the only one to see things the way I saw them. No one is that secure. But I wasn't going to say I didn't see them, either.

"She would not say she was not married when she was." Catherine of Aragon. Another queen, another adjudicated destruction. Paths of glory lead only to the grave.

"Where is this book now?" Belle asked finally.

"Wrapped up like the others, sitting at the studio," I said, forgetting that Diana-27's and Otterleaf's were at my apartment. "But you aren't interested in my theories. I'm sorry I bothered you."

The more I thought about Belle's remark—mild, really—the angrier I got. Either because it was true, or because she thought it was true, or because I needed to be angry.

"Who'd you get all dressed up for?" Belle asked.

"Stuart Hepburn." I stood up. "The man who killed Ilona Saunders and Ned Skelton. For the book. For money."

"What makes you say that?"

She was treating me like a patient; standing back and reserving judgment. But I hadn't come here for that. I'd come for a partisan, a friend, someone who believed the things I did.

But I already knew she didn't.

I'd thought we'd patched up our friendship. I'd thought things were going to be the same between us. I knew that Belle'd thought so too.

We'd both been wrong.

Why had I come here?

"Don't fucking patronize me; I'm going home." I felt enormously tired; alone and betrayed, which was gothic adolescent nonsense. I wasn't betrayed. Not yet.

"What did you think I could do?" Belle asked in her best psychiatrist voice, meaning *"Don't you think this is a lot of trouble to go to just to get out of a date?"*

"Tell your cop friend Hodiac that Stuart Hepburn had a motive. Ilona Saunders was his aunt, and his aunt Ilona claimed to have a family heirloom and turned up dead. Ned, who stole Books of Shadows for a hobby, stole *The Book of Moons* and wound up dead. I think that *The Book of Moons* and Ilona's heirloom are the same thing and the only person who could trace that connection is Stuart Hepburn and I'm the one with the thing now so could we please tell the police?"

"It makes more sense if Ned killed Ilona to get the book—by accident," Belle said.

"Then who killed Ned—and why?"

Ned would not kill someone for gain and then brag about his spoils later. I felt very protective of Ned, now that he was dead. He had no one else to speak for him now, to tell them that he'd meant well, or at least not as badly as things had come out. All his history and the bubble reputation that he'd sought (not in the cannon's mouth, but in living rooms like this one) were in my wardship now. There was no one else left to care.

"Bast, sometimes things just happen," Belle said helplessly. "You think that by weaving it all together into some enormous plot that only you can see, you can control it—"

"Sure. I'm sorry to take up your time." I headed for the door.

"Bast," Belle said, *"Karen."*

I stopped and looked back. Belle was invoking Karen Hightower, but she herself had helped me turn Karen into Lady Bast of the Wicca a lifetime ago. The woman she was calling—that woman's way of seeing things—no longer existed.

The lighting carved Belle's face, making her look the way she would when she was old. Once we had both believed the same things. She was the woman who had trained me. How could our internal landscapes have become so divergent?

"You don't need to mythologize your life," Belle said. "All of this criminal conspiracy—it's something you superimpose on what happens. It isn't *real.* People die. People are killed. There don't have to be reasons."

And Ned wasn't dead, nor Ilona. Possibly I didn't have an antique real-or-forged Book of Shadows on my shelf at work. I should have remembered that Belle, Lady Bellflower of the Wicca, did not believe in magic.

But she had, once. She'd told me that magic could transform the world. Which of us had changed? When had it happened?

"Stuart Hepburn had knowledge, opportunity, connection, and motive for two murders. I wish you'd find it in your heart to mention it to somebody at the police, Belle, because it's going to sound very weird coming in off the street from me. But I will."

"I think—" Belle said.

"Good night," I said. I opened the door and closed it, and as I walked down the hall I heard Belle locking up after me.

I sat in the subway heading downtown and felt cold, tired, and stupid. If Belle didn't know who I was, why did I think I was anything more than a figment of my imagination?

Too little sleep. Too little food. I'd missed dinner, and I couldn't remember having lunch, actually. I still thought I was right, but it'd been stupid to go to Belle's. What could she do?

It was weird to accuse Belle of judgmentalism, but in a way it was true. Belle wouldn't pass judgment on people, but she would judge events. And she had judged my events impossible, therefore she refused to see them.

It was, it occurred to me suddenly, the same reason Belle does not do magic, though once upon a time she'd at least talked about doing it. Magic is a part of Wicca, from the magical worldview to the spells braided into our daily lives, but Changing does no magic beyond visualization. A coven created in Belle's image.

As all covens reflect the worldview of those who form them. This was not news. And I was going to have to deal with Belle, and my anger at Belle, later. Right now I had to deal with reality. And perceptions of reality.

Cold on my bare arms. Unforgiving hard orange plastic seat sticky against the backs of my nylon-stockinged thighs. Fluorescent lighting turning my skin fish-belly white. This was reality.

Perception is a seduction. The willingness to see has to exist before anything can be seen, the encouragement of visualization that borders on the creation of phenomena without ever quite falling over the edge. To see you must be willing to see, and to place no limitations on what you may see.

The danger in that is that you may see what isn't there.

Was that how it had happened—the rift in the lute, which by and by makes the music mute? Had Belle and I, starting from the same place, both fine-tuned our perceptions of the world, hers to exclude magic, mine to include it? If two viewpoints contradict each other, mustn't one of them be right?

Or are both of them wrong?

Not in this case, I didn't think. The whole thing fitted together with a facility that was frightening. The events, at least, were real.

My mind flipped back to my first conversation with Stuart: "*I understand that the witchcult can trace its roots fairly far back,*" he'd said. He'd wanted information about Books of Shadows even then, but I'd been too blind to see it. He must have known almost nothing about *The Book of Moons* to begin with and been trying to get information at the picnic.

Had he seen Ned there—or heard him? Had he talked to Ned, somewhere in the dark hours before Ned's panic-stricken Monday call to me? Was that why Ned had left the books with me—to protect them from Stuart?

It made such a lovely plausible pattern.

Once upon a time, Ilona Saunders had a book. Say it was an Elizabethan forgery; it could be a forgery and known to be a forgery and still be incredibly valuable if it were four centuries old. She decided to sell it to save Lothlorien . . .

"*She's bringing someone with her. Nephew. New partner in Lothlorien,*" Glitter had told me. Her only living relative, Stuart had said tonight. If you make someone your partner, sometimes you tell them where the money's coming from.

The subway rocked, accelerating on the long express run down to Fifty-ninth Street. The money. *Cherchez la gelt.* And Stuart Hepburn, child of earls, might see no reason to plow such a chunk of capital back into the marginal bookstore that was all Ilona's heart.

Argument, as inevitable as gravity. I could hear his voice in my mind: "*Oh, don't talk a lot of rot, Auntie; no one cares about a place like this anymore. But this book of yours, this book is worth millions . . .*"

Where is it?

Where is it, Auntie, dear?

Let me see it . . .

A bright Beltane morning at Lothlorien Books. Stuart Hepburn, recently from England, has arrived, at Lothlorien to escort dear Aunt Ilona to Belle's picnic. It doesn't matter why or how the topic of *The Book of Moons* comes up, or why Stuart asks to see it. By May first, Ned has already stolen it—hadn't he told me Sunday morning when we were watching Morris dancers in the park that he had a surprise announcement to make at the picnic later in the day?

She tells him about the book. Stuart asks to see it. Is she willing? I could not imagine Ilona Saunders as anything other than forthright. She would produce it if she could.

But she couldn't.

The absence of the book must have been the cause for what came next—an accident that left Ilona dead, because why should Stuart kill her before he knew where the book was? If it was missing, they could look for it together, as allies. Or had things gone too far for that? But why kill at all when you can merely steal?

But something goes wrong and Ilona's dead. And try as he might, Stuart can't find *The Book of Moons* or a clue to its whereabouts anywhere in Lothlorien.

He could still have saved himself if he'd called the police then. Who knew?—if he'd called an ambulance immediately, Ilona Saunders might be alive today.

But he doesn't. Stuart Hepburn, murderer, leaves Ilona dead and goes looking for an alibi, for information—maybe even looking for Ned. Ned was Ilona's clerk. He was the next likely person to question.

And there was one thing I would bank on, the more I thought it over: Stuart *did* get to the picnic in time to hear Ned announce to everybody in earshot that he, Ned Skelton, had the grimore of Mary, Queen of Scots—Ilona's *Book of Moons.*

Did he mark Ned down for death then? Or was it later? Was he the burglar of Ned's apartment as well as the murderer? And why did Stuart kill *again* without proof that the book that was his ostensible goal could be gained by his actions?

I'd never know. But there was one thing I knew now: Stuart Hepburn did not act in good faith, not from the first moment I saw him. He mingled at the picnic, pumping all of us for information we didn't know we were giving. Looking for Ilona's book, for information about Ilona's book, for places such books could be found.

Maybe even trying to find out how seriously we Witches took Ned's claim, and if we would pay money for Ilona's treasure.

And presented himself as a seeker, without any of the round-

eyed wonder exhibited by new seekers who find the Craft. Stuart was determined to be unflappable, no matter how strange we were, because he wanted in . . .

That was the not-quite-rightness that had bothered me about him from the first. We are not mainstream, we of the Community, and you either love our weirdness or hate it. You do not ignore it as if it does not exist, not unless the stakes are very high indeed.

It took Stuart until Monday night to find out where Ned lived, or else to catch Ned's apartment empty. Assuming he was the burglar, he broke in looking for the book—only the book wasn't there either. I already had it. He came up dry.

So then he had to talk to Ned Tuesday night. Ned was frightened on Monday when he found out about Ilona, but he wasn't on Tuesday when he asked me to bless his apartment. Had he talked to Stuart in the meantime? Did Stuart convince him that he had nothing to fear? Stuart could be plausible; I was living proof of that.

So Stuart came to see Ned Tuesday night. And kill Ned Tuesday night. Frustration, or fear, or just covering his tracks; had Ned taunted him with the fact that *The Book of Moons* was beyond Stuart's reach?

But Stuart, for whatever reason, killed Ned without either getting what he had come for or even finding out where it was. And I was pretty sure that was what had happened, because that same night Weiser's, the Snake, and Mirror Mirror were broken into by someone who cleaned out their weird rare book sections.

Stuart.

Looking for *The Book of Moons* in the only other place he could think of. Finding nothing.

And then—and this new intuition made me slightly ill—coming back to his one inside informant on the witchcraft scene. Me. To dine and dazzle, looking for new leads.

Was the killer really Stuart? Who else could it be? There were too many indicators pointing in his direction.

Granted, Ilona's death could be the result of a random robbery that went wrong. But Ned was—what was Glitter's word for it?—professionally "whacked" within a ninety-minute early-evening window a full twenty-four hours after his apartment had been burgled.

Call that coincidence, too, if you're Belle. But answer a few questions first.

What was Ned's motive for leaving the package filled with Books of Shadows with me? For safekeeping? Why didn't he think his apartment was safe? How did he decide it wasn't safe *before* it was burgled? Did he know someone was going to break in?

And if he left the Books of Shadows with me so that I could return them, why include *The Book of Moons,* when he knew Ilona was dead? Who was I supposed to return it to? I certainly couldn't return it to the woman who had written it. Who was alleged to have written it. To Mary, doomed, manipulated Mary, thrown out of her French coven to die in a foreign homeland she could not remake in her own image.

And, if not Stuart Hepburn, then who found it necessary, the same night Ned was murdered to break into not one, but *three* occult bookstores? Had Ned told Stuart the book was in a safe place? Had Stuart killed him before finding out anything more?

I thought of the book and its hunters: a mad, Maltese Falcon chase down through the centuries. And now the *La Paloma* had docked and I was the new stalking horse, just as soon as *The Book of Moons* could be tracked to me.

I sat on the subway feeling spooked, but that was stupid. Knowing about Stuart did not change my life at all. We all live in cities full of murderers every day. It's just that we never look into their faces.

8

I felt like mugging bait walking home from the subway stop. I wondered if there actually was something to Lace's "clothing as victimization" rap. Either way, I thought I was going to give this damn dress and all its accessories to The Cat.

It was a little after midnight. Since noon I'd had two ounces of Scotch and a lot of adrenaline. If there was anything compromised about my locks it didn't register. I walked inside and closed the door.

Stuart Hepburn was waiting for me inside my apartment.

Realization came in a jerky series of epiphanies. The dishevelment of the space where I lived. The books on the floor. The curls of brown paper where he'd unwrapped the two books I'd brought back here. The bathroom light on, but the main room light out so I'd come all the way in.

And Stuart sitting on my bed.

Oh, yes, of course, was my first thought, tainted by faint self-reproach: after four burglaries and two murders, would the Stuart of my creation have stopped there?

"My door looked fine," I said. It was an effort to talk; my tongue felt thick and unresponsive, as if I were drunk.

"Occasionally I can be subtle. Where is it? It wasn't at that pesthole where you work."

There was only one "it."

"I don't have it," I suggested. I'd left it at the studio when I'd gone out with all the other books. Why hadn't he found it there?

Stuart smiled. He was still dressed as he had been earlier in the evening, in the expensive, understated dark suit.

"If you don't have it, I'll kill you," he said, smiling, and I knew it for the simple truth. "You have it or you know where it is. The card you left with poor Neddie was enough reason to search your office, but when I didn't find it there, I wasn't sure about you. Until dinner. Why else would you have run out on me except to make sure it was still safe?"

The truth, they say, will set you free.

"Because I knew you'd killed Ilona—"

"Oh, don't give me any of that witchy claptrap," Stuart interrupted scornfully. "If you had any supernatural powers you'd hardly be here now, would you?"

He had a certain point. I wished I weren't here now. But I simply hadn't been paying attention, in a city where inattention is fatal.

Stuart got up and walked toward me, and only then did I realize that the shock and fright had kept me standing there when I might have run. He took out a tiny gun, silver and pearl-handled, barely as big as his hand but big enough to kill. A .22 or .25; I knew this from a book on self-defense the studio did once.

I wondered if it was the same one he'd used on Ned and felt a wave of nausea fill my mouth with thick saliva. Stuart came and stood in front of me, pointing the gun.

"Ned had your card, darling, and for the longest time I couldn't figure out why—but you Witches stick together, don't you?"

It was so far from true that it was funny. I shook my head. Stuart thought I was arguing with him. Everything I said seemed to make him angry and I didn't know how to stop that.

"You have the book. Ned gave it to you. He didn't have it when we had our little chat, but he did have your card, right there by the phone. Who would he give it to, but you?"

Stuart's faith in me was nearly flattering.

"It's not here," I repeated, docile and truthful as a small child.

"I know that," said Stuart. "I've already looked. You're going to take me to it—I won't make the same mistake twice."

The little gun glittered in the overhead light. There was nothing I could do now. Magic could keep me from meeting the gunman. It could keep the gun from being drawn. But this was the real world, and no spell would stop a bullet.

"You thought you knew where it was before," I said, reasoning it out as if the right answers would save me. "That's why you killed Ned. You thought you had it, but you didn't."

"Bright girl," Stuart said approvingly. I shivered as if someone was pouring alcohol on my skin and might any moment set it alight.

"The book is mine," Stuart said. "I want it back. That's all. Stealing is a sin, you know."

I wondered what Stuart's views were on murder.

My mind seemed to be racing, as if I had to do all the thinking for the rest of my life in the next few minutes. I thought about the fact that death is silence and the involuntary archaic smile, that people killing or thinking about killing do not exhibit Stuart's drawing-room glibness. I understood the reason why in an instant: Stuart was hiding past and future murders from himself and pretending this was common social bullying. Plus gun.

I felt a desperate need to help him, to make polite conversation and conceal horror beneath a shield of metaphor and analogy.

"Where is the book?" Stuart said with surprising patience, and the millrace of discourse opened again in my mind: he said he'd searched the studio and he hadn't found it. But the studio was where I'd left it, and if he already knew it wasn't here, what could I tell him that he'd believe when the truth wouldn't help me?

I shook my head.

"I am waiting," Stuart said. "Where is the book now?"

My skin was dry ice, gathering moisture from the air. My eyes burned as sweat trickled down my face, down my skin under the dress.

The book. Mary's *Book of Moons.* The Craft must ever survive; this is built into our mythology—the Burning Times; six centuries when our struggle was not to stay alive, but to pass our tradition beyond our deaths.

As this shadow-Mary, wavering indistinct between history and fabulation, had. Her book had survived her beheading, taken and hidden by conspirators loyal, if not to her, then to their Goddess. Taken and hidden. And hidden, hidden, hidden . . .

"Of course it's at the studio," I said coolly, as if I could buy into Stuart's sociable lie. "Did you look inside the stat camera?"

"You're bluffing. Why would you hide it? You couldn't know I'd be looking for it," Stuart said. The gun gestured: flick away. Flick back.

"Witches hide their books, Stuart, from *cowans* like you."

Like so many of our words, *cowan* is Scots, and, as we use it, simply means "non-Witch." Stuart, however, seemed to be impressed with being a *cowan*, because he relaxed just a little.

"All right, Witchie-poo. Let's go back to the studio—and you can show me where it is."

I felt the immanence of violence retreat, enough to allow me anger.

"Afraid you'll shoot someone else too soon?" I said.

And Stuart hit me.

It was stunning; unexpected as a flash of lightning. It knocked me off those silly treacherous heels I was wearing. I fell to the floor, sliding on the linoleum. One of my big crescent moon earrings, torn off by the blow, slid across the floor and under the sink. I could hear the sound it made clearly. Then the pain rolled in, slow and heavy as thunder, while I lay on the floor in complete incomprehension of what had just happened to me.

"Get up," said Stuart, and understanding came. He'd hit me, maybe with the gun. I shook my head. Bright heat lightning danced over the surface of the pain-thunder, making me catch my breath in a jerky stutter. Blood eddied through my saliva, but there was no blood on the floor, only the cuts on the inside of my mouth that my teeth had made.

"Get up," Stuart said again.

I kicked my shoes the rest of the way off and got to my hands and knees. His shoes were very close to my face. I thought for a moment that he would kick me, and there was nothing I could do to stop him.

But he didn't. The relief made me almost grateful to him.

I got up and sat quickly down on my kitchen chair, shaking like an addict. I touched my face. It was hot and tender. My lip left smears of lipstick and blood on my fingers. Automatically I took out the remaining crescent earring. I could not look at Stuart.

"I like a girl who knows how to behave herself," Stuart said affably. I didn't say anything. I'd learned better.

"Come on, Witchie. Upsie-daisy. That's a good girl," Stuart said.

My boots were under the kitchen table where I'd left them last. I bent forward carefully and pulled them toward me. In nylon stockings my feet slid into them easily.

"Very nice," Stuart said. He was relishing this as if in retaliation for a lifetime's humiliation, but I could not imagine what I could have done to him that required this scale of vengeance. More than abandoning him during a date, surely? Who was I standing in for, in Stuart's mental landscape?

I got the boots on and stood up. The side of my face that he'd hit felt sunburned, and the ear was beginning to sting. My mind was rehearsing the possibility of future pain.

At the door I got my jacket, because shock, the body's instinctive response to threat, was freezing me to death.

I took the wad of keys off the shelf beside the door and stuck them in the jacket pocket. I picked up my hat and put that on, too, trying to convince some part of myself that everything was all right. Then I stepped out into the hall and Stuart followed me.

Stuart put the gun away, but not far away. He didn't let me lock the door when we left. It was foolish of him to give me such proof when I could still withhold what he wanted. But it was proof I didn't need. I already knew that, as far as Stuart was concerned, I would never come back here again.

The subway doesn't go there, Stuart had no car, and there were no taxis anywhere at this hour of the morning. We walked to Houston Graphics. Stuart held me by the scruff of my jacket and twisted it every time I moved my arms. The gun was in his pocket, handy to hand. This was New York. He could shoot me on this midnight street in perfect safety. No one would come if they heard a gunshot. No one would come if I screamed. No one would even call the police.

Life was composed of odd disjointed sensations. The wind, cold and fresh in the early morning. Distant sirens. Indignation, that I wasn't dressed right for a crisis. The pain in my face as I licked my bleeding lip. The knowledge that my boots were rubbing a blister into my right heel. Grateful relief, because now Stuart was behaving candidly—no more acts, no more deception.

As we walked he chatted companionably, as if he were not suspended between killings over the abyss in which lives the knowledge that there is no more external reason either to act or to refrain. I forgot each word as he spoke it. Incipient mortality scoured me into a desolation beyond ego.

We arrived.

Houston Graphics is not located in a neighborhood I would choose to frequent at this hour—as individual neighborhoods have gotten glossier, the whole fabric of New York life has rotted as if there were some metaphysical constant of niceness, and the concentration of it in some places has left others vulnerable to some existential plague.

There was traffic on Broadway, even now. While we waited for the light, a gust down the concrete canyon whisked my hat off. I grabbed for it reflexively, but Stuart yanked me off balance and I watched it vanish under the wheels of a cab.

"You won't be needing that, pet," Stuart said. My hat made a popping sound as it was flattened: echo of a gunshot.

Stuart hummed to himself. We crossed like law-abiding out-of-towners and Stuart led me to the doorway of Houston's building.

Where the door was covered with a steel shutter that I did not have the keys to open.

There was no way for Stuart to prove or disprove my story tonight. I felt a giddy wash of relief.

I was feeling safe when Stuart's hidden hand came out of the pocket with a wad of keys. He shoved them at me.

"One of these should fit. Don't gawp at me, poppet—our Neddie's been far more useful in death than he ever was in life."

I looked down at what I held in my hand—Ned Skelton's ring of master keys. Stuart's entrée to my apartment—and to Houston Graphics, earlier this evening.

I felt a dangerous and proprietary anger fill me, as if Ned were still alive to be hurt. But I held it down, concentrating on finding the key that would bypass the padlock, just as the padlock on the Snake's outer shutters had been bypassed Tuesday night.

The fifth one fit. I unlocked the padlock and loosened the chain and ran the steel shutter up, baring the door. Maybe its being open at this hour would look odd enough to stop a prowl car, but Stuart wasn't from New York; it didn't bother him.

I used my own keys for the rest. I thought I'd have trouble with the locks, but my hands had trembled far worse for much less than my approaching death. I opened the street door (two keys), then the lobby inner door that's supposed to be a security measure (one key). They're both glass. The outer door has a spring lock and dead bolt. It snapped shut behind me, but the crash bar would open it from the inside.

Of course, none of these measures would have been in place earlier this evening when Stuart had searched Houston Graphics. He'd done it while I was waiting for him at Top of the Sixes—that was the only time he could be sure I wouldn't be there. Ned's keys had gotten him into the studio, and I hoped for the sake of my fellow employees that no one had been there, because Stuart Hepburn seemed to think casual murder the ideal solution for Life's petty annoyances.

I wondered if the police had been to see him at all, or if that tale was just the one pointless lie that had unraveled Stuart so that I could see what he had done.

I think I had a plan.

The lobby was dim. I didn't bother to light it—that was a danger signal even an out-of-towner would pick up on, though in a few hours the building would be lit anyway, open for business.

A few hours. Such a short time when you're sleeping. Such a long time, when someone's pointing a gun at you.

We crossed the lobby. The elevator was probably locked down for the night, and habit made me choose the stairs anyway. Every step jarred my bruised jaw. Stuart, following me up, kept his gun pointed at my kidneys.

Houston shares the building's third floor with a theatrical costumer and a low-end typesetter. The door has a key lock, a snapbolt, and a key-turn dead bolt, none of which will lock by themselves. I opened the door's three locks and stepped inside.

"Where's this stat camera?" Stuart said.

On some level I'd managed to forget he was with me. I jumped when he spoke and dropped both sets of keys. He smiled and followed me in, shutting the door behind him. Neither of us locked the door or picked up the keys.

"Over there," I said. My voice was parched and tiny. I flipped on the overhead lights.

And then I turned around and looked, really looked, at what Stuart had done to the studio.

I groaned. Stuart chuckled, pleased. He took the gun out and waved it. Firearms, the chic urban accessory.

No one could have been here when he'd come. I imagined him, in his expensive, impeccable suit, ripping through everything like a spoiled child who would never be called to account for his actions.

Mikey Pontifex's desk rose up out of a nest of trashed paperwork: letters, memos, files. Its drawers hung open like the tongues of exhaustion. Ray's worktable was similarly trashed; boards and veluxes and transparencies blown up in a willful hurricane and all the billing hopelessly pied.

The bookshelves that line two walls of the studio were mostly empty, their books thrown on the floor, and around the white-painted corners of the carrels I could see a pale tide of jumbled ruined paper where Stuart had dumped the contents of everyone's storage shelves on the floor.

"Come *on,* Witchie." Stuart jabbed me in the back with the gun again. "I'd hate to think you were having me on."

What would you do if I were? I didn't say, and tried to stifle my own speculation about the answer. After two murders and two failures, I was pretty sure that Stuart was not going to shoot me until he was actually holding *The Book of Moons* in his hands. But there were so many other things he could do short of that.

"It's in the stat camera," I said. "Inside."

But it wasn't. I'd left it safely wrapped and labeled and in plain sight, as far as I could remember, and if Stuart hadn't found it, where was it?

I couldn't look for it now.

"Well, go on," Stuart said.

I walked over to the corner of the room where the big blue monster crouched. The stat camera is a reducer/enlarger, a camera, and developer all in one. It's eight feet long and four feet high and about three feet across. You put your original on the gray sponge mat with the white registration lines screened onto it and lock the glass plate over it to hold it still. Then you rotate the bed into an upright position and go back to the other end of the machine to make your stat.

You set the exposure time (by guess and experience and—as a last resort—by the manual) and you set the percentage of original size, from 25 to 250 percent, based on what you've run up on your scaling ruler.

The paper's loaded in twenty-five-foot rolls in a cassette that's kept inside the machine. You cut it to size by touch, with your hands stuck through rubber cuffs that keep the inside of the machine light-safe, and position it on the glass, and lock it down. When you press the button, there's a sound like main phasers firing, and the blinding light of the stat lamps. In the absence of paper, when the light is on you can stare down at a ghost image reflected onto the glass. It's helpful for positioning the photographic paper, but after a while you don't bother. At last—carefully, by touch, in the dark—you feed your exposed paper into the endlessly turning rollers and hope that *la machine* will send it through its various chemical baths and rinse and leave you, in the end, with a black-and-white photostat that you can use.

Every Tuesday morning Royce takes the cover off, mixes new

developer, changes the chemicals, makes sure the belts are aligned, and removes tiny shreds of paper from the gears. The job takes about four hours.

I walked over to the sink behind the camera and splashed water on my face. My face in the little mirror above the sink was red-eyed and set, unappealingly terrified, but serenity was settling over me with soft implacable weight. It would be so easy to let go of this world and robe myself in the *ekstasis* that made Indian warriors certain that painted shirts would stop bullets.

And then—without fear, without judgment—I would turn to Stuart and demand that he give me the gun.

No. Not now.

And a small inner voice answered: *not yet.*

I sorted through the wreckage at Royce's station until I found the stat machine's tool kit. The phone was here too, for some reason, sitting placidly on Royce's stool as if divorcing itself from the chaos below.

"What are you dawdling for?" Stuart said. He was standing by the door, waving the gun. It had a good chance of being inaccurate at this distance, not that that was any inducement to rebellion.

"Do you expect me to open it with my fingernails?" I snapped, brave because he was standing so far away. But he was standing between me and the door and I already knew he was stronger than I was.

The phone rang.

Here. Go, the inner voice said.

I lost all fear. I lost all sense of threat. I scooped it up and answered it—not for defiance, and certainly not because I thought the caller could help me—it was almost certainly, at this hour, a wrong number. But habit is that which is drilled into the nerves, beyond the grip of the mind. The phone rang, so I answered it.

"Bookie-Joint-Can-I-Help-You?" my voice sang out, assured and serene.

Stuart frowned, and shifted his weight forward, and raised the gun. I smiled brightly at him, having gone past the place where fear was.

"This is Sam. Is Karen there?" A male voice. A nice one, but worried.

"No," I said cheerfully, "she isn't here, can I take a message? Do you know what time it is?" I added, for verisimilitude's sake.

The clock on the wall said 2:00 A.M. There was a long crack down its glass that I didn't remember ever seeing before.

"Can you talk freely?" the voice asked cautiously. Stuart made "hang-up" motions at me as I smiled gaily at him. There was only the one phone; Stuart had no way of listening to what Sam-my-late-night-caller said.

"No, of course not," I said. "What kind of a moron are you? I don't know when your job will be ready. Don't call back."

"I understand," the voice said. Calm, alert, unknown.

Stuart charged for me. I put the phone back in the cradle.

"Who was that?" Stuart demanded, grabbing the phone away from me. His face was white and stretched, as masklike as mine had looked in the mirror.

The bright hysteric defiance collapsed. I bent forward as the world grayed out and left me shaking, weak, and nauseated. My mouth was dry and tasted foul. Magic—any extraordinary effort—takes its toll.

Stuart threw the phone across the room. It whipped to the end of its tether and landed with a jangle. The dial tone began to drone, loud in the early A.M. stillness. Stuart ran over to it and kicked it into silence. I could hear his breathing from where I was, and the sound finished anchoring me to my body and the world.

"Don't you do that again! Don't you ever do that again!" Stuart shouted, white-faced with fury. My eyes were drawn to the silvery flicker of the gun barrel, as if it were the most important thing in the room.

It occurred to me, distantly, that I was banking far too much on Stuart's reasonable self-interest. After two murders and several dead ends his grip on plausible normalcy was rapidly eroding, and unlike Witches and magicians, who cross the unmarked mental borders leading to the psychic shadowland frequently, Stuart did not have a way back into the territory of his daylight mind. The strongest social taboo had been broken: he had killed, and now he might do anything.

I saw him drowning in that knowledge, and realized that he could shoot me at any time, for any reason.

Or for no reason at all.

Who was it?" Stuart shouted.

"Someone for Royce," I said, and closed my eyes. I felt tears in the back of my voice and the serpent-terror that could get me killed by making me too reckless to live.

"Get to work," Stuart said. He rubbed the barrel of the gun against his jaw, then seemed to remember what he held and where it should be pointing. A smile appeared intermittently on his face; utterly meaningless. He no longer looked at all human.

I felt a megalomaniac certainty that I could handle this situation and I knew that I was wrong. I could wait, I could play for time, and when there was no more time I could wrap myself in the Goddess's light and let Her choose for me. That was all.

Carefully, as if Stuart's attention were a bomb I did not wish to trigger, I took off my jacket and put it on Royce's stool.

"I'm going to use the screwdriver to take off the cowling," I said aloud, as if I were defusing a bomb and every word was being recorded. To speak at all was an effort.

Stuart made another meaningless smile. I hoped he wouldn't shoot me when he saw the screwdriver in my hand, but after this long, it was getting hard to care.

Sweat poured off me as if I were desperately ill. I could smell myself; acrid and metallic. Fear sweat is different from any other kind.

I began hunting for the screws. I had to find them quickly. I was supposed to have done this before. I'd seen Royce do it lots and lots. If Stuart got tired of watching me do this he'd shoot me, and even though the stopping power of a .22 or .25 is minimal at anything other than extreme close range, I did not want Stuart to shoot me.

Not because I thought he'd kill me. But because I thought that once he fired the gun he would finally snap, and I did not want to be here when he did.

The amnesia of shock made me alternately forget my caller named Sam and obsess on him. I found myself believing that he would come and rescue me, and realized that hope was just another form of the terror that holds you still until you can be killed. He might be help, but I did not dare bet my life on it.

And I had a plan.

Without a plan I could not have built the fantasy of control that let me act in a way that would keep me alive. I actually managed to worry about what was happening to my unlocked apartment because I had a plan.

I had a weapon that Stuart didn't know about.

The photographic process requires two stages: the developer to bring the latent image out on the paper, and the fixer to halt the process before the paper turns completely black. The fixer, though

I wouldn't want to get it into my eyes, is a fairly mild chemical, but the developer is caustic. Once I got the camera disassembled, I'd have a bath of dilute acid in my hands.

I was going to throw it at Stuart and run. The door wasn't locked. Small handguns are supposed to be untrustworthy. I'd take my chances on the street.

If I could.

I found the screws and unthreaded them. There were eight. I pulled them out and set them aside. They rolled downhill, away from the machine. I lifted the cowling off the back half of the machine. It made hollow booming noises as it was shifted.

"Where is it?" Stuart said, shoving me aside. The cowling shifted in my fingers and cut them; it was thin metal. I set it down quickly. He stared down at what looked like a miniature printing press.

"I don't see it; if you're lying to me, you bitch, I'll—"

"It's in the camera," I said. "Underneath." Exhaustion helped make my voice flat and ultimately believable. Stuart backed off, waving his little chrome pistol.

"Hurry up," he said.

"If I hurry too much the book'll get wet. If that happens, it's ruined."

I don't know where this fund of plausible invention came from; I spend so much time learning to tell the truth that lying doesn't come very easily. But it was there when I needed it; the gift of the Goddess.

Stuart backed off.

And perhaps it was Her will as well that Stuart should take such an implausible story as mine seriously. But the Moon is the mistress of illusion; the Elizabethans believed Her light could drive men mad.

If I were Royce and this were any Tuesday morning, the next thing would be to lift out and clean the rollers, exposing the chemical baths. But if I did that, Stuart would see there was no place in the machine for a book to be hidden. Right now he was watching me closely; I'd never get the moment's grace I needed to work my plan while he was doing that.

I was calm, wonderfully so. But I didn't seem to be able to think very well. And if I stood here much longer trying to decide what to do, Stuart would get suspicious. I started removing the cowling from the front half of the machine.

Stuart retreated to the other side of the room.

I'd never seen this part done. It probably hadn't been done since the thing was assembled at the factory; it was no part of the maintenance routine, but Stuart didn't know that. The screws were frozen solid, and my fingers were slippery with blood and sweat. I finally had to wrap paper towels around my hands to get a grip on the screwdriver.

When I started to lift the cowling loose I realized there was something still holding it in place. I pulled anyway, and felt something catch, resist, tear, and finally give.

The sound of a footstep was loud in the room.

I jerked toward Stuart, but he hadn't moved. He was on the other side of the studio, staring at the clock and half sitting on Mikey's desk, jogging his foot in the air as if he were waiting impatiently. The gun was resting on his knee, almost harmless.

He hadn't heard the sound; neither had he made it.

The sound came again. Someone walking, but if I'd heard it, Stuart had to have, and he never moved.

There was someone else in the building, moving quietly. Moving toward me.

I looked at the clock. It seemed as if hours had passed, but it was only two-thirty. Half an hour since we'd gotten here.

Half an hour since the phone rang.

The stat camera is set along the short end of the rectangular bite out of the Houston Graphics studio space, which means that when you're standing near the sink at the head of the stat camera you're at the one place in the studio that isn't in sight of the door.

I set the cowling down and went back to the head of the camera. Stuart looked up, but I made sure I wasn't looking toward him when he did.

I began lifting the rollers out. They're almost three feet long and heavy; their weight is what holds the trays of fixer and developer steady. If I were a comic book hero I would have tried to bludgeon Stuart with one, but, choreography aside, I'm not certain that I could have managed to hit him with the force required to do any more than make him mad.

I lifted the rinse tray out and balanced it on the side of the machine.

Someone coming closer; a palpable certainty that raised the hair on my arms. Stuart noticed it at last, or noticed something.

He got to his feet and started toward me. I lifted the developer bath in my hands.

The door of the studio hit the wall with the sound of an explosion.

"Hold it!" someone shouted.

I threw myself flat, sliding in a puddle of chemicals. The machine blocked my view. My eyes watered with the fumes of spilled developer. I saw nothing. There were no loud sounds, only breathing and the scuff of shoes and some faint jingling sounds, and, after a moment, Stuart's voice, small and irritable:

"I didn't do anything!"

9

I t was a quarter of three Thursday morning, and things were different. Sam's last name was Hodiac. He was round, chocolate brown, and balding; dark-skinned and ten years and change older than I was. There was a gold shield hung on a chain around his neck and a gun on his belt and he looked open and friendly and reassuring, except for the eyes.

They were cop eyes, as giving as glass. That, too, was reassurance of a sort.

He was Belle's cop, and he was here.

"When Izzy mentioned Mr. Hepburn, you better believe I got moving," he said to me. "It's a good thing for you that I did. But we've had our eye on Mr. Hepburn for a while now," he added.

Izzy is Isobel. Belleflower. Who had, despite all our differences, made the phone call that had saved my life. If she'd waited until morning it would have been too late, unless my plan had worked.

I thought of telling Lieutenant Hodiac about my plan and decided he wouldn't appreciate it.

I was sitting in Mikey's chair behind Mikey's desk at the studio. We were in the midst of a full-blown crime scene, and no one had let me make coffee, a fact that grated irrationally on my nerves. We had Lieutenant Hodiac and two uniformed patrolmen and another detective whose case this actually was. There'd actually been four uniformed officers until two of them had taken Stuart away in handcuffs and Stuart's gun away in a little plastic bag.

Stuart maintained that he hadn't done anything.

"Stuart Hepburn killed Ilona Saunders and Ned Skelton," I said. I'd probably said it before. It was, I'd found, an opinion also held by our friends the police—who, until *The Book of Moons* was added to the equation, could not understand why Stuart would wish to do this.

"That shooter of his is going to tell us most of what we need to know," Hodiac said. He sounded pleased.

"Oh, good," I said inadequately. I felt numb, as if crying would be appropriate if only I could work up the interest.

A patrolman came in and handed something to Hodiac, who wrung it in his hands and then handed it to me. It was one of those cold bags that freeze when you twist them. I held it to my jaw, wishing everyone would leave me alone.

"Are you all right? Do you want someone to take you to the hospital?" Hodiac asked.

"I'm fine." I don't have insurance. "Thank you for coming," I added, feeling I had to say something.

Hodiac smiled. "It's our job, miss."

One of the patrolmen came back with coffees from the deli next door. Hodiac sorted through them and handed one to me. After what Stuart had done to the studio, our coffeemaker was probably broken anyway.

"Drink it, miss. It'll help."

"Bast," I said. "It's Bast."

Not Karen. Not "miss." Not "Witchie" or "sweetheart" or "pet." My name is Bast.

I sipped it. It was tepid and horribly sweet. I shivered.

"It isn't going to work out quite the way you see in the movies, but I think we'll be able to hold on to Mr. Hepburn," Hodiac said. "You may not have to testify in court." This was supposed to be reassuring. "Detective Larsen will explain the procedure to you, and what you need to do. Here's my card. You can call me if you need anything."

I looked for a pocket to put it in and realized I didn't have my jacket. I set the card on the desk, lining it up carefully with the edge. Lieutenant Hodiac was called away. I finished the coffee, winced at the sugar pooled in the bottom, and walked over to where my jacket was.

"It's mine," I said to the officer who'd followed me. He looked a young fifteen, if that, and had a white-on-black tag on his shirt that said his name was Sanchez.

I put on my jacket. It didn't make me feel any warmer. I realized the entire front of my little black dress was soaking wet and my nylons were nothing but snags. My boots were wet. Every muscle, without exception, hurt.

"Detective Larsen wonders if you could talk to him now, miss," Officer Sanchez said politely.

I wondered what he'd do if I said no. I was tired beyond imagining; I would gladly tell them anything in the world if they'd just let me sleep.

I slept not since the Conquest / Nor since then have I waked—

Mad Tom. Bedlam's boys are bonnie. I wondered if girls were allowed into their club. I wondered where you went to sign up. I walked back over to the desk.

Detective Larsen was an unshaven blond wearing a pale blue sport jacket over jeans and the gold shield medallion *du jour*. He was probably singing arias of thanksgiving at the prospect of being able to clear two murders off his caseload. I sat down. I smiled. He smiled. Meaningless.

He took particulars: name, address, phone number, profession. Had I really been working here this long? I wondered. Then we got down to specifics.

Detective Larsen interrupted me every other sentence with questions until I got the idea of what he wanted to hear. Had Stuart shown me the gun? Yes. Had he threatened me verbally? Yes—he'd said he'd kill me. Had he threatened me physically in any way? He'd hit me.

Detective Larsen seemed pleased that Stuart had hit me. I was glad somebody was pleased. We went on.

Stuart had broken into my apartment using passkeys stolen from his previous victim Ned Skelton. Stuart brought me to the studio at gunpoint, because I had told him that the rare book that Ned Skelton had stolen from Ned's employer—Stuart's aunt—and stashed with me, was here. No, I hadn't known what it was when Ned had left it with me; I'd found out later. No, I hadn't thought it was odd that he'd do that. Well, yes and no. Okay, never mind.

I'd been supposed to meet Ned the night he was murdered—

"Why?" Detective Larsen said.

"I was going to do a blessing on his apartment."

"Why's that?" Larsen said sharply.

Hodiac had come over to listen. I stared supplicatingly at him, feeling the fear that all of us fringefolk feel when our explanations may be twisted into unintended confessions.

"She's a Wiccan, Don," Hodiac said. "She blesses people."

"Oh," Larsen said, losing interest in that line of inquiry. "One of them. Go on, miss."

I went back to Tuesday night. I'd seen the police take Ned's body out of his apartment. We went over the time that Ned had called me and the time I got there, including why I thought those times were right and then (in my statement) I came back to the studio. I opened the box and found the book, and thought that Ned must have taken it from Ilona.

"Why'd you think that?" Larsen said.

Because it had been in a box with all the other Books of Shadows that Ned had stolen and Ilona's was the only place it could have come from, but if I told him that, what would he do?

"I don't know," I said unconvincingly. I rubbed the bridge of my nose. "Ilona was related to Mary, Queen of Scots," I said, and at the time it sounded like a reasonable explanation.

Hodiac said something to Larsen that I didn't hear.

"We can come back to that. What did you do then?" Larsen said to me.

I'd done nothing, wondering what to do with the book since Ilona and Ned were both dead. And Wednesday night, Stuart had been waiting in my apartment.

Reality, as simplified for the legal process.

While we'd been talking, phone calls had been made from the Rolodex—though not from the studio phone—once the police'd found it. Mikey and Ray would arrive as soon as they could make it from Fort Lee and Fort Hamilton Parkway, respectively.

Larsen walked off. Hodiac knelt by the chair, bringing himself down to eye level with me.

"Don's okay," Hodiac said. "He just wants to get everything straight for the charge sheet. You'll need to come down to the precinct to make your statement and so on; probably talk to the DA. I'm afraid it's going to take a while, but we'll try to make it as quick as we can. Are you ready to go? Sanchez can take you down. Don has a few things to finish up here."

"My apartment's unlocked." I guess I realized then I was going to live, and, living, had to take up my responsibilities again.

"I can have Sanchez take you by there on the way downtown. He can go up with you, check out your apartment, make sure everything's all right."

"Oh, good," I said.

"Why didn't Hepburn find this *Book of Moons* he was looking for?" Hodiac said. "Didn't you leave it here?"

"It was supposed to be here," I said. "But it wasn't here, and I don't know where it is," I said, and finally started to cry.

Mikey got to the studio a few minutes later. I was still there. Mikey Pontifex has tiny brown eyes and thin greige hair and stands five-foot-four in his socks. He looked at the wreckage of the studio, the cops, the remains of his stat camera. His face turned redder and redder and then he noticed me.

"You'd better have a good explanation for this," Mikey said to me.

I didn't. But I did have some advice that I earnestly encouraged him to take. Officer Sanchez put his hand gently on my arm and pulled, gently. I walked out with him. The hall was decked with yellow tape. POLICE LINE: DO NOT CROSS. We crossed it.

Where is the boundary between the real and the unreal? Between faith and insanity? Between the world of the Gods and the pleasant realms of Men?

I met Ray on the stairs.

"Jesus Christ, what happened to your face?" Ray demanded.

"Another beautiful day in Paradise," I said. He went up. Sanchez and I went down.

The material world was the flat fake dark that it only gets between well after midnight and just before dawn. I rode in the back of what Officer Sanchez called his unit and gave directions to my apartment.

When we got there, he got out of the car and came around to let me out. There are no door handles in the backseats of police cars.

We went upstairs. He called me ma'am and suggested I let him go first. His belt was covered with loops and pouches and boxes in black leather with nickel-plated snaps. He carried a revolver and a nightstick and a walkie-talkie as long as my forearm that murmured constantly to itself in *gematria* and static, but I wasn't afraid of him. He was safe.

I was safe.

No one had been in my apartment. Officer Sanchez pushed the door open very carefully and shined his light all around before he flipped the switch, but the place looked just the way Stuart and I had left it. Officer Sanchez looked in my bathroom. He looked in my closet. Nothing was gone. No one was there. No one had noticed this vulnerability.

I wondered if this was all that strength was: a vulnerability unnoticed through the exercise of random chance. Maybe nobody's strong, only lucky.

Officer Sanchez inspected my door. He told me that my locks were all still functional, but that I might like to get them replaced anyway; a secular charm against invasion.

He made me feel middle-aged and unworldly, and though I was happy to have him there I resented the fact that what had torn my life so far apart didn't seem to touch him at all.

I wanted to change clothes but he said not to. I compromised, grabbing socks for the boots, a warmer coat. My hands were shaking. Officer Sanchez locked my door for me and then handed me my keys. I clutched them so hard it hurt—distantly, as though the person being hurt were someone else.

We went back out into the night.

It was eight o'clock in the morning before I got back from what its inhabitants refer to—with varying degrees of facetiousness—as the Palace. One Police Plaza.

I had had bad coffee and vending-machine food. I had told my story to several detectives several times, and finally to someone from the DA's office; flurries of activity interspersed with hours of waiting while people waited for other people to show up. I carefully answered only the questions I was asked, and it turned out they didn't care a lot about Ned's package or my intuitions; they expected to match Stuart's gun to the bullet that killed Ned, and in the fashion of law as distinct from justice, were not going to bother with anything but their single strongest case.

The machine of bureaucracy, as adapted to enforcement. They took pictures of my bruises. I didn't see Stuart. They were careful about that. It was kindness.

I refused lawyers and EMTs and finally got to sign my statement. There was a grand jury appearance in the not-so-distant future, where the People of the State of New York would decide if what Stuart had done would merit a trial. It was a formality, Detective Larsen assured me. I might even not be called. They hadn't decided yet. There would definitely be a trial.

A marked car drove me home, clutching business cards and

form-subpoenas and a list of instructions. The daylight and color seemed wrong and unreal; a world of life and reason that I shouldn't be able to see, somehow.

The door was still locked. I unlocked it, went inside, locked it again.

I took off my coat and hung it up carefully. I took off my boots and put them neatly in the closet. Then I walked into the bathroom to assess the damage, feeling as though I was insulated from the world by a thick sheet of glass.

I'd washed my face at the station after they'd gotten some pictures of the damage, but I hadn't really looked at myself there. The woman in my mirror had dark purple moth-wing curves under her eyes and a flushed-red bruise on her face and looked as if she'd been dead for a week. My mind made the comparison before I realized it would be a long time before a joke like that would be funny again.

The ear the earring had been ripped out of was pink and smudged with blood, but not torn through. Small favors.

I washed my face again. The linen sheath would never look the same. I pulled it off carefully and hung it on a hanger over the showerhead. Dry clean only, the label said. I wondered if soaking it with photographic chemicals counted.

I'd put on my socks downtown; they stuck to the broken blisters now. I peeled them off carefully, but there was still a mess.

I washed my hands and my face again and peroxided the ear, putting a light silver post through it so the piercing wouldn't close while it healed. Just doing that made it start to bleed again, and the pale smears of blood made me want to weep. Shock. Sleep deprivation. Reality.

The phone rang.

There are very few people who phone me at eight in the morning. I picked up the receiver, glancing down at the phone. The answering machine tape was choked with incoming messages.

"Hello, Belle," I said. "I was right." Victory, as the poets say, is gall and wormwood.

There was a pause. "Bast?" Belle said. "Are you all right?"

I wondered what a truthful answer to that would be.

"I'm home now," I said unnecessarily.

"I tried to call you at the studio but I couldn't get through. I called Lieutenant Hodiac."

"Yeah, he came over and arrested Stuart."

I was so tired I was almost mumbling and the words came out

with arrogant matter-of-factness. Apathy is the secret to sangfroid. "Look, I'm really zoned, so I'll call you tomorrow, okay?" I added. Tomorrow and tomorrow and tomorrow, but tomorrow never comes. Or is it another day?

"Do you want me to come down?" Belle said.

I realized with a pang of leave-taking that there would have been a time, once, when I would have wanted that, but not anymore. From her worldview to mine was finally too far to travel.

"No. I'll be fine. I'll call you. Thanks for asking."

"Take care of yourself, Bast," Belle said.

Sure. If not me, who?

There was Tsing-tao in the refrigerator and Slivovitz in the cupboard. I administered both, plus a long hot shower. I scrubbed until I looked like a boiled lobster, until vast tracts of skin were abraded and raw. I came out and put on my one surviving Banana Republic jumpsuit and padded around the apartment with my feet surgically swaddled in aseptic white socks. Everything hurt.

I wanted to go to bed, but I couldn't sleep while my apartment bore such witness to Stuart's presence. I shuffled around it like a zombie, putting things away, making things right, finding my shoes and earrings. Doing for myself what Ned had wanted me to do for him, a thousand years ago.

The two still-unreturned Books of Shadows I put on the kitchen table, along with the biography I'd borrowed from Daffydd.

Mary, Queen of Scots. Who drew everyone in her orbit into intrigue and violence. Whose influence did not stop with her death. Did Mad Maudlin haunt Elizabeth's bloody chamber down the long years as Elizabeth watched Mary's son—the rival's son who would be king thereafter while she herself was childless—grow up across the border?

For to see Mad Tom of Bedlam, ten thousand miles I'll travel / Mad Maudlin goes on dirty toes, for to save her shoes from gravel . . .

Scotland's queen. Catholic or Witch—the Old Religion or the Oldest Religion? Always going home; never quite reaching it. Shadow queen and the proof—if it had been proof—gone once more.

By a knight of ghosts and shadows, I summoned am to tourney / Ten leagues beyond the wild world's end, methinks it is no journey.

Last of all I found the scattered pieces of my altar and assembled them again. It was almost noon, but I turned out my lights, lit my candles and incense, and petitioned my own Queen.

Thank you, Lady, for keeping me alive. Now tell me what I'm going to tell . . . everyone.

There was no answer. I hadn't expected any. I finished my beer, and snuffed the candles, and went to bed.

IO

P eople who are fond of justice or sausages, to adapt a phrase, should never watch either being made. My testimony to the grand jury consisted of answers to questions that seemed meaningless; maybe they were parts of a pattern I wasn't privileged to see.

Mary, Queen of Scots, was not mentioned. Ned Skelton and Ilona Saunders were killed by Stuart Hepburn. Here's the proof. End of story.

And because this was so, my involvement in the actual trial—whenever it occurred—would probably be only as a footnote. Detective Larsen might have been right, and I wouldn't be called at all. Who wanted my unwelcome complications introduced into this particular passionless play?

Bail was set at the hearing, and Stuart Hepburn did not make bail. I wasn't there for that; ADA Morales, the assistant district attorney who had shepherded me through the case—and who would be prosecuting Stuart in the sweet bye-and-bye—called to tell me, which was kind of her. I felt a distant, dutiful sense of relief; while there was very little point in his killing me now that *The Book of Moons* was gone, I felt that Stuart was the sort to hold a grudge.

With one thing and another I didn't go back to Houston Graphics for two weeks, but I got reports. Houston achieved full employment through having to let the freelancers bill for cleaning up the mess Stuart had made. Ray finally convinced Mikey that whatever I'd done, I'd done while being held at gunpoint by a deranged killer. I kept my job.

And life went on, just as if Stuart had never been.

Julian got most of his stolen inventory back when Ilona's apartment in the back of Lothlorien (where Stuart had been staying) was searched. The insurance company was delighted.

Ilona's cat, which had also been staying at the apartment, was adopted by Glitter, a move that did not bode well for the future of Glitter's gold-lace curtains. She told me later its name was Yarrow. I did not make the obvious pun about a yarrowing experience. I didn't seem to have much sense of humor lately.

Belle was able to trace both Diana-27 and Otterleaf and get phone numbers for them. I used the Criss-Cross directory at New York Public and mailed their books back to them anonymously.

Maria Stuarda played all six of its performances to what Beaner said was critical acclaim. I didn't go to any of them. Beaner said he now considered that opera in the light thespians viewed "The Scottish Play" and hoped Goddess would strike him straight if he ever sang Robin Dudley again.

I returned *A Rose in the Shadows* to Daffydd. He'd heard about Stuart; by now, everyone had. He told me that Mary had frequently been accused of witchcraft in her lifetime, but that during the sixteenth century C.E. such an accusation had been about as much of a distinction as being called a godless Commie in the McCarthy era. If he'd heard of *The Book of Moons,* he didn't mention it.

Lothlorien closed.

I read, I slept, I took long walks. I talked to Ned and Ilona when they came to visit. I did some work at the Snake, I read tarot (gratis) at Chanter's Revel, I hung out. I did my best to come to terms with what Stuart had done to me. Beyond the slap, beyond the threats, beyond attempted murder.

Because of Stuart Hepburn, for the rest of my life I'd be sharing my life with a monster. A monster born out of fire, brittle and inflexible as volcanic glass, something that would live beneath my skin and would die or kill rather than live with being that afraid again. Something for which death held less terror than helplessness did; a monster that could seize control of my life at any moment and make me follow not my will, but its. Because of Stuart.

I visited Belle, more out of a sense of duty than anything else. She told me that hate would be a healthy reaction that I could work through, but I didn't feel anything I recognized as hate. I told her

I thought I ought to take a sabbatical from Changing. We both knew what I really meant, but she didn't push me to make it formal.

I did a lot of ritual, I saw a lot of movies, and when the feeling that I needed to knock on my own door to make sure no one else was inside before going home was faint enough, I knew it was time to go back to work.

Monday, May 23, nine A.M. The day was overcast, hot and wet as a dog's breath. I got into the studio, doing my best impersonation of nonchalance. There was an almost full house of regulars, minus Royce. There was even a new hire, which was reassuring. Everything looked normal. We had a new coffeepot.

"Glad you finally decided you could make it," Ray said. He waved me over to his desk.

"Couldn't tear myself away." I came over and took charge of a dummy, spec sheet, and a folder full of type and photos. Virtue's reward. He'd saved it for me.

"You okay?" Ray said.

"Yeah, sure." Another inarticulate urban legend in the making.

I took the pile back to my carrel. Mikey was out on his rounds, so there was a certain amount of chatter. The official story, as current at Houston Graphics, seemed to be that I'd decided to work late at the studio and been surprised by a burglar. It was as good an explanation as any, and, best of all, did not involve Mary, Queen of Scots. I let it ride and accepted commiserations.

Tyrell thought I should carry a gun to prevent future incidents. Eloi spoke up enough to say that *he* never had any trouble (yeah, like somebody'd jump Bogie). Chantal said nothing like this ever happened in France, but it is Chantal's expressed opinion that all the evils of the Western World descend from the American insistence on using disposable grocery bags. Ray said that since I was going to sell my story for a Movie of the Week I'd become independently wealthy and could afford to hire a bodyguard.

Everybody's a comedian.

My work space had been carefully neatened by others to the point where I couldn't find anything. I spent the next ninety minutes putting everything back the way I wanted it. My coffee cup was missing its handle and would have to be replaced, but would do for today. I filled it with coffee and got to work as the studio settled down around me.

Royce got in around eleven. He was wearing a nice little

houndstooth check that had last been seen in the Bogart/Bacall version of *The Big Sleep.* I hoped Eloi could contain himself.

I went back to work. A few minutes later I heard the sound of high heels. I looked up at Royce.

"Welcome back," he said. "This is yours, right?"

He held out a flat, brown-wrapped package. I felt all my cozy, self-congratulatory assurance vanish like water down a drain.

I took the package. On it was a red-and-white label of the kind the studio uses, and on it was typed: "M Q o S: B o M."

Mary, Queen of Scots: *Book of Moons.*

"Where?" I said, as if it were a complete sentence.

Royce looked embarrassed. "I hope you haven't been looking for it too hard," he said. "I took it home with a bunch of my stuff by mistake the day before the studio got tossed—it was out on the table. Ray said it didn't belong to Houston."

"Yeah—and stop using our wrapping paper on your personal jobs, Kitty," Ray called from the front. I waved fingers at him.

"No," I said, with what I hoped was conviction, "it wasn't anything I needed. Thanks, Royce."

He studied me closely, trying to decide if I was being completely truthful with him. Like me, Royce is also into what we frequently call "alternative spirituality," but as his path is the achievement of the Holy Grail he and I don't really have that much to talk about.

"Yeah, anytime. Don't get yourself into trouble, Bast," he said. He went back to his desk. I wish I had half the self-assurance in heels that Royce does.

I looked at the package. I took a mat knife and cut away a little corner of the wrapping, exposing the edge of an old leather book—the old leather book, in fact, that I'd expected to see. I set it aside, out of harm and spilled coffee's way.

I was not forced to revise my view of Stuart's intelligence or posit supernatural intervention after all. Stuart hadn't found *The Book of Moons* in the studio because it hadn't been here to find. Somehow it had managed to go home with Royce and safely absent itself from the events that followed.

Which might be supernatural intervention enough. I didn't, after all, remember leaving it out on a table, but that Tuesday's events were pretty hazy in my memory. I could have. Whether I had, in fact, was just one more thing I'd never know.

It took me eight weeks to copy out *The Book of Moons*—in modern ink on modern paper, creating something with no verifiable link to the past. I copied each word carefully, straining at the archaic Elizabethan "secretary hand," although I had little Latin and less French, and not much of the book seemed to be in English. Maybe someday I'd do a typescript version and get the whole thing translated.

And when I was done making my copy I swaddled the original in neutral pH tissue and placed it in the pale gray archival document box I had bought to store it in. I bound the box tightly in acid-free tape, and when I had wrapped *The Book of Moons* for the last time I took it up to the Pierpoint Morgan Library and told them I was a messenger with a parcel.

Parcels do get messengered, even to libraries. They let me in.

I'd used a blank from Lightfleet messengers, the service the studio uses; it wasn't hard to slip one out of Mikey's desk and mark it up, and I picked the day carefully. Rainy, and just an anonymous messenger's bad luck that the call sheet that would tell who it was from and who it was to was sodden beyond recognition. Maybe the Pierpoint Morgan'd come up with plausible answers on their own. God knew they'd get no answers from Lightfleet.

I left it in the hands of a bored receptionist who didn't seem to care whether or not it was ever delivered, let alone who I was. I tried not to care what happened now; I'd done what I could for Mary and her cause. The Pierpoint Morgan has one of the most extensive rare books collections outside the Vatican, as well as a nearly complete Visconti-Sforza tarot deck. They'd know what to do with a book that was very, very old. If it was, in fact, even that, and not some modern forgery.

Magic or not?, so the question goes, but the real question isn't, in the final analysis, what is there, but what we see. Reality is a consensus, arrived at through polling the testimony of individuals. Truth and reality are both in a constant state of mutation, and all anyone can do is ride the crest of his particular wave. Alone.

In the end, everyone's alone. It was the middle of the day in early August. I was on my lunch hour. I headed downtown, back to work.

The Bowl of
Night

I

I hate Halloween. This might seem odd, but only consider how many people profess to hate Christmas—that frenzied end-of-year potlatch that has dragged Hanukkah down with it in a fine Judeo-Christian unanimity. December 25's certainly not a religious holiday anymore, and if not for the fact that retailers do 50 percent of their annual business during the month of December, the observance might actually die out. One of my co-workers defines Christmas as "The time of year when you buy people you don't like things they don't want with money you don't have"—which seems, on the face of it, to be a pretty good description of the entire winter gift-giving season, Kwanzaa included.

That much being said, I should also add that while it is actually possible for me to ignore the debasement of Hanukkah/Christmas/Kwanzaa/Yule (having no one to buy presents for), I have no such luck with Halloween. All Hallows' Eve is, after all, the climax of what passes for the liturgical year in our Community, and so I loathe the Real World "celebration" of it from the first sighting of Halloween candy at the grocery store to the last newspaper story about holiday vandalism; from the cute stories about Wiccans in your local newspaper to the green-faced Margaret Hamilton clones on every door, window, and trick-or-treat bag.

Those of you who hate Christmas will understand; I cling to the reactionary position that religious holidays—like Halloween—are not shopping opportunities. But then, my name is Bast, and I'm a Witch.

I don't want your ruby slippers, and you and your little dog can live in perfect harmony for all of me; what Hollywood means and what I mean by the "W" word are miles apart. What Hollywood means—after Bette Midler's last flop—is that bucktoothed broads on broomsticks are box-office poison. What I mean is that I'm a practitioner of a NeoPagan Earth-centered religion—Wicca—the majority of whose practitioners define themselves as Witches and then spend tedious hours on the political reeducation of everyone within earshot.

Not me. I'm a Witch, but I won't go on about my religion if you don't go on about yours. And like you, there are times when I don't think about my religion at all and times when I actually feel like an oppressed minority.

Times like Halloween. Or as we call it, Samhain.

In most Wiccan traditions, Samhain (pronounced "Sowwan," for those of you who didn't grow up speaking Gaelic) is the Feast of the Dead; the festival at which we followers of Wiccan and Neo-Pagan traditions remember our beloved dead, whether tied to us by kinship or simply by affinity. It is also the time, both in Christian traditions and ours, when the world of the dead and the world of the living draw together, and when past and future merge, just for an instant.

Or, in modern terms, it's a time for wholesale vandalism and the mass purchase of cheap candy.

My personal rebellion against the secular commercialization of Samhain has taken the form, for the past thirteen years, of an escape to HallowFest.

HallowFest is a Pagan gathering held on Columbus Day (observed) weekend at the Paradise Lake Campground in Gotham County, New York. A Pagan festival has certain things in common with a Christian religious retreat, except that HallowFest isn't restricted to one denomination, or even to one religion. People come from all over the eastern seaboard and from as far west as Ohio and Indiana; it's a Samhain celebration for most of us, but it isn't held Halloween weekend, because covens hold their private celebrations then.

This was the first year I wouldn't have a coven to go to—or with. I was hoping HallowFest would help me forget about all that. And as it turned out, it did; a salutary lesson in being very careful about what you wish for.

But that was later. This was Friday, and all I was thinking

about when I got up that morning was getting to Paradise Lake, which is about two hours' drive north of NYC on a good day.

Holding the thought of our planned two P.M. departure firmly in mind, I'd gotten myself and my duffel bag down to The Serpent's Truth promptly at eleven o'clock. Julian was just opening up. The van, which someone had been supposed to fetch earlier and leave parked out front, was nowhere to be seen.

The Snake (or, technically, Tree of Wisdom, the Snake's mail-order branch) has a table every year at HallowFest, selling those things—from Dragon's Blood resin to crystals to purpose-built athamés—that attending Pagans can't find in their own back-yards. Most years I drive the van, driver's licenses being in short supply among New Yorkers. Most years, I take one of the clerks from the store. This year I was taking Julian.

Yes indeed, Julian: ceremonial magician, my clandestine lust-object, and neurasthenic manager of New York's oldest and tacki-est occult bookstore, The Serpent's Truth—known to its intimates as The Snake. Julian the Un-Pagan was coming to HallowFest—for some reason having nothing to do with my company, sanity prompted me to suppose.

"Hi, Julian," I said brightly. He ignored this, but Julian tends to do this with conversation not to his taste. I stashed my duffel behind the counter and looked around. The stock for HallowFest, which ought by rights to have been already packed, seemed still to be on the shelves.

"So, are we ready to go?" I chirped, just to be difficult. We weren't ready to go. We'd never been ready to go on schedule in living memory. The festival didn't really open until tomorrow, but Summerisle Coven was running the festival this year and I knew Maidjene, its High Priestess, would let us come in and set up early.

"Here are the keys," Julian said, handing me the keys, park-ing voucher, and registration for the van.

Julian is an entirely satisfactory manager for the Snake, look-ing, as he does, as if he might have stepped full-blown from a nineteenth-century Russian icon, from his lank black hair and steel-rimmed bifocals to his rusty hammertail coat. He wears a Roman collar, too, which he may be entitled to, for all I know. But he doesn't drive.

I headed for the subway. Maybe he and Brianna would pack while I was gone.

I doubted it, of course, but it was possible.

*   *   *

The Snake's van is an ancient Ford, once black and now mostly primer gray, in a dramatic state of disrepair and with most of the lower body panels rusted through. Driving it is an adventure. Between the subways, the garage, and New York traffic—factoring in a stop for gas because anytime I get my hands on the van the tank is nearly empty—I got back to the Snake around one-thirty.

There was no legal parking left on the street. I double-parked in front of the shop and went in. Julian was just giving instructions to Brianna, the clerk of the moment, on how to handle the store while Julian—its manager—was gone.

Brianna is short, round, dreamy-eyed, and vague to a fault. She also has black hair long enough to sit on, something that I was pretty sure was not a factor in any decision of Julian's or Tris's (the Snake's actual owner) to keep her, considering Tris's sexual preferences and the fact that Julian is not known to have any, alas. Her continued employment is far likelier to be because Brianna shows up (eventually), is willing to work for something less than minimum wage, and doesn't steal.

"This key locks the top lock," Julian was saying patiently.

"Um-m," said Brianna.

Tris (it's short for Trismegistus, and probably not the name he was born with) usually hangs around when Julian isn't here, so there wasn't much chance for Brianna to get into serious trouble, but Julian is nothing if not thorough.

"The van is double-parked out front," I said at a suitable break in the conversation.

Brianna's gaze slowly wandered toward me. Her eyes are an unlikely shade of turquoise, which is natural so far as I know. There was a pause while she adjusted to the fact of my presence.

"I guess we better start packing the stuff for the festival?" she said at last.

In other words, business as usual.

I could tell myself I was putting up with this monstrous lack of organization for the pleasure of Julian's company, but the fact is that I do it every year whether he's going or not. It would be a real stretch to call this community service—and I'm not much on altruism anyway—so the only possible explanation must be masochism. As masochistic experiences go, this was a pretty good one; it was about four o'clock when Brianna, Julian, and I finally started loading cartons of books, Tarot cards, and Pagan jewelry into the van. The work went fast; Julian is stronger than he looks. But it was eight by the time he and I were well and truly rolling.

It was dark by the time we'd crossed the Willis Avenue Bridge (one of my favorite bridges, owing to the fact that the City of New York, in its infinite wisdom, has chosen to paint it a pale violet) and progressed, toll free (another reason I like the Willis), to the Governor Thomas E. Dewey Thruway (or *Twy*, according to the signs). Although this meant there wasn't much to see in the way of scenery unless you liked strip-malls and headlights, I still felt that same deviant thrill that leaving the metroplex for the land where the green things grow always gives me.

Once you become used to Manhattan's asphalt ecosphere, there is something perversely unnatural about suburbia, a land characterized by shopping malls and meaningless expanses of lawn. By comparison, there's something reasonable about the true countryside—which is defined as anything above commuting range.

We cut over from the thruway to the Sawmill River Parkway, stopped once for dinner at a Chinese place in Tarrytown (New Yorkers preferring their native cuisine whenever possible), once for gas when the tank got to half full, and once for groceries, because HallowFest is a demi-camping event: without tenting but with the necessity of preparing most of your own meals. In practice, this means I exist for three days on trail mix, tinned smoked oysters, and warm Diet Pepsi. Julian bought vegetables.

After that, we got lost—which was also a part of my yearly HallowFest experience, although it is something I try to avoid each time. All I know is that we reached New Paltz just fine and after that all is darkness.

Paradise Lake Campground does not, to my knowledge, waste money on advertising. There is only one small sign visible from County 6, and that sign directs you not to the campground, but up a long, twisting, one-and-a-half-lane road that goes on long enough for you to be sure you've missed your way. It is especially easy to think that at 12:30 in the morning after having been certain you were going the right way twice before.

Should you demonstrate the proper perseverance, the one-and-a-half-lane road offers you the opportunity to turn onto a one-lane dirt road with a hand-painted sign on it which merely says "Office." We passed "Office" a few minutes later, driving slowly because of the ruts in the road and the state of the van's suspension.

The Paradise Lake Campground consists of approximately one hundred acres, most of which are scrub, second-growth timber, and marsh. There is, as advertised, a lake, in which you can even swim if you are less squeamish about our woodland friends—leeches, water moccasins, and large pike—than I am. There are also outdoor accommodations for oh, say, 250 tent-and-RV campers on the meadow surrounding the lake, but the real reason that HallowFest chose the site and continues to use it is the indoor accommodations: the barn (dormitory style, sleeps between 100 and 125, depending on how friendly they are) and the cabins (of which there are four, suitable for holding between 2 and 10 people each).

Since HallowFest generally draws 250 attendees, tops, what this means in practice is that anyone who wants to sleep with a man-made roof over his or her head can. Some people do tent every year, and we get a couple of RVs, mostly from New Jersey and points west, but most Pagans, nature religion aside, are indoor people.

I stopped the van in front of the row of cabins. In the headlights they looked like miniature houses, all painted yellow. When I turned off the engine and killed the headlights the cabins and the rest of the campsite vanished.

I'd forgotten how dark the country was. I turned the headlights back on, praying the van's antique battery would take the strain. Julian handed me the flashlight he'd been reading by without comment. I opened the door. It was like opening the refrigerator and looking in. I'd forgotten how *cold* the countryside got, too.

The lights went on in one of the cabins and the door opened. In the diffuse light of the headlights (fading fast, dammit), I saw that it was Maidjene.

Maidjene is about my height and makes Nero Wolfe look like a famine victim. She has long brown hair and a taste for flamboyant dress that makes her well-over-an-eighth-of-a-ton even more impossible to miss, and a lacerating sense of humor, as befits the originator of Niceness Wicca, the Wicca for people who find Mr. Rogers too confrontational. Tonight she was wearing a neon-striped caftan with an orange fake-fur robe over it and looked like a Day-Glo Obi-Wan Kenobi doll.

"Bast? It took you guys long enough. I thought you said you

were getting up here before six," Maidjene said. I could tell by the broad vowels we'd woken her up; she's from someplace like Kentucky or Indiana originally and sometimes it catches her unawares.

"I didn't say A.M. or P.M. We got lost," I added feebly. Behind me, I heard Julian climb down out of his side of the van and come around to where I was. His glasses flared as the beam from my flashlight struck them and I flicked the light off.

Maidjene sighed. "Well, you might as well not have showed up if what you want is to set up; we can't get into the barn until tomorrow."

"What?" The Snake's table would be set up on the barn's second floor; I'd expected to spend the night there.

"Furnace broke last week. Heat's still off. Won't be on until tomorrow and even if Mrs. Cooper puts it on at six it's going to be *damn* cold in there unless I wanted to pay to have it turned on today, thank you very much, which is extra, *which* I didn't," Maidjene said, more or less all on one breath. "Why don't you all come on in?" She went back inside her cabin, leaving the door open.

I got back into the van and turned off the lights before the battery went completely dead and followed Julian (so I presumed) into Maidjene's cabin.

The cabin smelled of dust and damp; the odd blank smell of a place that people use but don't live in. The cabins at Paradise Lake are essentially single rooms, generally containing neither plumbing nor cooking facilities and only rudimentary furniture. This particular one had greenish wallpaper with a faded pattern of wreaths and roses on it. I resisted the totally unwarranted temptation to duck my head as I entered; the rooms are normal height, even though this one seemed more crowded than was strictly believable. It was filled with boxes and backpacks and groceries and duffel bags, suggesting that most of Maidjene's coven was already here. Somewhere.

"They're next door, since why should anyone else have to get the niceness up just because you and others of your ilk are late?" Maidjene said, seeing me look around. "Raven Kindred's coming, and Fred and Leigh and their guys, and some people got here earlier: Fireflower Coven from up to Boston and a bunch from Endless Circle, but they're camping out. There's Diet Pepsi in the cooler, and I think there's maybe some coffee in the Thermos," she added.

Coffee sounded good; I had the hollow watery feeling in my bones that comes from late-night long-distance drives, and I knew there was at least half an hour of shifting and hauling ahead before either Julian or I could think of bed. I searched for the Thermos while Maidjene looked for her paperwork; we struck paydirt at about the same time.

"Julian Fletcher, Karen Hightower," she muttered to herself, checking off the names we use on our checks in what is usually called the Real World. Our "real" names, though not by the yardstick most Pagans use. To Pagans and Witches, our real names are those we chose, for reasons of secrecy or sacrament, when we came to this place in our lives. It's always a minor shock to hear myself called "Karen." My name—my real name—is Bast.

And until now I hadn't known Julian's last name at all.

"Friday arrival, Saturday through Monday, Merchanting, Feast, Indoor, and Parking," Maidjene recited, confirming that we were intending to sell goods, were both participating in the Sunday Night "Feast" (the only meal HallowFest provides, and a logistical nightmare), required indoor accommodations, and needed parking. Every item had its own list, generated courtesy of Maidjene's computer.

I would not organize one of these festivals for dominion over all the kingdoms of the earth and real cash money besides. The picnic I helped Belle—that's Lady Bellflower, my former High Priestess—put on had been bad enough, and that was one day and local. I poured myself coffee into a clean mug I'd unearthed along with the Thermos. The coffee was still hot, but at this point I wouldn't have cared whether it was hot or not, so long as it wasn't decaf.

"License number?" Maidjene asked. I dug the paper I'd written it on out of a pocket and read it back to her. She made a note on yet another separate sheet, yawning.

"We were supposed to have the programs ready," she said, "but Bailey didn't get up here with them until late and they aren't collated yet. I'll give you your badges. Maybe sometime tomorrow," she added vaguely, referring, I hoped, to the programs.

Julian was standing in the corner by the door, keeping a wary eye on the piled clutter. He looked wildly out of place, assuming anything short of a Fundamentalist godshouter could be out of place at a Pagan festival. Julian is a Ceremonial Magician, which means that he is regimented, hierarchical, ascetic, disciplined, reasonably monotheistic, and 100 percent more organized (except when making road trips) than the average God-or-Goddess-worshiping NeoPagan. He is also, as you may have gathered, the oblivious focus of my unilateral sexual fantasies.

"So where are we going to sleep, if the barn's closed?" I said, when Julian didn't. Maidjene was digging through another pile of boxes with the patient late-night determination of a mole with a mission.

"So many kids this year, we're putting them in the barn in one of the big bunkrooms," Maidjene said, which wasn't exactly an answer.

"What joy," I said. The idea of trying to sleep in—or next to—a room full of children ranging from infant to ankle-biter, all with volume controls set at "Max" was not one that really excited me.

"You said we could have one of the cabins," Julian said. I turned around and stared at him. Maybe she had; Julian'd made all the arrangements having to do with the Snake.

"Well sure," Maidjene said, as if Julian were stating the obvious. "If we aren't using them for families with kids, *somebody's* got to be in them."

She came up with the box containing the badges and badge-holders and handed us two. I took mine, making myself the usual empty promise that I would fill my name in by the end of the weekend.

It didn't used to be like this. You didn't need to show a badge at a festival—just being there was proof enough that you had a right to be there. But that was before violence and gate-crashers of various stripes made it vitally necessary to know who belonged and who didn't. Now there are badges, and even something approaching security.

All forms of regimentation begin with an innocent desire for comfort.

"I'll just unlock the one on the end," Maidjene said, "and you can put your stuff in there and then shift the van on down to the parking lot." She handed me a placard to put in the van window to indicate that it, too, was a member of the festival, and picked up a set of master keys for the campsite that were attached to a Frisbee-sized piece of pine with the campground's name on it. "Here we go. I'll have it open in a minute."

"Do we get a key to the cabin, too?" Julian said.

Maidjene and I both stared at him blankly.

"So we can lock it?" he added.

The one last holdover from the Summer of Love in the NeoPagan Community—at least at the smaller festivals—is this: nobody worries particularly about keeping his possessions under lock and key. None of the inside rooms in the barn locked, and I'd never heard of anyone locking the cabins—even the Registration cabin—during a HallowFest.

Of course, this attitude is tempered by enough reality that most people still don't leave their wallets lying about unattended, but the sense of community—real or imagined—keeps the pilfering to a minimum.

"You won't need to lock it," I told Julian. "This is his first festival," I told Maidjene. Julian shrugged.

Maidjene led us down to the end of the row of cabins. It was quiet enough that the crunch of my boots on the gravel sounded loud and I could hear the sound that the wind makes when it blows through pine branches. The edge of the lake that gives Paradise Lake its name is just behind the cabins, and the reeds around it rattled as the wind passed through them. At a place and a time like this it's easy to believe that the Earth is a living and caring being.

"Are you coming or not?" Maidjene said from the doorway of the cabin she'd opened.

There was a bare bulb on a short chain, swinging slowly back and forth. The floor was a grungy green linoleum, flecked with white and yellow, and the walls were covered in a shrunken and aged paper patterned with yellow ducks carrying pink umbrellas on a pale blue background. There was a bare double mattress in a vinyl zip-bag lying in a corner.

"Okay?" said Maidjene. "See you in the morning." She wandered off again, keys jingling.

The cabin was about standard for HallowFest accommodations; it had more or less what I would have gotten in one of the bunkrooms, more than I would have gotten upstairs, and had the advantage of being quieter and more private. There was a door in the back wall, and when I opened it I found that Maidjene had really done right by us: there was a rudimentary washroom tacked on to the back of this particular cabin. I turned the tap and was rewarded with a hesitant trickle of brown water, which meant that the toilet would almost certainly be working, too.

Despite this luxury, the lodgings were probably not up to a standard that Julian was used to.

I turned back to him. He had an odd smile on his face.

"All the comforts of home," he said neutrally.

I felt the usual awkwardness of being in a situation where one person—guess who?—has an emotional agenda and the other doesn't. "Welcome to the lap of nature," I said. "Let's get the stuff out of the van."

We could have left the stuff in the van for tomorrow, but there was no guarantee we'd be able to bring the van back up here then, and I was damned if I was going to take the chance of having to schlep all this stuff up from the parking lot. Unloading the van took a little bit longer than packing it had, and while we were doing that another band of lost travelers arrived in a white oversprung station wagon with Rhode Island plates. I discovered then that Maidjene's coven was manning registration in two-hour watches, since once Maidjene had squared the newcomers away and directed them to the meadow—where they could amuse themselves by trying to set up the tent they'd brought with them in the dark—Maidjene woke up Bailey and went to bed.

By that time I was on my last load out of the van. Julian had pulled his share of the weight but he had more of an interest in being able to find things again in the morning than I did. When I brought in the last box he'd already started unrolling bedding and had even set up what looked like a small folding tray-table.

"I'm going to run the van down to the parking lot. I'll be back in a few," I told Julian. He waved, absently, turning to another box. I closed the door carefully behind me.

The parking area is a not unreasonable distance from the barn and cabins, but the walk back up the sloping drive was an eerie thing at something after one in the morning. With all the lifting and carrying I wasn't cold anymore, and from a familiarity with the area I wasn't worried about marauding bears or bands of Kallikaks. This year Samhain fell near the full moon, which meant that now, three weeks earlier, the sky was dark. The stars were brilliant, the air was clear, and the scurrying sounds from the woods were raccoons at the largest, and more likely mice. Nothing to feel threatened by.

What I did feel was a sense of complete isolation; a sense that not only was there no human companionship immediately available, but that even the future possibility of human companionship had been somehow erased, as if everyone else had gone and left me alone here forever. Standing in the dark, on the road that led back up to the cabins, I knew I was actually not only in the middle of civilization, but five minutes' walk, at most, from several other people, some of whom were even awake.

And it changed nothing. I stood there and wondered what it would have been like to live in a time, not so very long ago, when the entire human race numbered less than a billionth of its present total and I might have walked for days without seeing any sign either of civilization or of people. I decided that New Yorkers prefer social isolation to real isolation and continued up the path.

When I got back to the cabin, Julian was brewing tea.

He'd been busy while I'd been gone. Several boxes had been piled together and a red cloth spread over them: on this makeshift table were a lit candle, a smoking brazier, and a mirror, as well as various other odds and ends including a small glass bottle half full of dark oil. The incense was strong enough almost to overpower the burnt-dust smell from the laboring ancient electric heater we'd brought along.

Julian had also set up the folding table that would go into the barn tomorrow, and along its seven-foot length were arranged a little kettle on a ring over a flaming spirit lamp, a Rockingham pot waiting for hot water, a tin of English biscuits, and two white mugs.

It was not an unreasonable amount of gear to travel with—I have friends in the Society for Creative Anachronism who bring not only tables, but chairs, bedsteads, and entire yurts to their camping events—but it was a level of domesticity I'd somehow never associated with Julian.

He had his back to me and was opening another box, out of which he lifted a teardrop-shaped pressed-glass decanter, its stopper made leakproof with wax, and two tiny matching glasses. Those he set on the tray-table. Then he turned.

"I thought something hot would be good," he said when he saw me.

"Where did you *get* all this stuff?" I said, meaning, mostly, the clever method of making hot water without electricity.

"From my lab." Julian smiled. "Alchemy."

Which was not unreasonable, considering Julian—if medieval

alchemy (as distinct from its nineties offspring, spiritual alchemy)
didn't work, he'd want to know exactly why not. Julian is a spe-
cialist in the theory and history of magic, and, in his own quiet
way, a rigorous scientist.

I sat down on a stack of book boxes, which turned out to be a
mistake. Sitting still made me realize how damned cold it was in
here, and I knew from past experience that the heater would shut
itself off long before the room began to be warm. The cold didn't
seem to bother Julian at all.

I took my tea when it was ready and tried not to obsess on the
pile of quilts and sleeping bags on the floor. The *single* pile. I'd been
expecting to roll up in my sleeping bag in the barn—but then, I'd
expected that the heat would be on there, too.

"I thought it would be warmer that way," Julian said neutrally.
He was staring at the candle, not at the bed, and the mug of tea
and the biscuit he was holding made him resemble an impover-
ished English vicar. If this was a pass, it was a damned indirect
one—he might mean nothing more than what he'd said. I had a
sudden passionate curiosity to know what he wore to bed.

"Yeah," I said. "Warmer."

Sometimes my savoir-faire amazes even me.

If Julian had been Valentino himself I would still have worn a
T-shirt, sweatshirt, sweatpants, and two layers of wool socks to
bed; there's no sense in being a damned fool about things and you
try sleeping in an unheated cabin in Gotham County in the middle of October wearing anything less. I got first use of the bathroom, which might have been chivalry on Julian's part, except for
the fact that this also meant that I got the bed first, and Julian's
alchemical skills did not extend to conjuring electric blankets out
of nothing. I curled into a fetal ball under the layer of sleeping bag
and blanket and shivered, knowing I would be warm . . . someday.

Julian wore blue flannel pajamas to bed. Without socks. Ceremonial magicians are often ascetics.

He picked up the lit candle from the table and carried it with
him across the room to turn out the lamp. He set it on the tray-
table and picked up two full glasses that were sitting on the tray-
table beside a tiny decanter. He handed one of the glasses to me.
I sat up to take it.

"Skoal," Julian said, raising his glass.

It was syrupy-sweet and full of herbs—somebody's home-brewing—but as Julian'd drunk his, I followed suit. It was not the sort of vintage one allows to linger on the tongue; it had a nasty saccharine aftertaste, and one of the inclusions must have been *Capsicum*—red pepper to you—because I felt a rush of heat that went all the way to my toes as the liqueur hit my stomach. Warm at last, I burrowed under the covers again as Julian snuffed the candle with his fingertips and climbed in beside me.

Some time later—it couldn't have been more than an hour or two, as it was still too dark to see—I came bolt awake, the way you sometimes do out of violent dreams you don't afterward remember. The only light in the room was coming from the desperate coils of the electric heater, cycling on again before the Ice Age actually arrived. It made just enough light to see that Julian was not in the bed, but standing beside it.

I closed my eyes and prepared to go back to sleep. Julian got back under the quilt and put his hand on my shoulder.

The abrupt certainty of what I suddenly knew was about to happen jolted me with the pleasurable pain of an electric charge. I put my hand out and touched only skin, oiled with something spicy and ceremonial. The oil clung to my fingers. When he kissed me, the scent soaked into my skin. I could taste it.

I helped him push my sweatpants off. Neither of us spoke.

2

T he next time I woke up, the light was stronger. My sweatpants were shoved down to the foot of the mattress and my sweatshirt was bunched under my head. Julian was sound asleep beside me.

I felt as though I'd been hit over the head, or had expected to die but been miraculously spared, or any number of things that paralyze the cognitive faculties. I slithered out from under the blankets, excruciatingly careful not to let cold air in, and gathered up my outdoor clothes by the thin wolf-light of false dawn.

I was so girlishly rattled that I even went outside to dress. Although it wasn't that much colder out than in, the cold air was as immediate as a blow to the heart, and I sucked air and hissed as I struggled into jeans and parka. There was a stump a little way toward the lake and I sat on it to pull on last night's socks and boots. By then I could distract myself with the romance of being up with the dawn, something I actually see oftener than I'd really like.

As the sun rises, it turns the sky first indigo, then blue. Any clouds take on a ridiculous set of Disney colors: purple, pink, yellow—even green. The tops of the trees, or mountains, or whatever's highest, go to full color, while the ground is still shades of gray. After that the stages of the process are much less distinct, with areas of light and color slowly equalizing until all of a sudden you realize it's not dawn, but morning.

It was still dawn when I walked down to the lake. The lake was covered with white mist in a low bank, blurring its boundaries. Across the lake and to my left I could see two dome tents, an orange one and a blue one, rising like strange giant mushrooms from the grass. The grass would be green later; right now it was still grayish with night and fog. Down here the air was even colder and wetter; I decided the lake hadn't been my destination.

I turned right, following the lake around to where it dwindled into marsh. There was a wooden bridge spanning the disconsolate brown sludge; it was slippery with rime as I crossed over it. Across the meadow, the trail began that led up the hill and through a scrap of pinewood to another open space. When HallowFest had the site nobody camped there.

I was panting by the time I reached it; there's a more gradual trail that starts behind the barn but I'd taken the direct route and it's a pretty steep climb. By the time I got there it was full day and I had no trouble avoiding the fire pit in the middle of the clearing.

The fire pit is about four feet across and a foot deep, lined with brick and edged with big white stones. The reason nobody camps here is that we use this site for the Saturday Night Opening Ritual and for the Bardic Circle and Bonfire.

I went over and looked at the fire pit. It was full of dead leaves, charcoal, condoms, and the odd beer bottle, but somebody would be coming up to clean it out and fill it with firewood later.

I'd relaxed as soon as I'd gotten here, and it didn't take much to figure out why: Julian wouldn't be easily able to find me here, should he conceivably be looking. It was an irritating thought, and I couldn't face it right now; I hurried across the meadow and into the woods beyond as if I were following a ball of string through a labyrinth.

The meadow with the Bardic Circle is at the edge of a pine forest bordered on the west by the access road into Paradise Lake and on the north by the houses that edge Gotham County 6. The bulk of Paradise Lake's acres lie east and south; this patch of woods is mostly a buffer zone, leading nowhere. Once I reached the edge I'd have to go back the way I came; due east out of the pine forest is a drop-off too steep for me or anyone else with brains to shinny down.

I'd been walking fast, as if I had a destination in mind where there wasn't one, and the part of me that wasn't occupied in dithering had finally noticed that and was just getting around to questioning it when I saw . . .

I could say its stillness caught my eye, but that would be ridiculous: I was surrounded by rocks and trees and neither one moves much. I could say it was the color, but the colors were browns and blacks, just like the autumn forest. I looked, basically, to reassure myself that it wasn't what my mind was telling me it was.

But it was, and part of me wasn't surprised.

There was a man lying on his back on the ground. The trees had kept me from seeing his hands and face until I was right up on him; for the rest, he was wearing brown corduroy pants and black shoes and a brown woolly coat. It was an outside coat, a winter coat, and his left hand was still in its glove. The right hand was curled among the pine needles, waxy-pale and diminished. The nails were blue.

I knelt beside him on the forest floor and pulled open the unbuttoned coat. His eyes were closed and he might have been asleep, but I've seen dead people before, and I knew that he was dead, absent beyond any summoning back. The coat felt heavy; when I lifted it open, a gun slid out of the right-hand pocket and into the pine needles that covered the forest floor. It was, I decided tentatively, a .38 revolver. I didn't touch it. I hate guns. It comes of having had them pointed at me, I expect.

In life John Doe had probably been the upstate version of a redneck: fat, fair, and fiftysomething, clean shaven and closely barbered. He was wearing a red plaid flannel shirt and a white V-neck T-shirt. The only thing that didn't quite fit this picture was the aggressive gold crucifix bearing a muscular silver Jesus that he had around his neck. It was all of three inches long and he'd worn it on a heavy chain that would make it dangle about midchest. It was currently flung back over one shoulder and resting among the pine needles, as if it had flipped back when he fell. Only by looking very closely could you see the brownish spot, about the size of a quarter, on the front of the flannel shirt at about the place Jesus would have hung.

The shirt wasn't buttoned, which was odd. I pulled it open. There was a slightly larger spot on the none-too-clean T-shirt. The T-shirt wasn't tucked in, and a wedge of hairy bellyflesh showed at its hem. I eased the shirt up and looked.

In the middle of John Doe's chest, level with his nipples or a little below, was a weird puncture wound. It wasn't red and it wasn't bleeding; it was black and almost dry. A quarter, or a fifty-cent piece at the very most, would have covered it completely.

It wasn't a knife wound—which was to say, while he'd been

stabbed, as far as I could tell, it was with something that made three half-inch slashes that came together at almost right angles, like the center of a Mercedes-Benz hood ornament, or a radiation trefoil, or a peace sign with the bottom center stroke removed.

I pulled the T-shirt back down, feeling sick. And then I felt even worse, because I realized that the fingers that had touched him to lift the T-shirt were oily. When I lifted them to my nose I could smell cinnamon, and when I looked at the dead man's face again, I could see that there was a shiny patch on his forehead, a little darker than his skin—but then, cinnamon anointing oil *is* a dark reddish-brown color.

The marks on his T-shirt that I'd taken for poor laundry skills became blotches of reddish oil applied to the skin and now soaking into the cloth. I found myself staring fixedly at the white drops of resin oozing from the trunk of the pine tree he lay beneath, and then my focus shifted and I could see droplets of hardened cream-colored candle wax upon the fallen needles on the forest floor.

No.

I stood up and backed away, tripped over my own feet and crashed sideways into a tree hard enough to knock the wind out of me. I'd hit my head, too; the pain made my eyes tear and stopped me from doing something stupid. This was not a time for stupidity.

There was a man lying dead in the forest, stabbed through the heart with . . . something.

And sometime before or after he'd died, someone had anointed him with oil and burned candles at his head and feet. And this had happened in a campground already being filled by one of the biggest gatherings of Pagans, Wiccans, and magicians on the entire East Coast.

I knelt beside the tree I'd run into and scrubbed my fingers dry in brown pine needles.

There are things that you do when you find a dead person, and one of the important ones is to tell the police.

I'm not one of those steely-eyed adventuresses out of prime-time fiction who stumbles through battle, murder, and sudden death without even mussing her hair, but by now I've had enough bad luck in my life that John Doe didn't leave me really rattled for long. After all, he was dead; how much more harm could he do?

The walk back helped, too. On the way I thought to check my

watch and realized it was barely six. I entertained the craven notion of not mentioning what I'd seen at all—it was entirely possible that no one else would go up that way all weekend—and a
small irrational part of me was convinced that the whole thing was
only a sick practical joke that I was the victim of, and that when
I led someone else back up there, there'd be no one lying dead
among the pines at all.

I compromised with it by promising myself I'd tell Maidjene. She
ought to know, anyway, being the festival coordinator. And then
she could go with me and the police so that even if I was going to
look silly, I'd have moral support.

I tried the door of Registration. It wasn't locked. I looked in and
saw Bailey asleep in a pile of blankets, looking like a giant hedgehog. I closed the door again and went next door. The door there
wasn't locked either.

It was warmer in this cabin than it was either outside or in the
cabin I'd shared with Julian, but then there were eight people here,
crammed into a space roughly twelve feet by twelve. Fortunately,
Maidjene was near the front. I nudged her with my foot; there
wasn't room to kneel.

"Wake up," I said, trying to keep my voice down. I kept poking
her until her eyes opened. She blinked, then focused.

"Come outside," I said. "There's a situation." I retraced my
steps over puppy-piled bodies and waited outside. Maidjene and
I have known each other for a long time, even if she does live in
Jersey. She joined me outside less than five minutes later.

She hadn't bothered to undress from last night—rustic conditions encourage the layered look—and looked rumpled and wary
and ready to be mad.

"It's six-oh-fucking-niceness-clock in the morning, Bast," she
snarled in a stage whisper. "This had better be really exciting."

"How excited are you by a dead body in the woods up above
the Bardic Circle?" I snapped back.

She stared at me; I could see she didn't believe it.

"There is a dead body in the woods," I repeated more patiently.
"We need to call the police."

"You aren't making this up?" she said, after a long pause. I love
the amount of trust I engender in my friends.

"No. I saw him. He's really dead. Where's a phone?"

Maidjene didn't move. "Who is it?" she said.

It hadn't actually occurred to me until this moment to wonder.

"I don't know," I said slowly, thinking back. "I didn't recognize him. He was wearing a crucifix," I added, although that didn't automatically rule out his being an attendee of HallowFest.

And he'd been ritually murdered—both in the criminological sense and, possibly, in a magical sense. I thought about that and didn't say anything.

"Show me where it is," Maidjene said.

"Jesus fuck me gently with a chainsaw," Maidjene breathed reverently ten minutes later, staring at John Doe from a safe distance. She didn't need to get close to see he was there, and the police were not going to be best pleased by this becoming a high-traffic area. Because there really was a dead man at HallowFest, and now Maidjene had seen him too.

"We'd better tell Mrs. Cooper," Maidjene pronounced.

"We'd better call the police," I said.

In the end we had to do both, because although there was a pay phone on the outside of the barn, it didn't have a phone book. It only occurred to me later that I could just have dialed "Information," and later still that the reason for the lapse was that I felt like an outsider this far from Manhattan and was looking for allies before I confronted the Establishment.

Helen Cooper owns and runs Paradise Lake and has been very tolerant of HallowFest's free-range hippie foibles over the years. She's a stout gray-haired lady somewhere in her seventies by now; she wasn't young even when we started coming here back in the early eighties. She lives year-round in the building at the entrance to the camp, a large rambling white clapboard house with a porch around three sides and a wooden sign out front that matches the one on the access road that says "Office."

It was a quarter of seven when she answered the door, and by then I'd gone back to feeling twitched, certain that at any moment somebody else would trip over the dead man.

I didn't think we'd wakened her, but Mrs. Cooper was still in her nightclothes. She looked at us through the old-fashioned green-painted wooden screen door. There was a silence. I realized Maidjene was letting me take the lead and hoped I looked more respectable than I felt.

"We need to use your phone. We have to call the police. There's a problem," I said.

"What kind of a problem?" Mrs. Cooper said.

I suppose subconsciously I expected everyone to know in advance; every time I had to explain it bothered me.

"There's a dead man up in your woods," I said, restraining myself from phrasing it "seems to be" with an effort. There was no seeming at all: there was a man and he was dead.

"Just a minute—I'll go up with you and check," Mrs. Cooper said, starting to close the door.

"Mrs. Cooper," I said sharply. I would have put my hand on the door but I'd have had to open the screen first. She stopped.

"I saw him too," Maidjene said.

"He really is dead," I said. "And we have to call the police now."

It turned out to be the Sheriff's Department that we called, not the police. Maidjene and I stood in the dining room while Mrs. Cooper punched the quick-dial number on her kitchen phone. She spoke to someone named John and confided to him that "some girls" staying at the campground "thought they'd seen" a dead body in the woods. She assured "John" that we'd be here when the car arrived.

"Car'll be here in about ten minutes," Mrs. Cooper said, coming back to the dining room. "I have to go get dressed. Would you like some coffee?"

I would, Maidjene wouldn't. Mrs. Cooper showed me where the coffee things were, and I doctored up a cup while Maidjene peered out the dining room window, for all the world as if she were Ma Barker waiting for the cops.

"This," she said, "is going to be trouble."

I shrugged. It'd already been trouble.

"I can see it now," she went on mournfully, " 'Human Sacrifice at Satanic Sabbat.' "

"Oh for gods' sake!" I snapped.

Maidjene turned back to me. Her face was set. "You know damned well that's what they're going to say, and nothing *we* say is going to stop another—"

"Witch hunt?" I suggested sarcastically. Maidjene snorted.

She was right, though, especially if . . . I stopped. There were too many variables to settle on one good paranoid conspiracy. Who was dead, and how had he died? Who had killed him, and why, and—

Mrs. Cooper got back about the time the sheriff's car pulled up in front of the house. There were two deputies in it. The driver got out and Mrs. Cooper was already opening the door before I realized the driver was a woman.

She was wearing a pale tan Stetson that made me think of Texas marshals, a light shirt and dark pants and the rest of the usual paraphernalia: black leather belt and a truly enormous gun. Her badge looked oddly commonplace to me, and after a moment I realized why: Gotham County Sheriff's Office used a star-in-circle, just as Wiccans did, only their star was solid and had "Deputy Sheriff" written across it. She came inside and walked straight over to me.

"I'm Sergeant Pascoe," she said, holding out her hand. I shook hands with her; her grip was firm.

"This is the girl, Fayrene," Mrs. Cooper said.

"I'm—" I hesitated. "My friends call me Bast. Do you need my legal name?"

"Not if you haven't done anything wrong," Sergeant Pascoe said. "Do you think you can take us to what you saw, Bast?"

I must have looked panic-stricken; for a moment I wasn't sure I could find the place again. "There was a dead man," I said firmly. "Up in the pine forest above the"— I had to think a minute to remember the Paradise Lake name for it—"Upland Meadow. He really is dead," I said.

I must have sounded more frustrated than I realized; Fayrene put a hand on my arm. "Let's go see," she said.

"I'll stay here," Maidjene said firmly.

In the last few years I have found a dead body and barely escaped becoming one, but this time was different. Fayrene and I—and Deputy Twochuck, who drove this time—went by car back to the barn and up the road that led to the Upland Meadow site.

Deputy Twochuck looked maybe nineteen and kept staring in the mirror at me until Sergeant Pascoe asked him if he wanted to put the car in a ditch. That was how I found out his name was Renny. Renny and Fayrene, and their guns. I wondered how much trouble I was in.

They parked at the edge of the meadow; you couldn't take a car up into the pine forest even if you wanted to. Sergeant Pascoe got out and came back to let me out.

"You stay here, Renny. I'll call you if I need you." She turned to me. I pointed up the hill into the pines. Sergeant Pascoe sighed.

*   *   *

The body was still there.

It was more of a relief than I'd thought it would be; once I was sure it was there I stopped and leaned against one of the pines, catching my breath.

"Pretty worried, weren't you?" Sergeant Pascoe said.

"I thought . . ." I shrugged. "I don't know."

Sergeant Pascoe grunted and went to stand over the body, looking down.

"Anybody else been up here you know of?"

"I brought Maidjene up, but she didn't go any closer than this." I was standing about where she had been. "Somebody stabbed him," I said helpfully.

Sergeant Pascoe looked up at me from under the brim of her hat. She was blonde and had the color of eyes that often go with that shade of blonde, a steely sort of grayish-blue. I'd seen those eyes before in other faces. Cop eyes.

"Now how would you know that?" she said.

"I . . . looked," I said finally.

"Sure you didn't do anything else?" She didn't wait for an answer. "Go on back down the hill and tell Renny I told him to call the M.E. And tell him to bring me up the tape."

I went on back down the hill and told Deputy Twochuck what Sergeant Pascoe had said. He gulped and looked excited, and picked up the radio mike and started spouting 10-codes into it. I went back up the hill.

"Hey! You can't go up there!" he said.

"So stop me," I said, walking off. Which wasn't fair to him, but it hadn't been a very fair morning, all things considered.

"Why don't you tell me what happened?" Fayrene said when I got back. John Doe still lay on the ground. It didn't look as if Sergeant Pascoe had touched him.

"I got here last night about midnight," I started, and told her everything that was any of her business. "So around dawn I decided to go for a walk."

"And what made you come up here?" Sergeant Pascoe said.

I shrugged. I wasn't really sure anymore. "It was in the same direction I'd been going."

"So then?" she said.

"Well, I thought I saw a body, so I went to make sure, and it was a body—"

"Anybody you know?"

I shook my head. "People look different when they're dead, but . . . no."

"And how is it you happened to take a closer look at our friend?" Sergeant Pascoe said.

"I just— I guess I just had to be sure."

It didn't sound like the truth, and for good reason—what I'd been making sure of was that John Doe hadn't just been murdered; he'd been sacrificed. And I had no intention of saying so. At least not yet.

About this time Twochuck made it up the hill, carrying a big bright yellow roll of tape. He stared down at John Doe and gulped.

"Fayrene, that's—"

"Why don't you go and cordon me off a nice big chunk of real estate, Renny, while we wait for the suits to show up?" Fayrene said.

Renny stopped himself with an effort. So he recognized John Doe. That was interesting; about as interesting as the fact that Fayrene hadn't wanted him to tell me what he knew.

"Why don't you step back here with me," Fayrene said. We both backed away from the body, in the direction of the "Police Line: Do Not Cross" tape that Twochuck was stringing from tree to tree. We'd almost reached it when Maidjene and Mrs. Cooper got here. Either Maidjene had changed her mind about revisiting the scene or she was charitably keeping Mrs. Cooper company.

Mrs. Cooper was wearing green wellies and a black and red plaid jacket. She ducked right under the yellow tape and marched over to the body.

"Helen," Fayrene said. "You don't want to—"

It was too late. Mrs. Cooper stared down at John Doe.

"God damn," she said, as if passing sentence. She looked at Sergeant Pascoe. "That's Hellfire Harm."

Maidjene and I had both followed Mrs. Cooper.

"Jesus," said Maidjene, then: "Shit."

She'd been right. We were in trouble now.

Hellfire Harm—or as he was known to the HallowFest Community, "Jesus" Jackson Harm—had been a standing joke for years. He was a local character who'd sent long rambling letters to the *Tamerlane Gazette Advertiser* denouncing—among other things like vaccination, credit cards, and Suzanne Somers—our "unholy forgathering of Satanic Witches and Imps of Satan." These letters, which the paper resignedly printed in full on the editorial page, were written in a style that hadn't been much seen since Matthew Hopkins wrote his memoirs, and we'd used to read them out to each other over Sunday breakfast. While Harm had obviously been passionately serious, he'd just as obviously been several sandwiches shy of a picnic; a joke.

Not now.

"And you didn't know him?" Sergeant Pascoe said, looking at me.

We'd all gone back to the other side of the police line, and she'd sent Twochuck down to cordon off the path up from the meadow, too.

"No. If he's Jackson Harm, then I knew what he said about HallowFest, of course. But I only read about him in the papers."

And if he was Jackson Harm, the potential for publicity on this was, well . . . it'd probably make the city papers.

"Who killed him?" Maidjene demanded.

"That's an interesting question," Sergeant Pascoe said. About then two more marked cars joined hers at the bottom of the hill.

By New York City standards Reverend Harm got a lot of attention, but then, Gotham County probably didn't have as high a per capita homicide rate as my home turf did.

It was a learning experience. Fayrene, I discovered, didn't have the authority to pronounce Harm dead—that was left to the Medical Examiner. It took the M.E. about twenty seconds to confirm that the Reverend Harm was dead, probably from the stab wound, although he wasn't committing himself. The Crime Scene officer was hovering over his shoulder, waiting for him to finish. The photographer who had come with them was taking pictures of everything in sight, including the stab wound.

I wanted to ask what they thought could make a mark like that, but not as much as I didn't want to be noticed. Maidjene had already gone off with Renny—Fayrene wanted a complete list of everyone who'd been on-site between yesterday and this morning, and statements from them all. I wished her luck in getting them, or of getting any use out of them if she did get them.

The ambulance that would take Harm to the morgue arrived. By now the Bardic Circle was full of HallowFest attendees being kept from climbing the hill by three deputies in Stetsons.

Fayrene walked over to where I was watching the morgue attendants try to get their stretcher through the crowd.

"I guess we're going to need your name now," she told me. She'd gotten Maidjene's, and I imagine she already knew Mrs. Cooper's. "And you'll have to make a formal statement, but you can do that with Renny."

I nodded. It wouldn't be the first time.

I gave her my business card, wrote down my work and home numbers, showed her my driver's license, and even gave Lieutenant Hodiac as a character reference.

"You know Sam?" Fayrene said.

"Yeah." Well enough to mention his name and be pretty sure he'd remember me, anyway. Sam is Detective Lieutenant Samuel Hodiac, NYPD, Cult Crimes Division. Belle sometimes does advisory-type work for him, and besides, he saved my life once. "Some people I know do some consulting work for him sometimes." I was surprised she knew him, but then, the law enforcement community is probably as insular as the NeoPagan one.

"And you're one of those New York witches camping up here this weekend?"

There was no point in denying it. "Yes."

She sighed and shifted her weight. The leather belt she was wearing creaked.

"My boy Wyler's been bugging me to let him come up here and see what's going on ever since he heard about you folks last year." She sighed. "He's about sixteen, but he's getting to that age." At which, her tone implied, boys did not listen to their mothers, even if their mothers were heavily armed.

"Well, of course we wouldn't mind talking to him," I began slowly, trying to channel what my ex–High Priestess Bellflower, community outreach maven, would say in this situation. "But he *is* sixteen. He'd need his parents' permission before he—"

"Came out here and danced naked by the light of the moon?" she cracked.

"We don't do that," I said quickly, before I realized she was joking. Sort of. She hadn't been serious, and the reason was obvious: if there was anyone in Gotham County who knew exactly what we did at Paradise Lake, it'd be the Gotham County Sheriff's Department.

"You've been to a HallowFest," I accused.

" 'Bout ten years back," she agreed.

That would have been the year that we'd gotten deputies of our very own prowling the site at odd hours. What they'd been look-ing for, none of us ever found out.

"So you know," I said.

About then the Medical Examiner left and two people in plain-clothes arrived. I was introduced to Detective Lieutenant Tony Wayne and Ms. Reynalda Dahl of the DA's office. They wandered off with Fayrene for a few minutes and came back alone.

"So what did you think when you tripped over that body, Bast?" Lieutenant Wayne asked. He didn't look a thing like Bruce Wayne, or even Val Kilmer. I decided to forgot the obvious jokes. Detec-tive Wayne was a solid, dark-haired, ordinary-looking man with brown eyes, a bushy mustache, and a gold shield. I wondered how much ragging he got over his name, considering he worked in Gotham County.

"I thought I should call the sheriff," I said. "He was dead."

"You made sure of that," Ms. Dahl said. For a minute I thought she was accusing me of the murder. She looked formidably cor-porate; blacks storming the Establishment bastions have to look whiter than white, especially in this field. It isn't fair, but then, what is?

"I looked under his shirt," I said. Even I could hear how de-fensive I sounded.

"Why?" Lieutenant Wayne asked.

"I don't *know!*" I said. "I came up here, I saw him—he looked *dead;* dead people look dead." I stopped and took a deep breath and tried to cooperate. I was innocent; cooperation was my job in the great civil machine. "I got down beside him and opened his coat. You could see the blood on his shirt; just a spot." I remem-bered something else. "He had a gun. I didn't touch it."

Dahl whipped off to say something to somebody else.

"It would ease our minds considerably if we could fingerprint you, Bast. Sometimes people touch things without noticing," Tony Wayne said. He was good; he had the kind of presence you would instinctively trust.

"Okay." I wondered if my prints were still on file down in the city. "Do I have to go down to your office?"

"We can do it here." He gave me a smile. Practiced charm. Soothing the probably innocent. "What happened after you saw the blood on his shirt?"

I thought back. "It wasn't buttoned," I remembered, surprised.

"I don't remember whether it was tucked in. There was a spot on his T-shirt. Blood, you know? Shouldn't he have bled more?"

Lieutenant Wayne grunted; answering questions wasn't his department. Dahl came back.

"Crime Scene's got it. Smith & Wesson. Twenty-two."

In the words of Doonesbury's Uncle Duke: *"That thing wouldn't stop a hamster."*

"Something wrong?" Lieutenant Wayne asked me.

"I—" I said. "I don't like guns," I said feebly. Guns are a joke, until somebody points one at you. It wasn't so long ago that somebody had pointed one at me.

"So you saw he was stabbed," Lieutenant Wayne prompted me.

"He looked really dead," I said, knowing I sounded like an idiot and hating it. "I went looking for the police. It was about 6:30 when I looked at my watch."

"Helen's call was logged in at 6:55," Fayrene said. She'd come back without my noticing. "Her place is about twenty minutes' walk from here, cutting straight through."

"And dawn was around five today. That gives us a window of about ninety minutes. Are you planning to go anywhere?" Only this last was to me.

"When?" I asked blankly. I could tell the three of them thought it was funny. "I'm going to be up here through Monday," I said, nettled. "So are about three hundred other people from half a dozen states. Then we're all going to go home." *Please god.*

"Okay, that's about everything for now," Lieutenant Wayne said. "We'll be in touch if we need anything further. And we'd appreciate it if you didn't discuss this with anyone."

I nodded. Yeah, right.

"Come on." Fayrene took my arm. We went down the hill. Jackson Harm followed us down in a zipper bag.

There were a bunch of people, including Maidjene, standing around in the meadow.

"Sergeant Pascoe!" Maidjene called. Fayrene walked out to meet her.

"Look, are we going to be able to use this area for tonight?" Maidjene demanded, as soon as Fayrene was within hailing distance.

It was a reasonable question. There were cars parked on the grass, digging muddy ruts in it, and yellow tape was strung from tree to tree across the whole north side of it.

"You'll have to talk to Lieutenant Wayne about that," Fayrene said.

"The First Amendment—" Maidjene began argumentatively.

"Look, as long as we're on this side of the tape we're okay, right? And you guys are going to be gone by then, right?" I interrupted, desperately willing Maidjene to shut up.

"Nine o'clock?" Fayrene said, proving she knew as much about HallowFest as I'd thought. "Probably. Might be a deputy up there, though."

"That's okay," I said. Maidjene glared at me, betrayed.

"I'm glad," Fayrene said dryly. "Now if you'd all just clear out of here?"

I gave Maidjene the firm eye. She shrugged and walked back to the largest clump of watchers and started persuading them to leave for woods and pastures greener and fresh fields anew.

"It's like herding cats," Fayrene muttered.

"You don't know the half of it," I said. She looked at me, surprised I'd heard, I guess.

"So you don't think they're going to stay out of our hair?" she asked me.

It seemed to be a serious question, so I gave it serious thought. "I guess . . . a lot of us have too much confidence in our own abilities," I said.

She laughed. "I guess you do, but there shouldn't be much to mess up once we're done—and we photographed it all, anyway."

By now we'd reached her car. With two more cars behind it, it wasn't going anywhere soon. She opened the door and fumbled around in the glove box for a minute and pulled out a card.

"If you happen to remember anything else about this morning, you give us a call," Fayrene said. She wrote another number on the back. "Any time." It was not a social request.

"Yeah," I said.

I was dismissed. Fayrene went back up the hill again. I went off to help Maidjene clear the meadow.

It was about nine o'clock in the morning. The sky was blue, the birds were singing, the sun was even warm. And the Reverend Harm was dead, and public opinion—if nothing more—was going to point to someone at HallowFest as his killer.

"The deputies would like everybody to clear out," I said to a group of people I remembered faintly from other HallowFests. They were

all in SCA garb of the later MGM period, and one of them was wearing a silver pentacle brooch that must have been four inches
across. NeoPaganism, as interpreted for these current Middle
Ages.

"Tell them to leave us alone," the brooch-wearer said. I wondered when I'd been appointed police liaison for HallowFest.

"They better," one of the others said. I remembered her. Tammy
was what everyone called her; it was short for Tamar. "Or
Goddess'll zap them, just like she did Jesus Jackson." She giggled, as if it were all a joke.

"Payback time," a man with a large hunting knife on his belt
agreed. I wondered what we must look like to the forces of law and
order: knife-wielding hippie freaks? Or worse?

"They would like you guys to clear out of the meadow," I repeated. "Are you checked in yet?" I said on a sudden inspiration.

It turned out they weren't; that got them moving. I walked
away quickly. It had been a stressful morning, and people carrying on as if Jesus Jackson's murder were actually some sort of
supernatural seal of approval on their religion of choice did not
improve my temper.

I gritted my teeth and went down the easy path to the barn,
feeling like Cassandra booking passage on the *Titanic:* something
awful was going to happen, and there was no way I could stop it.

3

I walked through the barn: you can go in one door and out the other to reach the cabins if you're in a hurry. Deputy Renny Twochuck had taken over one of the smaller rooms. The door was open, and there was a line of people waiting to make statements. I ducked inside. He raised his pen when he saw me.

"I've got some stuff to do," I said, "and they're supposed to get my prints. When shall I come back?"

He looked at his watch. "If you could report back here at 11:30, ma'am, that would be very helpful. And if you see"—he consulted his notes—"Mrs. Wagner, could you let her know we'll need her records?"

I nodded. There was no sense in embarking upon long explanations of why he wasn't going to get them, and fortunately I knew who he was talking about. Maidjene was Mrs. Wagner, at least until the divorce was final, but as for getting the attendance records for the festival, I could foresee a pointless tussle and the invocation of the ACLU. I wondered what I could do to head it off. Belle would be the person to ask, and she should be getting here sometime today. Lady Bellflower of the Wicca comes from a long line of union organizers and civil protesters and would be a better judge of our rights under the law than some coven lawyer who'd gotten his ideas about our legal rights from old *Perry Mason* reruns.

I bid the police presence a fond farewell as Deputy Twochuck was explaining to someone, probably for what he felt was the ten millionth time, that he needed her *real* name, the one on her driver's license.

"That *is* my real name," Sparkle Starbuck said with ill-concealed triumph. "Here's my driver's license. See?"

I left before somebody asked me to take sides, and headed out the other door.

The HallowFest banner was hung over the door to the Registration cabin. It was after nine, and arrivals were starting to pick up. The space in the L-shape between the barn and the line of cabins looked like a cross between a kicked anthill and a madhouse: business as usual. There were some kids about toddler size running around underfoot while their parents checked in and unloaded. We call them our hereditaries, but I wonder myself if people who have had Craft handed to them without struggle will value it enough to cleave to it through all the betrayals and petty annoyances it contains. What view will they have of the Community, growing up in the middle of it? Will they see us too clearly—or not clearly enough?

Bailey was handling registration from a table underneath the banner. The murder was Topic A; I caught scraps of several conversations, some of which I fervently hoped the deputies would never hear.

"Do you know where Maidjene is?" he demanded when he saw me. "They want the registration lists and stuff, but I can't find them."

"They" being the Gotham County Sheriff's Department, and Bailey's excuse might or might not be the truth; Bailey is smarter than he looks. He's part Miwok Indian and resembles a shy hedgehog—a short one, which is apparently gods' curse on men, but Bailey doesn't act as if it bothers him too much.

"She was up at the meadow when I left, so she ought to be heading this way," I said, hoping I was telling the truth.

"I wish she'd get here!" Bailey wailed.

"Look, why don't you just give everybody badges now and sort out the registration later?" I said. He looked more grateful than the suggestion deserved, and I wondered what he knew that I didn't.

"Okay!" Bailey said, raising his voice and trying to sound authoritative. "Will everybody who doesn't have their badges please take them—and put them on? Everybody has to *wear* their HallowFest badge—"

I waved vaguely and headed for my cabin, feeling like a salmon swimming upstream. It was hard going. There were cars and vans and trucks pulled up haphazardly, blocking each other in, and people off-loading and generally catching up with one another since last year. An aura of high holiday seemed to suffuse everything and nobody much seemed to care about the inconvenience of it all.

Except me. I felt like the *memento mori* at an Elizabethan feast, certain that at any moment someone would notice I didn't belong here. It was a disturbing feeling, like waking up in the Twilight Zone. If I didn't belong here, where did I belong?

I was standing there feeling lost when a blue and white rental van pulled up, edging slowly through the crowd. I recognized the driver—and, by extension, most of the passengers.

Changing Coven had arrived at HallowFest. I abandoned my search for my own nametag and worked my way around to the passenger side. Belle slithered out the door just about the time I arrived.

Lady Bellflower of Changing Coven—to give her her full liturgical title—is short, round, blonde, motherly, professional, and (among other things) a very public Witch with a weekly radio show on WBAI. She's the woman who brought me in to the Craft and has run a Gardnerian-trad coven in New York City for the better part of fifteen years. She's been my closest friend for most of that time.

I looked at my watch. "You're late," I said. Not. It was all of ten A.M.—they must have left New York around dawn.

Belle shrugged and smiled. "So sue us," she said.

The others got out of the van. Sundance had been driving, of course, and Glitter, Beaner, The Cat, Dorje, and Actaeon—HallowFest veterans all—began unloading what was—as I knew from previous years—a pretty thoroughly stuffed vehicle.

"Topper and Coral should be here soon—they were coming up in their own car with the kids. Sallix had to work, and it's Ronin's weekend with the boys."

"Bummer." Ronin wouldn't dare jeopardize his visitation rights by bringing Ronnie and Seth to something like this. I caught Dorje's eye and waved. He waved back.

"So, how's it going this year so far? I heard Summerisle was running it, but now that Maidjene and Larry are splitting—"

"Summerisle's still running it, but there's been some differently-nice stuff coming down this weekend," I told Belle. It didn't take me long to fill her in on how I'd spent my morning.

"Is the Sheriff's Department being reasonable?" Belle asked. I told her about Sergeant Pascoe and Detective Wayne, and how they both seemed to be sane lawdogs with previous HallowFest experience.

"And they say we can have the Bardic Circle back by tonight so long as we keep out of the way now," I finished, "but they're asking everybody to make statements. I'm supposed to go do that as soon as I'm done setting up The Snake's table." I hesitated. "The Sheriff's Department wants to know the names and addresses of everyone attending HallowFest this year, and I don't think Maidjene's real happy about that."

"Turning over her records? She shouldn't have to. I'll talk to her," Belle said firmly. "And you keep out of things," she added.

"Me?" I said, surprised. "I haven't done anything." And I didn't want to, either.

"Well, don't," Belle said. "This is no time to be playing 'Lone Ranger of the Wicca.' The police can find out 'whodunit' without your help."

"I wasn't going to help," I said, nettled. "But—" It was on the tip of my tongue to tell Belle about the candles and oil, but something similar to prudence held me back.

"But nothing," Belle said firmly. "You aren't involved this time: you never knew Reverend Harm; there's no doubt that the murder's being properly investigated by the proper authorities. There's nothing for you to do."

It was a sentiment with which I wanted desperately to agree, but when I tried to something kept me silent.

"I don't want to borrow trouble," I finally managed. Belle beamed.

"Where are you staying?" she asked.

I pointed to the cabin, hoping she wouldn't ask the obvious next question. And she didn't, bless the Lady, so I didn't have to tell her that I was sharing the cabin with Julian.

"You'd better go ahead and get set up," she said. "I'll catch you later."

We went off in opposite directions. On the way back to the cabin I saw Hallie of Keystone Coven (they're in Pennsylvania, naturally) with an armful of the tie-dyed ritual robes she was bringing for sale. I knew Hallie slightly—she'd been in Changing when I first joined—but she took Third and went off to found her own coven out west almost immediately. I stopped her and we chatted—the usual conversation of acquaintances meeting after long absence. Keystone Coven had already generated daughter and granddaughter covens, and I felt a guilty sense of promises unkept, as if I were being pushed to accept a responsibility I wasn't ready for. I pushed it aside, concentrating on immediate business—setting up the Snake's table.

Julian wasn't at the cabin, and his absence was almost as much of a relief as Jesus Jackson's body actually being present up there in the pine forest had been. What *was* in the cabin was the long table and all the boxes he and I had schlepped in from the van last night. Even though Merchanting wouldn't open until noon, there was no reason not to get set up before my date with Deputy Twochuck.

Renny Twochuck. And people ask why I prefer to be called Bast.

I found my badge and pinned it to my sweatshirt, then went into the tiny bathroom and yanked on the light. I turned both taps on full; eventually they'd run clear. Meanwhile I stared at my reflection in the blotched and unsilvering mirror, wondering how I appeared to the Gotham County Sheriff's Department.

Single white Witch. Thirtysomething, five-seven in socks. Figure not too bad, but better out of a parka, sweatshirt, and baggy jeans. Black hair, shoulder length, two months overdue for a cut. Blue eyes. Three holes in one ear, two in the other, all full of earrings. No visible tattoos. No makeup.

Nothing here to inspire a lot of confidence in the police mind, but on the other hand, I didn't look like a crazed killer.

I hoped.

What *had* put that hole in Jackson Harm?

Nobody here had any answers.

I dumped the parka and decided to change the ratty sweatshirt for a slightly more respectable sweater and a silk turtleneck (it has holes in both elbows, but it still looks fine under a pullover). When I pulled the sweatshirt off over my head I could smell bergamot, chypre, and cloves. Julian.

What had he meant? What had I done?

And what were the consequences?

I'm old enough that my first worry was that I might be pregnant—a worry that lasted exactly long enough for me to realize that I shouldn't worry about pregnancy as much as I should worry about infection. I thought I'd rather die than grill Julian on his sexual history until it occurred to me that the stakes were precisely that high—and that it was already too late to be safe.

The nineties are such a lovely decade.

There was nothing I could do about either possibility—pregnant or infected—right now except curse my stupidity and pray for luck—neither of which is ever as useful as a little forethought. Being in denial, however, works nearly as well. For a while.

I got to work, wishing I could have moved this stuff only once. The table was the worst; it was big and heavy, and awkward even folded, but I had help before I was even out the door with it—one of the Raven Kindred folks. Between me and Lew, we got the table through the crowd, into the barn, and up the stairs that led to the second floor.

As you may have gathered, the Paradise Lake barn is not exactly a barn, at least not anymore. It was remodeled many years ago, and now has two floors, for one thing (only the ground floor is heated), and a kitchenette, for another. It also contains two dorm rooms, each of which can bunk thirty or so, and four other rooms, which are set up with bunk beds to accommodate various numbers of people. The rooms were starting to fill with members of my tribe, my nation, my extended family: Pagans.

"Thanks, Lew," I said, when we'd got the table upstairs. The upstairs was freezing cold; the sunlight that made everything outside warm wouldn't make a dent in this cold air mass for some hours. If ever.

"Any time," Lew said. He was wearing a Thor's hammer on a thong around his neck. "You need any more help?"

"It's just boxes. You and Janna better grab some bunks before they're all gone."

"See you tonight then," Lew said. He waved and went off.

I picked out a nice corner space under the joists and near the door, with a window at my back. No one else was setting up yet, but it was just as well I hadn't counted on being able to bring the van up this morning. I went back for the first of the boxes. Soon enough I wasn't cold at all.

On one of my last trips back to the cabin—Julian was still nowhere to be seen and that was fine with me—a battered station wagon with Jersey plates pulled up outside of Registration, and a Klingon got out.

I'm a classicist myself, but this was a movies-and-new-series Klingon with the ridged forehead—latex, I was relieved to note. He was wearing what might very well have been a genuine Klingon Army uniform, for all I knew: he was the size of a refrigerator and I counted at least five knives before he made it to Registration.

"Klash!" Maidjene shrilled in a register only bats and dogs could hear as she ran out to meet him. Klash shouted something back; it sounded like a jammed gearbox.

I looked back at the station wagon. Five more people got out. They were all wearing fringed sashes. Some of them were wearing latex. One of the women—a little smaller than Maidjene, but not much—was wearing a leather corselet with brass cups about the size of baby moon hubcaps for the '57 Chevy of your choice. She bared her teeth at me and growled.

"Bast, I want you to meet Klash. Klash is the Orm of Coven Koloth. The HP?" Maidjene added, in case I didn't quite get it. She looked frayed but indomitably cheerful. I guessed she'd got back from dealing with Our Friends the Police; I didn't see Bailey.

*"Tlingan ko da jattle a?"** Klash said.

"Hi," I said. I resisted the impulse to see if my ears had suddenly stopped working.

"This is their first HallowFest," Maidjene said. I looked around. I was surrounded by Klingons. "I know them from Jersey."

"Can we, like, register now?" said one of the Klingons. Klash said something to him in what was, probably, Klingonese. Finally, the penny dropped.

"Klingon Wicca?" I said in disbelief. Maidjene winced.

"Some people call it that," Klash agreed, fortunately in English this time. He smiled. "Want to join the Imperial Race?"

"I have to finish setting up my table," I said, at the same time Maidjene said:

"I thought you could maybe show Klash and the guys around." *And keep them out of trouble,* her tone implied. Like any good hostess, Maidjene wanted everyone to have fun at her party.

Klash ripped off another sentence in Klingonese and made a sweeping gesture. Two of the Klingons shrugged.

"Ron says, we can help you with that if you want," one of them said.

"Sure," I said. It was as good a way to introduce them to HallowFest as any. "Come on."

The two Klingons followed me back to the cabin.

The NeoPagan Community was self-created to display an infinite tolerance for anything its members might do. As wiser heads than

*"Do you speak Klingon?"

mine have pointed out, a community with no standards is no community, but, like science-fiction fandom and the bumblebee, the Community has survived infinite careful explanations of how it cannot possibly continue to work.

It is possible, however, that Klingon Wicca may be the bone of contention that breaks the camel's back.

While there are (my sources tell me) as many different approaches to it as to any other trad, and Klingon Wicca is only as accurate a label as, say, Norse Wicca is for Odinism, most Pagans understand Klingon Wicca to be a tradition of roughly Wiccan form and intention which takes its archetypes, mythos, and images from "Next Generation *Star Trek* Klingons—and, since there isn't all that much information available from the TV, they patch it together from a little Bushido here, a little Chivalry there until they've created a ritual and an identity.

What they've also created is a chasm between themselves and the majority of NeoPagans. Whatever else we say about ourselves, the one thing we all seem to agree on is that we are *reclaiming;* either the gods of our ancestors or the truth eternal; the path to perfect knowledge or the safety of the Earth. It is hard to maintain this belief when we see the same careful work and reconstruction put into something derived from a television show: How can we be serious if they are not? And how can *they* be serious?

They're not Pagans, say the Pagans, *they're fans.*

We're not fans, say the Klingons, *we believe.*

Where should the line be drawn?

Should the line be drawn?

And if here, then where else as well?

They guys' names were K-Rex and T'Davoth, I discovered shortly after they'd followed me off. They seemed more normal away from Klash ("His name's really Ron, but he doesn't like us to call him that," K-Rex explained), and willing to talk. It was a familiar story: they'd come to Paganism (however defined), as so many people do these days, after being exposed to it through SF. I wondered if they'd remain Klingons, or if the Imperial Race would become, in the end, merely another point of entry into our world.

With their help—"Strong backs, weak minds," T'Davoth boasted—I had the last of the boxes up to the second floor in two more trips. The cabin looked barren without them; all that was left was the mattress, my duffel bag, and Julian's things.

I told K-Rex and T'Davoth something about HallowFest, including the fact that the Sheriff's Department had found a body up on the hill this morning and wanted people to stay out of the area for a while.

"Cool," K-Rex said, which might mean almost anything.

I wanted to warn them that we didn't go in much for costumes, but that wouldn't have been entirely true. And ritual robes and Klingon battle-dress probably looked pretty much alike to outsiders, which seemed, at the time, to be a profound insight into the nature of reality. So what I did say was that I'd catch up with them after lunch to see if they had any more questions.

"Cool," said K-Rex again. T'Davoth nodded.

I didn't laugh at them. I didn't ask them their "real" names. Perhaps the actual example the Community tries to set isn't even tolerance so much as it is the freedom of allowing each person to define himself without discussion.

And maybe that won't work out either.

The guys went off to rejoin their Orm and I started unpacking the stock. I was the only one up here on the barn's second floor so far; it was peaceful and quiet, and provided the solitude I'd wanted this morning and never gotten. But what I'd wanted to use it for was lost just now. I worked instead.

Back in New York I'd taken the precaution of labeling the most important box in three-inch-high letters, so I had no trouble now in finding the cashbox (thirty dollars in ones and change-rolls), the tablecloth, the drape to cover the stock at night, and the credit card machine. After those things were on the table—and the top cover set somewhere I wouldn't bury it again, I hoped—I unfolded the two chairs and started in on the stock boxes. Fortunately I'd found the box-cutter early on, as Brianna had a free hand with a tape gun.

There was enough daylight coming in through the windows under the eaves for me to see; there are lights strung up here, but they're the pull-chain type and have to be turned on one by one, by hand, and it's a real pain. I knew the stock well enough to know what it looked like in the half dark, even if Julian had packed most of it.

So it was dark, and I was all the way back in the corner, away from the table bent over the box of jewelry, which was why the two of them didn't see me when they came in.

"I don't believe you had the nerve to come up here!" Maidjene said in a furious undertone.

"You're just lucky I did, now that one of your little buddies popped that fruitcake in the woods. You're lucky they haven't arrested you already, Philly."

"They didn't arrest me because I didn't kill anybody, Larry," Maidjene said, deadly flat. I'd already recognized the voice. Larry Wagner, Maidjene's survivalist-fruitcake soon-to-be-ex-husband.

"That's more than you can say for your so-called friends. I've heard them talk about karma and holy wars—and Harm was one of those funny-mentalist Christians. He was stabbed, wasn't he? Everybody knows that one of those weenies you keep inviting over to our house did it."

Larry Wagner was an ordinary sort of pear-shaped whiteboy, with light brown hair that was starting to go and horn-rimmed glasses that'd probably wowed 'em in college. He had the sort of mouth that looked as if it spent most of its time in self-justification; not quite petulant but not exactly prim. He was dressed, as usual, as if he expected to be called to active military service at any moment: jungle-pattern camo parka, olive pants bloused into gleaming paratrooper boots, and black leather gloves. He was probably also carrying a gun: Larry loved concealed weapons and showed them off at every opportunity.

"The only 'weenie' I see here is you, Larry. Now fuck off."

"I'm not going to let you ruin your life over this, Philly. These people don't care about you. Once you come to your senses you'll thank me—I've seen you go through these crazes before; remember that time you had that crush on David Bowie? Religion is a tool of the government; everyone knows that—"

Larry didn't seem to have cashed too many Reality Checks lately, but that was nothing new, and listening to him call Maidjene "Philly" (not her real name) was starting to get on my nerves. I straightened up slowly and looked out the window. There was thirtysomething feet of Winnebago camper parked right outside the barn, snarling traffic even further. I recognized it: the infamous "Warwagon," named out of the Mack Bolan books and Larry's pride and joy. One year somebody'd chalked *"Lasciate ogni speranza, voi ch'entrate"* on the side, and Larry left it there for most of a day until someone translated the Italian for him.

The Warwagon contained every form of paralegal radar detector and emergency band scanner known to man—at least it had used to—so I could take a pretty good guess that Larry's "sources" had been tuned to the sheriff's band. But were they really saying that *we* were responsible for Harm's death?

"Philly, all I want is for you to be happy," Larry was whining now. "When are you going to forget all this Wicca crap and come home? How are you going to manage on your own? You can't get a job—nobody's going to hire you the way you look." That was Larry all over, ever the gentleman. "Look, I'm sorry about your stupid book. If I'd known it meant so much to you—"

"You'd have done what you did anyway, seeing as it's just 'Wicca crap,'" Maidjene shot back with deadly mimicry.

"It's a stupid bunch of— You don't really *believe* that stuff, do you? If you stick around here, you're only going to get into real trouble this time!"

"Only if I kill someone," Maidjene said, in a voice that indicated it was a possibility.

"And I'd have to tell them that you people are anti-Christian— look, you come on home right now and that'll be that, okay? Nobody has to know anything," Larry wheedled.

"I've left you, asshole," Maidjene said, with frayed patience. "I have filed for divorce. We are separated. And I would rather starve in a ditch than ever have anything to do with you again. Okay?"

"Now look, Philly—" Larry began.

"You having problems, Jeannie?" a new voice said.

The newcomer was wearing a HallowFest T-shirt, shorts, and Birkenstocks. Larry was dressed like Bizarro Rambo. Guess who looked more dangerous?

Ironshadow has a mundane name—I think it's Pat—but he's known through the SCA and the Community by the name he puts on his knives: Ironshadow. He stands about six-four and is old enough for his black hair to be liberally streaked with gray. He has a face that looks as if it's been remodeled several times on barroom floors, which is probably not too far from the facts. He's also a pussycat—if he likes you.

"I want you out of here," Maidjene snarled at Larry. "I want you out of this *state.*"

Larry smiled unpleasantly; I could hear it in his voice. "I've got my membership paid up. I'm staying right here. I'm entitled."

"I don't think you need to stay quite this close," Ironshadow rumbled. He has the deep bass voice that my new acquaintance Orm Klash had been trying to imitate. Larry looked at him.

"You've got to move your vehicle down to the RV parking, for one thing," Ironshadow went on, with scrupulous mildness, "and then you'd better go and register and get your badge, if you're staying. And after that I guess you better go tell the Sheriff's Department where you were when Harm was killed."

Larry made a faint stuttering noise in the back of his throat, as if he were trying to talk but couldn't remember his lines.

"And if you keep bothering Jeannie, I think you're probably going to run into a tree. Several times. So I'd be careful, if I were you," Ironshadow said solicitously.

To say that Larry flounced out in a huff might be crueler than necessary. There was a sad side to the little sitcom I'd just inadvertently witnessed: Maidjene had changed, Larry hadn't. And Larry wasn't accepting the inevitable consequences with anything approaching grace. Which might have been unfair to Larry, but I didn't like him very well to begin with—he'd thought of HallowFest as his own Happy Hunting Ground for years and was notorious for hitting on the female attendees. I was glad Maidjene was dumping him.

"I don't know what to do." Maidjene was crying now. I felt guilty that I hadn't been the one to stop Larry and told myself that my arrival would only have raised the stakes of the confrontation.

"You'll do what you have to. You know that," Ironshadow said.

"Yeah. Well—Niceness Rules." Maidjene's voice was tired.

She turned and went down the stairs. Ironshadow followed her, but came back almost immediately with a suitcase. He must have left it on the steps before.

"You can come out now," he said to me.

I stepped from behind the joist and went over to hug him. It was about like hugging a tree: rock solid and full of energy. He hugged back, hard.

"I thought I saw you back there," he said after I caught my breath.

"I was setting up. I didn't want to interrupt them. But I would have if it got too nasty. Larry's such a weasel."

"He's got a few problems," Ironshadow agreed. "But not as many as the Reverend Harm seems to have gotten rid of."

" 'Marley was dead,' " I quoted, sourly.

"And you're the one who found him."

I nodded. It was hardly a secret, even if HallowFest weren't capable of fielding an Olympic-quality Gossip Team on five minutes' notice anyway. But Ironshadow didn't—gossip, at least.

"Look, 'shadow—if you wanted to kill a guy with a knife, how would you do it?"

He grinned. A short knife I hadn't seen a moment before appeared in his hand. Ironshadow throws knives as well as makes them.

I shook my head. "There wasn't any blood," I said, and heard the surprise in my voice. That was the thing that had bothered me all morning—had bothered me, in fact, from the moment I laid eyes on Hellfire Harm.

There was no blood.

"Then he didn't die by the blade," Ironshadow said. "Unless he was lying down when he got it. Standing up, even if you get him right through the pump, he's going to bleed for a couple seconds at least."

I nodded. Every mystery reader knows that. You bleed as long as your heart is pumping, or as long as gravity is draining the wound. There had been neither heartbeat nor gravity operating in the case of the Reverend Jackson Harm. There had been no blood anywhere around his body.

"Well, he *was* lying down," I said. "He was lying on his back." I went on to describe what I'd found as accurately as I could to the only person I could think of who might be able to answer my questions. I don't know how many of the tales Ironshadow tells on himself are true, but he's led a well-traveled life.

"Well, assuming he didn't get himself shot where you didn't see it, or overdosed on something," Ironshadow said, "assuming that what you saw killed him, then the only thing that fits is that the Reverend had to be stabbed while he was already lying down, and by somebody with one hell of a right arm on him."

"How come?" I asked, obligingly. Ironshadow snorted.

"You ever try to stab somebody through the heart, Bast? There's a lot of stuff in the way—bone and gristle and even muscle. You gotta grab 'em like this—"

Suddenly my back was to him and his arm was across my throat. I wrapped both hands about it as if I were going to chin myself. It was like grabbing one of the barn's cross-beams.

"—and then you gotta punch 'em *real hard.*" He tapped me lightly on the chest with his other fist, right about where the puncture had been on Harm.

"Or you aren't going to make it through all that," he finished, letting me go. "And getting there with an overhand blow from a kneeling position would be even harder."

I tried to imagine the choreography involved in that scenario and gave up. "Maybe he was asleep," I suggested dubiously.

But no. That theory required him to fall asleep—in the woods, in October, in street clothes—sleep through somebody half undressing him—neither his shirt nor T-shirt had been ripped, only stained—and continue to sleep while someone killed him with one powerful thrust to the heart.

"It doesn't make sense," I said.

"If it made sense, it wouldn't be Reality," Ironshadow said. "Look, watch this stuff for me a minute while I go get my table, okay?"

"Can I look through it?"

"Just don't break anything."

Ironshadow carries his stock in a battered suitcase. I laid it on its side and popped the latches. I lifted off the top layer of sponge padding and took a look. Ironshadow *athamés;* standard issue from Pagan Central Supply, most of them: six-inch double-edged blades with black lathe-turned hilts and your choice of decorator pommels: hematite, cloudy amber, even a quartz point. The union card for most Wiccans and their fellow travelers in the Earth Religions. There were a dozen of them; he might very well sell them all this weekend.

I lifted out the *athamés* and the sponge padding together and set them carefully aside. Next down was the expensive stuff, most of them probably special-order pieces being delivered here. One had a staghorn hilt with vaguely-familiar runes inlaid in silver and a blade so heavily greased that I knew it was iron, not steel; one had a rosewood hilt and enough jimping on the blade to make it look like fancy lacework. That one had a clear quartz marble slightly smaller than a Ping-Pong ball for a pommel-weight.

I coveted them both, mostly out of habit, while at the same time part of me was comparing every blade I saw to the mark on the late Reverend Harm and coming up empty.

There were a couple of other pieces—showpieces Ironshadow had little chance of selling here, but wondrous fair to look upon. I admired them all, taking my time.

The last item wasn't an *athamé*—or even a knife.

It had a short hilt of opalized bone that put it right out of my price range and the blade was a sickle-shape of pure copper that was already showing an oxidization rainbow.

"Four hundred," Ironshadow said, setting down a card table, a camp stool, and another suitcase. "It isn't spoken for."

I turned it over in my hands. A *boline,* the companion blade to the *athame.* Traditionally a copper sickle, used to gather and prepare spell ingredients.

"Nice," I said wistfully, setting it back among its kindred.

"I could hold it for you," Ironshadow said.

"Hah." There was no way I could afford to drop four bills—my day job wasn't that dependable, and the outside freelance money I counted on to fill in the cracks had been scanty lately. I looked at the opalized bone glinting in the dim light of the barn.

"I'll think about it," I said.

I went back to work on The Snake's table and found that Julian had been even more optimistic than Ironshadow was—he'd packed two copies of *La Tesoraria.*

La Tesoraria del Oro is a nineteenth-century grimoire drawing on a mixture of medieval French and Spanish sources. It's a Christian-based series of rituals designed, essentially, to obtain a bill of divorcement from God: to sever all ties to the natural world in order to study that world as a separate entity.

It had been my big freelance job last winter: every once in a while, Tree of Wisdom has a spasm and goes into the book publishing business, coming out with—usually—some expensive limited-edition grimoire that no normal occult publisher in his right mind would consider cost-effective. And so I happened to know that in addition to being freshly translated, typeset, proofread, and having all its sigils and diagrams redrawn, *La Tesoraria* went for about 250 dollars, hubbed spine, leather binding, sewn-in bookmark, fancy endpapers, and all.

For those less daring, Tree of Wisdom produced a plain hardback for 75 dollars, and we had one of those, too. I said Julian was an optimist. He's also probably the only person who'd actually have the patience to go through the year's worth of rituals and nasty-minded asceticism that the book demands and figure out a way around the joker at the end: the impossible condition the magician has to meet to complete the work.

Still, it's a pretty piece of bookmaking, even if it is—while not exactly evil—just about the antithesis of what I conceive Wicca to be. Still, it'd paid my rent when Houston Graphics hadn't. I set both copies out.

Merchanting was officially open by now; people started drifting in. I sold a few things while I was still setting up. I knew I
should go and keep my appointment with the law, but I didn't want
to leave the table unattended while there was a chance of the
Snake turning a profit for the weekend. Goddess knew they needed
to, from what I'd been hearing lately around the store.

It used to be that what you got at the Snake you couldn't get
anywhere else, and so the shop scraped by, even with New York
overheads. But today New Age is big business—Waldenbooks carries Tarot cards and shopping mall jewelry stores carry pentacles.
And by undercutting the specialty store's prices, the mundane
stores take away the profit margin that lets the specialty store
carry the serious ritual magic supplies that the New Agers have
no interest in.

And sooner or later, free market economics means no occultism
at all, something I hope to put off as long as possible. Fortunately
Julian showed up before one form of civic-mindedness won out
over the other.

He went over to Ironshadow's table first. The knives were all
laid out and glittering, making a pretty show in the sun. Ironshadow handed Julian one. Julian nodded, handed it back, and
Ironshadow wrapped it. Money changed hands.

This was interesting—almost as interesting as my love life. Julian buying an Ironshadow blade? Julian's a Ceremonial Magician,
not a Pagan. He considers most forms of polytheism to be beneath
him. What would he want with an Ironshadow blade?

"Thanks for setting up," Julian said, coming around the table.
"Why don't you come back at—five?—and take the cashbox and
charge machine back to the van for the night. And maybe the jewelry."

"Julian," I said, "there is something we have to talk about."

He looked at me, waiting. I gritted my teeth and told myself I'd
done harder things than this.

"About last night. I've got a clean blood test." I donate regularly.
"And you?" I kept my voice low; no one else was close enough to
hear.

There. It was said, and it hadn't killed me. Now all I had to work
on was my timing.

Julian smiled his detached plaster-saint smile, and I felt myself go hot all over. "Don't worry," he said. "You're safe. You're the
first." He turned away and started rearranging the table I'd just
arranged.

Julian was a virgin? An *ex*-virgin?

It was, I supposed, possible.

"Are you sure?" I asked, then heard what I'd said and wished I could be struck by lightning.

"Run along," Julian told me. "I didn't kill you."

But I would have been happy to kill someone—which made it fortunate, in a way, that my next date was with Deputy Twochuck. Not even I was self-absorbed enough to get in a sheriff's deputy's face out of season.

He started with my prints, which now made two law enforcement agencies they were on file with. Taking the print doesn't hurt. They roll your finger back and forth to get the whole image on the paper, resulting in ten square blotches on a stiff white form. It's kind of pretty, in a post-industrial way.

I was in the process of giving Renny a slightly more detailed account of myself starting at around noon yesterday when Sergeant Pascoe showed up. She had a carton of coffee in each hand.

"Don't say I never gave you anything," she told Renny, setting one down at his elbow. "And how are you?" she said to me.

As well as can be expected considering my sex life, I thought of saying. "Okay," I said instead. Cautiously.

"I asked Sam about you. He says you're a reasonable person." She pulled the lid off her cup and slugged the coffee back, letting the remark she'd just made lie there.

"I try to be," I said. "We don't want any trouble here." Platitudes "R" Us.

"Maybe you could fill in a little background for us, then. Bat wants to know. Tony," she amplified, seeing my face. "Lieutenant Wayne."

I suppose if your name were Wayne and you lived in Gotham County and were a cop your nickname would almost have to end up being "Bat." Geography is destiny.

"Okay," I said, still cautious.

"You done with her, Renny? Why don't we go for a walk?" Fayrene said.

Fayrene and I went for a walk.

"I thought maybe we could take a run down to the diner," she said. We were heading for the parking lot. "It's about the closest place around here to get coffee."

It was after noon; I realized that a cup of coffee at Mrs. Cooper's four hours earlier was no substitute for breakfast *and* lunch.

"Fine." And then whatever she wanted to say—or have me do—could take place in decent privacy. "You wouldn't know any place around here that does Chinese?"

She didn't. We ended up at a place called Mom's, a diner just up County 6 that was a retro vision in brushed aluminum and gold-flecked white Formica. I ordered coffee, lots of coffee, and the double bacon cheeseburger platter deluxe, figuring dinner was only a remote possibility.

"Now, Sergeant Pascoe, what is it I can do for you?" I asked, taking the war to the enemy, as the saying goes.

"You might as well call me Fayrene," she said. "There isn't enough space in the office I've got for my name and a title, too. And you go by Bast?"

"Most of the time." Ray at my workplace, Houston Graphics, calls me Kitty—either because it's short for "Miss Kitty" (Ray's a fan of TV Westerns) or because Bast is the Egyptian goddess of cats—but that's about it for theme and variations.

"Well, Bast, first of all you can convince your friend in the orange dress"—that was Maidjene—"to find her records of who's supposed to be camping at Paradise Lake this weekend, because if we don't get them, we just might have to decide to hold her as a material witness." Fayrene frowned at me.

A material witness, in case you didn't know, is just like a criminal, except with fewer civil rights—like arraignment, representation, and the chance of seeing the outside of the local jail before Hell freezes rock-solid.

"Uh-huh," I said. "What are you going to do with them? Are you going to make them public?"

"Now why should we do that?" Fayrene said back.

I hadn't the faintest idea. "It's just that people get jumpy, having information about them turned over to government agencies." Considering what a lot of it ends up getting used for. I wondered what the grounds for Maidjene and Larry's divorce were, and which of them was officially bringing suit, and whose files that information would sit in until the end of time. "If you could tell me what you want it for . . ."

"We want it to catch whoever stuck Hellfire—if that's all right with you," Fayrene said, starting to sound annoyed.

"But it won't," I said. "Not if you think it's going to tell you who's at the festival or when they got here."

I launched into Basic Explanation #71, about how anyone can call himself a Pagan—or a Witch—without reference to any accrediting agency whatsoever, and about how the forms the registrants send into HallowFest every year are generally for entertainment purposes only.

"Some people got here yesterday and went to the site—and of those, some told Maidjene they were here, and some haven't gotten around to it yet. Some got as far as the area last night and checked into a local hotel instead of going to the site." There are some around here, unlikely as that seems. "Some are getting here today. Some even live around here—well, sort of—and usually they put some people up, if they're coming from a long way away. But you can't tell from the forms. Some people just show up, because they've come every year."

"We'll just have to do our best without crystal balls and Tarot cards," Fayrene said sardonically. "And *with* the membership list. Consider yourself deputized."

I wasn't sure whether she could do that or not—and if she could, I'd prefer that she do it to somebody a lot more trustworthy.

And if she did, I at least wanted to get a badge out of it.

"I'll talk to Maidjene," I said. I wondered if I was going to have either a reputation or a nervous system left by Monday. "Do you think you're going to catch . . . whoever it was?"

"Well, we like to think so. Body's down to the morgue; we should know more by Monday."

"Like how whoever it was got him to lie down and strip?" I asked, ever helpful.

The waitress arrived, bringing my hamburger platter and a piece of pie for Fayrene.

"Go on," Fayrene said neutrally.

I explained my guesses, in between bites of burger. I left Ironshadow's help out of my story, but told Fayrene everything else, including things she probably already knew, like how strong the killer would have to be—and how lucky. "So who got Harm to hold still?" I finished.

And, I suddenly wondered, what had both of them—Harm and the murderer—been doing up there in the first place?

" 'How' is what you ought to be asking," Fayrene corrected my "who." "And we won't know that until sometime next week."

By which time everyone on the site would be gone.

"Anybody out there we should talk to?" she went on. "Maybe somebody with a really short temper? It can't be any secret to you folks that you weren't exactly Harm's favorite people."

"Nobody from HallowFest would do something like that," I said indignantly.

"Someone did," Fayrene said dryly, "or do you think our local boys light candles around people and slop them all over with perfume before they stab them?"

It took a moment for what she'd said to sink in. Then I closed my eyes and tried to keep my burger where it was.

"Hi, Mom," a gangling young local said.

4

J eff said you'd 10-70'd in from here. Did you know that old Hell-fire got himself murdered up with the Witches? Mom, can I go on up there, and—"

"What are you doing out of school this time of day?" Fayrene demanded, then apparently gave up the question as a bad job and said, "Bast, I'd like you to meet my son Wyler."

Wyler Pascoe was sixteen years old, an only child (as I found out later), and blond like his mother. He seemed likeable enough, which was a good thing, as it had apparently never occurred to Wyler Pascoe in all his young life that anyone wouldn't want him around.

"We had a half day today; I got out at noon," Wyler protested, all hurt innocence. He stared at me.

"Hi, Wyler. My name is Bast."

He took this as an invitation to sit down without otherwise acknowledging my presence; I moved over to make room for him.

"Hi. Mom, can I go up there and see them? I don't have to be at the garage until 3:00, and Felix doesn't like it if I show up early, and I *did* only have a half day, so I thought—"

I don't have much experience with teenagers, but my experience, they only talk that much and that fast when they are trying to put something over on their parents.

"No," said his mother. "Paradise Lake is private property."

"But Mrs. Cooper won't mind—she lets me go up there all the time, and—"

"But the Witches *would* mind. Wouldn't you?" Fayrene said to me.

Wyler seemed to really notice I was there for the first time. He stared at me, goggle-eyed and silent.

I welcomed the distraction from Fayrene's last bombshell, even if the list of things I was ignoring to concentrate on the present moment was starting to get ridiculously long.

"You're one of the Witches?" Wyler breathed in awe. "A real Witch?" He stopped, and I gave him points for not asking what usually turns out to be the next question, which is whether I can turn the speaker into a toad. My stock response is that I don't believe in improving upon Nature's handiwork.

"That's right," I said. "Wicca is a NeoPagan religion. There are a lot of different NeoPagan traditions represented at HallowFest this weekend." Belle would be proud of me. "And a lot of families bring their kids, too." Let's hear it for family values.

"So can I go?" Wyler demanded again. "I won't be long."

Fayrene frowned. I thought it best to be diplomatic.

"You'd have to have bought a membership several months ago—they don't sell them at the door." Which is different from paying at the door for something you reserved several months ago, and whoever was running it each year tried not to do that either. Besides that, we don't sell memberships to anyone under eighteen unless their parents are attending too, but there wasn't any point in mentioning that.

"Oh." There was a pause while Wyler digested these facts and Fayrene relaxed. "Can I have your french fries if you don't want them?"

I didn't want the french fries, I didn't want to be here, and most of all I didn't want to be the Sheriff's Office liaison to HallowFest. It didn't look like I was going to get what I wanted, except maybe with regard to the fries.

"Wyler, leave the lady alone," Fayrene said.

"Have them," I said, pushing my plate toward him.

"Is she the one that whacked him?" Wyler said, around a mouthful of fries. Fayrene snorted.

"Who would want to see Jackson Harm dead?" I asked, trying to ask detective-questions in the best amateur tradition.

"Other than everybody?" Fayrene said.

There was a pause while Wyler finished my fries, remembered somewhere else he had to be, and left. I drank coffee and tried not to panic. John Law thought Harm's was a ritual murder on a site full of ritualists.

"You knew, didn't you?" Fayrene said, when we were alone again.

"I saw the wax on the pine needles, and I knew there was anointing oil on the body," I admitted. I saw Fayrene's eyes flash and hurried on. "But I'm not a cop—a sheriff's deputy, I mean—and I didn't want to jump to any conclusions and tell you your job."

"You were just going to keep quiet and hope we'd miss it?" she said. Cops have this trick they do with their voices; the words sound like they're just making conversation, but the inflection they give things makes them sound as if they can mean anything at all. Or nothing.

I took a deep breath.

"I wasn't going to mention it because I couldn't see how my guesses could do you any good. And because I could be wrong. And because if there were really something to see, you'd spot it." And because I'd been praying I was wrong, but I didn't say that. I didn't have to.

"Well, suppose you start guessing now," Fayrene said, not letting me off the hook.

"About who killed Jackson Harm?" I asked, barely keeping the outrage out of my voice. "I don't even know for sure how he was killed—or when."

"Cautious type, aren't you?" she said, scowling. "Welladay, let's see. Unless he was poisoned, that pop through the heart was how he got it. As for when, I'm not the coroner, but rigor had passed off by the time we got to him, and the night was cold—which would delay both onset and release—so say somewhere between midnight and four A.M. Maybe as late as five, though—bodies are funny that way."

"Why are you telling me this?" I asked mournfully.

"Because you want to help us," Fayrene said, grinning with a shark-mouth full of teeth.

I supposed I did, once you defined enlightened self-interest loosely enough. I got back to the site about an hour later, armed with a mandate from the Sheriff's Office to do what I could to help—which boiled down to acting as a translator, mostly.

And to get Maidjene to turn loose of the Festival records.

I didn't see the Warwagon when I got back to the barn, so it looked as if Larry'd followed Ironshadow's, um, advice. There was a copy of the HallowFest schedule written out large and posted on the bulletin board on the side of the barn. Right now I had a choice between Woman's Herbalism of the Northeast (outside), Introduction to the Lesser Banishing Ritual (barn, upstairs, at the opposite end from the merchants), and Mediation for Coven Leaders (barn, downstairs). The herbalism workshop noted that its location had been changed from the Bardic Circle to the Lake Meadow. I noted the times for the Opening Ritual and Bardic Circle this evening.

There was a sign saying that Hoodoo Lunchbox would be playing at the Circle, and I was glad to see that Xharina had decided to make it up here. Then I thought things over and decided I actually wouldn't really wish this weekend on anyone I liked.

I tracked down Maidjene at the herbalism workshop after drawing a blank at both of the others. It was being held in an open space on the tenting field on the far side of the lake. The women were gathered in a circle around a gray-haired woman in her sixties who was wearing a crown of autumn leaves on her head. Fortunately, Maidjene was on the outer edge. I knelt down beside her.

"I need to talk to you," I said, keeping my voice down.

"Now?" Maidjene said.

"Now would be good," I said back.

The workshop leader was explaining that pennyroyal was no substitute for legal and political control of our reproductive rights—among other things, pennyroyal is an abortifacient, and damned dangerous when used for that purpose—and passing out flyers with addresses of various national politicos. Maidjene and I both took one, and then she stood up. I followed her.

She headed back in the direction of the cabins, but stopped on the bridge and stared down into the brack.

"You've got to give the police those records," I said. There was no point in being subtle.

"I don't have them," Maidjene said. She couldn't quite keep the smugness out of her voice.

"Find them. Look, Maidjene, they don't care about us. All they want is their killer."

"And they want to look for their suspect in the HallowFest registration forms. Forget it. Niceness Rules. I talked to Belle. I'll get a lawyer."

"You'll lose."

"Thank you very niceness much for the vote of confidence, Bast."

"They will arrest your niceness *tuchis*, Maidjene."

"I don't care. They're picking on us because we're different, Bast, and because we make good scapegoats."

"They'd ask anybody for this stuff!" I pointed out, getting exasperated. "The New Baptist Republicans, even."

"Sure." Maidjene looked tired. "But the New Baptist Republicans wouldn't get harassed out of their job once it got back that they'd spent the weekend having hot sex and Satanic drug orgies in Upstate New York." Her shoulders sagged. She looked every year of her age plus ten or so more.

"You should get out of your ivory tower more, Bast. It isn't like it was in the sixties," Maidjene—who was my age and thus too young to really remember them—said. "It isn't even like it was in the eighties. The hammer's coming down. And if you aren't right in the mainstream, you're going to get smashed. It's already starting: conform, don't make trouble, don't *need* anything—do you know what they're doing to the entitlement programs in Congress? I can't give the police those records. Not because of what they'll do with them now; but what about five years from now? What about then?"

Like many of us, Maidjene has slightly left-leaning views: most members of a racial/religious/sexual/political minority get radicalized early and often. I wanted to tell her she was crazy, but lying well is not one of my strong suits.

"Sergeant Pascoe said they'd keep it quiet," I offered feebly. "They only want to catch the killer."

" 'Love work, hate mastery, and seek no friendships among the ruling class,' " Maidjene said, misquoting Hillel ben Shahar slightly.

"Maidjene, have you really thought this through?"

"If they ask me, I'm going to have to tell them I don't have the records," she repeated stubbornly.

If she were actually telling the truth, HallowFest would be wiped out financially—next year's organizers wouldn't be able to tell who'd paid, or who to send registration forms to. Not to mention that we were probably going to lose this site anyway, records or no.

But if Maidjene were telling the *literal* truth, as elves and Witches often do, someone else might have the information the Sheriff's Office wanted.

"Try to see your way clear to helping them," I said. "Or else whoever's trying to make trouble for us gets what he wanted." I barely remembered in time that she didn't know that Harm had been anointed before he was stabbed, or about the candles. And I didn't see any reason to share that information, now or ever.

"You don't understand, Bast," Maidjene said. "This isn't just something I do on weekends. This is my *life*. I'm not going to say 'Oh, it just doesn't matter' any time it's more convenient to cooperate. I don't have a right to give up that list, even if somebody else in my situation was to feel differently."

Wicca wasn't a weekend thing for me any more than it was for Maidjene, and sometimes it was hard to count the friends and potential friends I'd lost to the choices I'd made. I thought she was wrong, but I didn't think I could change her mind. The martyr's crown bespells those of us who aren't Christians, too.

"Okay," I said, backing off. "I just thought I'd tell you."

"Sure." Maidjene smiled wanly. "May the Nice Be With You. And if anybody shows up waving a bloody knife, I'll point him in your direction."

"Do that," I said. She went back to the workshop. I crossed the bridge in the direction of the barn.

It would be really nice if the killer confessed—and turned out to be a local boy totally unrelated to HallowFest who'd popped Harm for totally mundane motives.

Unfortunately, a theory like that didn't wash. It couldn't. Harm had been killed right in our back yard, in a fashion that deserved at least a paragraph in "America's Unsolved Mysteries," by someone who used at least some of the bells and whistles of our practices. This left only three possibilities:

1) It was a religiously-motivated ritual murder by one of our HallowFest Pagans. This one was pretty hard to believe. Human sacrifice is the stuff of lurid rumor and afternoon talk shows, not reality. Certainly the occult tradition holds that there is power innate in spilled blood, and some of the older grimoires—like the *Tesoraria*—talk about ritual murder, but only as a symbol. It's a long way from theory and tradition to cold steel in the night. And a degree of religious faith ardent enough to encompass human sacrifice was something I didn't think I could find in Vatican City, let alone at Paradise Lake.

2) It was a secularly-motivated killing of Harm by one of us tricked up to look like a ritual murder. There wasn't much reason

for this either, unless the killer was already preparing an insanity defense. I supposed I could come up with a real-world motive sooner or later if I tried, though — not that it would be up to me. The problem with this idea was that none of us was really local — except for HallowFest, we really didn't have much chance to rub up against Jesus Jackson Harm.

3) It was a murder by a non-Pagan local who was attempting to frame someone — anyone — at HallowFest for it. It might be mere chauvinism, but I liked this idea much better than either of the others. It had a lot of built-in flex, including the fact that I didn't have to worry about a motive — hadn't Fayrene said everyone hated Harm? And we had written indication of how much he'd hated us. Enough to die a martyr's death, secure in the glorious resurrection to come, just to cause us trouble?

Maybe. Or maybe he'd been an unwilling sacrifice.

Mindful of my might-be deputization, my next stop was the Registration cabin. One of Maidjene's other coveners, a woman I knew as Sabine, was there to direct newcomers in the right directions. She had a sheet of paper in front of her and was copying out Sunday's schedule for posting. There were a pile of parking permits and a box of name tags on the table and no other paperwork in sight. A boombox in the background was playing a Charlie Murphy tape. She handed me a copy of the program (collated at last).

"So what are you doing about registration?" I asked, stuffing the program into a pocket.

"Oh, we're just giving badges to everybody. It'll be okay. I guess they'll send out next year's mailing from last year's list."

Not that they'd have to, I realized, unless the Sheriff's Office got the bright idea of subpoenaing Maidjene's hard disk from her home computer. HallowFest had a high-tech backup for those well-and-truly-sought-after registration forms.

"So what'd she do with the paperwork?" I asked, hoping the question sounded harmless.

"Over there," Sabine said. "We're going to burn them tonight at the fire." She sounded so unconcerned that I wondered if I was the only one here who had all my marbles — or, at least, a different set than were in general issue. "Hey, are you the one that found that guy's body?"

"Yeah." I looked at the box. I knew what I was thinking and I hated myself for thinking it.

"Isn't it great? I mean, not that he's dead"—Sabine didn't sound especially sincere—"but that *they're* finally getting some of what happened to *us*."

There is a mythology still current in the NeoPagan Community— and immortalized in popular song—that during the "Burning Times" (roughly four centuries, beginning with Dame Janet Kyteler in 1324 and ending around the end of the eighteenth century) nine million European women were burned for the "sin" of "witchcraft."

In addition to smacking unpleasantly of one-upmanship on this century's better documented holocaust, it isn't true: there weren't nine million of them and they weren't burned. And of the several hundred thousand who did die by the rope, the rack, and even the stake, most were Jews, heretics, and the mentally ill. Of course, there may even have been a few Witches among them, but I like to think they wouldn't approve of their deaths being used as an excuse for moral insensibility by their spiritual descendants.

"That doesn't make it right," I said. My voice was hoarser than I liked to hear it.

She looked at me, her expression of satisfaction fading into something like alarm. Belle tells me I have no tact, and after all these years I'm beginning to suspect she's right. I did what I could to repair matters.

"Look, do you want me to cover for you here? It looks like there isn't much to do, and I'm not too interested in this set of work-shops."

"Just about everybody's here," she agreed. "But maybe you could do, like, from three to five? Lorne was supposed to, but he's got to go to town for a firewood run, on account of we couldn't get up there this morning."

"Yeah, sure," I said, not looking at the box again. It had a Kinko's logo on the side, and was the kind that holds a thousand #10 envelopes. It was taped up, and tied with ribbons like a Christ-mas package.

"I'll check with Maidjene, but thanks for asking at least," Sabine said. "Look, I'm sorry if that guy was, like, a friend of yours."

"Oh, no." Some of my best friends, as the saying goes, but that didn't include the Reverend Jackson Harm, and if I'd only read about his death in the paper I would probably have had something like Sabine's reaction, if only in the privacy of my own mind. "It's okay."

But it wasn't. Only understandable.

I went back to the cabin, feeling like I was going in circles in more ways than the obvious. My palms were sweating, and I could still taste the burger I'd had for lunch, unhappy in its new home.

I like to think that it wouldn't have occurred to me if the box hadn't already been wrapped and tied like a virgin sacrifice. But if Maidjene was going to burn the records anyway, couldn't they just . . . disappear without anyone knowing?

And then the deputies would stop asking about them, and Maidjene wouldn't be arrested, and everything would be fine.

Right?

I knew what I planned to do and I hated myself. I was going to do my best to steal the HallowFest registrations before Maidjene burned them and turn them over to the police, unless something happened to stop me.

Why?

Because it was the lesser of two evils? Because it would save Maidjene from further hurt at a time she needed it least? Or was I just kidding myself? Maybe I was looking for a martyr's crown, too.

I soothed my conscience by telling it there was no way Maidjene would take Sabine up on my offer to baby-sit after our conversation this morning. I told myself that even if she did, I wouldn't be able to get into the box. And as I was telling myself that, I was loading the inside pockets of my parka with enough copies of the Tree of Wisdom mail-order catalogue to equal the weight of what I hoped to steal, and a box-cutter and a tape roll to camouflage my theft.

Now that the long table and the boxes were gone, Julian's altar was set up on the folding tray-table he'd brought up. I looked down at my face in Julian's mirror. *Oh, Goddess, don't let me fuck up*, I pleaded silently. *Let this be the right thing to do. Let my brains not have turned to Wheatena. And while You're at it, let me find out who the killer is so I don't have to do this at all.*

There was no answer, not that I was expecting one. But the air was charged with the *numen* I associate with good ritual. She was present, and She was listening, and I was acting in accordance with Her will.

I tell myself.

The door to the cabin slammed open.

"Bast! Come quick!" Maidjene bawled.

I bailed out the door of the cabin and followed Maidjene in the direction of Mrs. Cooper's house. I could hear her gasping as she ran; she wouldn't have enough breath left over to answer questions.

She didn't have to.

There was a crowd gathered in front of Mrs. Cooper's house. I heard them before I saw them. Maybe twenty people, a few of them ours. I saw Orm Klash, and a man named Ragnar, who I knew from other HallowFests, although I wasn't completely sure what his trad was. Ragnar is about the size of a backhoe and wears his hair in two long braids. But we weren't the only ones there.

Most of the people there were carrying signs—signs that said things like "THERE IS ONLY 1 GOD" and "WITCHES BURN IN HELL." One of them carried a blow-up photo of Harm clutching a Bible and looking insincere, but then almost anyone looks shifty in studio portraits.

Mrs. Cooper was standing on the porch, trying to be heard over the din. I put on speed and left Maidjene behind.

It's hard to reconstruct what happened next. At the time, everything seemed to happen at once, and all of it so loud and confused it was more bewildering than scary. And at the time I wasn't even sure who the demonstrators were; later I found out they were some of the more apocalyptic members of Harm's congregation, something I could have figured out for myself if I'd had the time.

Time. Everything comes down to time, in the end.

The demonstrator carrying Harm's picture climbed up on the porch. He had a megaphone in his other hand. Mrs. Cooper tried to push him off the porch. He started a long harangue through the megaphone; it merged with the rest of the noise. I heard various versions of it later; it was the usual sort of mudslinging about how we were evil and they were threatened, yadada, yadada, vamp till ready. The Pagans—and more were arriving every minute—began chanting "The Goddess Is Alive: Magic Is Afoot," drowning him out.

Then someone grabbed Iduna.

She's Ragnar's daughter and she's four—something I know only because she was born at a HallowFest when Sandy—her mother—went into labor two weeks early. She was wiccaned before she was a day old, with half the Pagan clergy of the Eastern seaboard in attendance. She didn't know what was going on, but she wanted her daddy, and went zipping toward him out of nowhere like a little blonde comet.

One of the demonstrators grabbed her in midflight and started going on about "rescuing the children." I got there just in time to grab Ragnar's arm as he went surging forward, and got banged in the jaw for my troubles.

A television van pulled up.

Maidjene made it to the porch. She isn't fast, but she's strong. She got the megaphone away from the godshouter. I don't know whether he fell or made a tactical retreat, but he ended up sitting at the foot of the porch steps.

"Let go," Ragnar said to me. He sounded in control, so I did. So did two other people. The van opened. Someone with a minicam got out, along with several people who didn't have minicams. Iduna was screaming. Ragnar pushed through the crowd, heading for her.

It sounds more orderly than it was—and quieter, and slower— but what it really was like was everything happening at once, and loud.

Ragnar plucked Iduna away from a man with glasses who was glad enough to let her go when he saw what was coming for her. Sandy ran up, screaming for her daughter. Ragnar handed Iduna to her. Then—in a calm, considered, in-control fashion—he punched the guy who'd grabbed Iduna bang in the face.

Everybody started yelling.

Mrs. Cooper—using the megaphone this time—started demanding that everyone get off her land. Nobody wanted to listen to her when they could talk to the local news crew. Maidjene went down and took the minicam away from the person using it. Ragnar helped her.

It was a mess.

I did my part for crowd control by making everyone who'd listen to me move back. Ironshadow showed up, having run all the way from the barn, and more people listened to him than to me. By now most of HallowFest had shown up to watch the raree show. I could see Mrs. Cooper down by the van, talking to the local television personality, with Maidjene hanging over her shoulder and some of the picketers trying to horn in. I wondered where Larry was; he'd love being ringmaster at a media circus.

While all this was going on, a black van drove up and found the television van blocking the road. The driver began leaning on the horn.

"It would really help if you guys would leave so those freaks didn't have an audience," I said for what seemed like the ten-thousandth time. Some took my advice. Some didn't.

A vision in black got out of the passenger seat of the van. She looked as if she'd come from an alternate universe where H. P. Lovecraft had done the costume design for *Annie Hall.*

Xharina.

Or to give the lady her full title, Xharina, Princess of Pain; the HPS and only woman member of a flourishing leather coven based in Brooklyn Heights. She was wearing black leather hotpants, artistically-ripped black tights screen-printed with skulls and roses, lace-up black paddock boots, a black lace merry widow, and a black velvet bolero jacket. The answer to an electronic journalist's prayer, although not to ours.

I couldn't hear well enough to make out what the representatives of the media were saying, but from the gestures, Xharina was inviting them to get their van out of the way. A sheriff's car pulled up behind Xharina's van, with all the lights on its lightbar flashing. I headed for Maidjene, hoping I wouldn't be followed. The film crew trotted over to the sheriff's deputy for a statement. The demonstrators waved their signs feebly.

"Need any help?" I said to Maidjene.

"Only if you can change time, speed up the harvest, or teleport me off this rock," she said, quoting *Star Wars* this time. "God damn them," she added, meaning, I supposed, the demonstrators.

The deputy was explaining that the demonstrators did not have the right to demonstrate on private property, but that they could walk up and down Route 6 all they wanted. The newscaster was trying to get the deputy to say that Harm had died in an "execution-style" killing. The demonstrators' spokesman was saying something about the heavy hand of divine judgment being made manifest, having apparently forgotten that it was Harm who'd died, not one of us. The guy Ragnar'd punched was nowhere in sight, for which small mercy I thanked the Goddess fervently.

"What the *fuck* is going on here?" Xharina demanded, New Yorker to the core.

"The local fundamentalist sphincter got hisself killed up here last night," Maidjene said. "Welcome to HallowFest."

"Jesus H. Christ," Xharina said reverently. "For real?"

Why did people keep asking that?

"He isn't only merely dead; he's really and sincerely dead," I said. Two can play at Dueling Quotes. "Hi, Xhar."

"Hi, Bast. Um, look, do you guys think we could maybe get up to the barn? We've been driving since six this morning."

Maidjene looked at the traffic jam doubtfully. "Maybe," she said dubiously.

I looked around. Were there fewer of Harm's congregation gathered 'round than there had been a few minutes ago? I watched as another one plodded down the road in the direction of his parked car. Yup. Apparently none of them was in the market for the martyr's crown today.

After that, things broke up in stages.

The TV people headed back to their van. Xharina ran back to hers. The sheriff's car backed out of the way, lights still flashing, and it and the other two vans did some fancy backing and filling before they got themselves sorted out. The two vans went in opposite directions. The patrol car pulled up in front of Mrs. Cooper's porch; it was driven by a deputy I hadn't seen before.

I didn't want to be here. Big-time.

"I gotta go talk to them," Maidjene muttered.

"I'll see you later," I said, and walked back up to the barn through a jumble of standing gawkers.

What was I running away from? It seemed like I hadn't done anything since I'd gotten here except try to be someplace else from where I was, and I was getting tired of the lifestyle.

There were some easy explanations. I'd more or less broken with Changing, which meant it was time to form a coven of my own, something I'd so far avoided. Belle would expect it. *I* expected it, come to that. But it was a step I'd hesitated over taking for years, for reasons that probably weren't very good.

And then there was Julian and last night. He wasn't the type for one-night stands. Why him? Why me? Why now? And what next? Did we have more of a relationship than having worked together on *La Tesoraria del Oro* could give us? Was this love? Infatuation? A death wish? Whatever it was, it was going to have to take care of itself for a while longer; I had too much else to do. But I was still tired of running away from it.

Xharina's people were unloading their van when I got back up by the cabins. I saw Cain, Lasher, and Arioch, all of whom I'd met before, and two others I hadn't. I wandered over.

"Welcome to HallowFest," I said in my most orotund voice.

Xharina laughed. "Come to the country; it's quiet and safe. Yeah, sure. Where should we check in?"

I was abruptly reminded that I was carrying a parkaful of burglary equipment to make a gypsy switch on the registration forms. "Um, well, they aren't checking registrations any too closely now, so why don't you just come and get your badges?"

"Sure. You haven't met Goth and Riff-raff, have you? Guys, this is Bast."

Goth and Riff-raff, like their brethren, were dressed in the fashion of Biker Sluts from Hell: lots of denim and leather and visible
tattoos, a look to which I am unreasonably partial. Goth had a glorious handlebar mustache and ferocious white sidewalls; Riff-raff
was skinny and blond. Goth held out a paw in a fingerless leather
glove. We shook. I could feel calluses scrape my fingers, and when
I looked down I could see stars and letters inked into his fingers,
blurry and dark.

Jailhouse tats.

It didn't make me suddenly decide Goth had killed Harm. But
it did make me think about the fact that many of us come to the
Community with a history of violence elsewhere. We've forged new
family ties after so much loss and pain that we would defend
these new families unthinkingly if the moment came. I remembered the psychic charge that had flashed through the crowd
when one of the demonstrators had grabbed Iduna. Had Harm
threatened one of us last night?

"Mars to Bast," Xharina said.

"Oh, yeah, right. Come on, I'll show you where you can put your
stuff."

The room where Deputy Twochuck had been interviewing people was still empty, for a wonder, and had bunks for six. Renny
and his ink pad were long gone; I showed Xharina and Goth in to
it. Goth dropped the duffel bag he'd been carrying in a corner. It
clanked.

"You can crash here; kitchen's around the corner if you want
to cook, but it's going to be mobbed," I said dubiously. It's a regular apartment-style kitchen; the fact that almost a hundred people get fed three meals a day out of it each HallowFest weekend is
one of Life's little miracles.

"Where are we playing?" Xharina said.

I remembered that I'd seen "Hoodoo Lunchbox Unplugged" on
the schedule for tonight.

"If it doesn't rain, probably up at the Bardic Circle, after the
Opening Ritual. I think—" I closed my eyes for a moment to concentrate on what I'd seen on the program when I'd skimmed it earlier. "Right. Lorne's scheduling the performers, so you'd probably
better talk to him."

"We're going on first," Xharina said. I wasn't the one to argue
with her.

"I'll help you unload."

*   *   *

It's amazing how much gear even an unplugged band travels with. Guitars, drums, flutes—all in cases—plus the usual bags, baggage, and unattached leather jackets. Not to mention the giant Coleman ice chest full of beer. I helped them stow everything and copped a brewski for my trouble, which I needed by then. Officially HallowFest is a "dry" site; in practice, this means a "don't ask, don't tell" policy on the part of Mrs. Cooper, and keep the bottles out of sight.

Xharina looked at my copy of the program doubtfully. It was a little after two, and according to the schedule we were missing "Fundamentals of Good Ritual," "Raising Pagan Children," and "Worshipping Aphrodite Safely." Maidjene had been ambitious— there was multitrack programming for most of the weekend.

"Um, we aren't really into most of this," Xharina said, looking from the program to me.

"Think of it as a networking opportunity. Some people go to them, some don't. And there's always the shopping."

"Oh, right, I heard Ironshadow was going to be here," Xharina said, picking up my allusion without a dropped beat. I wondered where she knew him from; she didn't look like the SCA type.

"Where's Bast?" I heard from outside the room, and, with a parting wave to Xharina, I went to see who wanted me.

It was Maidjene. And despite all probabilities, she asked me to cover Registration from three to five after all.

Half an hour later, I slithered into the registration cabin and shut the door—reasonable enough, as it was chilly outside. The box was still right where it had been when Sabine pointed it out to me.

I wondered what the Sheriff's Department was doing just now. I wondered if Harm'd had any next of kin to notify. I wondered who the "everyone" that Fayrene'd said hated him was. I wondered if I could find out.

And I wondered how it had happened that Harm had lain down and let someone—never mind who—pull open his clothes and stab him through the heart with whatever he'd been stabbed through the heart with. It occurred to me that Ironshadow would be a pretty good man to ask about edged weapons that made a Y-shaped entry wound. I made a mental note.

I knew what I intended to do here, and there was no point in putting it off. The doors of the cabins can be locked from the inside, and I pushed the lock button in on the knob. And that single act of commission opened the door for all the rest.

I didn't have to mean to give the forms to the Sheriff's Office, I told myself mendaciously. Just to keep Maidjene from burning them. In case she changed her mind.

But she wasn't going to change her mind. I knew that.

I slid the ribbons off the box. It was sealed with only a couple of licks of tape, and I sliced right through them with the box-knife. The registration forms were inside.

If Maidjene did change her mind before tonight and opened the box—or found out what I'd done in some other way—I would lose her friendship. Guaranteed. If she never found out, all the rest of the years of our friendship would be built on a lie.

What was important enough for me to betray a friend for? A dead man I'd despised?

Yes. Exactly that. Because Jackson Harm had been murdered. And if we do not count murder to be so extraordinary a crime that we will take extraordinary measures to punish it, we devalue human life, and with it, all hope of human dignity.

It was cold in my ivory tower, but I didn't mind it so much now. Because if the Goddess came to me and set a price that *I* would have to pay for justice, I knew now that I was willing to meet that price.

It is such folly to be wise.

I took the registration forms out of the box and put them in my jacket pocket and put the Tree of Wisdom catalogues into the box and sealed it back up just the way it had been. The ribbons would cover the cuts in the tape, if anyone bothered to look that closely.

I was easing the ribbons back into place when someone rattled the knob and then started banging on the cabin door. I froze like any burglar, clutching the violated box with both hands. Despite my lofty moralizing, I wasn't exactly eager to be caught.

"Bast?" A man's voice, elusively familiar. "Maidjene said you were in here! I've been looking for you all morning." The knob rattled again. "Open the door."

It was Lark.

5

I hadn't seen Lark in about ten years—he'd been the wild liber-ating fling I'd had in my twenties, when no one knew that sex could kill you and I'd been more willing to collect emotional scars than I became after I had a few. I don't know if we'd been in love with each other or just with ourselves—the mind edits memory, looking for the comfort level in history. Eventually, you even for-get why leaving seemed to be such a good idea at the time.

I flung open the door and it was like stepping back through time. He'd aged, but not much. Not enough to count.

Lark has blue eyes and long brown hair. He looks like some kind of beardless hippie Jesus, and I've never seen him wear much that wasn't denim. That hadn't changed. He had on jeans and en-gineer boots and a chambray shirt with a denim jacket over it. He held his hair back with a rolled red bandanna tied as a headband. There was a gold ring in his ear.

"It *is* you!" I said, which is what people say when the other per-son still looks the same. People had been telling me for months that Lark was heading back East, but seeing him still came as a surprise.

He hugged me but we didn't kiss—thus the nineties make cow-ards of us all. Why hadn't I been a coward yesterday, when it could have done me some good?

"Yeah. You're looking good, girl—somebody told me this morn-ing you'd got in last night, but every time I went looking for you, you weren't there."

"You were here?" I said.

"Since Thursday. I laid low until I saw Phil show up Friday and then I came down and said hello—god, she gets fatter every time I see her," he added with no particular malice.

"If you were married to Larry, you might, too," I retorted, moved to defend Maidjene after what I'd just done to her.

"Hell if I would," Lark said. "I'd give that cocksucker a Smith & Wesson enema and really make his day. Is he up here? Maybe I ought to go say hello?" Lark grinned at me.

"Oh no you don't." I dragged him inside. He flopped down on the villainous plastic couch in the boneless unselfconsciousness that old lovers have with each other.

"So what are you doing here? How long are you staying?" I asked. *Did you come to see me?* It would be nice to think so.

"Oh, well, looking up old girlfriends and generally hanging out," Lark said, waving a hand. "Just got back from a beer run; want one?"

I did, and he went out to his bike, parked outside. It was a top-of-the-line Harley, all gleaming maroon lacquer and streamlined farings: 25,000 dollars on the hoof; the price of a car. Lark lifted a six-pack out of one of the glistening steel saddlebags and came back inside. I used his absence to shove the ribbons all the way back into place on the box and dump it more or less where it had been. Crime accompli.

Then we sat there—with the door open, so Lark could watch his bike, which shouldn't be parked here anyway—and talked about people we'd known and things we'd done. I'd had reports of him over the years; probably he'd had the same about me. And it was just about the way it had been, except for the fact that we were both ten years older and everything in the world had changed.

"So I hear you've quit Changing?" Lark said, popping the top on a second beer.

Maidjene would have told him that; it wasn't exactly a secret, Community gossip being what it was. "Sort of," I said cautiously, not wanting to go into all the gory details. This was my second beer in half an hour, and on top of a night of very little sleep, I could feel it hit me hard. Alcohol makes me reckless, which is good in a few situations. A very few. Not this one. Covens are like families; leaving is a combination of divorce and graduation. The impulse, after separation, is to justify your position.

"About time," Lark said, and changed the subject before it

could get awkward. The conversation wandered on easily with no particular direction, until Lark remembered someplace else he had to be, and left to be there.

Once he was gone, I stared at the door and brooded—about something other than the state of my morals, for a change.

My breakup with Changing had been coming for years; Belle's style and mine had drifted too far apart, and enough had changed so that I was no longer willing to submit to her authority instead of to my intuition. The difference of opinion was irreconcilable and basic: Belle believed that magic was subjective and the Gods were allegories; that evil was a failure of social services and malice was a failure of perception.

It's a popular and comfortable viewpoint, which may be the reason I don't embrace it. Unlike Belle, I believed in the Goddess, Death, and Hell; in both true capital-E Evil and the lazy cowardice that often passes for it in the modern world; and also in a judgment that didn't wait conveniently on the sidelines until your next life.

And I wonder why I don't have more friends. But I didn't need more friends just now. I needed a coven, and the only way to get one was probably going to be to run one.

Lark had been Wiccan the last I'd heard, and probably still was if he'd come to HallowFest. He might be looking for an agreeable coven to join—or even to lead. It would be logical for us to pair off— I could hear the wheels turning in Belle's head from here.

But I didn't want Lark for my High Priest and working partner, I told myself, even if he was one hundred times more plausible material for the job than Julian would ever be (being, to begin with, a member of the same religion). Because Lark hadn't changed. I'd thought that the moment I saw him, and it was true, and seeing him again had reminded me freshly of all the reasons we'd split up.

He was charming. Yes, and thoughtless as well. He was compassionate. And had a violent temper. He was faithful—in his fashion. He was good in bed. And believed in that old double standard: men stray, women pray.

In short, Lark was the sort of person you probably couldn't stand unless you were in love with him.

And I wasn't. But there was enough friendship there to make part of me want to work to tip us back over the line into love—you can do that, if you work at it—and that would be a stupid thing to do, although it would probably feel very good for quite a while. And feeling good would be nice. For a change.

I didn't realize until I'd framed the thought that the emotional disquiet that had been vaguely dogging me all day came from the fact that my little tryst with Julian hadn't left me feeling good, answer to my girlish fantasies though it had been. Oh, not that it had been any species of rape, even by the PC rubber yardstick in use these days, but it had left me feeling unsettled, uncertain of my ground. A nice normal dysfunctional relationship with Lark would at least be something I could understand. That was the thought that led to me wondering how Lark and Julian would react to each other when they met, and the despairing certainty that they would meet, and I would probably have worked myself all the way up to quiet desperation if Glitter hadn't stuck her head in the cabin door.

Glitter is one of my (former) coven-mates in Changing, and a friend (still). In real life, Glitter is a probation officer for the City of New York, a gritty reality she offsets as much as possible by the way she dresses. To call Glitter's clothing "eccentric" is to be far too conservative—I honestly don't know where she comes up with some of her outfits, but clothes aren't clothes to Glitter unless they are purple or sparkly or, preferably, both.

Which meant that for a nature festival at a rural campground, Glitter had chosen to manifest in a deep violet sweatshirt and sweatpants combo liberally decorated with gold and fuchsia fabric paint, sequined rickrack, and the odd rhinestone. She was wearing an outdated down jacket made of metallic purple rip-stop nylon, which, fortunately, coordinated with the other pieces. To see Glitter and Maidjene together is to be aware of what a pallid, colorless world we normally live in.

"Oh, hi," Glitter said. "You're still here."

"Uh-huh," I said. "And if I'm still here in half an hour, I'm going to stick you with it—I'll have to close down the Snake's table for the night." And see Julian again.

"Oh, well, Lark said you were here," Glitter said. She sounded nervous for some reason. It couldn't be the murder, considering what Glitter does for a living, although it's different when it happens on your own time.

"He was right," I said. "Here I am. How are you?"

"Are you going to work with him?" Glitter burst out breathlessly.

In Paganspeak that phrase has only one interpretation: Glitter was asking me what I'd been asking myself: if I intended to take Lark for my working partner if—*when*—I founded my own coven. That I would have to find someone—and a male someone at that—was something neither of us questioned; it's a basic tenet of the particular branch of ritual magic from which Gardnerian Wicca is descended. Each coven has a High Priest and a High Priestess, male and female to mirror the God-and-Goddess duality that we of the Wicca worship.

"I don't know yet," I said slowly, although a moment ago I'd thought I had.

"Well," said Glitter, a little wistfully, "I thought if maybe the two of you were going to start another coven, I'd like to go in with you."

That was a facer, as they said in the nineteenth century, and I finally gave the logistics of starting my own coven serious brain room. Covens split all the time—I'd separated from Changing—but if I hived off formally, I'd be entitled to ask if any of Changing's current membership wanted to join my new coven. I wondered who'd accept that offer. Not Topper and Coral; they're headed for a coven of their own as soon as they're ready. But Glitter'd just said she wanted in, and maybe Actaeon, which would be good; men are scarce in the Craft.

"I thought you liked working with Belle," I said aloud.

"I do!" Glitter said quickly. "But, you know, she's talking about retiring . . ."

"She is?" I said blankly. It was true I hadn't been to a meeting of Changing in almost four months, but I still would have thought someone would have mentioned *something*.

"Not formally, exactly. But you know, fifteen years is a long time—"

And in the Community, where five years is a lifetime, Belle's decade and a half of activity made her one of the Great Old Ones of our religion.

"I couldn't have a coven meet at my apartment," I said, leapfrogging several intermediate questions.

"She wouldn't mind if we still met there," Glitter said. It was true. In fact, as I knew, she'd revel in it: Belle has been feuding with her landlord, who has been trying to take the building co-op, for years. He considers every visitor she has a potential illegal sublet barring him from reclaiming what is wrongfully his.

But Belle quitting? This was a different kettle of fish: if Belle was thinking of retiring from coven leadership, she was either thinking of passing the coven to someone else or freezing its current membership and finding new places for all its members before she stepped down.

I didn't want Changing—it was a basic disagreement with Changing's "corporate culture" that had led to my leaving. I could see Topper and Coral taking over the magical entity that Changing had become without any problem, although if they did, Changing would move with them to Co-op City.

But a new coven . . . Meeting at Belle's but not belonging to Belle. Something different. Something new.

Suddenly it began to seem possible.

"I'll talk to Belle," I said.

Glitter grinned. I felt a heart-clutching pang of responsibility. But I was getting used to it.

So I thought.

Sabine showed up a few minutes later—mostly to tell me I didn't have to hang out here anymore.

"Anybody needs any registering they can come find us over at the barn," she said. "Everybody's probably already here, anyway," she added. By Saturday at 5:00 they'd better be.

"Okay," I said. "You need any more help, just ask."

Glitter and I headed for the barn. The registration forms were heavy in the pocket of my parka. I steeled myself not to look back at the box.

I found that, in my absence, the rest of the HallowFest merchants had arrived and set up, including another bookseller and someone from the Witches and Pagans Outreach Network (WAPON). We were about eight tables all told, including Ironshadow's and the Snake's. Hallie's tie-dye robes were hung along a cord suspended between two nails driven into the low ceiling beams. At the other tables were a candlemaker, someone with oils and incenses, and a bakery sale table covered with things that looked better than any alternatives I had available for tomorrow's breakfast—or tonight's dinner, come to that.

Julian was sitting behind the Snake's table, reading the expensive copy of *La Tesoraria del Oro*.

"You're going to ruin your eyes, reading in the dark like that," I said. The surface of the table looked as if it had been rearranged. I hoped sales had been good.

"You sound like my mother," Julian said, setting the book aside. It wasn't one of our *Tesorarias*, I realized when I got a closer look: its leather binding gleamed with use and handling and the pages were no longer mashed flat in the way of book pages that have just come from the bindery. Julian's own copy, then. I wondered if he intended to do the *Tesoraria* Work.

He stood up. "What now?"

It took me a moment to remember that this was Julian's first HallowFest, just as it was for Xharina and the Klingons.

"Merchanting's over for the day. We pack up, then there's dinner. Ritual starts at eight o'clock, Pagan Standard Time. After that's Bardic Circle."

Julian removed his glasses and began pushing them on his coattail. It made him look younger. Maybe more accessible.

"I don't want to go to the ritual," he said neutrally.

"That's okay," I reassured him. Some people don't. I'd be there, because the Opening Ritual at HallowFest is one of my personal touchstones.

"Fine, then," Julian said, as if we'd settled something. There was a pause. "I'm going to be doing a working tonight. I'd like to use the cabin."

It took a beat, but I translated that without effort: Julian wanted privacy. I'd like to think he felt as awkward and off balance as I did about what we'd done, and given time, I might be able to convince myself he did.

"Yeah, sure; I can always sleep in the van." Which would be cold, but not much colder than the cabins, and I might end up sleeping somewhere else anyway. I wondered if there was room in Ironshadow's tent.

"Good," Julian said. "I'll let you close up, then." He tucked his copy of *La Tesoraria* under his arm and walked off. I paused a moment to get used to the sense of relief I felt at one more postponement of a confrontation with Julian. *If there's going to be a confrontation at all,* I emended scrupulously.

I walked around to the seller's side of the table and began to tuck things away. Out of the corner of my eye I registered that Glitter had come upstairs. She stopped first at the bake sale table and then drifted over to me.

"Want one?" Glitter said. She held out a muffin. "Banana–chocolate chip. Oooh, what's that?" she said, peering down at the table.

I took the muffin. "The same stuff you can see any day of the week in New York," I told her, biting into the muffin. It was a little sweet for my taste, but I ate it anyway.

Glitter was admiring a pair of sugalite "point" earrings. Sugalite is purple, which makes it a natural for Glitter, though not naturally pointed—or for that matter, crystalline. The Snake stocks a wide variety of carved pseudo-crystal "points." (My favorite is turquoise, as turquoise in its natural state appears in masses resembling cottage cheese, but thanks to the mercantile magic of New Age Crystal Power, even turquoise is vended as a six-sided point-ended cylinder complete with a specious set of mystic "properties.")

"I'll take them," Glitter said, fishing her wallet out of her purple rip-stop nylon fanny-pack.

I took her fifteen dollars—a mere three times what the things had cost wholesale—and added the money and the sales slip to the cashbox. Someone from Summerisle came through, ringing a handbell to close Merchanting.

Glitter told me I was welcome to join Changing for dinner. I told her I'd be there. Then she went her way, and I was left to my own devices.

I picked up the nearest empty box and put both The Snake's *Tesorarias*, the jewelry, and a few other small, high-end items into it, then set the cashbox on top. The rest of the stock—mostly books, plus a few small plaques and statues—could take its chances with the reasonably honest HallowFest membership. I covered the table with a cloth. Beside me, Ironshadow was also closing up. He was taking all his inventory with him, though; his wares were more likely to take a walk than the Snake's were.

I set the box I was taking with me down on a flat space on my table and idled over.

"How's business?" I asked.

"You made up your mind about that knife yet?" Ironshadow said. He held it up. In the sunset light the copper sickle looked as if it had been dipped in blood. The opalized bone glittered faintly.

"What was that special order Julian picked up from you today?" I asked. "I didn't see it out on our table." Sometimes the Snake commissions pieces from Ironshadow, then retails them at an outrageous markup.

"Personal," Ironshadow said. "Silver blade."

He made a face. Ironshadow does not like to work in metals that won't hold a cutting edge, even if most of his work will never cut anything more substantial than air. But he does do special orders, and some forms of ceremonial magic call for weapons of copper, silver, and even gold.

"Well, I hope you soaked him for it," I said amiably, and Ironshadow grinned.

"Some of us are having a private party after the Bardic Circle. You're invited," he said.

"I'll be there." Ironshadow's parties involve home-brewed mead. "And I'll take the *boline.*" I'd figure out a way to pay for it somehow.

He twirled it in his fingers and presented it to me butt first.

"I can't pay you for it now," I said, alarmed.

"You'll pay when you can," he said. "I trust you."

The vote of confidence made me feel absurdly mellow. I remembered the other business I had with Ironshadow.

"About Reverend Harm," I began.

Ironshadow grinned, showing large white teeth. "Yeah. I'd been wondering myself where the hell somebody in Gotham County came up with a *kukri.*"

If you've seen Alec Baldwin's beautiful but stupid movie version of *The Shadow,* you've seen a *kukri:* it's a Tibetan ceremonial knife with the sort of three-flanged blade that—if you stuck someone with it—would probably leave the sort of hole that had been left in Jackson Harm. In real life, of course, it doesn't fly around by itself, so someone had to have been holding onto it to make it do what it did.

What was unlikely about this scenario is that the *kukri* isn't really so much a knife as it is a knife *symbol* used in Tibetan Buddhism. It's cast, not forged; the only ones I've seen are dull as a letter opener, if not duller.

And, like Ironshadow, I couldn't imagine where anyone would get one around here.

I took the Snake's box of goodies down to the van, and took the opportunity to transfer Maidjene's registration forms from my pocket to a better hiding place in the back of the van. I still didn't feel good about what I'd done, but the hell of it was, I would have felt equally bad about any of the other choices I could see to make, some of which involved Maidjene's being arrested. I would have liked it if there had been someone else around to tell me what to do, but Witches don't even allow that privilege to the Goddess.

Speaking of Maidjene, Larry's Warwagon was at the other end of the parking area. I could see lights on inside, although the shades were down: Larry Wagner, doing his Charles-Bronson-in-*Death Wish* vigilante imitation and draining his RV's batteries. I wished I believed he'd stay where he was and spend the rest of the night communing with his technology, but I couldn't manage that.

I locked the Snake's van, then went back up to the cabin; if I was going to be shut out tonight I wanted my sleeping bag and toothbrush.

The cabin was empty when I got there, although Julian'd been back to it; the *Tesoraria* I'd seen him reading upstairs in the barn was on the tray-table altar next to the mirror, and next to it was a newspaper-wrapped bundle that was probably his new Iron-shadow knife. I grabbed my sleeping bag and pillow and tried to decide how much else I could carry in the one trip I was willing to make. I dumped the bedding by the door while I made up my mind.

Julian'd said he was going to do a working—what Pagans would call a ritual—tonight, and I saw no reason to doubt it. Lots of people took the opportunity presented by HallowFest to do some pretty intensive ritual. But Julian wasn't a Pagan; he was a Ceremonial Magician. What could *he* be working on, this far from all the special paraphernalia that magicians used?

The *Tesoraria*? I glanced guiltily at the door, then went over and unwrapped Julian's Ironshadow bundle. I saw the white gleam of fine silver—pure silver, not sterling, expensive as gold and just as soft—and the coarse, mock-ivory sheen of bone. This was out of *La Tesoraria,* all right. I knew the book reasonably well—although I'd only worked on it, not read it—the knife was part of the Adept's new tools, for use when *La Tesoraria*'s year of ritual preparations were complete. I wondered if it were really built to spec, and if so, where Ironshadow'd gotten a lamb's thighbone.

I wrapped the knife back up again, wondering why the sight of it made me so uneasy. The only thing a blade like that would ever cut or be able to cut was air.

"These our actors, As I foretold you, were all spirits, and Are melted into air, into thin air . . ." (*Tempest,* Act 4, Scene 1).

Suddenly I didn't care about my toothbrush and I didn't care about my clothes. I grabbed my sleeping bag and my pillow and fled as if there were someone there to chase me.

* * *

By the time I got back down to the van again the feeling was gone, and the aftermath of the adrenaline rush made me conscious of how tired I was. I glanced at my watch. Five-twenty. Four hours, at least, until the start of the evening ritual—assuming anything like an on-time start was being charitable. I opened the back doors of the van and climbed in, shutting them after me.

It was dark inside the van, and so cold that there was no particular smell to it, though I knew when it was warm the van ponged of all the oils and incense that had been spilled there over time. I spread out the dirty packing quilts to form a comfortable foundation, zipped my sleeping bag up into a bag again, and pulled off my boots and parka. Then I wriggled down into the bag, pulling my pillow in after me. HallowFest parties have a way of going on all night and I'd already been up for twelve hours at least on top of a short night; I was weary to the bone and thought I could best spend my time grabbing a catnap while the grabbing was good.

Once I was lying there, though, I felt false. Theatrical; as if I were not here to sleep, but, rather, to be *seen* to be sleeping for some unknown watcher who must be persuaded of the fact. I closed my eyes and tried to ignore the sensation, but it wouldn't go away, even when I actually did slide over the borderland into sleep.

Lucid dreaming is the flavor of the month on the New Aquarian Frontier; insusceptible to objective proof, like so much in our lives, because it relies on the subjective testimony of the participant. Put as simply as possible, to dream lucidly is to be aware that you are asleep and dreaming while you are doing so, and even to manipulate dream-events with the conscious mind. All of us do at least the former at some point in our sleeping lives. I prefer not to meddle, but to leave my dreams alone, searching for what they're trying to say through the mute symbol-driven interface dividing the conscious and unconscious mind.

And so I let myself be carried from reverie into dream, without really noticing the moment when I crossed over.

It seemed logical to me to be back up in the pine forest, since I'd spent so much of the day there, at least in spirit. I wanted to talk to Jackson Harm: I wanted him to tell me what he was doing here at this hour of the morning.

Associative memory happily presented me with the leopard

frozen in the snows of Kilimanjaro. No one knew why it had been there, either.

In my dream I realized that there was an appointment I must keep; a rendezvous that I was unaware of, although I'd begun planning for it years ago. The night was both Friday night and Saturday night—Jackson Harm was somewhere in the woods—alive—at the same time the Saturday bonfire blazed in the meadow below. The irrational conflation of images common to dreams made perfect sense, too, although they did cause me to suspect I was asleep. The bonfire shed no light here where I was, and there was something waiting for me in the wood.

Half-aware, I dismissed this thought as a shopworn Jungian archetype: the wood is a symbol of the preverbal unconscious, and there's *always* something waiting in it for the unwary traveler. But at the same time I knew that this wood was objectively real on some level, and so was what waited—a particular something, and no archetype—and whatever it was, to see it truly would change me forever.

To be changed like that frightened me even while I disbelieved in it: with my waking mind, I knew that the only thing that could be in this wood was the dead body of Reverend Harm, which I'd already seen. The dead body whose sight had changed me was in the past: Miriam Seabrook, whose murder I'd avenged, if not exactly solved. These woods are dark and dangerous, I'd told her once, but it had been too late to save her even then.

And when I remembered that, suddenly Miriam was here, clutching at me and demanding that I *see* before it was too late.

Now I realized these were dreams, not thoughts. I wrenched myself free and found I was standing at the edge of the fire pit, certain now that I was awake and pseudo-remembering that I had fallen asleep at the Bardic Circle. It was dawn, and I was thinking "what a strange dream *that* was" when I saw that what I'd thought were the campfire's remains were charred bones, burnt but recognizable—

And then I did wake up.

It was pitch-dark inside the van; I thrashed around disorientedly until I banged my face against the side and came completely awake, completely conscious of where I was. My heart was racing, and the dream images were already fading. The pine forest. Miriam. A dead fire of bones. A dream-pun that, I realized: bonfire = bone-fire; an etymology that Murray, among others, cites in her work on premodern witchcraft.

I sat up, rubbing my eyes. The glowing numbers on my watch-dial told me it was a little after six pip emma, but I didn't feel like trying for sleep again if *that* was the sort of thing that was wait-ing for me in Dreamland. Dead friends and an urgent sense of mission: now *there's* hubris for you. Lady Bast, Lone Ranger of the Wicca, off on another quixotic quest for truth, justice, and the Aquarian Way.

Forget it. There were real live police investigating this homicide, and no place in their investigations for a talented amateur, or even me. Fayrene had told me what help I could be, and I'd been it, and that was that. I'd get in touch with her tomorrow, probably, and give her (maybe) the HallowFest registration forms I'd stolen, and that would be that.

And though I've made a career out of listening to what I didn't want to hear and seeing when it would be more comfortable to be blind, I told myself there would be enough time later to see what needed to be seen in the landscape of my dreams. And so I wormed out of the sleeping bag in the darkened van, wishing I'd had the brains to bring a flashlight down with me. Wishing I was warmer. Wishing.

There's a lot of distraction to be found at a HallowFest on a Sat-urday night if distraction suits your fancy. I'd seen lights on in the cabin I now only nominally shared with Julian. I hadn't stopped.

The dinner hour was just getting under way when I got back up to the barn around seven. It was warm in the barn—a combi-nation of the now-functioning radiators and all the bodies packed into the area. People flowed into and out of the kitchen area in a random tidal fashion, sharing and offering food to anyone who passed; no one at the Festival would go hungry tonight. I mingled, searching out old friends and new acquaintances.

The Klingons had brought "Romulan ale"; whatever it was, it was luridly blue and wonderfully alcoholic. They'd also brought a whole Boar's Head deli roast beef, which they were eating in chunks off their daggers, which drew a few looks even from peo-ple who did the same thing themselves at SCA events. I introduced Orm Klash to Belle.

Belle was cool—she invited Klash's tribe to join Changing's meal and started trying to sell him on the idea of attending one of her monthly Pagan Leadership meetings. The fact that he was dressed out of a TV show and speaking every other sentence in interstellar Esperanto was something she appeared not to notice, but then, Belle was a red diaper baby and believes in Solidarity *Uber Alles,* which is part of the particular rock and hard place that's led to our (amicable) parting of the ways. I moved on, and found Lark partying with Hoodoo Lunchbox, as was (surprise) Actaeon. I joined them, and Ironshadow joined us, and everything was all right.

For a while.

". . . all I can say is, it'd be nice if somebody persecuted them for a change," Lark was saying after two or three beers. "Hell, what's wrong with one fewer Christo-Nazi in the world? Fire up the barbecue, boys, and throw another Christian baby on the coals, right?"

"*They'd* kill *us,* if they had the chance," a boy in this year's HallowFest T-shirt said solemnly. I wondered if I'd ever been that young.

" 'Never again the burning.' " Someone on the group's outskirts quoted the old radical tag line. It's a highly romantic concept: claim some suitably persecuted ancestors and write yourself a moral blank check for anything you choose to do.

"That is a stupid and evil idea," I heard myself say loudly.

"Well, who the hell are you?" T-shirt said.

Who do I have to be? as James T. Kirk is fond of saying. "Do you really think that anybody has the right to kill somebody else just because they worship a different god?" I said.

"Christians do," T-shirt said smugly, as if that were either entirely true or an answer.

"Look, he didn't mean anything," a woman next to T-shirt said. "You're overreacting."

"If he didn't mean anything he should shut the fuck up," I said, getting to my feet. "I'm sick of hearing people cheer on a murderer in order to pretend they're sanctimonious little right-thinking Pagans—especially you," I said to Lark. I felt my hackles rise: anger and power are closely linked; it's one of the tragedies of the Left-Hand Path. I headed out the front door before I either started crying or said something worse.

Before I made it outside I heard jumbled scraps of talk behind me: "Who does she think *she* is?" "Jonathan, you dickface." "She's the one that found Jesus Jackson." "Asshole." "I didn't *mean* anything."

Belle and Ironshadow were the ones who came out after me— not Lark. Ironshadow must have gone to get her. They put their arms around me to let me cry, but I couldn't. All I could do was quiver with trapped emotion and wish there was some barricade to clamber up onto.

"It isn't right they should be glad he's dead," I finally managed to say. It wasn't what I meant; that was too lofty a moral high ground for even me to defend.

"They're just assholes," Ironshadow rumbled soothingly.

We were standing just outside the "front door" of the barn, the main entrance that nobody uses during a HallowFest because all the action's in the other direction. There was enough light spilling through the uncurtained windows for me to see Belle and Iron-shadow's faces, and to see a worried clump of people silhouetted in the open doorway. People who cared about me—or cared about something at least. Maybe just their own self-image.

"I understand how you feel, Bast," Belle said. "It must have been very scary to be the one to find the body. Sometimes when something like that happens people feel responsible for the fact that it happened, and then, because they can't do anything about it, they get angry. But you're not responsible. Reverend Harm's death isn't anything to do with you."

No man is an island . . . any man's death diminishes me . . . Do not ask for whom the John Donne's, it tolls for thee. I shook my head, choking on the words I both wanted and didn't want to say. "You didn't see him," I finally managed, which wasn't what I meant, either.

"It's over," Belle said firmly. "We have to bless it and let it go."

"It isn't real to them," Ironshadow said. "You know that. It's just another TV show. That's why they're talking like that."

"Cowboys and Indians," I said, drawing a deep, hurting breath. Pagans and Inquisitors. Choose sides, and let the dead not be real people, but merely a convenient way of keeping score.

"That's right," Belle said, giving my back an encouraging pat. "You're upset, that's all. Nobody really wanted Reverend Harm dead."

"Someone did, Belle," I pointed out. I stepped back, breathing deeply to center myself.

"That is nothing to do with you," Belle said firmly. But it was, even if only to the extent that I had to hold an opinion about the morality of the death I'd discovered.

"All right," I said. Belle took it as an agreement, but it wasn't. Not really.

They took me back inside; I got a lot of soothing mothering, and Lark even showed up and apologized, although neither of us was certain quite for what. He put his arm around me and I leaned back against him, both of us pretending it was ten years ago and none of the time between had happened.

And then it was time for the Closing Ritual.

The Closing (Opening) Ritual doesn't begin HallowFest in any practical sense, since it's scheduled to take place at a time when the majority of the attendees have arrived. It's the one event at which most of the Festival's attendees can usually be found—though not, as I've said, all. The parents of the very young often stay away (although children are welcome), as do those who don't fancy a long walk in the dark for reasons of health or hedonism. This year more people than usual elected to stay behind in the barn, at least as far as I could tell from my place in the procession.

The ritual begins with the Closing Ritual that goes with the Opening Ritual of the previous year's HallowFest; closing the Festival just before opening it again (bad magical discipline though it is) is a conceit that helps us take the love and belonging we feel here with us through the secular year, as if in some sense we never leave this sacred ground.

Most people change into ritual gear for the opening, and I'd even brought my robe to the Festival, but it was in the cabin and I didn't want to disturb Julian at whatever his private devotion was to retrieve it. I had on the silver cuff bracelet that marks my degree in my particular Wiccan tradition and the pentacle I always wore and that was sufficient.

The flashlights people carried made brilliant erratic searchlights through the country night. It took maybe twenty minutes for all of us to reach the Bardic Circle, and members of Summerisle Coven were already there. They'd marked out the circle boundaries with battery-operated Coleman lanterns. The bonfire had been built sometime this afternoon and now stood ready, surrounded by carved and illuminated jack-o'-lanterns from the pumpkin-carving workshop I'd missed, flickering orange-gold with dancing candle flames. Even with fewer people than usual attending we made a large circle—possibly ninety people. Most of us knew what to expect from previous years. We waited.

Enough different trads come to HallowFest each year that it would be exclusionary for whoever was running it to use the ritual form of any specific tradition at this circle, so we don't. The organizers of the last year's Festival begin by closing last year's circle, then this year's organizers open this year's circle. Then one of our youngest Pagans lights the fire. In practice, this means he or she will throw a bit of burnt branch saved from last year's fire onto the waiting woodpile, then retreat to safety while an adult lights it. As theater it's simple, effective, and healing, which is, I suppose, one of the reasons it's evolved the way it has.

While the fire catches we go around the circle, making personal statements and introducing ourselves. Sometimes we make sacrifices to the flames — on the HallowFest bonfire one year I'd burned diaries and papers for Miriam Seabrook. I could see the ribbon-tied box that I'd tampered with earlier sitting at Maidjene's feet, and felt a guilty surge of relief. She'd burn it, and with it all evidence of what I'd done.

Unless, of course, somebody told her afterward.

Between them, the Coleman lanterns and the jack-o'-lanterns cast enough light that the yellow Crime Scene ribbons were visible at the edge of the clearing, an unwelcome reminder of reality. I could see the soon-to-be-fire in the fire pit: a stack of logs and split kindling almost three feet high, with a tinder-filled core for easy lighting.

Bailey from Summerisle stood in for members of Brightstone Coven in Vermont, who'd run HallowFest last year and couldn't make it down this year. He read out a short closing statement from them and then stepped forward and tucked the rolled parchment in among the logs in the fire pit.

Then Maidjene opened this year's HallowFest, while Sabine played "Banish Misfortune," an old Irish folk tune, on her flute. It was probably only my guilty conscience that made me feel Maidjene placed undue stress in her opening speech on HallowFest being "at a time out of time and a place out of the world, a sanctuary where hate and ugliness cannot enter."

I wished it were true.

This year Iduna carried the stick salvaged from last year's fire; she was wearing a light-colored robe that already had charcoal smears on the front and clutching Ragnar's finger as he led her up to the woodpile. There was a moment of negotiation before she'd let go and drop the branch into the kindling, and everyone clapped and cheered when she did. Ragnar picked her up and carried her back to the perimeter as she hid her face against his neck.

On the sidelines, Ironshadow lit a torch. It was a real torch — wax-soaked rags wrapped around the end of a stick, and he flourished it to make sure it caught before he handed it to another of Maidjene's coveners — Lorne, I thought. He was wearing a Summerisle tabard and looked as young as Wyler Pascoe. I wondered if that meant I was getting old, or merely jaded.

The people who'd brought drums or other rhythm instruments to the circle — and many had — began to strike them in time, falling quickly into synch. Lorne matched his step to the beat, holding the flaring torch high over his head.

It is at moments like these that the world seems to become truly real — as if the world that all of us occupy daily were truly, as so many theologians tell us, merely a veil for some unknown, but more brilliant and resonant, truth. It is this sense of intense reality — what C. S. Lewis called "joy" — that brings us all to our varied spiritual paths, and its lack that drives us ever onward, seeking.

Had Harm found this joy in serving his narrow and exclusionist God?

The question jerked me back inside my skin and made me feel cold and uncomfortable — and joyless. Lorne shoved the torch into a hole in the pyre, and as the kindling caught, the wood was illuminated from within like the Halloween pumpkins ringing the base of the fire pit. The drums, rattles, and tambourines exploded into an arrhythmic din, over which the sound of Rebel yells and wolf howls rang back from the surrounding trees. But the joy that others found, or seemed to find, here did me no good — I was cut off from it, trapped in my secular skin without the confidence in the Lady's presence that I'd come here to evoke.

The ritual proceeded. We went around the circle, each of us saying our piece, whether coven affiliation, geographical location, or witty tag line.

"I'm Brandy, and I'm from Summerisle."

"I'm Carol from Boston, and this is my first HallowFest." ("Welcome, Carol!" we all shouted back.)

"Treath and Dan, Endless Circle."

"Pain is Truth! And I'm Xharina."

"Ironshadow — and this sure isn't my first HallowFest." (Laughter. "Welcome, Ironshadow!" we shouted anyway.)

And on around the circle. "I'm Bast," I said, when it was my turn. "I'm from Manhattan." And nothing else.

By the time I spoke the fire was burning strongly.

"For those who have yet to find us — let their voices not be silenced!"

A woman I didn't know stepped forward and threw the tambourine she'd been playing onto the fire. The drumface of it had been elaborately painted, and knots of ribbons trailed from the frame. A collective gasp went up from all of us as it charred to black and then caught fire, and I thought again about Wyler Pascoe, who wanted to see "the Witches."

There were other gifts to the fire—someone's thesis; a photograph of a loved one who'd died since this time last year; even a *papier-mâché* Barney the Dinosaur filled with incense. It flared strobe-bright before becoming a thick column of scented white smoke.

Maidjene threw her box into the fire without saying anything; its impact sent up a shower of sparks.

The circle opened out away from the fire pit as the fire got hotter. Lots of people had brought instruments up with them; there was music going on, and singing; a jug of apple cider was passing and so was a box of cookies; everyone was settling into the familiar *ur*-ritual mindspace of a HallowFest Opening Ritual.

Everyone but me. No matter how hard I tried to concentrate on the ritual, I kept looking up the hill as if I expected Hellfire Harm to come striding down it brandishing a flaming sword.

Which was why I saw them.

The flickering firelight made for tricky seeing; at first I put the movement among the trees down to that. But it wasn't. There were people in the woods, coming down through them. Toward us. They might even be from the Sheriff's Office; I didn't know. I did know that their being here meant something was wrong.

We were making too much noise for a shout to carry, and half a lifetime's habit kept me from breaking across the circle to warn Maidjene. I grabbed the person next to me and pointed up the hill before stepping back to run *deosil* outside the circle's perimeter. As I ran I saw that one of the men was carrying a rifle.

A mob of Pagans is no brighter than any other mob. If we'd stood our ground and kept our heads, everything might have been all right. But someone screamed and then everyone was screaming, yelling, running in all directions. I grabbed Maidjene to keep from being swept away with them.

"Call the police!" Maidjene yelled in my ear.

Assuming these *weren't* the police. I let go of her and ran blind, taking the shortcut down the hill, straight toward the lake. Behind me I heard a gunshot.

6

I slammed in one door of the barn.
"There's men with guns up at the circle! Call the police!" I ran out the other door, moving fast, blessing the Lady that through luck and miracle I wasn't wearing my ritual robe: black, wool-blend, and eight yards of material in the trailing skirt alone. I ran for Mrs. Cooper's house because I doubted the ability of any of the barn's inhabitants to get the sheriff's deputies here as fast as she could, but I was gasping and winded by the time I jumped her front porch steps and banged on the door.

"Police," I panted, as she opened the door.

She let me inside. She was already on the phone—to the Sheriff's Office, as a matter of fact.

"One of them's here now, Tod," she said into the receiver. She looked at me. "I heard shots."

I'd forgotten how far sound carried in the country—she'd probably heard us howling, too. "Men with guns," I gasped. "Crashing the circle. Through the pine forest." My throat felt as if it had been blow-dried.

"She says there are men up here with guns," Mrs. Cooper told the phone. There was a pause. "Tod Fulton, do I resemble an utter fool to your mind? Of course I'll stay here and let you take care of it. That's what you're paid for."

She hung up the phone and came back to me. I was standing, bent over and blowing like a grampus who's just finished running the New York Marathon.

"Are you all right?" she asked. Her voice was kind.

I nodded, still puffing. My heart was a hard palpable thudding in my chest and my mouth tasted of salt and iron. I hadn't run that far that fast in years, and adrenaline—like magic—takes its toll.

"Come sit down," Mrs. Cooper said. "You're . . . ?"

"Bast," I said. "I've got to—"

"You stay right here," Mrs. Cooper told me firmly. "No one needs you running around in the dark."

It was good advice. Come to that, I really didn't want to go. I have the greatest respect for the power of a gun in the hands of an agitated lunatic. I'd faced one once, and it'd be fine with me if I never did again. I came and sat at Mrs. Cooper's kitchen table. She gave me brandied coffee and shortbread biscuits.

As I was sitting there I saw a red/white/blue blaze flash by the windows, then a few seconds later heard a squib of siren as the car cleared the road ahead. The Gotham County Sheriff's Department had arrived.

"John'll take care of things," Mrs. Cooper said.

"They're going to love coming here twice in one day," I said.

Mrs. Cooper laughed harshly. "More than that—I had them up here Friday in the pee em to toss Mr. Hellfire Jackson Harm out on his ear. I don't know what anyone else may have to say about it, but for my money, Reverend Harm's decease is the best thing that could have happened in all of Gotham County."

Loved everywhere he went, just as I'd thought. "Harm was up here Friday?" I asked.

Mrs. Cooper sat down opposite me at the kitchen table and sipped her own spiked coffee. "Hellfire was up here *every* year before you people were due in, saying I should throw you all out on your ears. I said to him Friday—just like I do every year—'Just you tell me, Jackson Harm, where I'm going to get another party—in October, mind—to rent the whole campground for three-four days'—well! Being practical was *not* any of Jackson Harm's particular virtues, let me tell you; he never did have an answer to that one. But this year he outdid himself."

I was burning to ask her how, but just then another police cruiser pulled up. This one stopped, and the doorbell rang.

"Just you look at this and see what I mean," Mrs. Cooper told me, getting out of her chair to answer it. She took a pamphlet out of a kitchen drawer and plunked it down in front of me, then went

374 Bell, Book, and Murder

off to the door. *"That's* what Mr. Harm was doing up here Friday,"
she shot back over her shoulder.

I picked up the pamphlet. It was cheaply done: black and white,
gatefold, probably just Xeroxed onto bond paper. It was typewrit-
ten, not typeset, and the columns ran crookedly up and down the
page—a home paste-up job.

"Satan's Handmaids!" the front page said, in large blurry letters. Press-type probably, or lifted from something else. There was
a hand-drawn Christian cross inside a barred circle beneath the
words.

I skimmed it quickly, then read it more carefully as I realized
that this wasn't just the standard sort of redneck godshouter rant,
but one directed specifically at *us*.

"You say that all gods are one god, but there is only One God,
who is the Christ Jesus, who has Truely [sic] said: Thou Shalt
Have No Other Gods Before Me . . ."

If this was an example of Harm's theology, he was on pretty
shaky ground: the speaker in that particular case wasn't the son,
but the father, and it was one of the commandments given to the
prophet Moses.

There was more. Our Goddess was no goddess, but the Scar-
let Woman of Babylon (which, speaking from the purely anthropological viewpoint, which holds that the gods of the old religion
become the devils of the new, was only true, but not in any way
Harm would've liked); our souls would dwell in darkness because
we preferred stones to the living bread of the Word; et cetera, et
cetera, ad nauseam, *und so weiter.*

I could not imagine anyone at HallowFest being converted by
this little tract: amused, yes, offended, possibly. It would offend
most of the Christians of my acquaintance, come to that. The
strangest thing about it was that apparently Harm meant this of-
fensive little morsel of liberation theology to have a positive effect.

I folded the pamphlet back together. The back flap was an
invitation—with map—for HallowFesters to join his Sunday Morning Rescue Prayer Service and be welcomed again into the whole
body of Jesus Christ, a process which sounded mildly cannibal-
istic, to say the least.

While I'd been reading I'd been half-listening to what was going
on in the background: Mrs. Cooper's voice interspersed with a
male voice I didn't recognize. Now both of them came into the
kitchen.

"I'm Sergeant Blake. You say you saw men with guns?" he asked me.

They grew them big in Gotham County—the sergeant was Fayrene's male counterpart, big and husky with the start of a spare tire around the middle, black hair instead of blond, and the addition of a large mustache. The gun was the same though: a Heckler & Koch .45 automatic with a ten-round clip. Businesslike.

"I saw a rifle," I said, not really sure now about *what* I'd seen. "And about five men. And I heard a gunshot."

"Roy's radioed for an ambulance," Sergeant Blake said, which did not reassure me. "I'll be back to talk to you in a few minutes, so I'd appreciate it if you stuck around here for a while, ma'am."

Sergeant Blake left. I heard the cruiser drive off, and the blips and yelps of the siren that meant he was clearing the way ahead.

"Isn't that the stupidest piece of trash?" Mrs. Cooper said.

It took me a moment to refocus my mind from Sergeant Blake and his gun to the Reverend Harm's little essay.

"Well," I said inadequately.

"Wanted me to hand them out! Free! And I told him, 'Jackson Harm, as sure as I'm standing here those people are just going to laugh in your face! And why should I do your dirty work for you?'— well! Then he started rabbeting on about equal time, and I told him that this was a campground, not a presidential election, and then he said—bold as brass, *if* you please—"

It occurred to me that Mrs. Cooper was one of those speakers whose conversation doesn't require participants, merely an audience, and then I thought that she probably didn't get too much of either one. And so I would have listened even if she weren't telling me things I really wanted to hear more about. Certainly she'd had as many jarring shocks as I'd had that day, but where were the people for her to share them with?

Now that I'd had a chance to actually talk to Mrs. Cooper I could place her type: New England liberal, of the breed who will defend her fellow citizens' eccentricities to the death and demand the same tolerance for her own. A kind not much seen in these parts in recent years, more's the pity.

"*First* he tells me that *God* doesn't like the way I'm running Paradise Lake—well, I told him that *God* could tell me that in person, rather than sending a nasty little errand boy like him!"

I laughed at the joke, as I was meant to. It's amazing how many people who profess to believe in an omnipotent, omnibenevolent, omnidirectional, detail-oriented god still manage to believe that this god doesn't have either the time or the inclination to run his own errands.

"And if he thought that I didn't have God's home address, after having him in my Sunday Bible classes all those years—"

Harm, I supposed she meant, and not Harm's celestial supervisor. "And?" I prompted, finishing my coffee.

She got up to get the standing pot. Her hands were shaking, and I put it down to age, but when she turned around I could see it wasn't age—it was fury.

"He had the nerve—the absolute nerve, that jumped-up little brass-bound bastard—"

I blinked in surprise. Profanity is supposed to be the exclusive preserve of the young and trendy.

"—to tell me that if I let you people rent the place again this year, I could kiss good-bye to the Summer Youth Bible Study Camp!"

"The Bible Study Camp?" I echoed, trying not to look as baffled as I felt.

"*They* have Paradise Lake for July. *All* of July," Mrs. Cooper said.

Now it started to make sense, and as usual, the bottom line wasn't about theology, but money. A campground is like any other small business, and the margin between failure and survival is slight. One month of her peak season fully booked and occupied might very well make the difference between Paradise Lake's success and failure for Mrs. Cooper.

"Could he do that?" I asked.

She snorted and refilled our cups. "Just between you and me and the gatepost, Jackson Harm wasn't quite the big stink he thought he was. But still . . ." Her voice trailed off. "Well, he won't be doing anything *now*, that's for sure!" she said in satisfied tones.

"And he was up here Friday?" I asked, just to be sure.

"Friday morning, bold as brass, preaching at me as if I were a public meeting for two and a half *hours*, until I had to call Tom down to the Sheriff's to disinvite him. And at that he left all of his damned pamphlets behind!" She jerked her chin and I saw three suspicious-looking boxes piled in the corner of the kitchen.

"And Saturday morning he was dead," I said.

"Up in my woods, which is pure meanness on his part. Have another cookie," Helen Cooper said.

* * *

So I did, while Mrs. Cooper regaled me with more local color from Jesus Jackson's glorious career. In addition to Mrs. Cooper, the Reverend Harm had harassed the local paper, the local radio station, and even the welfare office in Tamerlane, which is twenty miles up Route 6 and the closest thing to a city there is in Gotham County.

It occurred to me I'd just been handed a motive for murder that the Sheriff's Office would have no trouble understanding. Mrs. Cooper's.

She had motive—Harm was trying to drive away the customers on whom her livelihood depended: the Bible Camp and HallowFest. If she wanted to do a frame-up, she had enough experience from previous HallowFests to do a fair job of imitating our handiwork. And she'd had opportunity—by her own admission Harm'd been here Friday afternoon.

But so had Maidjene. And Lark. And probably even Larry Wagner in his Warwagon, all set to fight World War III and convinced that the world was against him.

No, I couldn't believe in Mrs. Cooper for the killer. If she were to kill someone—something I didn't doubt for a moment she was capable of—she wouldn't use a knife. A shotgun, maybe—I'd be surprised if she *didn't* have one. But Harm hadn't been shot. He'd been stabbed. And I didn't think Mrs. Cooper had the physical strength necessary to stab Harm, let alone the inclination to get him half-naked first.

The doorbell rang again. I glanced out the parlor window, but didn't see any flashing lights. Mrs. Cooper went to open the door.

"I just couldn't tear myself away," I heard Fayrene Pascoe drawl.

She came into the kitchen, still in uniform, this time with the addition of a dark green nylon bomber jacket.

"Hi, Fayrene," I said.

"You in trouble again?" she asked me amiably. The walkie-talkie on her hip chattered on intermittently, with flashes of static and 10-codes I wished I could interpret. I caught a burst of someone telling someone else to "secure the area," and hoped it meant the trouble was over.

"Some boys are up here bothering my campers!" Helen Cooper said fiercely.

"Jeff and Johnny are probably taking care of it, Mrs. Cooper;

don't you worry. I heard over the radio one of your friends got shot, though—nothing serious," she added to me. "So I thought I'd come over and see the fun. What were you doing up there this time of night?"

"Trying to pursue that freedom of religious expression to which the Constitution theoretically entitles me," I said. I sounded as if I were spitting nails. "Sorry," I said after a moment. "It was our Saturday bonfire—"

"I've seen 'em. We had one of our units on a short drive-by tonight, but Tony didn't think we needed anybody out here," Fayrene said. After a moment I placed the name: Mad Anthony Wayne, our detective-on-the-spot.

"Well, we were all just standing there, and these guys started coming down from out of the pine forest, and one of them had a gun—rifle or shotgun, I don't know—and I ran like a rabbit," I said.

"More people should do that," Fayrene said.

When Fayrene walked me back up to the site it was glaringly lit by the searchlights of two cruisers and looked pretty well trampled. More cars not belonging to the festival were parked nearby, and I counted six uniformed deputies, not to mention the EMTs and their big orange-and-white truck, just now arriving. The deputies were herding the HallowFesters into little clumps and chasing after the ones who just wanted to leave. Babies were crying, and I looked automatically for Ragnar and Iduna. I didn't see them, but I did see Xharina, standing next to Klash and looking worried. There was an eerie continuity between the two sets of leather, straps, buckles, and elaborate makeup. I looked away before we could make eye contact, following Fayrene.

There were flashlight beams as the deputies walked the wood, blazing emergency lights, and blaring radios. Fayrene sliced through the chaos as if it were familiar territory, swapping jokes with the other deputies. In the middle of it all, the bonfire Maidjene's coven had so painstakingly constructed and lit blazed on, even with no one there to care.

As is usual—though not, as I am starting to suspect in my case, typical—I was on only the very fringes of the whole thing and had to piece it together out of what I found out later. Which was this:

It wasn't religious bigots so much as it was a case of Saturday night and nowhere to go—and Paradise Lake and its exotic visitors very much in the forefront of the public mind, thanks to all

THE BOWL OF NIGHT 379

the coverage in the paper and on the local news about Harm's death.

When I passed one of the cars I was surprised to see there was someone in the back—an older man, with the undefinable air of being Not One of Us. He was wearing handcuffs and looked bored and irritated, which was better than I would have been doing in the same situation.

"So, John-boy, you managed to make any arrests yet?" Fayrene was addressing Sergeant Blake, whom I'd met earlier. "Oh, and I already took the statement of the original complainants."

Sergeant Blake looked at her, and then past her to me, then back again.

"Local boy," he said to her. "Nothing much. We can hold Arnold here on menacing—he had the shotgun. The worst we can charge his friends with is harassment, maybe a little conspiracy. They took Reece Wheeler off to Taconic Hospital—somebody plinked him with a .25 or a .32, and none of the boys here was carrying anything like that. So they say."

He looked back at me, while I figured the rest out for myself. Someone had been wounded tonight, but not someone from HallowFest. The victim had been one of the local party animals, one Reece Wheeler. And if Wheeler had been shot, and his fellow Jukes and Kallikaks disavowed it, the only other possible candidate for shooter was one of us—and no one was admitting to possessing the gun that had shot him.

"I didn't shoot him." I barely kept myself from saying I was glad he was shot and hoped it hurt. I was not prepared at all for the sheer triumphal fury that shook me at the thought that one of our attackers had been shot. At that moment, I wanted them all dead, as slowly and painfully as the hand of Man could contrive. I'd been terrified and I wanted revenge; it was a stupid, childish, clockwork reaction, and I tried very hard to regret it. "I don't know who shot him. I wasn't here." I had a witness to the last statement, at least.

"Any of your friends carry guns?" Sergeant Blake asked. "Anyone here we should talk to?"

"Not that I know of." And at that moment, I wouldn't tell him if I did. Fortunately the need to lie, if not the impulse, was absent.

Childish, like I said.

"Find it yet?" Fayrene asked.

Sergeant Blake made a spread-handed shrug that took in the entire scene, including the clumps of Pagans standing and watch-

ing. The entire area around the fire was littered with things people had dropped in the confusion: hats, wands, Pepsi cans, baby
bottles—even an *athamé* or two.

"In *this*, Fay? We're going to sweep the woods in the morning,
but sure as you're born that pop-gun's at the bottom of the lake by
now. Nobody saw a thing, and Reece says he doesn't want to press
charges, so you know how much rope the DA's going to give us."

"Well, that's mighty white of Brother Reece," Fayrene drawled,
her flat upstate accent becoming more pronounced.

"Are you the officer in charge of this investigation?" It was
Maidjene, sounding small and scared, but there. I raised my hand
in greeting. Her eyes focused on me for an instant, then flicked
away. Her face was whiter than it'd been this morning by Harm's
body, an occasion that seemed a thousand years ago now.

Sergeant Blake turned to her. "I'm Sergeant Blake," he said.

"My name is Phyllis Wagner. I'm the organizer for this festival."
Maidjene hesitated. "Can you stop them from coming back?"

"I don't think they'll try anything else, Ms. Wagner," Sergeant
Blake said soothingly.

"You didn't think they'd try this, or you'd have left someone
here to protect us," Maidjene said, shaky but dogged.

Blake looked at Fayrene, and some cryptic cop-thing seemed
to pass between them.

"We'll have someone walk the area a few times tonight,"
Sergeant Blake told her. He didn't seem to know about the material Maidjene was supposed to turn over to his department, or
maybe he was just being subtle. "Now, do you want to lodge a complaint?"

"I—" Maidjene hesitated, although I could tell she was mad and
scared in just about equal portions. If she lodged a complaint there
might be a trial where she'd have to testify, and that would be an
awfully long commute for somebody who lived in Jersey and currently had no visible means of support.

"I'll complain," I said harshly. "I saw them coming down the hill.
I saw the gun. I'll do it."

Maidjene's look of gratitude did little to salve my aching conscience.

"Are you sure about that, miss?" Sergeant Blake said, in that
tone that suddenly makes you sure of nothing at all. I'd dealt with
the law before, though, so I stood my ground.

"The fire was bright. He was close. The barrels reflected—on the
rifle; even if they were blued, you could see them; they were metal.

I knew he had a gun, and I knew he wasn't a member of Hal-lowFest. We had trouble this afternoon. You probably saw it on the news. I thought this might be connected."

Blake asked for my name and address, and I gave them. I vol-unteered that I was selling here at HallowFest, and Maidjene told them that I was helping the committee running the festival, which was not really that far from the truth, all things considered.

"Did either of you see a shot fired? Anyone with a gun?" Sergeant Blake said, but not as if he expected to get the truth.

I shook my head. I'd been running down the hill when I heard shots.

Maidjene shrugged.

"Do you know anyone here who might have a gun'?" Sergeant Blake went on. They must give out these lists of numbered ques-tions in Famous Law Enforcement Officers Training School.

Maidjene and I got the same idea at the same moment, and stared at each other with identically transparent looks of horror.

"Larry," Maidjene said in a strangled voice. "Larry's got guns. Lots of them. He always takes them with him."

Not that I suspected Larry. The question was, had someone borrowed one?

The four of us went down to Larry's trailer. Along the way Maid-jene filled them in: soon-to-be-ex-husband, survivalist, possessor of various firearms, and free-range pain in the ass. Neither of us had seen him up at the Circle, but that wasn't much in the line of an alibi.

I didn't think any more of it than that it was another episode in that embarrassing real-world sitcom: "The New Adventures of Larry," but as we got closer, it occurred to me that Fayrene and Sergeant Blake didn't share my insouciance about the upcoming interview. They stopped Maidjene and me at the edge of the park-ing lot and told us to stay here.

"Which one is it?" Sergeant Blake asked.

Maidjene pointed. There was that silent conference between the deputies again, then they both started forward. Their feet made almost no noise on the gravel. I could see that Sergeant Blake had his gun out.

"Mr. Wagner? This is Sergeant Blake of the Gotham County Sheriff's Department. Could you come out here? We'd like to talk to you," Sergeant John Blake said.

He and Fayrene were standing on each side of the door, their backs pressed against the side of the Winnebago, and it suddenly occurred to me that they were—not expecting, precisely, but *planning* against the possibility that Larry would choose to come out armed and shooting.

"Who's there?" I could hear Larry's voice faintly even from where I stood.

"This is Sergeant Blake from the Sheriff's Department, Mr. Wagner. Could you step outside for a moment, please?"

"Philly?" The door swung open, and there Larry stood in all his sweatshirted and fatigue-painted glory. He came down the steps looking for Maidjene, and only then saw the deputies.

"What's going on?" Larry bleated.

"Could you keep your hands away from your sides, Mr. Wagner?" Fayrene asked, with steel courtesy.

There was enough light coming from the open doorway for me to see his face go slack when he realized that, beyond all expectations and nightmares, this was *real*.

Beside me, I heard Maidjene sob as between them Blake and Fayrene had Larry turned and spread and patted down before he could figure out quite what to say.

He was lucky he wasn't armed. But he wasn't, and when they found that out the tension eased. Nobody seemed to be going to shoot anyone today, so I headed over. Maidjene followed.

I didn't think Larry was the shooter—not really—but like Maidjene said, I knew he always traveled with a number of handguns. Had he given one—intentionally or un- —to whoever'd popped Reece Wheeler?

"Where've you been for the last half hour, Mr. Wagner?"

"Was anybody with you?"

"Did anybody see you come back here?"

"Who'd you talk to today?"

"Can I take a look inside your RV, Mr. Wagner?"

Larry's head ping-ponged back and forth as the questions came at him. He fumbled through some answers, but as I watched, I realized that Blake and Fayrene didn't care as much about the answers as they did about the reaction to the questions.

"What's this about?" Larry asked, when they finally let him. "Philly? You all right?"

"A man's been shot, Mr. Wagner," Sergeant Blake said, "and we were hoping you could help us figure out who did it."

Larry stared helplessly at Maidjene. I watched her, seeing her soften, because even if the breech between them was permanent, it wasn't solid yet.

"He wasn't up there at the Circle," Maidjene said softly. "I would have seen him. He wasn't there."

"Do you have a gun, Mr. Wagner?" Sergeant Blake asked.

Larry did. Larry, in fact, had several. The deputies didn't like that much, and when he brought them out they confiscated all of them, tipping them into evidence bags. Blake and Fayrene'd seemed to have had the same idea I had, and the guns were going down to the main office for testing.

And so was Larry, apparently.

"Just a formality, Mr. Wagner. You're going to need to make a statement."

Sergeant Blake went back inside with him while Larry got his jacket and wallet. While he was in there, the ambulance containing Reece Wheeler came slowly down the hill and headed off for the local hospital, lights silently flashing.

Maidjene was crying quietly.

"Mrs. Wagner," Fayrene said gently, "why don't you go back to the barn and rest? There isn't anything you can do here."

"Come on, Maidjene," I said, and took her arm.

Despite the Gotham County Sheriff's Department's best efforts at crowd control, people were spread out all over the Paradise Lake Campground. It was a lot harder now than it had been this morning to find a quiet place to take statements, and it would have been impossible if almost everyone here hadn't already been through it once.

The patrol car with Arnold the Shotgun Man came gliding, shark-smooth, down the road while Maidjene and I were walking up. A few paces further on we ran into Bailey, and I handed Maidjene over to him.

"They're taking Larry down to the station to talk to him," I told Bailey.

"Hope they fry the ratfucker," Bailey said, and his voice was so amiable it took me a moment to realize what he'd said. "C'mon, Maidjene."

I went back toward the parking lot.

Fayrene's car, driven by somebody in uniform, passed me on the way, and when I got back down to the lot, Sergeant Blake and Larry were just getting into it.

"You just bring that back here in one piece, you hear me, John-Boy?" Fayrene said. Blake waved, and backed it around.

I closed the distance between me and Fayrene.

"I do hate amateurs with guns," she said to me.

"So do I," I said feelingly. There was a pause while I remembered something else I had to do. "About those registration forms?" I said. I tried not to look toward the Snake's van and twitched instead, body language I somehow suspected Fayrene would have no trouble reading.

"A little bird told me that we were going to have some trouble getting those after this evening. I truly do hate to lay paper on Mrs. Wagner, but I'm not sure she's giving us a lot of choice."

I hesitated. Fayrene had obviously heard that the forms had been burned; considering that all of Summerisle knew, a leak wasn't too surprising. But of all the things Maidjene needed in her life, a subpoena wasn't one of them.

"If you could wait until Monday, probably we could work something out," I said reluctantly. Reluctantly, because I knew that tomorrow I was going to go and tell Maidjene what I'd done and try to convince her to hand the documents over freely. And if I couldn't manage that, I'd hand them over myself, but I wouldn't lie to Maidjene.

"Could we." Fayrene's voice was flat. "You sleeping down here?" she added.

"Maybe," I said. "I haven't made up my mind yet." And she hadn't told me whether I'd won my reprieve.

"What about your fella?"

It's disorienting to be on close terms with the police; they're always coming up with conversational icebreakers based on confidences you don't remember telling them.

"You mean Julian?" It's best to get these things clear. "He wanted some privacy tonight." I wondered where Julian was right now, not that I suspected him of shooting anybody.

"Hm-m." Fayrene was noncommittal. "If we wait until Monday, you are going to hand me those HallowFest forms." It was not a question.

"I will or Maidjene will," I said, and felt the weight of *intention* make my scalp tingle. As though, somewhere, *She* was listening and taking note of what I'd said.

"Mm-n," Fayrene said, letting me off the hook for now. "Is there anyplace a person can get a cup of coffee around here? Or do we have to go back and wake up Helen?"

Privately, I doubted if Helen Cooper ever slept.

"I think there's a pot on up at the barn. She told me Reverend Harm had been up here that Friday?" I asked. There was nothing wrong with checking.

"Mm-n. The way Bat figures it, Harm came back later looking for trouble. And found some. Now, about that coffee?"

"Come on."

We headed back for the barn at an ambling pace. Fayrene was content to be silent, and I had meditations of my own. The sheriff's deputies hadn't found the gun used in tonight's shooting, and conventional wisdom said that if they hadn't found it yet, the odds were good they wouldn't find it.

But what about the knife?

They hadn't found that either, and like Fayrene said, the thing that had made that hole in Reverend Harm wasn't any Buck knife. So where was it? At the bottom of Paradise Lake with the gun?

Maybe, but I doubted it. A gun is a gun is a gun, interchangeable and anonymous. Even if they found it, if they didn't have the good luck to have the bullet out of Reece Wheeler for a ballistics match, they wouldn't be able to weave a chain of evidence. But the knife, by its particular uniqueness, would retain a stronger connection to its wielder. Latent prints, occult (which is to say, *hidden*) blood, even someone, somewhere who'd remember the murderer buying it or showing it off. The wise murderer wouldn't do something as rash as simply throw it away. It could all too easily be found.

And that was only assuming this was murder most secular. Once you assumed that the murder had taken place in a ritual context, it was even more unlikely that the murderer would get rid of the knife. In most schools of magic-with-a-K, the knife— *athame* to us Witches—is the symbol of the will, and in magic, the symbol not only represents the thing itself, the symbol *is* the thing.

No magician would throw away his will.

So where was it?

And would I recognize it if I saw it?

Mirabile dictu, there was an actual percolator set up inside the barn. It was on a card table, and there were three boxes of Dunkin' Donuts next to it. Ragnar was standing beside the table, doughnut in one hand, the other supporting Iduna, who was slung over

one shoulder like a bag of laundry, fast asleep. He was talking to
a uniformed deputy, and both sets of body language told me they
were meeting as equals. Hell, for all I knew Ragnar might *be* a LEO,
when he wasn't being here.

It's a strange dichotomy that our Community has. Thirty years
ago the counterculture was politically homogenous: liberal and
left-leaning, white and upper middle class. These days there are
a thousand countering cultures, and my particular slice of it—
NeoPaganism—contains left- and right-wingers in about equal
numbers. It would be possible, if you looked long enough, to find
among us representatives from both sides of the barricades at Kent
State and Chicago.

"Well, I better go put Punkin to bed. You let me know if there's
anything I can do for you, Lieutenant Dix," Ragnar said, wandering off.

Fayrene drew herself a cup of coffee. So did I. I usually take it
light and sweet, but tonight drinking it black seemed more appropriate.

While we were standing there, Detective Wayne came in
through the front. He looked like he'd been seriously interrupted
from something that he liked doing better than this, and zeroed
in on the coffee by what seemed to be some kind of preconscious
radar. He didn't speak until he had a cup in his hand.

"Whadda we got?"

I listened while Fayrene and Lieutenant Dix gave it to him all
over again. By now I'd heard the evening's events described over
and over to the point that their real-life randomness was starting
to take on symmetry and meaning.

"Nothing to do with your case, Bat," Fayrene said. "They weren't
even members of Harm's congregation."

"Neither was whoever shot Reece," Mad Anthony Wayne said,
"but I'd sure like to have a chat with him."

"Shooters don't usually change their luck that way," Fayrene
mused. It took me a moment to realize it was shorthand for: *"He
probably isn't the same person who stabbed Harm, because . . ."*
While I was piecing that together, she continued: "John-Boy's
down at the shop taking a statement from a Lawrence Bernard
Wagner, the soon-to-be-ex of the woman running this thing. Mr.
Wagner came up here with a number of personal firearms and no
permits."

"Did he?" Wayne said with interest.

I restrained an impulse to defend Larry. He hadn't stabbed Harm (probably), or shot Reece, and the Sheriff's Office knew it.

Probably.

"I tell you," Wayne said to nobody in particular, "I ought to shut this place down, and if one more thing happens, I will, I swear to God. Sometime tomorrow I'm going to try to get some people out here to drag the lake, and I don't want to have to do it while the Dance of the Sugarplum Fairy's going on."

I thought of mentioning that Paradise Lake'd be deserted inside of forty-eight hours anyway, but decided he didn't want to hear it. As for Sugarplum Fairies, the Transgender Ball is held at Paresis Hall in NYC, not here. I didn't mention that either.

Coffee in hand, Wayne wandered off to find someone else to talk to, and Dix went with him.

I looked at Fayrene.

"He's just cranky 'cause he doesn't think we're going to get this one. I think he's right," Fayrene said. "It's looking like anybody could've helped himself to one of Mr. Wagner's guns," she added in disgust, which was about as close as she was going to come to leveling with me.

In fiction we'd unbosom ourselves to each other and become fast allies with a *simpatica* that transcended job barriers. I would become her trusted eyes and ears in the NeoPagan Community, and she'd become my judiciary *imprimatur,* to be wielded at will once I'd scoped out the villain. But this was reality, and things didn't work that way—at least I was pretty sure they didn't. There was no reason for Fayrene to suddenly treat me as her equal. For all she could know, *I'd* popped Jackson Harm.

"So what do you think?" Fayrene said to me.

I shrugged. "I think it would help to know *why* Jackson Harm was killed." Never mind that if you know *how* you know *who,* to quote Lord Peter; if I knew *why* I'd be able to make a better guess at the killer.

Take a stab at it, so to speak.

Fayrene blew out a long sigh. "It would that, not that we're likely to ever know. We won't have the complete autopsy report until next week, but the M.E. can tell now there wasn't any unusual trauma. Our boy just lay down and took it like a man."

"Did he come here to meet somebody?" I asked, because whether she'd tell me or not, I was curious.

"When you find out, you let us know. You take care of yourself now, Bast."

I was dismissed.

The rest of the evening, like so much of life, was anticlimax. The deputies pulled out in increments, still without finding—so gossip ran—either the shootist or the shooting iron. A couple of people got to join Larry down at the station to make extended statements. I wondered if Bat Wayne would get his wish and be able to drag the lake tomorrow, and if so, what he'd find.

Some determined people went back up to the bonfire to have a Bardic Circle in spite of everything, but I wasn't one of them. I'd gone to the interrupted ritual for a healing and relinking that'd gotten overtaken by events, and I felt peculiarly unconnected from the warp of myth and deity in which I usually spend my life. There wasn't, as the headshrinkers say, *closure.* The evening felt unfinished, though considering how it had started, maybe that was a blessing.

And Jackson Harm was still dead.

The whole campground was alive with the separate lights of various tents—all battery operated, because of the fire regs. The fire at the Bardic Circle was plainly visible from lakeside. I prowled around for a while and finally found Lark.

He was sitting on the edge of the party that had gathered around Ironshadow's tent with a guitar on his knees and a bottle by his ankle and for just a heartbeat it was forever ago and none of us would ever grow old.

"Yo, Bast," he said, looking up. I knelt down beside him.

Across the party, I could see Ironshadow holding court under the tent awning, the usual ladies-in-waiting around him in long skirts or embroidered jeans. I wondered if I could brace him for backup when I faced Maidjene. Doing that was something I wasn't looking forward to, but the alternative was forfeiting my own good opinion of myself. And I was willing to go through a lot to avoid that.

"You feeling better?" Lark asked tentatively.

"Oh, sure, getting rousted by weasels with weapons and then doing the masochism tango with our friends the police sets me up real good," I shot back without thinking.

"Hey," Lark said, with only a little edge to it, "I thought you *liked* the police."

I looked up at him. The unwavering lantern light left his face half in shadow, the brights and darks making it hard to read.

I thought about it. "Not really. I like justice."

"Justice." Now Lark sounded definitely bitter. He handed the guitar off to someone else, who took it willingly and began to re-tune it. He picked up the bottle and stood up. "Go for a walk?" he asked. I walked with Lark away from the lantern light, out between the oases of parties.

"You still living in that place in Brooklyn?" he asked.

I remembered the place in Brooklyn, though it's been about ten years. It'd overlooked Fort Hamilton Park and there'd been six of us living there, some of us running away, some of us running to. More than the apartment, I remembered the bed, which had been lumpy and untrustworthy and had tended to collapse at inopportune moments. I remembered Lark.

"No; I got Van's old place when he moved back to Ohio." Common friends, common history. I slid my arm around his waist. Lark had muscles I didn't remember from the last time I'd seen him. I wondered what changes the years had wrought in Lark's body. I wondered if I was going to be self-destructive enough to try and find out.

"What? That coffin down in Alphabet City?"

This was unfair. My apartment is bigger than a coffin, though not by much, and it's several blocks north of Alphabet City. At least five.

"Yeah." And would Lark have looked so attractive if there hadn't been Julian? Was Lark my anodyne to that sweet nepenthe? And who would be my antidote to Lark when that time came?

"Damn if it's big enough for two. Too bad; I'm kind of looking for a place to crash for a while," Lark said regretfully. "You know of anybody with crash space?"

Once I'd been younger, with infinite optimism and resource. In those days I would have invited Lark to move in with me anyway, certain that rising above the cramped inconvenience would be an adventure. I am older now and no longer certain there is that much generosity of spirit anywhere in the world.

"Maybe Belle," I said, thinking it over. Belle has four bedrooms and a landlord she likes to annoy with the specter of illegal sub-lets. "I can ask her."

"But you're not in Changing anymore," Lark said, as if I needed reminding. "That going to make a difference?" I thought again about what Glitter had said; that Belle was going to give up the coven, and that she might let me use her space to run one of my own. If I started one, something that looked more likely by the moment.

"It was an amicable separation," I said dryly. "And you can ask her yourself if you'd rather."

"Not me," Lark said hastily. "You do it, okay?"

"Yeah, sure," I said. It wouldn't make any difference, and I thought Belle would probably do it. I wondered just how Lark was planning to keep himself in cigarettes and gasoline while he was here; when I'd known him last he'd been working in a bookstore, but that had been in the eighties and we'd all been pretending we didn't want to be yuppies.

Of course, *I* was still doing what *I'd* been doing in the eighties.

Behind us, the guitarist swung into the opening chords of Gwyddion's "We Won't Wait Any Longer," that confrontational marching song of the (Not Very) Old Religion.

"So, what do you think's going to happen to us?" Lark said. It took me a moment to realize that Lark was using "us" in the greater cosmic sense—i.e., the attendees of HallowFest.

"Nothing much," I said. "They'd like to find the gun that townie got shot with." *And I'd like to find the knife Jackson Harm got stabbed with, come to that.* "But they don't have much in the way of suspects."

Lark sneered. "You don't have to be a weatherman to know which way the wind blows," he misquoted. "They'd rather it was one of us. They'll look till they find out it is."

City people are sometimes surprised at how fast the United States turns redneck, once you're outside of the major population centers. And anyone with half a brain can see that the winds of change are blowing very cold on the fringes of society these days. While it hasn't yet gotten to the point that difference itself is a criminal act, I wondered how many things were being assumed about us by the Gotham County natives on the basis of the knives we carried and the clothes we wore. Which prejudgment is not in and of itself an uncommon act, but usually the stakes aren't as high as murder.

Lark put his arm across my shoulders and offered me the bottle. I stopped and tilted it back—Ironshadow mead and worth the trip all by itself. I drank and passed it back, and Lark drank. We walked on. His arm was still around me.

"So who's that guy you came up here with?"

"Julian?"

Was Lark jealous? Flattering if true, but I was smart enough to know that it probably wasn't Lark I wanted, really, so much as the gilded past we'd shared.

And what about Julian? Gratifying to think of having the need to choose between them, if unlikely.

"He runs the Snake—the Serpent's Truth; that big occult book-store down in—"

"I've heard of it," Lark said. "Didn't it get bombed last year?"

"Something like that," I said. "It happens a lot." Which is true, actually.

"And nobody cares—because it's us. If it was one of us got popped up here, do you think the cops'd be running around like headless chickens trying to pin it on somebody?"

"Now that you mention it, yes. That's what they do. Pin things on people. Usually on the ones who did them."

We stopped again. Lark drank. He passed the bottle over to me conscientiously, but we were on the edge of an argument all the same.

"Come on," I said. "Let's go back."

He grunted noncommittally but turned around. His fingers dug into my shoulder, even through my parka and sweater, as if he'd forgotten I was there.

"How long are you going to stick up for them?" Lark demanded, and although it's a clichéd question, it sounded like he really wanted to know.

"Some things are right, Lark, and some aren't . . ." I waffled.

"And so it doesn't matter who you've got on the same side as you, so long as they're right?"

It sounded logical, but not the way he put it. "No. I mean, yes." He always could confuse me. "You know that—"

"You don't know what you're talking about," Lark said flatly. Irrationally, that irritated me more than any other sort of insult might have. I pulled away from him. He let me go.

"See you later," I said, walking away fast before either of us could say anything else.

I stopped at some other parties, ingested an alarming array of mixed drinks, and tried not to brood too much. Nobody mentioned Harm's murder; in fact, even tonight's shooting incident wasn't the main topic of conversation. In fact, it was a Saturday night much like other Saturday nights at other HallowFests. I was the thing that had changed. I was seeing these people — my kin, my clan — the way an outsider would; and the more I realized that the problem came from within me, the more irritated I was with them. Over and over I found myself judging my fellow festival attendees as if I were seeing them for the first time. It wasn't a comfortable mindset.

Eventually I wound up back by Ironshadow's tent. Lark had moved on, so I stuck there for a while. Ironshadow gave me my own bottle of home brew, and I took it down a couple of inches chasing homemade beer and damiana wine and even some authentic absinthe, brewed from a recipe that *Scientific American* published (in its innocence) a few years back.

The company was good and the mead was better and the guitar was playing Richard Thompson and Mike Longcor and the works of other cute guys with beards. But my thoughts weren't pleasant company — for me or anyone else around Ironshadow's tent — so after a while I left there, too.

On my way down to my cold and lonely pallet in the back of Julian's van I noticed that every light in the barn was on, even the ones upstairs, where nobody was supposed to be right now. Maybe I wasn't the only one who felt the uneasiness in the air, as though the dead who were supposed to ride three weeks from now had come through the Gate Between the Worlds early and stalked among us now without our knowledge.

The parking area seemed cold and deserted after the Lake Meadow, but I was still full of Ironshadow mead, and between the packing quilts and my sleeping bag and the fact that the human body, left to itself, can radiate quite enough heat to warm even as uninsulated a space as the inside of the van, I certainly wouldn't freeze. I pulled the doors shut behind me and locked them. There was no real point to getting undressed; I pulled off my boots but left my parka on this time. After all, my friend Lace sleeps in her leather jacket even at home, so she tells me; I didn't feel too far outside the normative curve.

And, I thought with woozy romanticism, if Julian wanted privacy for ritual, a certain fellow-feeling and noblesse oblige required I give it to him. Too many of us have too little safe space in our lives for ritual, and I could not manage to begrudge it to anyone, even if it did leave me sleeping in the parking lot.

I did not worry about a lot of things that I ought, in retrospect, have worried about, from improbabilities such as being murdered in the van to the likelihood of more nightmares. I didn't worry about what Lark was thinking of me and I didn't even worry about my relationship with Julian, or about what ritual he was doing—and why.

I went to sleep.

7

I knew exactly what time it was because my wristwatch glows in the dark. What I didn't know was why I was awake, soberly and completely, out of a dreamless, alcohol-assisted slumber.

A gunshot?

It was possible that something like that could have awakened me without my remembering hearing it. I did not want to think of what, other than a loud noise, could have done it; psychic summonses and other staples of occult literature, while part of my worldview, tended to lead to rendezvous even less pleasant than those heralded by gunfire.

What was a fact was that I wasn't going back to sleep. So I could either sit here in the dark for three hours until sunrise, read while running down the van's already weak battery, or find some other way of amusing myself.

I found the flashlight and turned it on. It failed after I'd found my boots but before I got them on. I groped my way out of the back of the van by touch. It was colder outside than in; no surprise.

Once on my feet and reconciled to insomnia, I tried to look on the bright side of things. It was my favorite time of night, and a time that I, being a freelancer able to set my own hours, see more often than not, when that part of night that begins with sunset has run its course and the part that's a dry run for dawn hasn't started. The bowl of night; the unchanging moment in a world of change. It was calm (wind is a part of dawn) and dark, and very nearly quiet.

And now at last I felt what I'd searched for in vain earlier this evening. The breath of the Goddess on the back of my neck; the immanence of deity. It was a good feeling—the security that children leave behind in childhood, that adults have left on the barricades of the Industrial Revolution; an incontrovertible sense of belonging to a world that is complete and whole. It was a gift, and such gifts demand reciprocation. What gift could I make in return?

I knew the answer to that, but the question really was, what gift was I *willing* to make?

I started up the path to the barn, but I didn't end up going to the barn. It was dark, full of sleeping Pagans, and it wasn't my destination anyway. Julian's cabin was dark, too—Registration, at the other end of the row, was the lone light, and I didn't have the feeling there was anyone awake there, either.

I remembered other HallowFests, where three A.M. would not have meant silence and darkness, where the Bardic Circle had lasted until dawn and we'd cooked breakfast over the embers of the fire. But that was long ago and in a far decade, and those Pagans had changed—gone on to other paths, or just grown up.

It struck me with a sudden unwelcome force that of my circle of NeoPagan friends and Aquarian acquaintance from the early eighties, I was almost the only one left. Van was dead, Thomas had left us for the Christians, Belle was about to retire, others had moved on, grown up, gotten out. *"And I alone am escaped to tell thee . . ."* I felt the same sort of spooky embarrassment that you feel when you've just realized you've stayed too long at the party. It was time for me to move on, too—talk to Belle, talk to Lark, take the next step of becoming teacher and leader.

But if I did that, someday that would end, too. That was the underlying truth of what I was resisting; change is a movement forward in time, and everyone knows that such movement someday ends.

Or, as in the Reverend Harm's case, is ended prematurely.

I circled around the cabins, and then around the lake. I had no particular destination in mind; eventually I might go up to the bonfire. There'd be people there; someone always kept firewatch until the embers were cold. But I wasn't really looking for people.

I thought. Until I heard the voices.

I was across the near side of the meadow that surrounds the lake, off into an area that's slowly being taken over by second-growth timber. People camp there some years, but the prime camping area is around the lake, and this year everyone had been accommodated there.

"Life is pain."

I could make out what they were saying about the same time I saw the light—closer than was really prudent, but rocks and straggling bushes had concealed the area. Which was one of the reasons they'd chosen it, of course.

"Pain is truth."

It was a tiny fire; mostly charcoal on a bed of sand in something that looked like an institutional-size wok. Something that would leave no trace in the morning's light. There were candles in hurricane lamps at three points, putting the wok-fire in the center of a triangle.

"Truth is life."

Xharina was standing in the ritual space, across from one of her coveners, wearing a black corset that offered up her bare breasts like cupcakes, and a long skirt that looked like it was made of animal tails. Her tattoos gave her arms a mottled motile surface as though they were wreathed in snakes. She was holding a knife in her hand.

It wasn't one of Ironshadow's polite carriage-trade *athames* with the maidenly double-sided six-inch blade. Xharina was holding a point-heavy single-edge Bowie knife with an eleven-inch blade. It flashed like a mirror in the firelight, and leather tails were braided over the hilt, ending in a tassel as long as hilt and blade together. She held the flat of the blade to the flames for a moment.

One of her coveners—Arioch, I think, though I wasn't sure— was standing opposite her. He was bare to the waist, wearing jeans that were black or leather or both.

Xharina cut him.

She started just above the nipple and cut careful diagonal marks into his pectoral muscle—they'd look like the marks of the Sioux Sun Dance when they healed. She pulled the blade along slowly, painstakingly, like a child trying her best to color inside the lines, and I could hear Arioch first catch his breath, then breathe slowly and raggedly, as if what he was feeling were not pain. She cut six lines, evenly spaced, working from bottom to top so that the surface she was working on was always dry.

"I am the shadow where three roads meet; I am the durable fire.

I am the night-howling dog; the mortal wound of love; the madness of fear; and the exercise of power. I am mastery and desire, and all roads lead to me. I am the sword in the hand; I am the scars on the soul. I am the whip that drives you; I am the flesh beneath the lash. I am the shadow where three roads meet—"

Against the sound of Xharina's voice the others murmured an antiphon, too low for me to hear. Arioch's head was thrown back, in a gesture I'd have difficulty not recognizing as ecstasy, but other than that he had not moved.

I should not be here. I'd stumbled into a mystery of which I was not initiate; the worship of a more primordial Mother than the aspect my tradition's rituals courted. The power raised here was rawly seductive; gooseflesh hackled on my skin and I felt as if someone had opened the door of a blast furnace in my face.

Xharina dabbled her fingers in the blood and wrote the sign of the horns on Arioch's forehead with it. He knelt, and she stepped around the fire to approach him. I used the cover of their movement to get away, hoping they hadn't seen me.

I was more intent on distance than destination; the next thing I knew I was down by Mrs. Cooper's house, along the road that led to the outside world. My heart was pounding as if I'd run to get here; I was flushed and shaking, and once again, like an unwanted guest, I could feel the projected outrage of the outsider inside my skin.

But what Xharina and her people were doing was not wrong by any standard—Goddess knew it was consensual. I'd seen Arioch with Xharina before; nothing in the way he acted indicated that he was someone trapped in a ritual relationship that had gone wrong in any of the many ways those intimate relationships can. Arioch had been happy where he was yesterday, and would still be happy tomorrow morning.

I believed it; I had felt no threat when I'd accidentally stumbled into their ritual. But the outsider in my skin wasn't convinced. People don't cut people, people don't hit people because they love them.

Yes they do, I told the inside Outsider. Yes, there was blood, and yes, Xharina had cut him—but it had been done with love, and was not, when all was said and done, so much more abhorrent than the accepted practices of more established faiths. Xharina's coven's was a shamanic tradition—nothing more.

But it was so far from the self-perceived norm of NeoPaganism that I began to understand why Xharina's people were so skittish about networking with the rest of us. The greatest taboo in the Gardnerian-derived traditions is to allow blood to touch the ritual blade—Craft tradition holds that such a blade must be destroyed at once, and a new one consecrated. But Xharina's coveners must blood their blades regularly, if what I'd inadvertently witnessed tonight was any indication.

All unwelcome the malicious monkey part of my mind demanded attention, assuring me that those who were willing to cut shallowly could cut deeply as well—and that Reverend Harm had died of a knife wound.

They had no motive! I told myself sharply, as irritated as if some stranger had made the suggestion. And it was true—Hoodoo Lunchbox had never been to Paradise Lake before; this was their first HallowFest. They could certainly not have had any previous exposure to Reverend Harm.

But if I were going to pardon shamanism, my mind insisted, surely I should admit that human sacrifice was a part of magic as well?

Fortunately this was too ridiculous for even me to take seriously; it broke the spell of my overheated internal monologue. It was a long way from a little shamanic bloodletting to murder; you might as rationally accuse a cigarette smoker of being a pyromaniac. Yet the fact remained that Harm had been ritually murdered. Or, I thought again, had been made to *seem* to be ritually murdered, because once I had ruled out magic and religion I could imagine no nonsecular motive strong enough to actually motivate the deed.

I knew where I wanted to go, now.

It was hard to reach the pine forest without crossing the Upper Meadow where the Bardic Circle was, but I managed it by dint of a long detour and a scramble up the steep slope I'd avoided yesterday. If there was a deputy posted up here I didn't see him, but there was no reason for him to be standing right over the murder site, after all.

We were almost out of the bowl of night, now; in less than an hour there would be hints of dawn in the sky.

I'd dreamed this, I realized suddenly. I was standing in the forest, just where I had been when I'd seen Miriam. Ahead of me— toward the Circle—I could see the "Police Line—Do Not Cross" tape glowing brightly yellow in the reflected light of the fire in the meadow below. The firelight edged the downward slope sharply, giving me the illusion of enough light to see by.

Here was the last place Jackson Harm had come to alive. He'd met his killer here, and died.

It took a bit of casting about to find the exact spot where the body had been. The police don't outline victims' bodies in white paint the way you see in the *Naked Gun* movies. But I'd been here three times, under circumstances which enforce the vividness—if not the accuracy—of memory, and I found the likely spot eventually. There was a short stake with a bit of red ribbon tied to it stuck down into the forest mulch; I didn't remember seeing it before, but probably the Sheriff's Department had left it to mark the site.

I knelt down, the way I had . . . was it only this morning? I tried to still myself and open myself, and do what good divination does, allowing myself to see what there was here to see. I touched my fingers to the ground where Harm had been. *Tell me who killed you. Tell me why.*

I felt a chill reasonless excitement; the adrenaline rush that comes before the conscious mind understands the reason for it.

There was a sound.

It brought me out of half-trance like a slap in the face; it was a real-world sound; the sound of a broken twig and someone trying to shuffle quietly through the dark. I jerked to my feet, and all I could think of was that I was guilty of trespassing and about to be caught.

But I wasn't the only one.

"Uh . . . hi," Wyler Pascoe said.

I could just make him out in the darkness; a teenaged blob of light and dark, identifiable mostly by the T-shirt I'd seen him wearing yesterday at the diner. Wyler Pascoe. Sergeant Fayrene Pascoe's underage son.

"What are you doing here?" I said. It wasn't particularly gracious as opening gambits go, but he'd scared me. And now that I'd had time to think about the consequences of his being here, I wasn't any less worried.

He made an inarticulate gesture—at least it might have been inarticulate and was certainly a gesture. I couldn't see him very well. The fire was not as bright as it had been at its height, and was at the bottom of the hill besides; most of what I could make

out of Wyler was his pale skin and pale hair and the glinting silver pentagram he wore around his neck. I couldn't remember
whether it'd been there in the diner or not.

We didn't need this. I didn't need this. *HallowFest* didn't need
this.

"Uh . . ." Possibly Wyler wasn't sure himself. "Hey, you're Bast,
right?"

"Right." I thought about heavy-metal gangstas and rock music
Satanists and that Wyler seemed to be out pretty late for a boy
whose mother, presumably, knew the worst that Gotham County
had to offer. I thought about the fact that Wyler probably knew
Jackson Harm by sight and could easily have gotten close to him,
and that murderers get younger every day, and that here he was,
now, at the scene of the crime—or back at it.

Of course, so was I.

"Is there something we can do for you here, Wyler?" I said, in
my best customer service tones.

He looked from me to the fire, much as if he was missing an
appointment he longed to keep.

"I came to be a Witch!" he blurted out.

I shook my head; not at him. At the situation, if at anything,
and the fact that life goes on.

"No!" Wyler protested. "I really did. I just wanted— I just
thought that . . ." He stopped.

"Everybody's asleep," I said pointlessly.

"No they aren't. Not down at the bonfire. Mom was saying that
there'd be somebody up by that all night, and I just thought . . ."
He shrugged again.

"There'd be somebody you could talk to?" I suggested.

I walked back toward the edge of the forest, where the light was
better. Wyler followed.

"Yeah," he breathed. "Mom doesn't understand, you know?
She says it's just a passing phase, and if it isn't, I can look into it
when I'm older. But I'm old *now*," Wyler added, with the exasper-
ation of the sixteen-year-old self-perceived adult. "And I want to
be a Witch. I've always wanted to be a Witch."

"What do you think a Witch is?" I asked him gently, part of me
remembering that this was one of the first questions Belle had
asked me nearly fifteen years ago.

Wyler stared at me; a good kid, I theorized from limited experience, trying hard to bring an honest answer out of the inarticu-
lateness of teenagerhood.

"Is there somebody up there?" It was a shout from below, nervous and belligerent; one of the people on firewatch. I recollected sharply that the last people heading toward the fire from this direction had been armed, and there was still a gun unaccounted for among my fellow happy campers.

"It's me," I called down. "It's Bast." Hoping it was somebody I knew.

"Oh, hi, Bast." A new voice: Bailey of Summerisle, thank the Goddess; someone who knew me. "We heard voices?" he went on.

"I'm up here with a friend of mine," I said mendaciously. I walked forward and looked down the slope. Bailey and a couple of other members of Summerisle were standing around the fire, looking up toward me.

"You're not really supposed to be on that side of the tape," Bailey said apologetically.

"Yeah," I said. "We're coming down. C'mon, Wyler."

No one else at the Festival knew that Wyler was Fayrene's son, and probably neither Bailey nor I knew everyone here this weekend on sight. Wyler could easily be taken for one of the campers; there wouldn't be any immediate awkward questions.

I was prepared to drag Wyler along with me by force, but apparently he'd already imprinted on me and followed, agreeable as a duckling, as I led him across the Upland Meadow and through the sleeping campground toward the parking lot.

Along the way I learned that he'd ridden over here on his bike, which he'd left down on Route 6; that he'd always wanted to be a Witch but hadn't known that was what it was called; that he'd attended Reverend Harm's Bible Summer Camp once when he was younger; and that he'd been reading as much as he could find on the subject of Wicca but that the Tamerlane Association Library wasn't much use.

"And it's what I want! I want to worship the Goddess—I *belong* to the Goddess," Wyler said.

We'd reached the parking lot by this time and didn't have to talk in whispers. Wyler glanced skyward, but at this point in the night and her cycle, Lady Moon had set long ago.

The most I'd been planning to do was drive him home and forgo the lecture on prudence he probably deserved and wouldn't listen to. It was that gesture, I think, that convinced me to help him get what he wanted, even knowing full well his mother the deputy sheriff wouldn't be best pleased.

"Okay, look," I said. I stopped and turned to face him. "Here's the deal. You go home and don't come back."

"But—" Wyler said, drawing breath to argue.

"While the Festival is on," I said over his protest. "You do that, and I will pick out a basic Wiccan reading list for you to start on—some of the same books I started with. You come here Monday, pick up the books, and pay for them—before noon, which is when the Festival will be over and we'll be gone. Everything else you've got to square with your mom. She's got my home address, if she wants you to be in touch with me."

I watched him argue with himself over whether he could get a better deal elsewhere; whether I was being straight with him or just trying to blow him off. Kids today are so suspicious.

"I want to join a coven," Wyler said in a small strangled voice.

"I know," I said, as gently as I could. Fayrene was going to kill me, no doubt about it. "But it'll be two years before you're eighteen and can even join an Outer Court"—the pre-Initiation study and training group that most traditions use—"and you'd still have to read the books"—though every tradition's reading list is slightly different. "This way—if you want—you can practice as a solitary."

There are some people—not many, as the position is even more Old Guard than some of the ones I hold—who'd say that what I was doing now was proselytizing, something strictly forbidden to the Hidden Children of the Goddess. There were others who'd say that by selling Wyler the books I was selling training, something as disgraceful as being a fee-charging literary agent.

But the look on Wyler's face when I held out even that prosaic hope was enough to show me that I was far too late to proselytize; he already belonged to Our Lady and he'd train himself, just as we all do. There's no central regulating body that can compel you to magical discipline; you either have it and stay or you burn out and leave.

I tell myself.

"I can be a Witch?" Wyler said.

"You're a Pagan right now if you say you are," I pointed out. "If you want to be a Witch you need coven training and initiation, but you can be a Goddess-worshipper without that. I'll give you a catalog, too—you can order more books mail order." And maybe Belle had brought some copies of Changing's introductory reading list up with her that I could swipe to tell him which ones those ought to be.

Wyler hesitated, plainly afraid he was being sold a bill of goods.

"Are they very expensive—the books?" he finally said. "I don't have very much money."

"What can you afford?" I said, trying to remember if Julian had brought any copies of *What Witches Do* by Stewart Farrar up to the festival with him. When I'd come in to the Craft, it had been one of the handful of accurate books available, and I still liked it for unsensationalized descriptions of Wiccan practice and the fact that it didn't promise its readers a lot of cheap New Age miracles.

Wyler hesitated again.

"Look," I said. "I'll put together the books I think you should have in the order you ought to buy them. You come on Monday and buy whatever you want."

Wyler relaxed—Goddess knew what kind of Florida beachfront scam he'd been expecting me to field him.

"And can I buy an *athame,* too?" he said. He pronounced it "ar-thaim," which gave me some idea of the kind of books he'd been reading so far.

"Start with the books," I said. "You can save up for an Iron-shadow blade later." I would have been willing to *give* him a blade—a gift to ghosts of my own—but I couldn't afford to buy one of Ironshadow's and I didn't think the Snake's HallowFest inventory included any. Even Julian knew there wasn't a lot of point to bringing knives, with Ironshadow dealing cutlery at the next table at one-third the price. "Now get in the van. I'll run you home."

And hope Fayrene hadn't noticed he was gone, or I'd have to do a lot more explaining than I wanted to just now. Or ever, if I had my choice.

We stopped back on Route 6 to pick up Wyler's bike—it was carefully chained to a road sign, which struck me as slightly ridiculous—and then I pulled a three-point turn (traffic at fourish A.M. in Gotham County is nonexistent) and headed in the direction of Tamerlane and Wyler's home address. At least if I saw him into the house I could swear to Fayrene later that I'd brought him home.

Home, for Wyler and Sergeant Fayrene Pascoe both, turned out to be a double-wide in the Hidden Valley trailer park—lower-middle-income's answer to the high cost of new housing and the higher cost of upkeep in the Northeast. The sky was perceptibly light by the time I got there, and out of the corner of my eye I could see Wyler fidgeting nervously.

"What time does your mom get up in the morning?" I asked.

"She's on nights now," Wyler said. "She gets home about six."
Which explained how he'd come to be over at Paradise Lake.

"But sometimes she gets home earlier," Wyler added mournfully.

I pulled carefully into the entrance of the park, past the bank of ganged mailboxes that looked like some bizarre form of birdhouse. The road curved around the park in a horseshoe fashion with trailers parked on both sides of it—pink and white or beige and brown, with the odd-man-out aluminum Airstream hitchtrailer. The trailers in the center backed on each other, but the ones on the outside of the U had nothing behind them but the scrub woods and ACREAGE FOR SALE signs that edged most of County 6.

I drove slowly down the serried ranks. The plots of grass beside the trailers ran heavily to yellow plastic daisy windspinners and foot-high preformed plastic picket fences. There were lawn chairs and barbecue grills and occasional forsaken children's toys. Most of the trailers' windows were still dark, but even at this hour—I checked my watch, 5:15—lights were on here and there.

At Wyler's direction I pulled into the asphalted parking spot beside a white trailer that looked more like a house than some of the others here. If Fayrene was home she was keeping quieter about it than I would in the same circumstances.

"Got your key?" I asked Wyler.

He gave me a funny look. "It isn't locked," he said, as if that were something everyone should know.

I left the van idling as Wyler slid out of the passenger seat. We got his bike out of the back; he propped it against the side of the trailer and bounced up the steps—it wasn't locked, as he'd said—and a moment later returned to wave me an "all clear."

I got back into the van and backed carefully out of the space. The secret of his midnight visit was safe with him, but that was no guarantee I wouldn't hear about it from Fayrene—one thing that experience has taught me is that most people give up their secrets far too easily. I reached Route 6 again and turned left, leaving behind me the housing made of ticky-tacky that all looked just the same.

When I was younger Life was simpler—I could have guiltlessly deplored the entire dehumanizing idea of living in a trailer park in the low-income housing enforced conformity of the blue-collar

yahoo who existed only to destroy my own infinitely more interesting slacker demographic. I could have waxed lyrical on how life
in a trailer park was a living death, creating an army of *volkskultur*-
ingesting Eloi who were a threat but not of interest, and on how
I, through sheer puissant superiority, would forever evade such a
fate.

I still thought most of those things—well, some of them, anyway—but I'd ceased to believe that living in a New York City apartment was some index of moral superiority. Maybe I was wiser now,
or maybe just tired; the main thing that struck me about Hidden
Valley trailer park was that it must be nice to live somewhere you
trusted your neighbors enough to retain the old country habit of
not locking your doors at night.

And then again, maybe they just knew that anyone could get
into one of those things with a large screwdriver and an unkind
word, so why bother?

I hate seeing both sides of every question.

Mom's Diner was on my way back to Paradise Lake. I almost
stopped for an early breakfast before it occurred to me that
Fayrene was probably in there right now, and that the last thing
I actually wanted was to have to explain to her what I was doing
out here in the real world instead of safely tucked up in my comforting fantasy.

I was no fit company for man nor beast, anyway. Or for woman
or deputy, for that matter.

The sun was well up and the day was getting started when I
slipped the Snake's van back into its parking place at Paradise
Lake. This time I had no trouble falling asleep.

8

The next time I woke up it was to the sound of slamming doors. I looked at my watch. Ten-thirty, and I had the feeling I'd been supposed to open the Snake's table about half an hour ago.

I jammed on my boots and opened the back door of the van. The day was bright; at least we'd been blessed with good weather this weekend.

Xharina was leaving.

Both back doors and the side were open on the black van with the flaming guitar painted on the side, and boxes and guitars were being loaded with a speed and skill that suggested this activity was one that Hoodoo Lunchbox performed frequently.

I didn't see Arioch anywhere. The events of the previous night came back to me suddenly, vivid with the immediacy of memory, and I found myself flushing.

Xharina turned and saw me. After that, I couldn't just walk away pretending I hadn't seen her and them without it seeming highly suspicious. Besides, it was partly at my insistence that they'd come to HallowFest at all, and I owed them common courtesy at least as much as I wanted to cover my tracks.

I went over. "You're leaving early," I said.

This morning Xharina was wearing riding breeches—the old kind that are tight to the knee and have the lagniappe of fabric at the thighs—with her paddock boots and a sleeveless black silk camp shirt. Her tats burned jelly-jar bright in the sunlight. I still wondered how Xharina, being Xharina, managed to walk in foot-gear with heels that low.

"This isn't exactly the kind of place we belong," Xharina said tactfully. "So we thought we'd cut our losses."

So to speak.

Arioch appeared, leaning out of the van to take something from one of the others. He was wearing a white T-shirt under his vest this morning, and I was almost sure I could spot the bulk of a thick gauze dressing under the tee. He saw me and grinned.

I felt myself lose it completely; a blind deafman would know that I knew what he'd been doing last night. Fortunately, Arioch wasn't paying attention.

But Xharina was.

She turned her back on the others and took a step away. I followed her.

"We were doing some ritual out in the woods last night," she said when I reached her. I found myself unable to meet her eyes, a sensation I analyzed for its strangeness even while it unnerved me. I took a deep breath and held it, forcing my diaphragm muscles to relax. I didn't think I was ashamed of either of us, and I certainly had no desire for anyone to carve *me* with a Bowie.

"I couldn't sleep. I was out walking last night," I said.

"And what did you think?" Xharina said. Her voice wasn't neutral now. It was angry.

"I think what I saw wasn't any of my business," I said honestly.

"Sure it wasn't," Xharina said bitterly. "But that isn't going to stop you from phoning all your friends and telling them all about it. Why not?—it isn't as though we're really Pagans or anything."

I thought of telling her that I didn't have any friends, but Xharina didn't need stand-up comedy right now. "It was a ritual. What I saw I didn't have any business seeing," I repeated. "I'm not going to tell anybody."

"And I suppose we'll just take your word for that?" Xharina said.

"What choice have you got?" I said, starting to get angry myself. "I've told you twice it was an accident—do you think I went out looking for you?"

"Maybe." Xharina looked me up and down in a way that was meant to be insolent and succeeded pretty well. "Maybe you were looking for—what we have."

There was no use denying I knew what that was, and knee-jerk denials are not my specialty anyway. With toxic fair-mindedness, I remembered waking up out of a sound sleep and going looking for . . . what? Them? I shook my head. Even if Xharina were right—and she might be—I could see no happiness for myself down that particular path, and given a choice I wouldn't walk it. There are degrees of separation from the mainstream; I could see Xharina's from where I was, but that didn't mean I wanted to go there.

"Maybe," I said reluctantly. "But I didn't mean to crash your ritual. I'm sorry."

"Okay." The word came on a sigh, an indication of how wired Xharina was. There was a pause. "Nobody else noticed," she said. "I knew there was someone but I didn't know who, and I thought . . ."

That it was Jackson Harm's killer trolling for new victims? Or something darker?

"Cheer up," I said glibly, "I'll keep my mouth shut and they'll make stuff up about you anyway."

That made her grin. Xharina wasn't averse to bad press and living the legend—except, I realized, when there was truth to the rumors.

"I'd say you should come party with us sometime," she said, "but I don't do women. I know some people, though."

I wasn't sure whether the offer was serious or whether she was still trying to jerk my chain, and on this particular morning I wasn't even sure which I wanted it to be.

"I'll keep that in mind," I said, settling for neutral politeness. "You folks have a safe trip home."

"See you at the Snake," Xharina said, and strode back to her coven.

I took the long way up to the barn, rearranging the inside of my head into something that wouldn't get into my way and trying to push the brilliant flash of the blade in Xharina's hands back somewhere into unconsulted memory-space.

And doing that made me forget about most of what else had happened last night, too.

It was only after I got up to the barn that I realized everything I needed to have to open up the table was down in the van. By the time I got back down to the parking lot again, Hoodoo Lunchbox was gone, which was, all things considered, a relief. I was pretty sure Xharina hadn't killed Jackson Harm, but I couldn't feel as certain about her boys—jailhouse tats, biker colors, and all. There was no reason other than bloody-minded suspicion for me to think any of them *had* done it, of course, and when I faced that thought, I realized that my subconscious didn't want to pin Harm's murder on Hoodoo Lunchbox as much as on their equipment.

It was, after all, a similar case to Reece Wheeler's shooting last night—a weapon appears, is used, and vanishes again. But even disappearing knives have to come from somewhere, and I suspected that Hoodoo Lunchbox traveled with a lot of them.

Of course, so did the Klingons. I wondered where Orm Klash and his brethren and sistern were this morning.

I got the cashbox and the jewelry and a few other odds and ends and headed up for the barn.

This time I didn't miss my chance to swing by the cabins and see if Julian was there. He wasn't. I wondered which of the workshops he was attending—without the cashbox, he probably wasn't up at the dealer's table. Imagination failed. I could not imagine Julian—ascetic, cerebral Julian—engaged in any of the well-meaning anarchy of a HallowFest.

As if to underscore this, the cabin was as neat as a monk's cell, with everything folded and put away as if Julian intended to make a habit out of living here. The scent of cold incense smoke covered the cabin's mustiness with a sharp tang: frankincense, mostly, and—

And amber, cinnamon, bergamot, and myrrh—at least if Julian was following the *Tesoraria* rituals, which that silver knife he'd gotten from Ironshadow indicated he was.

Interesting, but hardly of immediate importance. Julian is a student of magic; he's nearly always engaged in some magickal operation or other. Something niggled at the back of my mind, then, but I ignored it in favor of getting set up for the day. I wondered where I'd be sleeping tonight. I didn't think I could manage another night in the back of the van.

I had customers waiting when I got upstairs and no Julian in sight, which kept me busy supplying catalogs and making change for the next half hour. Since this was Sunday, business was picking up—people had done their window-shopping yesterday and now were ready to buy. One of my customers volunteered to go downstairs and get me coffee and I bought a couple of trail-mix muffins from the bake sale table next door (chewy, but filling) and settled down at the table.

A Welsh trad named Gerry came and asked me if we had any ritual robes—he'd seen Hallie's and didn't like the informality of the tie-dye. I was sure we'd packed some on Friday, but a quick search of the boxes under the table turned up altar cloths and Tarot cloths and everything but. I promised to keep looking, and Gerry promised to come back later, and possibly both of us would keep our promises.

Business slacked off with the start of the eleven o'clock workshop. It would probably pick up again at the lunch break, and then there'd be a last go in the late afternoon before Merchanting was shut down for the night. Tomorrow there'd be no workshops; the merchants would be able to open for a couple of hours before loading to leave. The last event of the weekend would be the "opening" ritual for next year's HallowFest. The closing ritual for this year's Festival was still a year away.

Ironshadow wasn't here yet, but he'd partied hearty and late last night and had the added advantage of merchanting a small and portable stock; I supposed he'd be here when he felt like it, if he didn't just decide to deal what he had left out of his tent today instead. *I* would have, given the option; the day outside was one of those bright autumnal glories that actually make people want to live in the country with kamikaze skunks, woodlice, and attack deer. I'm a city girl, myself.

It got to be noon. I wondered how Larry's evening on the cutting edge of law enforcement had been, and tried to remember if I'd seen him around the Warwagon this morning. I wondered where Julian was, since he wasn't in the cabin and didn't seem the type to go for long nature rambles. And then, for a change of pace, I wondered why Lark hadn't come around to see me this morning. It was true we hadn't parted on the best of terms, but with Lark that didn't mean a helluva lot, unless he'd changed more than I thought. If I was even thinking about tapping him for my working partner I was going to need to know exactly where I stood with him and whether he was, in the quaint patois of Organized Crime, a "stand-up guy."

And if not Lark, who? I began going over all the males of my acquaintance who were (a) semidetached and (b) initiate Gardnerians, trying to think of who would do for me. Assuming, of course, that I would do for them. When that got frustrating enough, I looked around for something to do and realized I hadn't brought a book with me—not a problem, you'd say, since I was running a table for a bookstore, but Julian had brought up a collection of books I'd either already read or wouldn't read if the alternative were illiteracy.

He doesn't like the stock bent anyway.

So I read the more expensive of the two *Tesoraria*s for a while but got bored with that too, since a grimoire's got as much plot as a cookbook—a really boring one.

Aside from its particular purpose of ending all spiritual outside influence on the petitioner, *La Tesoraria* is similar to other grimoires of the period. Its rituals require a detailed knowledge of Latin, Greek, Hebrew, and astrology, and a list of ingredients that not only keeps stores like The Snake in business but guarantees that the legitimate magician will never find himself with time or excess money on his hands. Needless to say, I am not drawn to the more esoteric reaches of Ceremonial Magic; in fact I have a suspicion that the rituals in most grimoires—like the advice in their distant cousin, the *Kama Sutra*—are mostly designed to be read and not done.

For example, at the end of working of *La Tesoraria del Oro* there are two acts the practitioner must perform. They're impossible, of course, but, like Welsh riddles, once you've gotten that far you have to solve them to finish the game. In order to receive his theurgical bill of divorcement, the petitioner, once he has completed his year of abstinence and observance, must first slay himself, and then have congress with himself—as the translated Spanish so quaintly puts it. I'd gotten that far in the read-through of the translated manuscript when I asked Julian if he had me working on the world's longest Polish terrorist joke (you know, the one that ends: "—first me, and then all of my hostages!"). He'd just given me one of those smug cat looks.

I suppose it *was* a dumb question. The similar impossibilities mentioned in most alchemical texts are treated by modern commentators as metaphor for a purely psychological transmutation; most magic is, these days, when only allegorical angels dance on the head of New Age pins. Depending on the inclination of the magician, there are a number of different ways to interpret what *La Tesoraria* says, ranging from simple animal sacrifice and bestiality to a rather airy-fairy congress of the spirit, but the book itself is quite explicit. *La Tesoraria* calls for human sacrifice. I wondered which allegorical reading Julian was going to give its injunction when he got there. (In this it is not, as I've said, out of line with other medieval grimoires, whose recipes suggest that no one short of Giles de Rais has ever properly mastered the Black Arts, but it is also not particularly legal, ethical, moral, or PC. Of course, neither is your classic floor-model magician.)

I'd given up on *La Tesoraria* and was just about to have to choose between *Cats Are Angels Too* and *New Aeon Crystal Power* when Ironshadow showed up to save me from the sin of literary criticism.

"And good morning to you," he said cheerfully. He was looking particularly pleased with himself, which meant that *somebody*, at least, was having a good HallowFest.

"I may rise, but I'm damned if I'm going to shine," I answered with moderate good grace, and his grin widened. Ironshadow has enormous white teeth that make him look as if he's capable of eating trees for breakfast. His smile is particularly unsettling if you have the least bit of a guilty conscience, but fortunately mine was almost clear.

"My, my—did we get up on the wrong side of the van this morning?" He set his suitcase down on top of his card table and popped the locks. I watched as he arranged his last few *athames* and the other samples of his art on the length of black velvet: single-edged, double-edged . . .

But nothing that could have made that hole in Jackson Harm, my helpful brain reminded me.

I decided to think about the late Jackson Harm and how he got that way for a while, as it was more fun than thinking about Lark, Julian, or whether I was still going to be friends with Maidjene after I told her about that gypsy switch I'd pulled with the HallowFest records.

A gypsy switch is where you hand someone a package—usually containing valuables—and they hand it back. Or so you think, but the package you get back is never the one you handed over, and the substitution is called after its originators by those in the bunco know. The image set up a faint nagging warning in my backbrain. A gypsy switch—had someone swapped one knife for another to make the knife that killed Hellfire Harm disappear?

And if so, how? What killed Harm had left a distinctive entry wound, to say the least; the knife that made it would be instantly recognizable. But I was the only one who'd seen it. Nobody else would associate a *kukri* with foul play, so if the killer had helped himself to somebody else's knife to do the deed, its owner might be walking around with it this very moment, having no idea that he was carrying around evidence in a murder investigation.

And tomorrow he—along with everyone else here at Paradise Lake—would go home, and the chain of evidence would be broken forever.

As a theory it was pretty unworkable, since Harm had been killed early Saturday morning and not too many people had been around then to loan the murder weapon to Harm's killer, but I was equally willing to entertain the theory's evil twin: that the killer had stashed the knife he'd used among others somewhere here at the Festival, hiding it in plain sight.

Competing theories—all in need of more baking than they'd currently had—jostled and proliferated in my head until the only thing I was sure of was that I wanted to turn HallowFest inside out looking for something I wasn't even sure I could put a name to. I wondered if our friends the police felt the same way.

"Reality to Bast," Ironshadow said.

"You call this reality?" I snarked. "I could pull a better reality out of a hat."

He just grinned in a self-satisfied way and settled himself behind his table. "You hear they're out there dragging the lake this morning?"

"What?" I hadn't seen anything like that when I came in. I hoped my co-religionists weren't giving Bat Wayne too much grief.

"They were just getting things set up when I went by. Big-old gasoline generator, winch, seining net. Going to pull up every carp and Coke can in the whole damn thing, take forever, and find them exactly zip."

And Maidjene would be right there reminding them about our Fourth Amendment rights, no doubt. I had an appointment with her that I didn't want to keep, and the addition of the Sheriff's Department to the mix didn't sound calculated to improve her forbearance or the idle hour.

"And speaking of guns and their nuts, have you heard anything about Larry?" I asked.

"He wasn't booked. Jeannie had to go down to the station in Tamerlane and pick him up, though." Ironshadow looked disapproving; Maidjene had a lot of friends and none of them liked Larry.

"Is he still here?" I asked. It would have been lovely to be able to pin Hellfire Harm's murder on Larry, but I really found it hard to imagine Larry stabbing anybody, although I could certainly see him *shooting* someone, probably by mistake.

"The Warwagon," Ironshadow remarked to the ceiling, "has not left the grounds, either yesterday or today. It would, of course, be amazing if it had, with four flat tires, but . . ."

"You didn't!" I yelped, laughing in spite of myself.

Ironshadow turned the blandest of bland gazes upon me. "That would be vandalism," he said solemnly, "which would be illegal. And as young Lawrence has not so far disturbed the peace of the Festival, it would be wrong of someone to chastise him."

I hoped Larry Wagner had Triple-A. I hoped they'd send someone who could either patch a flat on a Winnebago or tow one. And while it was wrong of me to take such unholy delight in Larry's probably-deliberately-engineered misfortune, I did feel that the punishment fit the crime.

So what crime had Harm committed to merit *his* punishment—and did it fit as well?

I was abruptly cross again and might have said something regrettable, but fortunately Julian finally showed up. He was dressed, as always, in severe and funereal black—clerical collar, hammertail coat, trousers to match the coat, and glossily shined shoes. He stood in the doorway of the barn's second floor, polishing his glasses with a handkerchief and blinking as his eyes adjusted to the relative gloom after the bright light outside.

Julian is not a creature for bright light. He looked jarringly out of place here, but tomorrow the creature of the night would return to the night.

I reminded myself that I really ought to bear in mind that all this Gothic nonsense about Julian was the product of my imagination and not his lifestyle. People aren't like works of fiction, with every piece matching perfectly. At some point in his life Julian must have gone to kindergarten and the dentist and had birthday parties and the flu just like everyone else. Had what mainstream America would call a *normal* life.

In theory.

He was looking toward my table, and so he was looking toward the windows. The light shone full on his face; smooth skin, smooth shaven (it seemed unreasonable to think that Julian shaved, but he must) that granted the superficial illusion of youth, but the tiny lines around his eyes revised his age upward from Generation X to Woodstock I. It was odd to think of Julian not only subject to time but as a person somewhere near my age, although I'd known he wasn't young. If nothing else, it takes time to master the magical skills that I knew he had. He put his glasses back on and came toward me.

"I'll watch the table for a while," Julian said. "There isn't anything else to do here," he added, dismissing the Festival and all its workshops with a shrug.

"Sure," I said. I started to tell him about the morning's transactions and the state of the stock, but Julian wasn't interested. He came around the table, sat down in the chair I'd been standing beside, and pulled *La Tesoraria* over to him, much as if I wasn't there. I could smell cinnamon and oranges; the formula from *La Tesoraria*.

If I hadn't still been morbidly sensitive I might have stayed, since, interesting or not, I'd missed the start of the workshops and didn't want to come in late. But this particular morning that feat of detachment was beyond my skill.

When I got to the first floor of the barn it was practically empty. Both doors of the barn were open to the October sunshine and a perfunctory hand-lettered sign announced that the workshop on "Finding Your Faerie Guardians" had been moved to the Bardic Circle. Further investigation revealed that the Woods Walk had met down by the bridge and would be gone for two hours, and "Ritual Swordsmanship" had been moved from the Lake Meadow to the lower parking area. There was a notation "due to Faschist [sic] Pigs" on the paper after that one. From the direction of the lake I could hear a lawnmower-on-steroids sound that was probably the winch engine, and a lot of businesslike male voices making shouted conversation over the din.

I looked around. Nobody in sight through either door or the windows. I turned around and went through the door to one of the main bunkrooms.

There are two of them, and they occupy most of the first floor of the barn. Each one sleeps around thirty, in two rows of double-decker bunks. I remembered Maidjene saying that one of the rooms had been given over to parents with small children (Iduna sprang to mind). Out of a lunatic sense of expedience she'd made it the one nearer the bathrooms; I went into the other one.

It showed the signs of untidy overoccupancy by a tribe not noted, by and large, for its housekeeping or wilderness survival skills. Sleeping bags were in the minority; most of the bunks were

piled with patchwork quilts and satin-edged blankets, Holofil com-
forters with Kliban print designs, and assorted stuffed animals.
The luggage consisted of duffel bags and backpacks and plain
cardboard boxes and the odd Samsonite suitcase; ritual robes
were hung off the foot of most of the upper bunks, uneven hems
trailing on the floor.

It was a familiar homely clutter; one I was so used to that in
any year but this I would have walked in and simply taken it for
granted. This was the way things were.

But this year was different in so many ways. I found myself
thinking that there was no way I could search this mess even if I
wanted to. It looked like an explosion in the Department of Lost
Luggage.

All but one corner.

There were—I blinked, but they didn't go away—*footlockers* at
the foot of two bunks in the corner and the beds were made up
with black satin sheets. There was a banner hung on the wall between the two footlockered bunks, and another one covered the
window. Everything was militarily neat and precise.

I moved closer, carefully negotiating the encroaching-or-
escaping collections of personal possessions. Someone had
brought what looked like six cases of Classic Coke with them this
weekend and was doing pretty well at emptying them, if the clear
trash bag full of empties was any guide. Considering that I was
surviving the weekend more or less entirely on smoked oysters and
warm Diet Pepsi I wasn't in any position to throw stones, but still,
there are limits.

I had no idea what I was looking for or why, and I even more
certainly had no right to look for it—only a nagging unsatisfied
might-be hubris that told me I had to search for . . . something.

I suspected I'd found the Klingon Wiccans.

The Klingons had made their encampment into a complete
home away from home. There was a rug on the floor—gray, shaggy,
and real fur—and a small table in the corner with a candle in a
glass chimney on it. I looked up and realized the banner on the
wall wasn't quite what it seemed. The stylized bird design was
composed of knife sheaths, and every one of them was filled.

I reached up toward it.

"What do you think you're *doing?*"

It was the Klingon woman with the hubcaps, the one I'd seen
on Saturday with the elaborate leather armor almost as impres-

sive as Orm Klash's. She'd either slept in her latex appliances or found some way to put them on even under HallowFest's rudimentary sanitary conditions, and I don't think she'd internalized the love-feast protocols of the New Aquarian Frontier.

"Hi, I'm—"

"You stupid touchy-feely fuck—you were going through our stuff!" She hadn't waited for an answer; Lady Macbeth had her own script and she was happy with it, thank you very much. She took another step toward me and I could smell the sharp chemical tang of cheap-cured leather mixed with the need for a shower and some sweet resiny scent I couldn't immediately identify.

"Look," I began, gesturing toward the banner, planning some only slightly mendacious explanation.

She backhanded my hand away from it. I am not a small woman, but the Klingon lass had a few inches and a lot of pounds on me and she was wearing armor to boot. The metal studs on her wrist-guard dug into my skin with a bright, stinging pain and I heard her grunt: with satisfaction, with exertion.

I have received worse slaps from worse people, and because of that, I no longer handle being threatened in a particularly sensible manner. The spider kiss of adrenaline sang through my veins. I lunged for the banner again and this time ripped it off the wall, too furious to be wise.

I whipped the banner toward me like a matador playing the bull and its sheaths spilled knives. Blades hit the floor while others, still caught in their sheaths, clanged against the bed frame as the felt wrapped around it. "Sorry," I said, in a tone that turned the word into a threat. She'd struck where I was brittle, and I'd shattered.

Lady Macbeth was probably more terrorized by that than my grabbing her national flag. I think she tried to run for it but there wasn't a lot of room between the bunks; what she did instead was shove me hard enough to knock me off balance. I barely managed to turn the fall into a hasty collapse to the mattress. It gave us both a breathing space; I was still angry, but now not crazily so.

The Klingon hesitated over the spilled knives.

"Step away from the little lady," a high voice quavered uncertainly.

Lady Macbeth and I both froze.

Larry Wagner was standing in the center aisle near the door. He was still dressed in the Weight Watchers version of paramilitary chic, but, unlike the last time I'd seen him, he was holding a gun. I wondered if Ironshadow would hear me if I screamed.

"Jesus!" said the Klingon.

I endorsed the sentiment if not the deity. It takes an enormous amount of either chutzpah or stupidity to go around brandishing a gun just after the local Sheriff's Department has spent the night asking you with all due politeness if you've shot somebody.

"Oh, put that away, Larry," I snapped in irritated relief. I was betting on stupidity. "Move!" I barked at the Klingon, who took the opportunity to bolt out from between the bunks. She looked like she'd be happy to get the hell out of here completely if Larry weren't standing in her way.

I didn't have that kind of problem. I walked over to Larry and belatedly realized that someone who'd walk up to a man who was holding a gun intending to clock him one was not as grounded on the Earth Plane as she might think.

But I do not take well to being threatened.

"Good thing I had this, huh?" Larry said. "Right?"

I barely did not hit him. "Put it away." The gun was tiny and brightly chromed; it was hard to take something that looked like it came out of a box of Cracker Jack seriously. Or maybe it was just Larry I was having trouble taking seriously.

Larry put his combat-booted foot up on one of the mattresses and pulled up his pant leg, exposing hairy calves and a concealed holster that had that "loving hands at home" look. He actually patted the gun as he tucked it away.

My hands were starting to shake from the aftermath of the adrenaline rush, and I was beginning on a headache for the same reason. It's amazing what your body can do to you if you give it half a chance.

"Good thing I came along, right?" Larry said. "I saw you heading this way and if I hadn't followed you, you'd be in real trouble now."

There was something childishly gleeful about the iteration, and I realized that if I didn't get Larry out of here reasonably quickly Lady Macbeth would realize he wasn't all that dangerous and either come and clock him herself or go for reinforcements. You might respect the damage he could do, but you'd never respect Larry. I glanced back. She was standing with her back pressed against the wall, her expression a mix of vulnerability and growing anger.

"Come *on,* Larry," I said. "Walkies."

I grabbed him by a fold of his jacket and towed him out of the bunkroom. He followed me willingly, as if we were allies in some grand adventure, and I decided that the barn's main room wasn't far enough away. For one thing, there was a couch out there, and Larry is far from trustworthy around couches, especially when he feels you owe him something.

We went outside.

The sound of the winch down by the lake increased exponentially as soon as we were in the open air. Straight ahead was the wide dirt path with the cabins on the left and bushes on the right. The lake was beyond the cabins; ahead, the road went on past the cabins and then split, half doubling back behind the bushes, heading down until it reached the parking lot, half going straight on past Helen Cooper's house. It looked like a reasonably safe and public place to have a conversation with Larry Wagner. I didn't like Larry, but I prefer being in the right at all times and noblesse oblige until proven guilty was part of that.

I looked back. Lady Macbeth hadn't followed us. I turned around, waiting for Larry to say something and reining in my temper. Larry regarded me with the sort of limpid brown eyes that make people want to take up vivisection of small helpless animals. There was a kind of desperation in the way he waited, as if he expected me to guess why he'd come after me. I could not understand why Maidjene had ever married him, but we so rarely understand what it is that people see when they look at other people.

The sun was warm enough that I contemplated taking off my parka, and remembered that I'd been in these clothes, what with one thing and another, since Saturday morning. I ought to get my stuff out of the cabin while I knew where Julian was and maybe take a bath in the sink.

It finally became obvious that Larry wasn't going to say anything.

"Did you want something from me?" I said, as politely as I could manage under the circumstances.

"You've got to talk to her for me. She'll listen to you. Hell, she's always listened to you; anyone but her husband."

"What do you want me to say?" I asked. I kept my face bland and my voice neutral. The discipline of eyes and face is the earliest survival mechanism, gained by instinct under siege.

"*You* think of what to say!" Larry said vehemently. "You and all your smart-mouth friends making her think I wasn't good enough for her—*you* figure out what to say to change her mind."

I stared at Larry blankly. I had accepted the fact of Maidjene and Larry's divorce so thoroughly that it took me a moment to realize that Larry hadn't.

"You tell her I still love her just like I always did—Wagner & Wagner, just like it started out; I don't want her going off like that." Larry stopped abruptly, breathing hard. His face, pale and pasty from junk-food diets and indoor weekends, was turning red; his breathing had quickened.

What could I say that was both kind and honest? Never kick a man when he's down, as the saying goes; he might have a gun.

"I think that Maidjene has probably pretty well made up her mind about things," I said.

"She doesn't mean it!" Larry said desperately. "She needs me— nobody else is going to take her in—she's just in one of her moods. She'll listen to you."

Not if I told her to go back to Larry she wouldn't, I bet. I wished I wasn't here listening to Larry whipsaw between insult and pleading; a man who despised what he needed.

"Larry, I can tell her to be sure she's thought things out thoroughly, but . . ."

"I don't *want* you to tell her to think! I want you to tell her she's making a big mistake. She thinks— She thinks I don't love her— but I do. I always have." His face twisted up in earnest and got redder. For a moment I thought he was going to cry, and I tried to feel sympathy for him and failed. Maybe Maidjene had finally failed at that as well.

"Larry, you've been making passes at everything in sight for as long as I've known you, and right in front of her—is that love?"

"Men aren't like women," Larry said. "I didn't do anything anybody didn't want me to. Philly understood that—at least she did until she started up with all this Goddess crap. It was bad enough when she was Born Again—and now I'm supposed to believe that a bunch of girls standing around naked in my bedroom can make something happen just by wishing and Philly tells me that some *god* told her to get a divorce?"

I'd bet dollars to broomsticks that Maidjene had said no such thing.

"Larry, I'm sure the two of you were very happy once. But people change, and Maidjene—"

"Don't you go calling her that! Her name's Phyllis. Phyllis Eileen Wagner, just like on our marriage license, and she's *my wife.*"

He said it the way he might say: *my car,* with as much entitlement and as little honest affection. And I was tired of this point-less conversation anyway.

"Look, Larry, what exactly is it that you want me to do? She doesn't want to be married to you and I can understand that: *I* wouldn't want to be married to you. Hell, I don't know why she married you in the first place—"

"Oh, you just think you're the cutest little thing, don't you?" Larry snarled. The down-home twang in his voice was stronger by the minute: he sounded now the way he looked, like a nasty-minded good ol' boy, the kind of reactionary that doesn't want to be bothered with the facts.

"If this is the way you ask for favors, Larry, I'd just love to see you try to piss somebody off," I snapped. "I couldn't do what you want even if I wanted to. Now leave me alone."

I already felt guilty; sufferance is not among my virtues. I tried to tell myself that a tonic dose of disenchantment would be the best thing for Maidjene's soon-to-be-ex but I couldn't really make my-self buy it. What I needed was someplace to go that would put a final end to the conversation. I settled for walking off down the road. Maybe Helen Cooper would give me another cup of coffee.

"Who are you to judge me?" Larry yelled after me. "Who do you think you are?"

I stopped and turned around. You cannot reason with people like Larry, but sometimes, out of a despairing sense of civic duty, I still try.

"I'm me," I said. "Everybody judges. It's called being alive."

"Yeah, well, you didn't like it so much when Hellfire Harm did it, did you? Called you Satanists and said you'd all better come to Jesus? You stuck-up bitch—maybe you didn't kill him but I bet you're glad he's dead. You're too gutless to pop him yourself but you'd sure love for *somebody* to do it; fall all over yourself crown-ing them hero of the fucking Revolution and be *happy* to do what they wanted . . ."

They could probably hear him on the other side of the lake. I saw the Klingon woman watching us nervously from the doorway, and when I looked up I saw Ironshadow looking down from the second-floor window. At least there were plenty of witnesses.

"Larry, go away," I said. At least I could eliminate one suspect: if Larry were the killer there was no way he'd back off from call-ing in the "favor" now.

He smiled nastily. "Fine. I'll go away and leave you alone, Miss Witch Queen of the Goddamn Universe. But you aren't going to like what happens when I tell Philly about what you've done. You aren't going to be so high and mighty then."

We are none of us without guilt. The first thing I thought was that Larry had found out about my switching the Festival's registrations, and I almost fell into the trap of trying to reason with him that disclosure would serve no purpose. But he might be bluffing. Or he might be thinking of something else entirely. And at any rate, it was blackmail.

"Fuck off, Larry," I said, and turned again in the direction of Mrs. Cooper's house.

Larry trotted after me at a safe distance, trying to restart the conversation—which, since it had consisted of whining threats from Larry and abortive reasonableness from me, wasn't something I could see any point to, even if Larry hadn't succeeded in pissing me off royally. I would have preferred to feel compassion and understanding, but what I felt mostly was embarrassment. I wished he'd go away.

When I finally reached Mrs. Cooper's house, Larry was still following, but now it didn't matter. Lark's dark red Harley was parked beside the porch, and Lark was straddling it, talking to Mrs. Cooper. I walked faster.

Lark grinned when he saw me. The grin widened when he looked past me; I glanced back over my shoulder and saw Larry shuffling off toward the parking lot, trying to look as if that had been his destination all along.

"I sure hope he wasn't planning on going anywhere—not with four flat tires," Lark said when I reached him.

"And good morning to you, too," I said. I wondered who'd done the actual slashing of the Winnebago's tires, though at the moment I was almost willing to have done it myself.

"Well, I can't spend all day here chattering," Mrs. Cooper said to Lark. "You just go and do what I told you and you'll be fine." She went in the house and closed the door.

The deep porch cast the front of the house into shadow, making it possible to see inside. Through the lace curtains at the window I could see Mrs. Cooper cross the dining room toward the kitchen.

"Look," Lark said to me. "You want to go out for lunch or something? There's a diner up the road."

I checked my watch. Noon. If Deputy Pascoe had got off work at six o'clock this morning, she probably wouldn't be hanging around the diner now. Not that I had a guilty conscience or anything.

"Sure," I said.

"Hop on," Lark said. I guessed we'd forgiven each other for last night.

I swung my leg over the seat behind him. He handed me a crash helmet, a bowl-shaped thing painted the same deep heart's blood color as the farings on his bike. I Velcroed the chinstrap up and put my arms around his waist. Lark kicked the bike to life and swung it around, heading down the dirt road in the direction of County 6 again.

There's something about riding a bike that's like flying. Your mind turns the engine roar into silence and you seem to glide effortlessly through the world. Everything's close enough to touch, and it's as if the bike goes away too, and all that's left is you and the speed and the wind.

I rested my cheek against Lark's denimed shoulder and tried not to obsess on what Larry might tell Maidjene and who was going to yell at me when I got back to Paradise Lake and how Arioch's blood had looked in the moonlight. I wondered if I'd come back here next year. I wondered if I'd be let to come back next year. I wondered if there'd *be* a next year. If the Klingon woman complained to Maidjene and was willing to complain to the Gotham County Sheriff's Department, they'd probably arrest Larry for waving a gun around today, but while I was even willing to believe that he'd given or sold or loaned the gun that had done last night's shooting, there was no way he could have either done the shooting himself or stabbed the Reverend Jackson Hellfire Harm Friday night. Not without bragging about it today.

The motorcycle's engine vibrated up through my spine, making my scalp tingle. I wished, now, that I'd gotten a better look at the Klingon knife banner I'd had my hands on so briefly. My impressions weren't very clear, but it seemed to me that it'd been heavier than it would have been if it contained ordinary flat-bladed knives. Had one of the *objets decoratifs* been a *kukri?* And had Orm Klash loaned it out—or had it borrowed'?

But no. The Klingons had gotten to HallowFest *after* Jackson Harm's body was found and long after he'd been stabbed; none of them could be the murderer. But what if they'd found, or been given, or had the knife substituted for one of their own *later?*

We arrived.

9

We settled into a front booth in the diner where Lark could keep an eye on his bike. The waitress came. I ordered coffee. Lark ordered beer.

"So was Larry giving you a hard time or what?" Lark said.

"He wanted me to talk Maidjene into going back to him," I said. I wondered what Lark and Mrs. Cooper had found to talk about.

"Asshole," Lark said comprehensively.

The beer and coffee arrived and we ordered—bacon cheeseburger platters all 'round. I told my arteries I'd be virtuous later, although living in the Big Apple is such a health hazard by itself that it hardly matters what else you do with your life.

"So," I said, when the waitress had gone. "Where are you heading off to tomorrow?"

"Down to the city." "The city" means New York, always; every other local habitation has a name, but New York is the only city.

Lark pulled the sugar caddy over to him and began grouping the little packets by the designs on the back. "I figured it was time to start over. You know—live down my mistakes and all that?" he said with a crooked grin.

"Sure," I said, though I couldn't think of any mistakes Lark had made lately. As far as I knew, the biggest mistake in his life was his parents', who had named him Elwyn. I stared at the acreage for sale across the road. There was a stand of white birch, all in yellow fall leaves.

*Nothing gold can stay. Robert Frost. Márgarét, are you griev-
ing/Over Goldengrove unleaving? Gerard Manley Hopkins.* I felt as
if I was saying good-bye, and I didn't know why.

"You know," said Lark, "I was kind of hoping I could work with
you, you know? I had a group out in Anaheim, but after what happened they decided not to know me. Big talk. *All* talk," he added
a little bitterly. "Some justice."

After *what* had happened? Whatever it was, clearly it was something he thought I already knew.

"It's better than no justice, I suppose," the half-remembered tag
of an old "I, Claudius" springing to mind. Lark snorted eloquently.
He finished his beer and called for another and I started to worry
about riding back with him. We were probably about five miles
from the campground; walkable, if long. I could make up my mind
later. Lark drank half the second beer in one pull, straight from
the bottle.

"God, I missed that. Look, who are you—"

The burgers arrived.

Who are you working with? he'd been going to say. Who was
my working partner? A reasonable question, since everyone but a
Ceremonial Magician had one. Would it be him? It was a question
I'd been asking myself all weekend; a question I'd had in the back
of my mind ever since I'd accepted the reality of the split from
Changing. But now that he'd brought up a subject I was determined to talk to him about anyway, I found myself unable to continue with it, tongue-tied as a nervous virgin. Which we were not,
to each other, in any sense.

So why couldn't I get off the dime?

Lark devoted himself to lunch in a fashion that suggested he
hadn't been fed for weeks, but he had to come up for air sometime.

"So who are you going to be working with?" he said when he
did. "Anybody I know?—not that I know anybody out here anymore."

"Why did you leave?" I said. It wasn't a question I'd thought I
had any interest in the answer to, but I've been wrong before.

"I was young and stupid." His inflection gave the sentence neither regret nor irony.

"And you're older and wiser now?"

"Older, anyway. And Second. And Long Island," Lark said, reminding me that he was not only a ranking member of our tradi-

tion, but that he came from the same branch: the Gardnerians who could trace their lineage back to the Long Island Coven founded back in the sixties by Rosemary and Raymond Buckland, whose spiritual mandate—for what that was worth—had come from Gerald Gardner himself.

"You know we work well together," he added.

"Not for ten years. It'd be like starting over."

"You'd be starting fresh with whoever you pick."

"I haven't even made up my mind. I've never run a coven."

"I have. Goddammit, Bast, you've been around for years and watched everything Belle does—what are you waiting for, a handbook?"

"Yeah, well, maybe," I admitted.

"So write one. What about it?" Lark said.

He was doing nothing more than echoing my own thoughts back to me, but things seemed to be moving too fast; everything he said sounded as if it ought to be the right answers, but I felt as if I were being pushed into making a choice that I wouldn't make if I had time to think about it.

"Lark, you've just gotten back. It's been a long time; this isn't the time to be making decisions like that. I mean, somebody stabbed Jackson Harm, and—"

"And you think I did it," Lark said, deadly flat. I felt a warning prickle of the little hairs on the back of my neck. "Hell, why not—what's a little murder among friends?"

He thought I already knew. I didn't, but I managed to piece it together from what he said then. He'd been working in a family-planning clinic in Orange County, California, which had gotten the same flack that clinics everywhere get in these antichoice times. And then one day it had burned in a highly suspicious fashion.

"So I figured if Heather Dearest could bomb a GYN clinic she ought to expect a little Christian charity in return."

And Lark had felt that biblical retribution was in order. An eye for an eye. A building for a building.

"Local merchants wouldn't let the place reopen—bad for business, they said, and everybody knowing that good old Reverend Heather Grace Barrows had been yapping about 'cleansing fire from heaven' in her sermons for weeks, so 'who will rid me of this turbulent priest,' right?" Lark snarled. And two years ago this month—they make you stick close during your probation—he'd been released from the Orange County Correctional Facility after serving eighteen months of a three-year sentence for arson.

"Honest to Goddess, Lark," I said helplessly. It was, I supposed, justice of a sort—bomb a clinic, get bombed in return—providing any of what I'd heard was true. But it was vigilante justice,
and a society which allows individuals to take the law into their
own hands is doomed.

"The bimb wasn't home. Nobody was; I checked—which was
more than she did for us. And that tax-dodging bitch could afford
a new coat of paint."

"But Lark—"

"And you know what the real joke was?" He looked into my eyes,
smiling his twisted grin. "Everybody in Ocean Circle'd been saying it was time for some Instant Karma—only when it came down,
all of a sudden it was nobody's idea but mine."

Oh, Lark, what did you expect? I shook my head sadly. Even if
what he'd done had been legal as church on Sunday he probably
wouldn't have gotten the support he'd been expecting—as I knew
to my cost. Our Community isn't a Community, not really. It's an
assemblage of chance-met fellow travelers, singularly unwilling to
make moral judgments.

"Judge not, lest ye be judged," the rabbi from Galilee is rumored
to have said, and his followers have always assumed it was a command, even as they ignored it. But it's not a command. It's a reality. Judge and be judged. No one here gets out alive.

"So you just stay wrapped up in your sanctimonious little
shroud with that silver-plated virgin looking down on you from
Heaven, sweetheart. Some of us are living in the real world."

Lark dug a twenty out of his pocket and tossed it on the table.
He was out of the booth and halfway to the door before I realized
what was happening.

"Come back here you son of a *bitch!*"

I caught up with him just as he reached his bike.

"Don't you talk to me about the real world!" I said, grabbing his
arm. "And don't you go using it as an excuse."

I didn't have the slightest idea what I meant. All I knew was
that all the adrenaline left over from the Larry and the Klingon
episode had finally found a home.

"Maybe I did do it," Lark taunted. "Yeah, here I am: the Horned
Avenger, doing what you're too scared to!"

I wished I knew why everybody was so convinced I wanted
Harm dead. Before this weekend I'd barely known he existed.

"I just love the odor of sanctity you're exuding—is that a new
cologne?" We're never so eloquent as when we're flaying old lovers.

"What makes you think that murder has suddenly become a moral act?"

"It's better than moral cowardice," Lark said. "You're afraid to stick up for what you believe in—and you're afraid of anyone who does."

"I sure as hell hope that pedestal is comfortable," I snarled back. "Seeing as you're going to spend so much time up there."

Lark jerked away from me and swung his leg over the seat of the bike.

"*Did* you kill him?" I said to Lark's back, more to piss him off than because I cared about the answer just now.

"Sure," Lark said. He kicked the bike to life. "I shot him right through the heart."

I watched Lark skim off down the road. It wasn't me he was angry with, although the realization wasn't particularly comforting. I was standing in for Ocean Circle, and everything they hadn't done.

I hadn't known about Lark's prison record until just now, but once I did, it didn't take much of a leap of imagination to wonder if someone who'd firebombed one anti-abortionist might not have killed another. It would have been damned unlikely that Harm *wasn't* anti-Choice, given the rest of his platform. Or Harm could have recognized Lark—I imagine Lark's trial and conviction had been front-page news with pictures in the *Godbotherer's Gazette.*

But Lark—who'd been mad enough not to choose his words carefully—had said that Harm had been shot, just as Larry had. It was a reasonable assumption, but it wasn't the truth. Harm had been stabbed.

Was it an ignorant-therefore-innocent assumption? Or had Lark learned tactics in the last ten years?

I went back inside the diner.

Everyone stared at me when I went in. I went back to the booth, sat down, and tried to ignore them. The dishes hadn't been cleared away yet. I tried my coffee. It was cold.

"Have a fight with your boyfriend?" the waitress said sympathetically. "I could ask Charlie can he give you a lift as far as Tamerlane. You could get a bus from there."

"Thanks," I said, "but I don't think I'm going that far." I looked at the ruins of two Double Bacon Cheeseburger Deluxes and decided I could call the campground to see if Ironshadow or someone could come and get me. Or maybe there was something approaching a taxi service. Or I could walk it, which would at least have the advantage of keeping me out of trouble. "Do you think I could have some more coffee and the dessert menu?"

Lark came back about the time I was finishing my apple pie à la mode and a third cup of coffee.

"You coming back to the campground or not?" he said ungraciously.

"You want dessert?" I said without looking up. Lark waited until it was obvious even to him that I wasn't moving and slid back into the opposite side of the booth.

I had the hopeless feeling that today's lunchtime theater was going to be a report on somebody's desk before dinner. I wondered what they'd say and do. The fact that I wasn't going to be the one in trouble was scant comfort. I finished my pie, although it wasn't easy.

"I'm not going to apologize," Lark said.

"So don't," I said.

Lark stopped the bike by Mrs. Cooper's house and I got off. He fishtailed around in a spray of dirt and gravel and sped off again. I thought he'd come back eventually, but I wasn't completely sure.

I wanted to go home. I wanted my own shower and my own bed and my own refrigerator full of beer. I wanted to stop dealing with murder and other quaint native folkways not my own. The more I considered Jackson Harm's unsought quietus, the more I thought the identity of his killer wouldn't be anything I'd end up wanting to know.

I should go talk to Belle and arrange for Lark's crash space out of a vindictive sense of moral superiority. I should go up and take over the table from Julian. I should go find Maidjene and give her a pound of flesh.

What I did do was go back to the bungalow.

You could lock the door from the inside, so I did. I wanted a bath and compromised with an unsatisfactory scrub in the rusty sink and a change of clothes, which made me feel a little better but not much. I'd never really gotten unpacked, so it didn't take long at all to bundle my stuff back into the duffel I'd brought it in.

Maybe I could talk Julian into packing and leaving tonight. He already had his Ironshadow blade; picking it up had to be the reason he'd come to the Festival. The selling was all but over and we could load the van tonight and be back in the city by four A.M. at the latest. Julian hadn't wanted to be here in the first place, and by now neither did I.

Having a plan cheered me up; I took my duffel down to the van and loaded it in, feeling optimistic enough to roll my sleeping bag up and tie it, ready to go. But by the time I got back up the hill to the barn, I'd changed my mind again. I didn't want to be here, but I had the superstitious feeling that leaving would be worse—although tomorrow at noon it would become a moot point. Tomorrow at noon the Festival would be over, and everyone would leave.

Including Harm's killer, if he—or she—were one of us. I kept a wary eye out for Larry and any stray Klingons as I headed for the barn.

The news reached me before I reached it.

"Larry Wagner's been arrested!" Lorne said. Lorne was a member of Summerisle—if Maidjene's soon-to-be-ex had been arrested, he'd know.

I stopped and stared at him, and as I stood there wondering what to do, I heard the back door bang and Glitter came running toward me.

"Is it true?" she demanded.

"What?" I stared at her. Maidjene and Belle had followed her out. I walked over toward them. Glitter and Lorne followed.

"It isn't true," she told them.

"They took him away!" Lorne said. Maidjene had been crying, and she started to cry again.

"Why didn't you *tell* me, Bast?" she said.

"I was going to, but . . ." I said.

Maidjene shook her head, shutting me out. "I could have done something!" she sobbed, which even in the confusion clued me that she could not be talking about my stealing the festival records.

"You know what Larry's like," Belle said to Maidjene, soothingly. I looked at Glitter. The expression on her face said that things were not good.

Larry arrested? "What's going on?" I said.

"Larry said this Klingon beat you up," Glitter said. She inspected me critically. "You don't look beat-up."

"A Klingon did not beat me up." I stared at Maidjene. "And you *believed* him?"

Maidjene shook her head. "But she said he had a gun, and she went and told one of the deputies down by the lake, and we couldn't find you, and—"

"It was kind of a mess," Belle admitted. "Everyone was looking for you because you were the only one who'd seen him with the gun besides Rhonda."

Rhonda must be the Klingon.

"I went down to the diner," I said feebly.

"What nobody could figure out was how he still had a gun," Glitter said with interest. "They found it on him," she amplified.

And possession being nine points of the law, Larry was now getting an even closer look at the judicial system of Gotham County.

" 'Still'?" I asked.

"Well, he didn't exactly have permits for the others, so they sort of confiscated all of them," Glitter, mistress of modifiers, said.

"You should have said something!" Maidjene said, and while it was true, I could also not see how it could have changed the course of events, unless I'd talked Rhonda out of reporting Larry.

"I'm sorry," I said.

"Look," said Lorne to Maidjene, "why don't you come on and lie down, okay? They aren't even going to set bail until tomorrow morning, and the sonovabitch sure had it coming. And you've got to go make a statement," he added to me.

I opened and closed my mouth a couple of times, and gave up. Lorne led Maidjene away.

"There somebody still here?" I asked, and Glitter made a rude noise.

"Follow me," she said.

Glitter and I got to ride down to beautiful downtown Tamerlane in the back of one of their green-and-whites so the Gotham County Sheriff's Department could take my notarized statement in comfort. They were not really pleased with the idea that I'd just figured that the firearms display was just another case of Larry being Larry and therefore hadn't bothered to mention it to anybody. My vagueness earned me a long session in a private room with a detective and a stenographer. The room smelled of dust and Lysol and ancient cigarette smoke. The bulb in the ceiling was protected by a wire cage. There was a battered gray table in the middle of the room and four chairs that looked like they didn't want to have anything to do with it. The floor was covered with multiple coats of battleship gray enamel, and the walls were painted a shade of greenish yellow that looked as if it wanted to be chartreuse but didn't have the energy. There was a frosted glass window in the wall opposite the door, and the walls had dingy two-color-process posters explaining the Heimlich maneuver and giving information on the "Cop Shot" hotline. It was just like the last copshop I'd been in, even though that one had been in Manhattan.

I did my best to give them what they wanted, but it was hard to explain to anyone who hadn't been around for the last fifteen years about how Larry had always had guns—usually cheap small-caliber hideouts—and was always showing them off with the zeal of a Fuller Brush salesman. I finally explained that Larry had been trying to get me to effect a reconciliation with his wife, and I'd been so interested in getting out of there that I wasn't thinking very clearly.

Which brought my story around to Lark. Lark with his prison record, Lark with his *motive*—for Jackson Harm's death, if no one else's. My conviction that he was innocent wouldn't carry as much weight as his prison record would.

I told them I left the grounds with a friend. I had to give his name. But I was also able to cite Helen Cooper as a witness that he'd been nowhere near the barn, nor the trouble with Larry.

Finally I got to leave.

When Glitter and I got back to Paradise Lake it was late and so was I. When I got upstairs in the barn there were customers three deep around the Snake's table.

Lark was there, too. I felt a moment of appalled self-consciousness, as if the only thing he and Julian could possibly be discussing was me. It turned out I was right.

I slid in behind the table, next to Julian, who removed his attention from Lark and started making change.

"Where've you *been?*" Lark demanded, at the same time someone else wanted to know if Three Kings Incense was the same as pure frankincense (it isn't).

"Down in Tamerlane, making a statement to the police."

Lark and Julian both stared at me. Lark's mouth had a set expression that reminded me—forcibly—of our lunchtime conversation. I wondered about the chat he and Julian had been having before I got there. It was hard to think of two people who had less

common ground. Dionysus and Apollo; Sun and Moon; Wiccan
and apostate . . .

"It wasn't what you think," I said feebly. Julian handed me a
stack of books to bag. "Larry's been arrested. I had to make a statement."

"About *what?*" Lark asked with suspicious disbelief.

"He had a gun," I said. ("No shit?" one of the customers asked
with interest.) "I saw him with it," I added. Which wasn't quite the
whole story, but the whole story wasn't for an audience.

"Okay." Now that this had been settled, Lark remembered he
was mad at me again. He glanced at Julian.

"He wondered where you were," Julian said to me. His tone was
neutral, but I could tell he was amused. "He thought I might tell
him." He regarded Lark over the top of his glasses. Lark glared at
him, not quite sure of the subtext but knowing he didn't like it.

"I'm right here," I said ungraciously. Then I had to tell somebody why there were three Waite decks on the table and explain
why they all had different prices. Albano-Waite; U.S. Games; and
shot from original art, if you're interested.

"I'll see you," Lark said, while I was in the middle of that. His
inflection made it something in the nature of a vow, but I didn't
know which of us he was talking to.

"I'm certain of it," Julian murmured sweetly. I felt my face grow
hot and hoped it wasn't as noticeable as it felt. Business picked
up further. I started making change and supplying bags and tried
to stop thinking about Lark or anything else.

The fin de siècle shopping frenzy was intense but brief; a little later
I dumped the last packet of Three Kings Incense into the last red-
and-black paper bag and made change for the last customer. The
second floor was still crowded, but people were standing around
in the open space, not clumped near the tables.

I glanced over at Ironshadow—his table was bare of everything
except the museum pieces and he gave me the "thumbs-up" sign
that indicated business had been good. Hallie's rack of tie-dyed
robes was almost empty, and the baked goods table was completely gone.

"So how'd we do?" I said to Julian.

"Well enough," he said. "Look, are you . . ." There was a pause.
"Are you coming back to the cabin tonight?"

Coming as it did, while my mind was full of Lark, what might be a perfectly innocent question seemed remarkably fraught. Was this Julian's bid to retain my favors, or his acknowledgment of my might-be relationship with Lark? I opened my mouth to suggest leaving tonight instead, but finally remembered a good concrete real-world reason why I'd been so reluctant after all to leave tonight. Tomorrow morning Wyler Pascoe would be coming for his books, and I'd promised him I'd be here. I might even find time tonight to get that reading list from Belle.

But that left tonight to get through. And asking Julian whether he wanted me to come back to the cabin tonight would be playing into all those old boy-and-girl games we're supposed to have left behind now that we've entered the Aeon of Horus. So I said, "I haven't made up my mind yet," instead.

Julian smiled coolly and stood up. "I don't think I'm going to go to the party," he said. "I've got some reading to do. You could drop by if it gets too noisy for you." He walked away before I could collect enough brain cells to field a reply.

The sharp snap of the locks on Ironshadow's case jarred me out of my woolgathering. I looked around and saw him closing his case and starting to fold up the table.

"Nothing left to sell," he said happily. "And I've got to hit the road early tomorrow."

Ironshadow lives somewhere in New Jersey—or, as its habitués refer to it, *Fucking*jersey—and has a trip home that is longer by several hours than the one I was facing.

"Good luck," I said. "When do we see you again?"

"I'm going to be in the city for Twelfth Night; maybe then."

"Call me," I said, meaning it. He grinned a toothy troll-grin and picked up his table, chair, and case.

"Too bad about Larry," he said, and his tone made the words into an epitaph, "but that boy was definitely asking for it."

Yeah, a traitor part of my mind said, *but what did he do besides want to be a hero?*

People began to wander downstairs from the selling floor. There was still light in the sky outside, but it was that lucent misleading brilliance that comes just before you realize it's dusk, when things seem very clear but relationships are hard to judge. Eventually it was just me and someone I didn't know well who had a table full of herbs and oils. She started clearing her table and packing her stuff away. It was about time for me to do the same.

The Gotham County Sheriff's Department had not objected to

my plans to leave the county, providing I was willing to come back if they asked. I was, even if not very, and at the moment the thought of getting back to the big city had an obsessive glamour to it. Only the thought of packing the truck in the dark—and the knowledge that, come hell or high water, I still had to talk to Maidjene and meet Wyler—kept me here.

I tried to distract myself. Monday would be a short selling day, with a long load-up at the end of it, but I had a pretty good idea of what I needed to leave out for Monday's last-minute impulse shoppers, and I might as well pack the rest of the stuff now. When I got back to New York it'd be early enough that maybe I'd call Lace and we'd have a big Chinese dinner and then maybe cruise her favorite bars.

Unless Lark . . .

Damn Lark. And Julian, too, for good measure.

Meanwhile, I could get together the books I'd promised Wyler, that he might or might not be back to buy. And I still had to ask Belle about getting Lark a place to stay, which meant after that I'd have to go and find *him,* and . . .

I started to work.

Every year it's the same thing; Julian sends more stock than any six Festivals could absorb, on the theory that Goddess forbid he should miss a sale. Every year 90 percent of it goes back to the shop untouched. Julian is not daunted by this—and I did have to admit it would make filling Wyler's shopping list easier, since who but Julian would bring Wicca 101 books to a Pagan Festival where everyone who came had bought and read them years ago?

I found Buckland's *Complete Book of Witchcraft* and Dion Fortune's *Psychic Self-Defense* without much trouble, but I wanted to include *What Witches Do* by Stewart Farrar and I was pretty sure I'd seen Julian take a copy of it off the shelf back in New York. The only question was, where was it now?

I packed while I searched, trying to group titles by subject and get all the remaining copies together into the same box, although since I wouldn't be the one unpacking them in New York there wasn't a lot of reason for me to bother. An inventory to check things off against would have made life ever so much easier, but every year the van is packed at the last minute and there's no time to do one.

It was while shifting the half-full boxes that I came on the full one.

It was under and behind everything, shoved into a corner and sealed, and if I hadn't had a suspicious nature I would have thought it belonged to Paradise Lake and not to me. But I knew this corner had been empty when I set up and so it must be mine.

Right?

The first thing I saw when I slit the tape was a bundle of cloth, which annoyed me. This must be the wizard's robes that I'd spent the morning looking for; I'd known we'd brought a couple and if I could have found them I'd have been able to sell them. I lifted them out. Maybe I could find Gerry sometime tonight and tell him they were here.

Under the robes was an odd collection of things—cheap brass incense holders, some of the eight-inch beeswax candles that we retail for thirteen dollars each (wholesale they're somewhere around $4.50). Not stuff that we wouldn't have brought, but stuff that shouldn't have been packed together. And at any rate, stuff I might be able to sell tomorrow.

I lifted the candles out, annoyed and puzzled, and saw beneath them one of the Ziploc bags that the Snake uses to pack jewelry, specula, and other small objects up in. Some moron—I had my candidates—must have packed the candles on top of a bunch of jewelry, and it was pure luck and not planning that there wasn't something heavy on top of the candles, because beeswax candles are brittle rather than soft and will break given the right encouragement.

Then I took a good look at the bag.

Those who don't believe in the power of the abstract threat reject the power the imaginative mind has over the body. What I saw had no ability to hurt me, but I looked into the box and felt a sudden rush of adrenaline that made my hands shake and my ears ring.

Lying in the bottom of the box in one of the Snake's Ziploc bags was a *kukri*.

It was not like the Tibetan ones. Its three-flanged blade was made of brass or bronze, and the hilt was a plain shaft of white bone—antler, I thought—finished with a flat brass pommel. There was a dark line where the hilt met the blade. It *could* be epoxy. But it was so much more likely that it was blood.

I stared at the knife in the bag. I had no doubt that I was looking at what had killed Jackson Harm. And it was here. In the Snake's stock.

I looked around. The herbalist was gone. There was nobody up here on the barn's second floor but me. I picked up the bag. It was sealed; there was crumpled white tissue bunched loosely around the knife. I broke the seal on the bag. Trapped air huffed out, redolent of clove and bergamot; chypre, cinnamon, and civet . . .

Julian's ritual oil.

There were any number of people who could be wearing a mix like that, I told myself. And it was true, but I knew too many facts to take that easy out. Holding the knife carefully through the bag I held it up and angled it to catch the weak bulb-light. Its entire surface glinted, even the hilt, glossy with the oil that had been used to wipe it clean after it had been used; the reason that it and the bag reeked of the mix now. I sealed the bag shut again and knelt there holding it.

People who've never experienced it talk all the time about feeling desolated, when what they mean is the mild disappointment of a missed opportunity. Real desolation is when you've lost everything, including things you hadn't known you had. Like innocence. Like ignorance, because now I had the answer that I hadn't wanted.

I'd suspected everyone else this weekend, but never Julian—Julian, who had been out of character from first to last, in coming to HallowFest at all and then in everything that followed. Julian, who made no secret of the fact that he was doing *La Tesoraria*—if you knew what the indicators were. And I did, but I hadn't looked until now. Either at Julian, or at the end of the operation, at the two acts that must be performed.

Love and Death. But as metaphor, as simile—not literal, not actual, not real. The language of magic is metaphor. The requirements of the *Tesoraria* were supposed to be allegorical; their accommodation a symbolic one. I did not expect a real death to proceed from the *Tesoraria* work any more than the Catholic expects his priest to hand him a chunk of bleeding human meat at the Communion rail.

And so I hadn't looked at the most obvious suspect—because to me he'd been the least possible suspect. Julian. Who was, first and always, a Ceremonial Magician.

And a killer?

No! He's a magician, and magic is real, but there are LIMITS. Nobody commits MURDER in the name of magic, for Goddess's sake, no matter what their beliefs!

Yet the true magician is amoral, and recognizes no law but his own—that's what the books say, isn't it? What was the distance, really, from my perception of the immanence of the Goddess, to the Klingons' embrace of a culture that never was, to Xharina and Arioch in the moonlight, to . . .

To Jackson Harm, dead not for anything he was or had done, but because his death was the last component of a ritual? I looked down at the knife in my hands. The end does not justify the means, nor the means, the end. Human life must be valued so highly that it can never become a component in a marketplace transaction; not for slavery, and not for murder. Someone had killed Harm, that was simple fact. And the oil on the body would match the oil on the knife, on Julian.

On me, Friday night. I swallowed hard.

But I wasn't sure, I told myself. Not sure enough to make the ghastly unbelievable accusation. Julian could have been performing *La Tesoraria* and Harm could have been murdered, and these two events might have only a psychic connection. Or be sheer coincidence, something I'd seen enough of to believe in as devoutly as I did in magic.

I'd said I was willing to pay any price for justice, back when the question was an abstract one and the price was only friendship. But now the bill had been presented, and the price was higher than I could have imagined. And if I was going to pay it, I had to be sure.

IO

I put the bag with the knife in it into the pocket of my parka, where it seemed to burn with malignant intention. Blood shapes the purpose of the blade for once and all; I could barely imagine the shape of the intent in a blade that had been used to kill. I didn't want to hold it any longer than I had to, for fear of the consequences, yet Julian had been willing to sell it.

That made things even worse, but if one thing was true, the other was, too. The *kukri* had been packed up with the rest of the stock and would have been going back to New York tomorrow, to the glass case in the front of the shop, to end someday in the hands of someone ignorant of what it had been, and what it might still do . . .

If it were the murder weapon.

If Julian was the killer.

I had to know.

But when I left the barn, it was not to confront Julian. I went instead to the beginning of things; to the place I'd been drawn to all weekend. To the pine forest where Jackson Harm had died.

It was dark outside now, and cold. Traffic was all the other way, toward the barn, and light, and dinner. I met no one on my way to the Bardic Circle, and up the hill beyond. The winch and the net were gone from the lakeside. Even the deputies seemed to be gone.

I knelt where the body had lain, and reached for the knife. My fingers were cold and clumsy, and the bag in my pocket was slick and unpleasant to touch. Overheated imagination? Or the exercise of directed intuition that is the gift of every magician and Witch? I laid the bag with the knife in it on the pine needles and breathed slowly, letting my imagination and subconscious build a narrative without censorship from my daylight mind. Guided imagery, the New Agers call it, though the whole point is not to be guided. I called the Guardians to stand around me, and protect me from what I was about to see.

It was the blackest part of night, and Harm was here. Where were the leaflets? His plan had been to distribute them at the gathering; he'd left some with Mrs. Cooper, but he couldn't have counted on her to hand them out.

—*Give them to me. I'll pass them out for you.*

Who was speaking? I didn't know. The words echoed in the mind's ear, unattributable as a line of print.

—*I'll pass them out for you.*

Harm had felt no fear, only trust in this ally. He'd given—

He'd taken—

I could see the silver flask glinting in the moonlight; the sportsman's friend.

The flask in the moonlight.

—*Here, why don't you . . .*

I jerked out of trance state, unable to retain the detachment I needed to be there. The white hilt of the *kukri* on the forest floor seemed to glow balefully in the last of the twilight. There was a coppery taste in my mouth: the fight-or-flight reflex of danger.

The sweet musty undertaste in the wine that first night. I'd never slept better—or more soundly. I hadn't heard Julian get up at all. Who sleeps that soundly in a strange place?

"*I didn't kill you.*" Julian's words to me the following morning. I'd been too embarrassed at the time to pay close attention, but had there been the slightest, most scrupulously accurate stress on the last word of the sentence? "*I didn't kill YOU.*" Who, then, if not me?

Where were the leaflets? That was the real-world proof I had to have. I could not believe that Harm hadn't brought them with him Friday night. They'd been the whole point.

I picked up the *kukri* and put it back in my pocket.

*   *   *

It was after eight o'clock when I got to the bungalow, and I was shivering inside my parka from standing so long in the chill. It had been easy to get to the Bardic Circle, hard to make myself leave it. Harder still to cross the bridge over the lake to reach the path that led to the bungalows. I was filled with a desperate reluctance to take each step, an unwillingness to force the conclusion. Only an act of will kept me moving forward; the trained will that is the root of magical discipline, the training that links the magician and the Witch.

I could see the light on in the bungalow. I knew that Julian was waiting for me; that he knew I was here. And I knew that I would have to move first; the opening gambit in a chess game that could have no winner. How different were Julian and I, if both of us were willing to sacrifice everything for our beliefs? I opened the door.

Julian had been sitting on a folding stool, reading. The light flashed on his glasses as he looked up, dressed as always in clerical black and white, the collar that would have made Harm trust him on sight, there in those midnight woods.

I tried to speak and couldn't. The room seemed to be filled with reflective surfaces, all dazzling me. The knife against the red cloth. The silver-framed mirror. The lit candle.

And beneath the table, a box.

I knelt before it, moving as if Julian weren't there. It wasn't taped shut; I pulled open the flaps and felt weak with relief when all I saw was wadded newspaper — some stock from the Snake that hadn't made it upstairs.

But there was something wrong with the newsprint. I reached for it. Pulled some out. Saw what I didn't want to see beneath, even while I saw that the newsprint and design on the sheet I held were all wrong for any of the New York papers — and why should Julian have packed anything in pages from the *Tamerlane Gazette Advertiser?*

It was the same newsprint I'd seen wrapped around the silver knife, and where would Ironshadow have gotten a *Tamerlane Gazette* when he was home in New Jersey wrapping his custom orders for delivery at the festival? Julian had unwrapped it to look at it, and wrapped it back up in a fresh sheet of newspaper from the box. That was what I had seen without seeing when I was here before. That was why I'd been afraid.

I stared down at stacks of Harm's pamphlet.

Here. Give them to me. I'll pass them out for you.

"You didn't pass out his pamphlets, Julian," I said without moving. "You have to keep your promises."

"I didn't say *where* I'd pass them out," Julian answered.

I stood up. Every muscle ached. Turning to face him was agony. "You killed him," I said.

"Who?" Julian said calmly. Julian, who'd killed to complete *La Tesoraria*. Completed the work and achieved his result. But when you obtain a bill of divorcement from all that is, what do you have left? What did Julian have left?

"Did you kill Jackson Harm?" I said evenly, because nothing must be subjective, nothing left to interpretation.

"Yes." He turned a page in his book.

"*Why?*" I said despairingly.

"You know why," Julian said reprovingly.

Perhaps I should have been afraid, but I knew Julian too well for that. "It's only a *book*," I said.

"If you don't follow a ritual exactly, don't be surprised when it doesn't work," Julian said. "I knew it would come to this when I started *La Tesoraria*. I was willing to pay the price."

"And what about what Harm paid?" I said.

Julian shrugged. "I didn't choose him."

No. Fate or luck or the guiding intelligence of *La Tesoraria* had done that. And it could as easily have been Maidjene, or Lark, or anyone else who'd been here that night. It could have been me.

"And what will you do now?" I asked him.

"The *Tesoraria* work is over. It's served its purpose. I'll write up my notes." And maybe even publish them—safely, because no one would want to see the truth. Just as I hadn't wanted to.

I looked at Julian. He was watching me with uninvolved interest, the cool dispassion of one who has made the decision that ends decision for all time.

"Would you like a drink?" Julian said.

He lifted a silver flask out of his pocket; the one I'd imagined, though I didn't remember ever seeing it before. A few drops of its contents in my glass of wine had made me sleep. A mouthful had made Harm helpless. What would a glassful do? And if I drank it, who had made that choice?

"No," I said.

Julian shrugged. Disappointed, but that was all. Julian had bargained with the spirits for perfect knowledge, and perfect knowledge casteth away fear.

"And what are you going to do?" he asked me.

"I haven't made up my mind yet," I told him.

But I lied. I knew what I was going to do. All I had to find was the courage.

It took me an hour of driving around Tamerlane to find the sheriff's station again, and the closer I got, the less certain I was of what I should do when I got there.

It seemed so much more likely that the whole thing had never happened. I could throw the knife in the lake; it wouldn't cause any trouble there, and the Sheriff's Department wasn't likely to drag the lake twice. I could forget Julian's confession. It was probably his idea of a joke, anyway, just to see how gullible I was. *I* was the one who professed to believe in magic, after all. Julian professed no beliefs.

It would be so easy to let everything go. Keep my mouth shut for twenty-four hours, and the weapon would be gone, the killer vanished. Gotham County could search forever for motive and weapon, and find neither. There had been no motive. And eventually the investigation would be dropped. Unless I told the Sheriff's Department what Julian had told me.

I parked in the lot beneath the sign that said VISITOR PARKING and went inside.

"I need to talk to Sergeant Pascoe—is she here?" I said to the uniformed man behind the desk. He'd been watching me for trouble from the moment I walked in; I suppose I looked like an accident waiting to happen.

"Can I help you?" the sergeant said. I tried to remember the name of the detective investigating the Jackson Harm case, or even of the one I'd talked to this afternoon. It was after seven—would either of them still be here? Why hadn't I just found a phone and called? I could even have remained anonymous, somehow. Maybe.

"Or Detective Anthony Wayne," I said, retrieving the name from memory. "Is *he* here?"

"Your name?" he asked.

I wrenched at a mental clutch. "Karen Hightower. It's about Jackson Harm."

The names got me a seat in the room where I'd spent most of the afternoon. It was even more depressing at night. I wanted to leave, but it was already much too late. I'd given my name; they had my address. The chess pieces were in motion; the game had to be played out.

Detective Wayne came in.

"Good evening," he said. He was carrying two mugs, looking dapper yet rumpled. "Want some coffee?" He set the cups down on the table and juggled with a notepad. "You're . . . Bast, isn't it?"

"Yes." I gave him points for taking the trouble to get not only the name, but the right one.

He handed me a cup. It was black, and had oily beads on its surface. I drank, and tasted the bitterness in my nose and all along the lining of my throat.

"And you said you wanted to talk to me?"

He sat down next to me at the table. I saw a little cloisonné bat-pin from last summer's big movie pinned to his jacket. So the man had a sense of humor.

"I know something," I heard myself say, insanely. The coffee slopped in the cup as I tried to gesture while holding it, and that made me angry. I'd been through this before. This time was no different.

Tony Wayne waited me out.

"I wanted to tell you something. It's probably nothing." I felt myself trying to remember something I'd known too well a lifetime ago, but the words wouldn't settle into any order. *Ego te absolvo*, and all my sins forgiven. Confession is good for the soul. Wash me in blood and my sins will be whiter than snow.

"Someone told me they'd killed Jackson Harm," I said. I sipped the coffee, and to my disappointment, Detective Wayne didn't jump up and down and demand details. I tried to get his interest. "I've got the knife in the van. It's in a bag."

"Can we look in your van?" Detective Wayne asked noncommittally.

"Sure." I pushed the keys across the table. "Here."

He got up and went over to the door. A deputy who must have been standing just outside leaned in, and they spoke. The deputy took the keys and went off.

Detective Wayne came back over to the table.

"Who told you they'd killed Reverend Harm?" he said.

I wanted to say the name. I tried, but it wouldn't come; I felt myself gag on it, victim of the secular sorcery of shock.

"It wasn't because he was him," I said instead. "It could have been anybody." It could have been me, if Julian hadn't had another use for me—and maybe some human vestige of self-preservation, even then. A last cry for help, in the midst of self-destruction. "The point was, it had to be the first person he saw, just like in the old fairy tales, you see? It was because of *La Tesoraria*—he was doing the ritual in *La Tesoraria* and he got to the end. Julian's a magician, you see—" I'd done it; I'd managed to trick myself into saying his name. I felt my throat close with tears, choking me.

"Julian Fletcher?" Wayne said.

I nodded. It was easier, now. The first betrayal is always the hardest. "Julian Fletcher killed Jackson Harm. He told me he did. I found the knife in our stock. I asked him and he told me."

"When was this?" Wayne said.

There was a knock at the door. The deputy came back in, carrying the *kukri* in its Ziploc bag, now rebagged in an evidence bag belonging to the Gotham County Sheriff's Department. I realized that not only the knife but the bag it was in had just become evidence and thought I ought to care about that more.

"Is this the knife?" Wayne said.

I nodded. "I think it has blood on it. The oil on it will match what's on Harm."

And there was beeswax around the body; could they tell that the candles were ours? That Julian had brought them here for just this purpose?

The knife went out again. Tony Wayne leaned close to me.

"Now listen to me, Bast." There was only a slight hesitation before my name and I liked him for that. "This is important, and we really need a straight answer on this. Are you telling us that Julian Fletcher killed Jackson Harm?"

"Yes," I said, feeling defensive anger. "Ask him yourself. He'll tell you, too."

It was long after midnight when they were done with me, and they kept asking me if there was anyone I could stay with tonight, just as if I weren't up here at a campground with two hundred and fifty of my closest friends, most of whom wouldn't want to know me after this. I thought about Lark. Maybe we had something in common at last.

The door opened, and Fayrene came in with a bag of Dunkin' Donuts and a large coffee. She set them down in front of me.

"We brought Mr. Fletcher in," she said. "They're processing him now. I thought you'd like to know."

I pulled the lid off the coffee. Black. Fayrene reached into her pocket and pulled out a handful of sugar and creamers.

"Can I see him?" I asked. The unshed tears were a hard weight at the back of my jaw.

"No," Fayrene said. There was a pause. "You'll see him soon enough."

I wasn't sure what she meant, but it sounded frightening and final. I pulled the lids off four of the creamers and dumped them into the coffee. Fayrene winced, gently.

"You know," she said, seemingly inconsequentially, "my boy thinks the world of you."

I looked up, startled. She smiled. "Oh, we don't keep many secrets. First he does what he doesn't think I'm going to approve of—then he tells me about it afterward. He told me you were going to pick out some books for him to read?"

"Yeah," I said. "I promised. You have to keep your promises." It seemed important to repeat that, but I wasn't sure who I was telling.

Then I thought of something.

"Fayrene," I said, and there was so much urgency in my voice that she whipped around to face me. "You don't need the HallowFest registrations now, do you? You've got Julian. You've got a *confession*. You don't need them, right?"

She stared at me for a long moment, and I could almost see her thinking.

"No. I guess we don't need them now at that."

That was when I finally started to cry.

What is the demarcation line between reality and fantasy? Was Klash, with his insistence upon being a Klingon, deluded, or merely playing out a role? And what about Julian, who followed the *Tesoraria*'s strictures with murderous exactitude? Where does science—or religion—cross the line into madness? Do the borderlands shift every generation, or are they fixed for all time?

The real question was, could any of us stop what we were doing if we wanted to?

No.

Maidjene couldn't—she'd destroyed her marriage and risked jail to follow what she saw Wiccan law to be. I'd alienated my oldest friend for much the same reason.

THE BOWL OF NIGHT   447

For his magic, Julian had killed.

It was a difference not of kind, but degree. The same divergence that causes one Christian to picket a Planned Parenthood clinic and another to bomb it. And we say one is permissible, and the other isn't, as we must.

But if it is, *as* it is, only a difference of degree, then where is the line drawn that makes one act right and the other wrong—the line not of law, but of morality? Where is the border between good and evil? How often does each of us cross it every day, and how can we know when we do?

It was dawn by the time they finally let me leave the sheriff's station, and I didn't go back to the campground. I went to the nearest motel. Lark came later. I never asked him how he'd found me.

On Wednesday morning I found out what Fayrene had meant when she'd said I'd see Julian soon enough. I saw him that day, in the courtroom where the Gotham County grand jury brought in a true bill of murder against Julian David Fletcher, and the case was bound over for trial.

In the end, I spent several more days in Gotham County than I had time or money for, and the trial itself was still in the future. Lark stayed with me a while, and then he left. Wyler Pascoe stopped by, too. I asked him for a favor. He promised he'd do it. I can't remember what else I said to him.

It was a cold, gray, empty day when I finally drove back to Paradise Lake to pick up the Snake's stock. Everyone, even Maidjene, was long gone. It was almost November; the campground was closed. I got the keys to the barn from Mrs. Cooper. We didn't have much to say to each other now.

The inside of the barn was as cold as the outside, and all the electricity was shut off for the winter. Someone had thrown a sheet over the table on the second floor to keep the remaining merchandise clean. I finished packing and sealing the cartons. I even put the books aside for Wyler; The Snake, I figured, owed them to me. Then I carried everything downstairs to the van. There was one more thing I had to do before I was free to go.

In the fire pit in the Upper Meadow Wyler Pascoe and I burned the two copies of the *Tesoraria* that The Snake had brought to sell. When the leather binding was reduced to ash I filled the fire pit with the wood he'd brought, and when the fire was burning hot and strong I burned the HallowFest registration forms one by one, along with the pamphlets Jackson Harm had left behind.

> *O yearning heart! I did inherit*
> *Thy withering portion with the fame,*
> *The searing glory which hath shone*
> *Amid the Jewels of my throne,*
> *Halo of Hell! and with a pain*
> *Not Hell shall make me fear again—*

> —*Tamerlane*, Edgar Allan Poe